"A charming story of family and a young woman's courage to be obedient to God in the face of adversity. I loved the historical detail. Choose a long, quiet day to curl up with *The Calling of Ella McFarland*. You'll want to finish it once you get started."

—**CARYL MCADOO**, author of historical and contemporary Christian fiction

"Davis knits together an intricate, multi-level tale, leaving open threads for more ... a book where the author and the characters share flesh and blood and story, and the reader gets folded right in."

—**ALLISON PITTMAN**, award-winning author of historical fiction

"... Ella McFarland ... a woman worth knowing ... a complex character filled with the strength of her convictions, but tethered by the same human frailties as the rest of us. I found myself transported to turn-of-the-century Oklahoma Indian Territory ... Davis does a beautiful job of weaving together a lovely romance and a powerful message of God's enduring, steadfast love in even the most trying of times. *The Calling of Ella McFarland* is a powerful debut effort."

—**KELLY IRVIN**, best-selling author of bestselling author of *Through the Autumn Air*

"It's easy to see why this book won First Place in Jerry Jenkins' Operation First Novel. The characters captured my imagination right from the beginning and drew me into this wonderful story. Linda Brooks Davis is definitely a talented writer and I hope to see many more books from her!"

—**ANN TATLOCK**, best-selling, Christy award-winning author of historical and contemporary fiction

"This is an amazing book. It reminds me of books I read as a child—ones that kept me turning the pages, enthralled with the story and captivated by the characters. It is beautifully written … I found the book inspiring … **This is a jewel box of a book**—a love story, a story of trial and heartache, but also of victory and joy. I highly recommend it.

—AMAZON READER

"I received this book as a gift and had intended for it to get me through those sleepless nights with a newborn. I finished all 357 pages in two days! I was enraptured by Ella's fierce spirit, faith in God and passion for the underprivileged. Davis did an excellent job giving life to each character and successfully transported me back to the early 1900's. Not only was it easy to read, I found myself deeply connecting with the characters through the triumphs and trials of their faith. The end brought me to tears. Amazing read. Hope there is a second in the works!"

—AMAZON READER

"… I loved these characters, their values, their faith, their determination to make a difference. It is quite an impactful tale, with main characters you can root for, who don't play silly games. Well done! An inspiring, enjoyable read."

—AMAZON READER

"… Ms. Davis has shaped a very interesting and sympathetic protagonist who stands in the threshold between traditional feminine roles/behaviors and the onset of suffrage. The story lines explore old-fashioned and respectful romance, self-discovery, the vagaries of family bonds, the security of a godly lifestyle, and the delivery of justice, all amidst a study of domestic violence during an era when women were considered the property of men … I have already recommended the book to several friends and purchased a paperback for another who isn't as tech savvy as my Kindle-oriented friends."

"... Ella is a character who elicits multiple reactions from the reader: Admiration, Chagrin, Indulgence and Understanding. She is young and beautiful, moral and respectful of God, parents and people with whom she lives and encounters. She is impatient and sometimes impulsive toward the ones with whom she finds fault or distrusts. She is a loving and compassionate advocate for the downtrodden, especially women. She is intelligent, resourceful, educated, refined and wise for her age. At times she succumbs to the frailties of her youth, inexperience and naiveté and makes rash decisions with sometimes favorable, sometimes not so favorable results. She is a believable character with whom the reader can identify. I really liked this book and recommend it to other readers.

THE CALLING *of* ELLA McFARLAND

LINDA BROOKS DAVIS

BROOKSTONE
PUBLISHING GROUP

Copyright © 2015

The Calling of Ella McFarland
Linda Brooks Davis

Brookstone Publishing Group
P.O. Box 211, Evington, VA 24550
BrookstoneCreativeGroup.com

ISBN: 978-1-949856-04-0 (print), 978-1-949856-05-7 (epub)

Ordering Information:
Special discounts are available on quantity purchases by corporations, associations, and others. For details, contact
Brookstone Publishing Group at the address above.

Cover art by Carpe Librum Book Design: carpelibrumbookdesign.com

This novel is a work of fiction. Names, characters, places, and incidents either are the product of the author's imagination or are used fictitiously. Any resemblance to actual events, locales, organizations, or persons living or dead is entirely beyond the intent of the author or publisher.

IN MEMORY

MY GRANDMOTHER, MAMA

ELLA JANE

You buried two husbands and five daughters, yet never lost your faith.
Thank you for leaving a name worthy of a great-great-granddaughter.

. . . My grace is sufficient for thee . . .

—2 Corinthians 12:9a

DEDICATION

For my granddaughter

ELLA JANE

I loved you first.

463 The Cross is Not Greater

May be sung as a Solo and Chorus.   Com. BALLINGTON BOOTH

1. The cross that he gave may be heav-y, But it ne'er out-weighs his grace,
2. The thorns in my path are not sharp-er Than com-posed his crown for me,
3. The light of his love shin-eth bright-er, As it falls on paths of woe,
4. His will I have joy in ful-fill-ing, As I'm walk-ing in his sight,

The storm that I feared may sur-round me, But it ne'er ex-cludes his face.
The cup that I drink not more bit - ter Than he drank in Geth-sem - a - ne.
The toil of my work groweth light-er, As I stoop to raise the low.
My all to the blood I am bring-ing, It a - lone can keep me right.

REFRAIN.

The cross is not great - er than his grace, The storm can - not
hide his bless - ed face; I am sat - is - fied to know
That with Je - sus here be - low, I can con - quer ev - 'ry foe.

CHAPTER 1

*E*lla had aimed for this day all her life. She would allow nothing to spoil it.

Perched on the edge of a tufted chair, she slipped off her gloves. A corset stave bit her flesh, but she held herself erect. Worthington School for Girls expected no less of their teachers.

"Miss McFarland, we insist you understand ..." The chairman of the three-member board gestured to a colleague on either side of the table. "Female teachers who marry are dismissed."

She nodded. "I read the school policy paper, sir."

He cleared his throat. "You see, unlike for men ..." The man's tone had turned as severe as his starched collar. "Marriage divides women's loyalties."

Women, more prone to divided loyalties than men?

Ella itched to spout a challenge, but she suppressed the urge. A Worthington teacher knew her place. "Rest assured, sir, I'm wedded to teaching."

Perspiration dribbled down her spine. Was 1905 the Twin Territories' hottest year on record? She plucked a handkerchief from a sleeve and dabbed the cleft in her chin.

Mr. Chairman stifled a cough with a fist. "Your loyalty notwithstanding ..."

Ella's shoulders tightened, and a tremor threatened. Had she forgotten the Lord Himself brought her to this fine institution of learning? She inhaled a goodly portion of library air—as much as her irksome corset allowed—and willed herself to relax.

"We've reached deadlock." The chairman delivered the news as if it were trivial.

Her insides clamped. "You've reached consensus *not* to reach consensus?" A recalcitrant spiral of golden hair slipped from its pin and dangled near her eye.

A younger board member, one whose dark hair had turned neither gray nor *loose*, covered his mouth with a hand. Had he hidden a grin? Unlike the other men's ties and stiff collars, an open-necked shirt peeked from beneath his brown serge coat.

"Suffice to say we must deliberate further." The third board member's expression had tightened, rather like his gray vest. Light reflected off his pate.

Ella had interviewed six weeks ago. These men required even more time? Undoubtedly, a panel of three women would find deliberations a simple task. But she held her peace. "Far be it from me to—"

"Well then." Mr. Chairman tapped a stack of papers into precise lines, as if doing so dismissed her.

To the contrary, she would make a reasonable inquiry. "Can you tell me, sir ..."

The man's eyebrows curved into question marks.

"How long might your deliberation take?" She met his stare with a steady gaze.

Mr. Gray Vest tapped a fist on the tabletop. "We refuse to be rushed, young lady." His head bob sent a tremor through his jowls.

The junior member, having squelched his grin, lifted a hand. "May I, sir?"

The chairman nodded and slumped with an elbow on the arm of his chair.

The genial—and ever so handsome—young gentleman turned to Ella. Clear blue light shone in his eyes. "Good morning, Miss McFarland. I'm Mr. Evans."

"Pleased to meet you, sir."

"As you know, I joined the board when the former member met with an unfortunate accident."

"Aye." She'd read the newspaper report. Tragically, the hard-of-hearing widower, caught in a hail storm in the path of an oncoming train, left five fatherless daughters.

God bless them.

"Filling that fine man's shoes is a responsibility I take seriously," he continued. "I'm afraid further deliberations are in order—on my account. Can you return in two weeks?"

Despair threatened, but she forced a smile. "Of course." Tugging on her gloves, she rose. The three men stood in tandem, their bearings as precise as the pinstripes on their suits.

Mr. Evans extended a hand. "I'll see you out."

"That's not necessary, but thank you." Neither the man's smile nor his fleeting dimple dispelled the unease tussling in her middle. His glum associates exchanged a glance, as if communicating unspoken thoughts.

Something was amiss.

Pausing at the doorway, Ella straightened her cotton shirtwaist and faced the panel. "There's more to it, isn't there?"

Mr. Chairman eyed her like a whooping crane spying a minnow. "See here—"

"We *are* divided." Mr. Evans stepped nearer with a conciliatory expression.

She gave him a nod. Thankfully, she'd chosen her simple linen hat. Her wide-brimmed straw would've bobbled in an unseemly fashion. "May I ask the cause of your disagreement?"

An expression not unlike regret skimmed his features. "You see—"

"We've learned of other … considerations." The chairman all but shouted.

She turned to him, her gaze steady. "You've learned I'm not a capable teacher?"

"Of course not. You've an admirable record."

Aye, nothing less than excellence was required of a farmer's daughter in need of connections. And a stable income.

"But under the circumstances of your family's—"

"My *family*?" She puffed a curl off her forehead.

"Your family's reputation. We have our students' good names to consider."

Gossip had reached even to Worthington?

A finger of ire picked at her restraint. "My parents must account for your uncertainty?"

"Why, no. Gavin and Betsy McFarland make a fine Christian couple."

"So it's my twin brother?"

"To the contrary, Cade McFarland's known to be industrious and honest."

"I see. It must be Hannah, my twelve-year-old sister." She had vowed to bridle her saucy tongue or die trying. Would she write her own death warrant this very day?

"Young woman, you know precisely of whom we speak."

Indeed. 'Twas the third McFarland girl, the dark chestnut-haired, golden-eyed beauty. Viola.

She returned the chairman's unflinching scrutiny. "Thank you for your time. Making such decisions must be … difficult."

Shaking Mr. Evans's hand, and catching a whiff of sandalwood, she strode from the library with her pride intact. Ella was a McFarland. She'd behave as such.

Retrieving her parasol from the foyer hall tree, she nodded to the receptionist and helped herself through the double oak doors. As she descended the steps, her dark gored skirt puffed outward with each footfall.

She paused at the bottom step and scanned the billowed sky. July's simmering sun and a blanket of reluctant rainclouds had created a sweltering ride to Worthington. Her blouse clung to her damp skin, but she set aside her discomfort. A two-hour drive stretched before her with household tasks yet to accomplish before dark. She must hurry.

"Miss McFarland." A strong, yet kind, male voice halted her at the buggy.

It appeared Mr. Evans was persistent as well as gentlemanly. She reached for the buggy's folding step.

"Here, let me." He bent to release the latch and pressed the handy amenity into place. Sunlight glinted in his hair, as dark a brown as black walnut shells. He touched a hand to her elbow, and she caught another whiff of the manly scent. Bay Rum aftershave, perhaps?

"Thank you, sir." She placed a button-shoed foot on the tread. Her legs wobbled, but she settled into the seat without stumbling.

"Don't give up hope, Miss McFarland. I'll do everything I can."

"You're very kind, Mr. Evans. Thank you." Shaking off the disconcerting effect of the man's cobalt eyes, she released the foot brake and flicked open her pendant watch. Ten o'clock. She should make it home in time to help Mama with the noon meal. Five miles of back roads and a bridge over the Canadian River would take her into Indian Territory. Just past the Washita River, she'd catch sight of the home place where her family awaited news.

Ella was their best hope, but hope was growing scarce.

Securing her hair with a comb, she squared her shoulders. The snap of the whip belied her crumbling emotions as it urged her mare Bunny onto the thoroughfare toward home.

CHAPTER 2

The McFarlands' tin roof jutted above the distant treetops. Ella couldn't face her family while in such turmoil. Perhaps Rock Creek would bring relief.

She eased Bunny onto a bridle path to a picnic area Papa had cleared for his family, set the brake, and secured the reins. Sliding the pearl-tipped pin from the hat atop her pompadour of curls—thick and nothing short of irksome—she tossed the headpiece aside and climbed down.

At her mare's satisfied snort, she leaned against her faithful companion and allowed her pent-up tears to flow. She snatched a handkerchief from a sleeve and snorted, not unlike Bunny.

Stumbling toward an elm tree, her skirt caught on a bramble, but she tore it away. Who cared if it ripped? She wouldn't need it for Worthington. She'd patch it like countless other garments. And don her work clothes. Nothing but home and field drudgery awaited her, all under a cloud of scandal.

She fell prostrate on the mossy bank. "Hasn't my family lost enough, Lord?"

Just that morning Viola and Hannah had complained that assuming their elder sister's household tasks was unfair. Papa abandoned his chores to oil the buggy springs, apt to squeak of late. Mama delivered the laundry early, not to her customers' front doors as was her custom, but to the family store, an inconvenience for all.

Lately customers seldom darkened the door of McFarland's General Store, but the welcome bell down the street rang without ceasing. Morgan Mercantile, with its swirly cutouts in the windows and candy counter, had taken more than half of Papa's business. The owner's daughter, a girl too proud to look beyond gossip, had broken Cade's heart. And saw that the Girls' Club rejected Hannah.

Ella had counted on the county school's teaching position. But the headmaster filled it without explanation. So she applied to Worthington, but now …

"How I long to work in a classroom, not a cotton field, come September, Lord."

During the harvest, the family would toil until dark, even on Saturdays. Cade would shepherd his sheep, and Mama and Ella would see to the laundry business while the morning dew was still on the cotton bolls. And after supper.

The Lord's Day remained inviolate, save when dark clouds portended disaster. On those Sundays, the family would don their field hats and long-sleeved shirts and pull the locks from the burs as long as the Lord gave them light. Alongside a few hired workers and sharecroppers, Ruby and Lily Sloat, the McFarlands would offer their sacrifice of praise between rows of cotton.

Industrious Miss McFarland barely managed her jams and produce business.

Mama wouldn't admit it, but the scandal had taken a toll on her health. Ella welcomed an opportunity to help provide for her family and ease the strain on her mother.

Cotton prices were plummeting, but the McFarlands must harvest the crop even for a pittance. Life had changed in recent months as surely as the plowed soil would give way to winter's frost.

The Worthington job would've saved her family in more ways than one.

All lost at the hands of a sister she loved fiercely, albeit a mother with no husband—Viola.

Vexation nipped at Ella's heels until she pictured baby Joshua with the dark, auburn-streaked waves. The family loved him no less for his fatherlessness. His babble filled the McFarland home with joy, but Viola's refusal to name his father multiplied the family's troubles. Thankfully, laughing Joshua was nearing his first birthday oblivious to the turmoil.

Mama and Papa had chosen to spare her the news of his birth while she was away at normal school. She would've shared her family's trial had they given her the choice. As it was, the news greeted her two months ago in the face of nine-month-old Joshua.

Snatching her handkerchief from a pocket, she blew her nose. Unlike other growing girls in times past, she'd helped out at her family's store and chose her studies over games and outings. She rejected suitors from as far away as the next county and tossed aside well-meaning friends' remarks about her beauty and desirability as a wife.

Ella McFarland was wedded to teaching.

Had the Worthington men witnessed her foregoing school parties to sell her canned goods on innumerable market days, counting her pennies and depositing them into her school account, they'd have need to deliberate no further.

"Nothing brings me such joy as teaching, Lord."

Cicadas and frogs created a racket. Dragonflies and their tiny cousins, the damselflies, dipped and flicked the water. Even insects created ripples. Yet Ella McFarland—her family's best hope, with all her passion and learning—couldn't wrap her hands around her one solitary dream.

"Haven't I done enough to please You, Lord?"

She dabbed her eyes and discharged a heavy sigh. She must leave aside her tears and return home. Hadn't she more blessings than she could count? Faithful Christian parents. A spirited but loving family. A solid home and a soft bed. Health and strength for her daily chores. And a teaching certificate.

Turning toward the old buggy and faithful Bunny, she held up her head. She must deliver unwelcome news. Again.

Ella halted Bunny at the barn, and Papa looked up from horseshoeing, his expression hopeful.

She averted her eyes. How could she disappoint him?

Just that morning Papa had helped her harness the buggy. "I'd drive if you'd let me."

"You've work to do. I can take care of myself." She waved off his concern and scampered down the back steps of their weathered farmhouse.

"Rifle's under the seat, daughter."

"I've my pistol, too." She patted a pocket.

"God be with you, my Ellie."

"And with you," she called with a flick of the reins.

Had she and Papa spoken those words only hours ago?

Wringing her threadbare apron into knots, Mama met her at the porch. Her hair, smoothed into a bun streaked with gray, gleamed in the sunlight. "How'd it go?"

Ella ran a hand along the sharp angles of her mother's shoulders. Mama possessed a steady presence that hearkened to her solid Irish roots, quieting her child's misgivings. "They postponed their decision two weeks."

"Why, lass? Did you remember your manners?" Although slight of stature and a head shorter than her eldest daughter, Mama possessed a strength of will and faith that rivaled ten women. But time had stamped lines around her eyes and in her brow.

"My manners were impeccable." Opening the screen door, she waved her mother inside and hung her headpiece on a hook. Later on, she'd fluff it, encase it in tissue, and set it in its box, protected from the dust.

The comforting aroma of ham and boiled cabbage permeated the kitchen.

"I'll get coffee." Mama kept a pot of coffee warm even in summertime.

Sitting at the hand-hewn oak table, Ella ran a fingertip over marks three generations of McFarlands had etched, scars her mother refused to sand away. Perspiration rolled down her chest, and a stave poked the tender flesh beneath an arm. She itched to be done with the pesky garment.

Mama set glasses of cool Chickasaw plum juice on the table and settled into her chair. "Tell me about it." The set of her jaw signaled her resolve.

Ella glanced around. Papa's reading chair sat empty, the lamp lit, and his weekly paper lay strewn on a hassock. "Where are the girls?" She hadn't caught a glimpse of either.

"Upstairs. Hannah has her nose in a book. And Viola's napping with Joshua."

"My sisters are reading and napping while you prepare a meal? While Papa bends over a horse's hoof? And Cade toils in the fields? Did they at least finish the ironing?"

"You mustn't fret about me, daughter mine. Let it be. It's not good to kick against a cattle prod."

So her sisters were the prods. And she, the stubborn mule? Pitching the image aside, she trained her eyes on her mother. "The committee's deadlocked."

"Deadlocks can be broken, child." Steadfast and full of faith, Mama's confidence in her daughter was unshakable.

"I suspect their minds are made up."

"They'd reject a scholarship recipient and outstanding graduate? Surely they know what a boon you'd be to their school." Mama's heritage peppered her speech and temperament, but she'd learned to curb her fiery inclinations. She trusted the Lord.

"They recognize my qualifications, but they must please wealthy families."

"Why would your being on the faculty displease anyone with sense, wealthy or nay?"

"*My* record isn't the problem. It's ... "

Mama's cheeks reddened, deepening the gray in her eyes. She splayed her hands on the table and rested her head on them. The lamplight sparked silver in her hair, though golden strands battled for their place. "It's Joshua, isn't it?"

"More rightly, it's Viola."

Mama sat up, her eyes flashing. "Where's their Christian charity? Their grace? Haven't they known both at one time or another?" Exasperation flaring, she slapped the table and stood with a huff. But—truth be told—she'd be on her knees soon.

"I can explain neither the men's deadlock nor their acquaintance with mercy." Save, perhaps, Mr. Evans whose kindness rang true.

The door ground open. Papa stepped inside and slung his hat onto a hook. Pulling a rag from his pants pocket, he mopped sweat from his face and neck. His tanned skin bespoke years of farm labor. "Got news?"

His daughter picked at a cuticle. "Not what you're looking for."

He pulled out a chair, and Mama poured his coffee. His curls, once buckeye brown, had silvered along with his eyebrows. "Out with it."

"They're deadlocked. Postponed their decision. I fear I won't be joining their faculty."

"And why not?" A storm had amassed around his eyes.

"It's our family's supposed reputation."

Six feet tall and broad shouldered, Gavin McFarland presented a fine form of a man. He plowed a field as well as he handled a steer. He slurped steaming coffee, and his eyebrows narrowed into a V. He plopped down his mug, sloshing dark liquid over the edge. "What're we gonna do about it—after I give 'em a piece of my mind, that is?"

"Settle down, Gavin." Mama found her commanding voice when called for. "We'll take it to the Lord."

One parent, ready to battle with words—or a fist—and the other, on her knees? Ella had gotten the lion's share of the former and a measly portion of the latter. But one trait they'd given her in spades—a will of iron.

"Please act on none of your reckless urges, Papa. Do what you're called to do. Pray. I'm twenty-one years old. I'll decide what comes next."

CHAPTER 3

Grateful to be relieved of her vexatious corset, Ella picked up her embroidery. The family's afternoon naps afforded her a measure of peace.

She glanced out the window. Thunderheads blocked the sun. Easing closer to the lamp, she threaded a length of black through the needle. Even a moss rose design required dark threads. For depth. And interest. So it was with life. She repositioned the birch hoops, tightened the screw, and pulled the fabric taut.

"Daughter?" Mama spoke from the hallway.

Ella squinted in the lamplight. "In here."

Dressed in a soft gray summer dress suitable for company, Mama took her husband's reading chair. The lines around her eyes had softened.

A roll of thunder passed overhead.

"The Lord's talking to us, child."

Ella set down her embroidery. Folding her legs beneath her, she smoothed her skirt over her knees and leaned onto the arm of the chair. "I'm sorry about Worthington."

"I'm not." Her mother picked up the embroidery. Forced an embroidery needle into the fabric with a thimble. And pulled the thread through. "I was miffed, but now that I've had time to pray, my spirit has eased."

"Don't you want Worthington for me?"

"Only if God wills it."

Lightning cracked open the sky, illumining the murkiness. A rumbling peal answered.

"Why wouldn't He? A position at Worthington would restore our family's reputation and ease the strain of making a living."

Mama laid the handwork in her lap. "The Lord sees what we cannot. So we trust Him."

Hadn't Ella resolved the same only hours ago. Now the thought chaffed. "You toil in the field wearing a threadbare work dress. Bend over hot, soapy laundry water. Just look at your hands, fiery red from lye. I want to set you in a place of ease."

"What would I do with myself in such a place?" Mama chuckled. "Our roots'll never be anywhere but in this soil." She reached over and cupped her daughter's chin. "Make your own life. The rest of us can see to ourselves."

"I want the best for you." How often had both parents spoken those words as they scrimped and saved so their children could have better than they? "But I confess I did you a disservice, expecting you to corral your sisters. And you no more than a little one yourself."

Indeed, the McFarlands had endured hard times—Papa busting sod, Mama burning the blocks for supper's fire, and their eldest chasing rats off the roof with broomcorn. Many a day Ella would've picked wildflowers or pursued other carefree endeavors had she not been expected to watch her sisters. But what was Mama to do?

"It's taken all of us to make it, but I want to ease your burden, Mama. If I were a Worthington teacher, the Girls' Club wouldn't deny Hannah membership. That prissy miss in town might reconsider Cade's proposal. And folks would shop in the store again."

"You put a heap of stock in Worthington."

"It's the finest of girls' schools. It prepares students to enter society at the highest levels."

"That what you figure the Lord has in mind for you, preparing rich girls for high society?"

Mama's words stung. Hadn't Ella spoken similar words when Viola wailed about her common existence? "I'd be teaching literature, not manners."

"I want you to have the desires of your heart." Lights of love had clustered on Mama's face. "You want the same for me. We must take care our desires are in line with God's."

Ella sighed. "I'll do my best to seek God's will while I wait on those stiff-necked—"

"Watch your tongue, Ella Jane."

Expelling a sigh, the recently teacher-licensed, firstborn child of much-esteemed Gavin and Betsy McFarland, gathered her wayward thoughts into a tidy bundle. "Sorry. I'll put on my work clothes in the morning. There's a riot of weeds in the cotton. You can stay inside."

Mama set aside the embroidery. "I hear stirring upstairs. Time to get supper. Zach and Ollie will be here before you know it." She peeked out the window. "If the weather lets them."

Ella dried her hands on a kitchen towel and checked the boiling peas. The thunderstorm had left a muddy road for the Irvings and stifling humidity for all. She fanned herself with her apron and stepped to the back door. Perhaps a breeze would ease through the screen.

Leaning on the jamb, she observed Cade at his chores. He checked the sheepfold gate and tromped through the cow lot, now a muddy manure pit. Were his thoughts on his broken engagement? Foolish girl, rejecting the McFarland name. She'd live to regret it.

Ella eyed the table, as bare as fallow farmland. How was she to corral her sisters? "Where's Hannah, Papa? I need help with supper."

He set aside his paper and strode onto the porch. "Hannah, come help with supper."

She glided up the steps from the bottom tread like a swan—with nary a ripple.

He adjusted his wide-brimmed hat and strode past her. "I'm going to the barn."

The youngest McFarland girl entered the kitchen with a book under an arm and the corners of her mouth nudging dimples into her cheeks.

"*Little Women.* Lost track of time."

"That's what you said the last time. And the time before that."

Setting her book aside, she tied her light chestnut waves into a tail and fluttered her daddy-long-legs lashes.

"You'll get nowhere batting your lashes at me, young lady." Ella gave her cheek a gentle pat. "Set the table please."

Hannah's ivy-green eyes, so like Grandma Mac's, flexed downward. "Wish you'd act more like a sister and less like a teacher or a ma."

A sense of soul weariness threatened Ella's composure. How would this child learn to tend house and care for a family with her head in the clouds, dreaming of other times and places? At Hannah's age, she was already doing chores *and* school assignments.

"As your elder sister, I stand in for Mama when she's busy. Hurry now. The Irvings will be here soon."

Heat rose from the cookstove's water reservoir, adding another layer of dampness to Ella's skin and irascible curls. She swiped her face with a dress sleeve.

"Where's Mama, anyway?" Hannah pulled a step ladder to the hutch.

"Resting." Ella hooked a thumb upward. Their mother prided herself in girding her loins with strength as the proverb said, but rampant gossip had taken its toll on her nerves.

"And Viola?"

"Down at the creek, but—"

"She's to be given every consideration." Hannah planted her fist on her hip. "We all get tired of it, you know." She retrieved the cedar box of Mama's good tableware, the knives and forks and spoons that matched.

Aye, they all knew. Viola's willful streak knew no bounds. The baby on her hip would forever attest to that truth. "Do unto others—"

"As I'd have them do unto me, another thing I know well enough." She stepped down with a basket hooked onto each arm and the box in her hands.

"Let me help." Ella eased the box onto the table and nodded toward an arrangement of canned goods. "There's pickles, chowchow, okra, and pearl onions."

Hannah set out utensils and napkins and twisted off the lids of the pickled goods, freeing the pungent aromas. Mama's recipes originated in Ireland, but her rearing in the Ozark Mountains added the zest.

Ella tapped a forefinger on her chin. "That's tableware for the six of us, plus Ollie and Zach. Plenty of napkins. Salt and pepper. Hot sauce. And Joshua's spoon."

Her head-in-the-clouds sister undertook her chores, humming.

"Hannah?" Ella lowered her chin. "Hannah!"

Her sister's head snapped up. "Yes?"

She gave a dismissive wave. "Never mind." She must curb her teacher tendencies.

Hannah shrugged and whisked the novel under an arm.

The door squealed opened, and Viola stepped inside, whistling a lull-aby and nestling a baby. This dark chestnut-haired McFarland girl had received all the beauty God dispensed the day she was born.

"Stop the noisemaking, Vi." Did Hannah spout her every thought?

The young mother hung her bonnet on a hook and ran fingers through her waves. "Busy making trouble, I see." She scraped her muddy boots on the straw mat.

"At least I helped with supper." Hannah headed for Mama's sewing chair. "And I didn't traipse in with mud on my shoes."

"Did you forget I have a baby?" Viola set Joshua in his chair and wiped his face with her apron.

"How could I?" Hannah positioned her book in the best of the lamplight.

"Here, Vi. Wash Joshua's hands." Ella thrust a towel under the pump. A couple of pulls on the handle saturated the fabric. She squeezed out the excess water.

Viola might've been eighteen years old, but at times she behaved like a twelve-year-old. If it weren't for her sisters, Joshua would be in a sad state. If only the girl would name the man who fathered her son, perhaps the child could anticipate a decent future.

"I'm awful hot and tired." A persistent whine tinted Viola's voice. "Mind seeing to my boy while I rest?"

Joshua's father ought to be listening to Viola whine.

Ella smoothed her nephew's tar-black locks. "Check on Mama while you're up there. And don't think you'll be resting long. Company's coming."

Viola trudged up the stairs.

Hannah burrowed into Mama's chair.

How Ella ached to teach students, not her sisters. But she must put aside such longings. And mash a bit of carrots.

Baby Joshua favored carrots.

CHAPTER 4

"There's Zach and Ollie." Papa stepped onto the porch. "In their new Packard."

"You don't say." Mama craned for a better view. "Road wasn't too wet after all. And lookey there … Frank's with them."

Ella's insides knotted, and her hand stilled over the pump handle. The Irvings' son wasn't expected home from the university back East for a month. Time enough to relocate to Worthington. Or so she had planned.

She forced down the pump handle, topping off the pitcher. "Would someone *please* fill the glasses?" She hadn't meant to speak like a miffed schoolmarm, but the words were said.

Mama bristled. "You feel all right?"

Lowering the cookstove door, Ella flinched as heat barreled over her. "Why wouldn't I be?" She pulled out a pan of browned yeast rolls and set it on a trivet.

"Your cheeks are flaming red." She touched her daughter's forehead. "Working too hard and eating too little, I'd wager."

"Just the heat." She shooed her mother toward the door. "Greet your friends."

How was she to bear greeting Frank?

Mama scurried to the porch. "How good it is to see you, Ollie. And you brought Frank with you." She tucked her oldest friend into her arms.

"He met us at the port of Philadelphia with news he was coming home to get a start in banking with Zach." As Ollie received Mama's embrace, her filmy dress ruffled like blue cotton candy. This blonde, blue-eyed wife of a prosperous banker knew every advantage—beautiful home, latest fashion, and travel—but she remained a simple, loving girl from Arkansas.

Mama gave Zach a one-armed hug. "Thank God you're home safe."

He smiled and nodded. "And with more luggage than we took. We bought half of Europe." Impeccably dressed as always, the successful businessman sported a string tie with linen shirt and trousers. Ever the gentleman, he doffed his hat.

Their son stepped onto the porch in an open-collared, fine cotton shirt tucked into iron-creased slacks. With hair as black as Poe's raven and eyes to match, he could play the rake in a cheap dime novel. "Thanks for having us for supper."

"You're like family. You know that." Mama cupped his chin as she had her daughter's.

If her mother knew this scoundrel as Ella knew him, she'd bar him from the house.

He gave Mama a peck on the cheek and stepped inside.

Ella whipped a retreat to the stove.

"Hello, fair maiden." Frank's deep, distinctive drawl sent a shiver through her.

"You're home earlier than expected." She spoke without looking back, as if to the peas.

"And glad to be here." He neared and pressed a hand to her waist.

How she longed to tell the blackguard what she thought of him. But not here. Not now. Their families' friendship depended on her discretion.

"Let's sit on the front porch, Ollie." The two women chattered toward the front.

Papa took to his reading chair, and Zach and Frank followed, their conversation turning to crop prices and bank interest rates.

Ella poured out the peas, releasing a blast of vapor. She dropped a spoon into the bowl and fanned her neck. They ought to be taking a picnic, not adding to the heat with this old cookstove.

Feet clomped on the porch. Cade stepped inside, bringing with him the odor of sheep. Like a burly, good-natured bear, he stood tall and represented all that was good and noble in a man.

How dare any silly girl break his heart.

"Home to visit?" He offered Frank a handshake.

"Nothing for me in Philadelphia." The black-eyed rascal glanced at his father.

Zach cleared his throat. "Frank starts at the bank tomorrow. Keeping books."

Frank was home for good? Strength evaporated from Ella's fingers. A serving fork clattered to the floor, and she scooped up the utensil. What happened to his job in Philadelphia? He wouldn't last a week keeping books at his father's bank.

She speared the beef roast and transferred it to a platter.

Floorboards complained as Hannah skittered down the stairs.

Frank stood like a proper gentleman. "You're prettier than ever."

With eyes sparkling, she blushed and sat on the bench at the table.

"Will someone call Vi?" Ella ladled gravy into a bowl.

"I'm coming." Viola's voice lazed downward from the landing. Conversation halted. New slippers peeked from beneath her petticoat ruffles. Joshua's chubby legs kicked against her skirt. She'd donned her Sunday best. Whatever for?

As she stepped off the last step, she hiked up Joshua and blotted his lips with his bib. Flipping a dark tress over a shoulder, she turned with a grin slightly askew. "Hello, Frank."

"Fine looking boy. Whose is he?"

"Mine." One eyebrow peaked. Joshua gurgled. "No one told you?"

"I … haven't been home in so long. I guess Mother neglected …"

"He's growing." Zach's comment eased the collective discomfort.

"Where's that baby?" Ollie entered the house with her arms out-stretched. "Come here and give Aunt Ollie a hug. You're as beautiful as you were a month ago, Vi." She embraced mother and child as one.

Viola grinned, deepening her dimples.

"My, how handsome." Ollie kissed Joshua's cheek.

"He comes from good stock." Viola handed her son to the older woman.

How could a child of Gavin and Betsy McFarland possess no more sensitivity than a pea? "Supper's on the table." Ella grumbled the words.

The group tossed aside Viola's careless remark with the ease born of lifelong friendship.

As they circled the table, Frank pulled out a chair. Viola plopped into it with Joshua on her lap. Frank took the last empty place. Beside Viola.

Joshua slapped the table, rattling the dishes. Viola pushed her plate aside.

Frank drew away from the child.

Papa spoke a blessing, adding a special thank you for Frank's return. Hannah handed Cade the peas as Joshua stuffed a fist into his mouth. Drool ran down his arm. Frank ladled gravy onto a slice of beef and offered the bowl to Viola.

"Would you hold Joshua?" She tilted her head, and the light painted red streaks in her hair.

The little one's gaze curved upward toward the dark-haired stranger.

Hesitating, Frank glanced around the table and back at Viola. At length, he held out his hands, and Joshua fell into them. He jostled the boy with his face turned away, his lips quirked into a snarl.

Perhaps it was the way the light set Joshua's eyes and hair ablaze like fireflies at midnight or his ears peeking through his curls. It might've been the shape of his mouth or the depth of color in his skin. So like …

Icy hot foreboding crawled through Ella. Her breath abandoned her.

So like Frank's.

She pressed her lips together and stared at her plate. Shock held her eyes wide. The same couldn't be said of the other diners who served their plates and chatted as always. No untoward reality marred their banter.

Were they blind?

She raised her gaze to Viola's own. And to her grin.

The girl cared not a whit what lurked on the fringes of supper conversation.

Ella cared. Deeply. And she'd learn the truth.

But first, she must make it through supper.

Unable to sleep, Ella stared at the bead board ceiling. Supper had seemed interminable. Cade had closed his door, and the household was finally silent save Papa's snores, the rasp of the rocking chair next door, and Joshua's whimpers.

Hannah lay sprawled like a rag doll across the bed they shared, her features slackened in slumber.

The next-door rocking ceased. Viola hummed, no doubt laying Joshua in his crib. Her door clicked open and closed.

Throwing aside her sheet, Ella padded across the floor and stepped into the hallway.

The young mother stood at the stairway. A shaft of moonlight silhouetted her womanly form beneath her nightgown.

"Vi."

Viola ignored her sister's whisper-shout and disappeared down the stairs.

Ella followed.

Moonlight streamed through the kitchen windows, rivaling the sun at dawn. Viola sauntered to the icebox and poured a glass of buttermilk.

Lighting a lamp, Ella took a seat at the table.

Her sister licked a ring of white from her mouth and joined her.

"Joshua's Frank's child." Speaking the words made them all too real.

The bridge of Viola's nose crinkled. "Whatever do you mean? He's been in Philadelphia."

"He came home for Thanksgiving in '03. Joshua was born the following August, the year I couldn't come home from school."

"I don't remember such insignificant details." Viola's eyes shuttered the truth.

Ella grabbed her forearm. "Did he force himself on you?"

Her sister jerked away. "Frank's never had to force himself on anyone."

Resting her head on the back of the chair, Ella released a heavy breath. "He's written all over the boy. Why no one else has noticed, I can't imagine."

"Imagine is right. You're the one imagining." A shadow darkened Viola's countenance. "Don't be coy. Frank has always had eyes for you." She inspected a fingernail. "You for him before you went off to school. But something changed. I saw the way you acted around him tonight. You hid it from the rest of the family but not from me." She drained the buttermilk.

Ella refused her sister's bait. "If your dalliance with Frank hadn't resulted in a child, I'd understand keeping the secret to protect Mama and Papa. But Joshua's welfare is at stake. Zach and Ollie would be devoted to him."

"For heaven's sakes, leave me alone." Viola flicked a wrist. She set her empty glass in the dishpan and leaned against the counter.

"Unless you admit it soon, I'll—"

"Tell no one what you think you know." Viola craned forward, her gaze locked on her elder sister's. "This is my life. Stay out of it."

Naught but the pump's drip into the dishpan broke the silence. Blood bound the sisters, but a great chasm of loss gaped between them. Ella's heart ached.

"Some truths are bitter, but they must be ingested, Vi. Your family has borne the—"

"Shame? Are you ashamed of us?"

Ella's shoulders sagged. "No ... the uncertainty. We love you. Gossips have made this a disgrace, not your family."

"I can see it in your glances and the way you stammer when folks pry."

"You see what you want to see. We would introduce Joshua to the world if you'd allow it. How do you expect others to respect the McFarland name if you don't?"

"I have my reasons for not exposing my boy to the citizens of Needham and for hiding the identity of his father ... for now." Ice encased her words. She wheeled toward the stairs, her bare heels pounding a warning on the hardwood floor.

Why wouldn't Viola admit the truth?

Why hadn't Ella exposed Frank herself? Mama and Papa deserved to know the true character of the man they treated like a son. But the truth would evoke such pain.

She refused Frank's darkness and wanted none of it for her sister. Still ... Frank must be held responsible for his son's future. But he couldn't—he mustn't—join the family circle.

Nor would she let her sister traipse blithely forward, pursuing a man she didn't know. Ella loved her too much. She padded up the stairs and stood at Viola's door. Choosing not to knock lest she awaken sleepers, she turned the brass handle and nudged aside the door.

A lamp's dim glow outlined the young mother on the edge of her bed. Her son lay in his crib, his legs entwined with a stuffed bunny's. She looked up as if she were expecting her elder sister.

"I've loved you fiercely since the day you were born." Ella spoke in a near whisper. "I can't let this continue without telling you. Frank—"

"I won't hear a word against him."

"But there's something you need to know."

"I don't want to know." Viola stared into the shadows. "Nothing will make a difference. Just leave."

Ella lay awake long into the night, imagining what brought her dread—family life around the McFarland table with Frank Irving a part of it. Forever.

CHAPTER 5

$\mathcal{G}$uilt picked at Ella in the cotton field the next morning. How long could she withhold the truth? Shoving a damp curl under her field hat, she raised her eyes. "Ever keep secrets, Mama?"

Her mother leaned on her hoe handle. "A woman hides a little something now and again."

"How does she decide which secrets to keep and which to share?"

"That's the trouble with secrets. Why?"

Eager to direct Mama's ever-so-familiar, searching gray eyes elsewhere, Ella nodded toward a pair of laborers, the only other White women among sturdy, dark-skinned men. "Ruby and Lily are hiding more than a little."

"Sloats're proud."

"The poor woman's back is as curved as a bow." Ella palmed a drop of sweat from her nose. "Lily's just a girl, but she'll be as hunched as her mother one day."

"Hunting bow serves a worthy purpose, same as a woman's labor." Mama pulled off her bonnet and dried her face on a dress sleeve. "Even so, Ruby's lot would bend any back."

Across the field, Ruby yelped and leaned forward with a hand at her spine. Lily dropped her hoe and stretched for her mother.

Ella tossed aside her own hoe. "I'm going to—"

"You'll do nothing of the sort." Mama laid a calming hand on her arm. "Help the Sloats if they ask. Not before." She gestured to a bur oak at the edge of the cotton patch. "Let's rest a spell."

Her daughter surveyed the endless rows of dogged weeds. "No, too much to—"

"I'll brook no arguments, Ella Jane." Her mother spoke in a tone honed to a no-nonsense edge.

"All right. I'll rest … for *your* sake." The dutiful daughter removed her hat and shook loose her bundle of corkscrews, a thick matted mess in the heat.

"There's gold in your hair, daughter." Mama ran her fingers through her waves.

"And silver in yours."

"Too bad the silver and gold's not in our pockets."

What Ella would give to put gold in Mama's pocket. Her mother insisted on helping in the fields even when baking, ironing, and scrubbing waited inside. How had she managed while her eldest daughter was away at school?

They let their hoes plop to the ground, scattering the scent of freshly turned soil. Although worn to a frazzle, this farmer's daughter was smitten with love for the land. She desired no other spot on earth for a home.

Mama led the way to the oak and sat in its filigreed shade.

Ella had packed a basket with a Mason jar of well water and four slices of bread spread with Chickasaw plum jam. The jar sweated like her scalp, in lazy trickles. She set it against her cheek and offered her mama the first swig. "Still cool."

Mama shook her head and leaned against the tree trunk. "You first. Drink your fill."

Ella downed half the water, a balm for her parched throat, and bit into the jellied bread.

"What came over you last night?" Mama finished off the refreshment and set the jar into the basket.

"Stood at the hot stove too long."

Her mother paused, as if ruminating. "Frank's ready to settle down."

Oh, to be free of such probing. Rolling up her long sleeves, necessary in the blazing sun but disagreeable in the shade, she fanned herself with her hat brim.

"He's grown into a mighty handsome man."

"Never favored black hair and eyes in a man."

"What's changed between you and Frank?"

"Just grown up." A lie could serve a noble purpose, couldn't it?

"He has a good future, good family. I'd give him a chance."

Ella scanned the horizon. "What about the job in Philadelphia?" If only he'd stayed there. Nothing good could come from his nearness.

"What he wants is here. Or should I say *who* he wants?"

If Mama knew the secret her daughter harbored, she'd thank her to keep away from the Irvings' son.

Scrambling sounds drew their attention to the turn row where Ruby and Lily trudged toward a bucket hanging from a nail on the wagon. Dipping tin mugs into the canister, they brought them to their lips dripping water.

Ella scowled. "Ruby and Lily don't have two nickels to rub together."

"Your papa pays as much as he can, better than others."

"Seems they should have more to show for their labor."

"Gotta do the best we can with what we're handed."

"Couldn't we hand them something better than hoes? We plug away in our own fields to keep costs down. They don't have a choice, not with a man of the house like Walter."

"Best not tread in other folks' affairs."

"Ever see Lily smile?" Ella stood and offered her mother a hand.

"Don't reckon."

They returned to the field with the noonday sun on their faces and the faithful soil beneath their feet.

"Lily ought to be giggling like other girls. Like Hannah." Ella drew her hair into a knot and stuffed it under her hat.

"Your sister has more to giggle about." Mama slipped on her gloves and nabbed her hoe.

Grateful for a hat that shielded her skin so apt to sport freckles, she nodded toward the Sloats. "I intend to learn what's troubling those two."

Mama pitched a wary glance. "Take heed, daughter mine. You could uncover a nest of vipers under that rock."

Rock Creek outlined the south side of the town of Needham. Along the way it curved to create a horseshoe of land no one cared to venture onto. Walter Sloat's property.

Ella intended to change that. She mounted Bunny and directed her toward town.

Two days of rain had kept laborers from fields and customers from town. Johnson's Tobacco Shop and Phillips Realty were shuttered. Morgan's Mercantile was opening in anticipation of Saturday afternoon shoppers, as was Papa. Cade was mending the sheepfold back home.

A rutted path diverged off the road at the edge of town. It ended at a rickety bridge that spanned a dry irrigation ditch once used by farmers, now grown over with brush.

A leaning fence with an open gate peeked through unsightly growth. Bunny's hooves clomped on the rough planks and softened to plops on the trail. A lone tree frog croaked, and a cicada screeched, not unlike those on the other side of the creek.

A peculiar stillness settled, as if a curtain had suffocated the noisy creatures. Ella's skin pebbled, but she nudged Bunny forward.

She reined in outside a tar-paper house where the screen door hung at a haphazard angle. A single wild yew sprouted near the stoop, and stone-hard soil spread its fingers around a well and outhouse. A spindly cow grazed on Indian grass the color of ashes.

Ruby's young son slouched on the stoop with a pea shooter in his hand. His ratty overalls exposed a swarthy shoulder and muddy feet.

"Hello, Donnie." She offered a smile and a wave.

The boy nodded and aimed the pea shooter at a bird on a low-hanging tree branch. A brown bean skidded past the bird, sending it fluttering away.

"Your mama home?"

"Doin' wash. At the creek."

"Is there a footpath?"

"Pa says it's just for Sloats." Light shimmered in the dark depths of his eyes.

"What if I'm calling on Sloats?"

"Can't rightly say."

"If you don't mind then, I'll find your mother. May Bunny drink at your trough?"

"I reckon."

The saddle leather stretched and whined as she dismounted.

Donnie took the reins and waddled to the well on legs as bowed as Ruby's spine.

Rickets. Compassion warmed Ella. No wonder the boy didn't work in the fields. "I've a tin of cookies. And honey." She held out a knapsack.

He turned, and his mouth sagged open. "Thank you, ma'am."

She set the bag on the stoop and strode around the house along a poorly tended path. Bees droned amid broom weed sufficient to supply Mama's medicine basket with a healing salve. Wild sumac bushes dripped with berries, another of the McFarlands' staples, their tea good for swelling. Mama had learned the art of healing from her own mother in the Ozark Mountains. For as long as she could remember Mama tended the wounds of her children, as well as neighbors and field workers. Even Doc Butler praised her skills and called on her for assistance.

Rippling laughter and sloshing water drew her toward the buttonbush shrubs that obscured the waterway.

"Stop that, Lily!"

"Just returning the favor." The girl's reply was laced with mirth.

Ella entered the shade of a sycamore surrounded by packed soil. Wet skirts and blouses, pants and shirts, and underclothes created a checkerboard over shrubs.

"Had us a good bath even without soap, didn't we, my Lily?"

Ella stopped short. They were bathing. No time for a social call.

Laughter spilled through the vegetation.

"Better get home. Your pa could pull up anytime."

"Why can't he leave for good?"

"Careful what you say!"

Alarm flashed through Ella.

"I'm near full grown. Pa or no pa, I'd like to tell that man—"

"Don't you back-talk your pa!" Ruby's voice reeked of trepidation.

The eldest daughter of Betsy McFarland knew better than to eaves-drop. Shame pawed at her. She whirled and broke into a run, stopping at the trailhead to calm her breathing.

She stepped around a heap of rusty cans and whiskey bottles, a graveyard instead of a garden. Ignoring Indian Territory's prohibition on liquor, Walter added to the pile while his wife and daughter toiled in the fields. As a sharecropper, the man had long claimed a portion of Papa's crop sales in payment for labor, but he never lifted a finger in the fields. Ruby and Lily earned the living.

Standing by a fire beneath a walnut tree, Donnie stirred the contents of a black iron pot. He gave Ella an impassive glance.

"Mind if I sit?"

"Don't reckon."

She squatted on a log and bunched her skirt around her booted feet. The boy's steaming pot drew her appraising eye. "Dinner?"

"Beans. Want some?"

"Maybe later."

He sat on the opposite end of the log and picked up his whittling.

She eyed the boy's handiwork. "What're you making?"

"Crutch."

For his bowed legs. She flushed with embarrassment.

Voices careened around the house as Ruby and Lily approached.

Ella stood.

Their smiles faded, and they jolted to a stop. Their hair dripped water onto sacking dresses that did little to conceal their wafer-thin frames. Or Ruby's shepherd's-crook back.

Their unexpected caller eased forward. "Hello."

They stepped back in tandem.

"I won't stay long."

"Leave!" Ruby extended an arm in front of her daughter.

"But—"

"Walter could be here any minute."

"Just wondered if I could visit now and then. With friends."

"Ain't likely. No place for you." Ruby shook her head, scattering droplets.

"Let her stay, Ma." Lily tugged her mother's sleeve.

Ruby gave her surprise visitor a prolonged stare. The woman's hair hung limp, the color of tarnished pennies. Her leathered skin testified to hardship, but her eyes hinted at a quick mind, a fiery spirit.

Ella raised her hands to ward off Ruby's concern. "No need to get upset."

Lily pulled on her mother's arm. "Please, Ma. Pa ain't comin' home for days."

At length, the woman of the house nodded. "While Walter's gone, you can visit Lily. But not me."

"I want to know you, too."

"My lot's set." The haggard mother studied the ground and bent a lone blade of grass with a bare toe. "But my Lily girl's something else."

"May I come by tomorrow after church?"

"Suit yourself." Ruby tossed her a backward glance and shooed her children inside.

CHAPTER 6

"They're scared spitless, Papa!" Ella hammered her fist on the table. She eyed her parents through the dim light of a kerosene lantern. Unlike herself and her parents, the sun wouldn't rise for two hours.

"Settle down, daughter." Mama raised her hands as if to ward off her child's ferocity.

"I'm worried about them." She drummed her fingers.

"You've reason enough to fret." Papa tapped his tin mug with a forefinger. "But we can't bury our noses in other folks' lives."

"If you could see their faces ... their eyes. And the hopelessness." Her lips tensed. "Oh, I'm itching to—"

"Now, Ella Jane . . ." Her father peered at her from under one arched eyebrow. "Your itches more times than not—"

"More times than not she gets things done, Gavin." Mama folded her arms on the table and leaned toward her ever-so-earnest daughter. "What about Worthington? The board's considering your application, and you're lining up a year's worth of chores."

Ella pictured Lily's tired young face, her cheeks hollowed like an old woman's. She longed to see the girl laugh or even smile like the child she was.

"She needs someone to come alongside her. I've a plan for how to do that whether or not Worthington makes me an offer."

Papa glanced at Mama and gave his girl a guarded perusal. "Let's have it."

"With knowledge comes power. So I'll teach her to read."

"What about her helping with the Sloat living?"

"Knowing how to read would open doors to a different livelihood. For now, helping with my canned goods and produce business is a way to start." She paused to let the idea settle.

"Your enterprise has done well, but it's not enough to make a living." Papa's cocked eyebrow signaled his dubiousness.

"The two of us can increase production. And split the earnings."

"What about Vi?" Mama said. "She's always been a part of your dealings."

Ella rolled her eyes. "I'm sorry, but as much as I'd love for Vi to partner with me, she sits to the side and gripes. She prefers selling her sweet-smelling soaps and sachets anyway."

Papa leaned back. "Your idea sounds reasonable. Gotta sell Walter on it though."

"He'd be crazy to oppose more coins in his pocket." Ella pushed away from the table. "I'll see what Ruby thinks."

"How do you plan to teach reading?" Mama persisted in her query.

"Same way you taught me—with the newspaper and Bible." The county school ended after third grade for girls and eighth for boys, but Mama insisted her girls continue through eighth and then at home. The upcoming school year would be Hannah's last at the county school. Mama's patient teaching had inspired Ella's own dreams.

She set her cup in the wash pan and turned with a pointed finger. "There's McGuffey's *Eclectic Series* and Peter Parley and Cousin Sarah stories in the attic. The classics, too. Plus, I have the complete set of Ellen Cyr readers. California's considering them as their adopted school texts. I especially like her *Third Reader* because it presents women and girls who take action."

"Best have the details laid out before Walter gets back," Mama said.

"That gives me a few days, according to Lily."

"Who's to take your places in the field?" Papa said.

"We'll read before work, at noon, and at the end of the day."

"What about chores, yours and Lily's both?"

"What I don't get done daily, I'll make up for on Saturdays."

"Ella Jane." Papa's gaze bore into her.

"And I'll help her with chores on Sundays."

"The Lord's Day?" Papa taught his family to revere the first day of the week.

"Helping Lily's nothing short of benevolence."

"My, how you can plow a piece of ground."

"Somebody has to." She headed for the stairs.

"That somebody needs to consider what the folks she's planning for think." Papa leaned toward his daughter. "What about Walter?"

She stopped, remembering the dread on Ruby's face. But hadn't the poor woman given her permission to visit Lily? The so-called man of the house needn't know. Taking two stair steps at a time, she leaned over the balustrade. "I'll talk to Ruby."

Papa's question—what about Walter?—pinged in her mind like bird shot, but it wouldn't turn her aside.

The sun had yet to reach its zenith when Ella slipped from the church the following day. No time to volunteer in the widows' pantry. She'd render service of a different kind. Dressed in a riding skirt and simple waist, she freed the bun at the nape of her neck and tied a bandana around her quarrelsome tresses. Chewing on a corn fritter, she directed Bunny over the hill toward town.

She prayed until she reached the Sloat house. A few resolute chickens pecked for their meager meal. The rooster as dingy as sun-bleached poppies eyed her. Several items drooped on the clothesline. Tethering Bunny, she stepped onto the porch and knocked.

Donnie greeted her through the screen.

"Your mamma here?"

"Out yonder in the privy."

"And Lily?"

"Lookin' for bullfrogs."

"I'll wait out here."

"Suit yourself."

The outhouse door squeaked open. Ruby's stooped form materialized like a wraith.

Ella cleared her throat. "Howdy."

Ruby stopped mid-stride, squinting. The morning light outlined her disfigured shape in painful clarity. "That you, Ella?"

"Got a minute?"

"I reckon." Ruby joined her under the tree.

"I have a proposition. I need a partner in my produce business. Lily needs to learn to read. What do you say we trade services?"

As Ruby stared at her, Ella silently prayed she'd go along with the idea. Would her pride get in the way? *Lord, please let her agree.*

Ruby turned her eyes toward the creek and pursed her lips as if she'd bitten into a bitter herb. When she brought her gaze back to Ella's, a look of determination had replaced signs of uncertainty. "You teach my Lily to read, and she'll give you a hand all you want. But I stay out of it. It's that or nothin'." Ruby paused. "If Walter gets his tail over the line 'bout this, we'll all pay."

"Come on, Donnie," Ruby said. "We're going out yonder for broom weed."

Lily approached, whistling. She smiled around yellowed teeth and held up a string of bullfrogs. "Want some hoppers?"

"Maybe another time. But I have something for you, Lily." She offered up a knapsack. "Chickasaw plums and supper leavings."

Tall and willowy, Lily approached. Grime—the kind a bath without soap never could remove—splotched her face. A length of twine held back her hair. "Thank ya." She cradled the sack. The dirt under her fingernails could sustain a crop of melons.

Lily turned without explanation and scampered toward the house, and her visitor strained to keep up. The girl opened the door and let it slap shut, barely missing Ella's nose.

Ella composed herself with a steadying breath and stepped inside.

The odor of accumulated filth assaulted her. Unwashed bodies. Overripe food scraps. Neglected floorboards. She held a hand under her nose, lest the stench bring up breakfast.

"Have a seat." Lily spoke from the dim interior.

Ella allowed her eyes to adjust. The sun revealed a bare plank floor. A nail keg supported one corner of a three-legged table. Crude sycamore chairs and upended logs served as seating.

She settled into a chair, its surface worn smooth.

"Want some blackberry tea?" Lily pointed to a blackened stew pot above a fire grate. An iron skillet and two tin pans sat nearby.

"I'd love some."

Lily ladled hot water into a teapot, chipped and sporting the faded outline of a pink posy and powder-blue ribbon. She covered the pot with a saucer and set it on the table with two cups.

A vaporous finger laced with the fragrance of blackberries meandered from the spout.

Ella sniffed. "Smells good."

"Ma saves it for when Pa ain't around."

"The Bible says a worthy woman looks well to the ways of her household."

"Ma talks to us 'bout the Good Book." Lily poured the tea. "Ain't never read it, though."

Ella raised her cup and sipped. The pungent flavor told her the girl had used a fresh batch of dried berries. "Reading from the Good Book's daily fare under Papa's roof."

Lily ran a calloused finger around the rim of her cup. "I can't read much more 'n what's on yonder sacks and cans. And the Sears catalog." She pointed to a cupboard without doors. Tin cans with torn labels and sacks with faded lettering read Flour, Cornmeal, Beans, and Salt, all provisions from Mama's pantry.

"I'll teach you to read." The recently licensed teacher sipped her tea.

"You will?"

The plea in Lily's voice gave the teacher in Ella a gentle shove. She set down her cup and leaned toward the girl. "Indeed I will."

But what about Worthington? There wouldn't be much time . . . She disregarded the snippet of doubt. She'd help this girl even if it meant setting her alarm an hour earlier.

Lily smiled, the first time to do so. She spread plum jelly on bread and made more tea. "Let's sit over yonder." Lily pointed to an old ladder-back chair beside a chest near the heath. An oil lamp sat atop its soot-blackened surface.

Ella examined a carving that graced the lid: RLD 1775. "It's lovely."

"Ma's granny's." Lily settled on the floor beside the chest and gestured for her guest to take the chair. Without prompting she spoke of her longing to read and wondered about the world beyond Rock Creek.

Ella spoke of possibility and promise.

Lily absorbed her new friend's enthusiasm like a dry sponge takes in water. They'd finished off the leftover pork roast and emptied the teapot before they exhausted their storehouse of words.

This day was about building trust. Teaching would come later.

A dusky sunset was slanting through the windows when Ella said her farewell and mounted Bunny. She turned at the bend in the trail and looked back. Lily lived in a tar-paper prison, but starting tomorrow those bars would come down.

Walter Sloat would do well to stay out of Ella's way.

CHAPTER 7

"Lily's coming for her first lesson this morning." Ella set the last plate on the table and reached for the napkins.

A knock drew her to the back door, and she held aside the curtain. "She's here. In a skimpy dress. Where are her field clothes?"

Mama peeked around the window covering. "I'll swan."

Ella opened the door and stood aside. "Good Monday morning. Join us for breakfast?"

"I'll wait out here 'til you're finished." Lily stood with hat and knapsack in hand.

"We have plenty."

"That ain't it." Her tone had softened.

Ella stepped outside. "What is it?"

"Ain't fit to sit at your table." She lowered her head.

"Of course you are. But do you care to get started reading then?" A breeze picked up, rocking the swing in a jig. A pad of paper, two pencils, and the Cyr reader awaited them.

"Can I get a bath 'fore I sit at your table? I can smell my own self." She turned a bare foot side to side. "I'll hoe a extra row of cotton for the sight of clean feet."

Ella's face warmed. The poor child must've noticed the bath tub when she helped with laundry. "Of course. But you won't turn an extra clod." She glanced toward the horizon where the sun had just risen. "Time enough for a bath before breakfast."

"Don't wanna pester you none."

"Go on to the shed. I'll bring hot water."

Lily bounced off the porch with her knapsack and hat. Her single braid swung like a stiff rope dancing in the wind.

Ella entered the kitchen and chuckled, drawing five sets of eyes to her own.

"What's got you tickled?" Mama angled her head at a questioning slant.

"We need hot water in the shed."

"For what?" Papa spoke behind his newspaper.

"Lily wants to wash up."

He lowered the paper. "She can do that at the well. Can't she?"

"She wants a whole bath."

"Before work?" Frowning, Viola set out an assortment of jams.

"Before breakfast."

"Thank heavens." The sachet-scented beauty mumbled and rolled her eyes.

"What about her lesson?" Cade entered the kitchen, shaven and buttoning a cuff.

Ella raised her hands to halt the questions. "We can read if we have time. Meanwhile, let's pour up the hot water from the reservoir and turn up the heat under both kettles. Got any lemon verbena, Mama?"

"Good idea." She scurried toward her bedroom. "I'll bring towels."

Rummaging through a basket on the lower shelf of her mother's reading table, Ella set aside nail care items. More digging produced a tin of beeswax and a bottle of mineral oil. "Got any Brilliantine, Papa?"

He nodded and walked with a purposeful gait to his bedroom.

Cade bounded toward the mud room. "It's milking time."

"Coward," Papa called from down the hall.

Papa and Ella carried four buckets of hot water to a bench outside the shed, and Mama followed with bathing products.

Ella found Lily in her underclothes on a bench. She'd filled the tin washtub half full of cool well water and folded her shift into a neat square. A bucket of clear water for rinsing waited nearby.

Hair like weathered hemp drooped across her shoulders.

What colors lay beneath the grime? Ella caught a whiff of an odor like the Sloat house. She must send the girl home with a jug of vinegar and lye soap.

Sachet bags added to hot water produced a bouquet of lemons that drifted upward in balmy clouds. Next, a bar of Pears soap on the bench. Towels. Nail tools. Baking soda and a toothbrush.

She dipped a finger into the water. "Feels right." She spread open a dressing screen. "I'll be along later to help with your hair."

"My bonnie lies over the ocean." The lass sang in a sweet, clear voice.

What was Ella getting herself into? She'd return to Worthington soon. Surely someone could pick up with the sweet girl's studies if …

She forced away her unease. Already curriculum ideas were forming—the alphabet, phonics, numbers, table manners, and personal hygiene. Strolling toward the house with her hands in her pockets, she allowed her thoughts to scurry to Scripture, then to her tongue. "The worthy woman's household is clothed in scarlet, and she gives tasks to her maidens."

She descended the cellar steps alongside the house. The door opened without a sound, and a cool draft whooshed around her. She lit a lantern with a match from the wall dispenser, and light flooded the paneled space. Shelves heavy with Ella's canned goods created rows as in a library. Mason jars of summer vegetables and fruits all labeled and arranged in alphabetical order, dried berries, and herbs. Viola's specialty ointments and sachets in tightly lidded jars were lined up on one shelf.

A writing table and straight chair sat beneath a vent that provided circulation. On the table lay a stationery box, newspaper, pencils, and pens, Ella's private spot for reading and studying.

Crossing the dirt floor, she entered an interior room that retained the underground chill. Moisture clung to the motionless air. Crates of root vegetables packed in saw dust lined the far wall. She examined each container and etched figures in the air with a finger. At the table she prepared her tasks amid pen scratching and the rattling of newspaper print. She returned to the wash shed with her mind cluttered with calculations.

The notes of an old tune, off-key but earnest, greeted Ella at the wash shed. She rapped on the door. "Ready?"

"Come in."

She peeked around the screen.

Lily leaned forward in the tub with a goodly portion of her thick mane drooping down her back and the rest trailing face-first into the bath water, hiding her face. She sputtered. "I used the soap. Three times."

Ella doused her new friend's head with rinse water. "Run your fingers through it and squeeze." The liquid poured through the girl's long locks and into the tub in gray rivulets. At the second rinsing, it ran clear.

She laid a towel over the edge of the tub. "I'll straighten up while you dress."

When she rejoined Lily, the girl was sitting on the bench in home-spun drawers and a chemise with *Gold Medal* stenciled across the bosom. Her hair covered her face like a mop, the damp towel wrapped around her shoulders.

Ella spread a dab of Brilliantine between her palms and kneaded it into the damp strands. She wrapped the towel around Lily's head to form a turban, revealing her shoulders and back.

Air rushed into Ella's lungs. Scars, some faded, others fiery, stretched from Lily's shoulders along her back as if a malfeasant hand had sprinkled sizzling grease. "What's this?"

"Quirt tracks." Lily covered her face with her hands. "When Ma irks Pa, I get a lash. And she gets mine. You don't want to see Ma's backside."

Ella's fury bubbled. "Your father used a horse whip on you? This is a crime! We're reporting it to the sheriff!"

"No. Please." Lily pleaded with her face turned away. "Don't do noth-in'. He'll kill Ma!"

What was she to do? "When's Walter coming home?"

"'Nother few days, I reckon."

"We'll have to figure out something." Unstopping the tub, she released the water through a pipe system that irrigated the property. She collected bath items, swabbed surfaces, and gave the floor another swipe. "I'll take these things to the house while you dress."

When she returned to the shed, she knocked and walked through the doorway. "Ready, Lily?"

"I reckon."

The child turned, and Ella gasped.

CHAPTER 8

"Lily?" Ella stepped nearer.

The girl's hair spun around her shoulders and down her back, exposing her features. Her eyes radiated bright green light. Her hair glistened like copper. Her teeth gleamed. Her nails were spotless and trimmed. Her freckles were sprinkled over apricot skin.

A magnificent creature had emerged from a cocoon of dirt. Would she unfurl her wings and fly away?

She pointed the unsuspecting girl to the mirror. "You're a beautiful butterfly. Look."

As water trickled from the tub, Lily inched forward and lifted her eyes.

Like a kaleidoscope, she'd been transformed. Such a change would extend far beyond her appearance. It would creep into the crevices of her world.

Ella studied a silky tress. It caught the light and slipped through her fingers like satin ribbon. "What're we to do with you now?"

"Work on what's inside yonder girl?" The transformed young one nodded at her image.

"What's inside yonder girl is beautiful too. We've only to bring it out."

But how? What would Walter say? Surely he wouldn't begrudge his daughter a bath. Or learning to read. Would he?

She grasped Lily by the shoulders. "Are you ready to read, dear girl?"

"Been ready all my life." She offered a lopsided grin.

"Would you like a pair of shoes? And some boots? I've an extra pair of each."

"I reckon I would." She leaned forward and wiggled her toes.

They finished straightening the shed and spread the wet towels across the tub.

Ella gestured for Lily to follow her to the house. She stepped into the kitchen where her family was waiting breakfast.

"It's about time." Viola rolled her eyes.

Ella closed the door and leaned against it. "Something's happened to Lily."

Five pairs of eyes snapped to hers. Cade jumped to his feet.

"What is it?" Mama's eyes had widened.

She extended her hands in a calming gesture. "Nothing's wrong. But prepare yourselves."

Opening the door, she coaxed Lily inside.

"Dear Lord, what've You done now?" Mama spoke in a whisper.

Papa scratched his head.

"That you, Lily?" Hannah tilted her head and squinted.

Viola frowned, and Cade stared.

Ella proffered a sweeping hand. "Meet Lillian Sloat, belle of Glover County."

The child's smile added fullness to her cheeks, her gemstone eyes a sharp contrast to her crude dress. The girl from the other side of Rock Creek was nothing short of a beauty. She shifted her feet and looked down at her hands, as presentable as Viola's. "Weeds're waitin' out yonder. You reckon we can eat now?"

"You're too pretty for a cotton field." Cade spoke the words as if in a trance.

"Ain't nobody too good for honest work."

Ella smiled and guided Lily toward the table. With only days until she returned to Worthington and hopefully a position, how could she do this deprived child justice? She could only try. But first she'd feed the girl.

The family stood around the table set for seven, the three McFarland girls on one side, Lily and Cade on the other, and Mama and Papa at either end. Joshua babbled in his baby chair between his mother and grandmother.

Cade pulled out a chair. "Have a seat, Miss Sloat."

She blushed and ducked her chin, and they all claimed their seats.

Papa said grace.

Mama passed their guest the bread basket. "Have some biscuits and gravy."

Lily set a biscuit on her plate.

"For goodness sakes, girl, get you some breakfast." Mama plopped down three more and upended the gravy dish over them. "Eat up. That field's calling."

Their copper-haired guest grasped her fork as she would a broom handle and leaned toward her plate. "Good groceries, Mrs. Mac." She mumbled around a gravy-laden lump.

Viola brought her napkin to her mouth and turned aside.

Ella flashed her sister a warning glare. "Here, Lily. Have some ham."

"Ain't had hog meat in don't know when." Nutrition starved, she stared at the bounty.

"Take that big piece." Cade set the platter between them.

She speared the ham and tore off a hunk with her teeth.

Viola glared at Ella who returned it in spades.

"Pass that meat down this way." Papa gestured with his chin.

The family shook its collective head, spell broken. Breakfast-time chatter made its way around the table as they filled their stomachs.

In time, Papa leaned back and patted his belly. "Some of that nectar'll do it." Hannah passed him a bowl of the golden concoction. "This here's straight from Heaven." He poured the syrupy mixture over a biscuit.

Lily's gaze slipped from Papa's plate to her own. She drizzled the mixture on the last biscuit and scraped the bowl with her spoon. "How you make this, Mrs. Mac?"

"Just butter, sugar, and egg. And a little vanilla."

Ella raised an eyebrow. "Don't let her fool you. She learned a secret trick from Grandma Anglin. Whatever it is—she didn't pass it on to me." She pointed with a fork to the specks in the sauce. "That's browned egg and sugar."

Lily spooned a portion of the dripping confection into her mouth and ran her tongue along her lips. She closed her eyes as her mouth churned. "That there's ... What'd you call it, Mr. Mac?"

"Nectar of heaven."

She jerked a nod. "That's it." When she consumed the last morsel, she lifted the plate with both hands and slurped.

Ella dispatched a warning glance at Viola, daring her to speak an unkind word.

Lily must learn table manners, but the McFarlands were sure to learn plenty from the girl from the other side of Rock Creek.

"Go on, you two. Hannah and I'll do the dishes." Mama shooed them toward the door.

Downing the last drop of coffee, Ella pushed away from the table. "Let's sit outside."

"Thanks for pulling out my chair, Cade." Lily turned to Mama and Papa. "I 'preciate you givin' me a place 'round your four-legged table. You filled me plumb up." She smiled at Viola and gave Joshua a gentle pat on the head.

Ella waved her outside with a flourish. "Have a seat. Today's lesson is the alphabet."

With Ellen Cyr's *First Reader* between them, the teacher pointed and spoke. And her student listened and responded, one letter and its sound after another.

"Looks like you learned more from sacks and cans than you thought."

The girl's cheeks blushed rosy peach.

When the sun warmed their necks an hour later, Lily pointed to the field. "It's time."

The door opened, and Cade stepped out. "Sun's dried the dew by now."

"Field's calling then." The young beauty pulled her tail to the crown of her head, plopped on her hat, and tied the twine under her chin.

The family lined up beside Cade.

"Thanks for the bath, Mrs. Mac." Lily strode off the porch. "Pay you in trade." Her long strides took her across the yard and around the clothesline and outhouse without a backward glance.

"If that don't beat all." Papa positioned his hat atop his head.

Mama turned her head side to side, pensive-like. "Never saw anything like it."

Hannah gazed toward the field with a wistful expression. "I want a lemon verbena bath."

Viola returned to the kitchen without speaking, and Cade stared toward the back fence.

Why hadn't Ella reached out to Lily sooner? How many whippings might she have prevented had she only known? She must speak with Mama and Papa about Walter.

But what would happen to the student if her teacher moved to Worthington? Trepidation raised its ugly head, but she set it aside. She'd permit nothing to come between her and her newly found pupil.

CHAPTER 9

Supper conversation at the McFarlands' table consisted of nothing but Lily.

"Her eyes." Hannah gazed upward. "They're like Mrs. Scott's emerald ring."

Who'd've thought apricots hid under all that dirt?

Viola remained silent as she scooped peas into Joshua's mouth.

"Copper." Cade set an elbow on the table. "Always did favor copper-colored hair."

"Oh!" Ella whirled from the table. "I promised her shoes." Her heels tapped the floor planks like single-minded woodpeckers.

Papa raised a halting hand. "You could be stepping on toes doling out charity."

"I already asked." She halted at the first step. "You should've seen her smile."

"We'll do it then." Mama followed up the staircase.

Hannah skittered behind them. "I have extra ribbons." She opened her wardrobe. "Here's a pair of slippers. I'll see if Cade has some shoes for Donnie."

Viola emerged from her room. "She can have this pinafore."

"That's old and stained. Give her something that bears wearing." Ella pulled a tatting-trimmed pinafore from Vi's wardrobe. "Like this."

"Not my best!" She snatched the garment, and the edging ripped. "Look what you've done! It's worthless now!" She crushed it into a tight wad and threw it at her sister.

The seamstress assessed the damage. "I can fix it."

"I'll not participate another minute in the dressing of Lily Sloat!"

Viola stomped down the stairs and out the door.

"Oh!" Ella grimaced and tightened her hands into fists. "Sometimes I'd like to—"

"But you can't." Mama offered her a carpetbag.

She set the shoes in the bag. Undergarments, skirt, waist, dress, and ribbons followed. Imagining her young friend's expression at the sight of the clothing brightened her spirit. "Where's that old cupboard, Mama?"

"In the shed."

As his eldest child bounded down the stairs, Papa let his newspaper crumble into his lap. "Best take care, daughter."

She halted with a fist at her waist. "How could a man object to a cupboard with doors?"

"I don't know how some men can do a lot of things, sugar."

"No field work tomorrow. Can't we take Ruby some things and let her decide?"

Mama gave a pert nod. "A woman enjoys a surprise now and again, Gavin."

He scrutinized his wife and daughter. "I reckon you can, but be ready to bring it back if Ruby hesitates."

Ella took to the sewing chair with the torn pinafore in her lap. On the morrow she'd mend Lily's world, Walter Sloat or nay.

Tuesday morning brought a bevy of activities.

The women packed baskets with seldom-used pans and utensils. Mama supervised Papa's and Cade's wrestling match with the cupboard and cookstove. "Careful, Gavin! Look out, Cade!"

"Go inside, Betsy." Papa would tolerate no interference.

Mama ventured a peek out the window. "They're handling those things like bales of hay."

"Come on, Mama. Morning's half gone." Ella scanned the kitchen a final time. "Put the peas on to boil, Vi. And heat the flatiron."

Perusing a *Ladies Home Journal*, Viola ignored her.

Papa tied his buckskin Cherokee to the wagon and took the driver's seat beside Mama. Cade mounted his bay gelding, Braun.

Climbing into the wagon, the eldest McFarland girl assumed her teacher stance and issued instructions to Hannah on the porch. "Clothes are sprinkled and rolled up." Papa whisked the reins, and she called out a final time, "Stay away from your journal. Too much to do."

They rumbled down the drive in a wagon overflowing with goods and their hearts with anticipation.

Lily was waiting outside the rickety tarpaper house.

Ruby joined her daughter and focused on Mama. "Betsy."

Mama alighted and nodded. "Ruby."

"Can you use these things?" Ella offered Lily the carpetbag.

Ruby responded with a hard shake of her head. "Can't take 'em. Walter won't like it."

"Can't we hide 'em, Ma?" Lily's pleading expression was heart rending. "Pa never goes out yonder to the lean-to."

Ruby lowered her eyes, chewing as on a cud. "I reckon we can lock 'em in the chest."

Relief swept over Ella.

Mama pointed to the furniture in the wagon. "Can you use those things?"

"Don't take handouts." Ruby's tone said she'd brook no arguments.

"You can take them in trade. Help with the canning, maybe?"

Lily whispered to her mother.

With a look of resignation, Ruby propped open the door. "Bring 'em in." She nodded to Donnie. "Pick some mint. And haul in a bit of wood."

The McFarland women stepped into the Sloat shanty. Steam threaded from a stew pot over dying embers. The fragrance of blackberries masked the patina of odors.

The men wrestled the cookstove and cupboard inside and settled them where Ruby directed. The women deposited the supplies, utensils, and cookware in the cupboard.

Ruby raised an arresting hand. "Too much. I'll never get it paid for."

"I'll help." Lily slid a hand around her mother's waist.

"Excuse us, ladies." Papa donned his hat, "We'll be on our way now."

The men strode outside, and Donnie slipped inside. He laid a bundle of leaves on the hearth with two logs. "We burn cow patties most days. This here's for special times."

Lily filled a cheesecloth bag with mint leaves and dropped it into the stew pot.

Ruby stood beside the old chest. "Bring those clothes over here."

Inside the trunk lay a *Holy Bible* and a veritable treasure unlike any Ella had imagined Ruby owned—a lace-trimmed garter, an old brocade miser's purse, a pair of silk stockings. And what looked to be a journal. Perhaps a book. Where in the world had they come from?

Lily laid her garments atop Ruby's treasures. "Ain't never seen nothin' like this finery."

Experiencing a spate of shame, Ella recalled the many times she and her sisters had rejected the garments Lily received as if fit for a queen.

By noon the women had finished cleaning. Floors were mopped with lye. Pots were hung on the wall and towels on hooks. A jar of wildflowers and rag rugs brightened the table and floor. Canned and dried goods lined the cupboard shelves. The kitchen radiated warmth.

Ella noticed a McFarland's General Store calendar on the wall. "There's a circle around next Saturday, the twenty-ninth. Special day?"

"My birthday." Lily grinned. "I'll be thirteen."

The germ of an idea sprouted. They would surprise Lily with a party.

Papa's former warning rang an alarm, but she silenced it. Should Lily be denied a party because it would chap Walter's hide?

No. The eldest McFarland girl would stand against such neglect and remedy it. She surveyed the house with a thumbnail at her teeth. "Is the old bedstead in the shed, Mama?"

"Yes. So is the wardrobe."

"We'll pay for 'em." Lily extended a halting hand.

"In time." Ella answered with a dismissive hand, already planning future deliveries.

"Thank you, folks." Ruby's eyes had moistened. "You'll get what's owed you."

Mama hugged her. "Like I said, you can help with the canning."

"Let us know when it's time." The destitute woman straightened, proud-like.

Ella waved a farewell, and Donnie returned the gesture.

Ella abandoned her Friday meal preparations. "I'm not interested in stepping out with Frank." Would her father ever understand?

She glanced at Viola feeding Joshua a scoop of red beans. If Papa knew who fathered his grandson, he'd pester her about Frank no longer.

"My elder sister wants to be an old maid." Viola spoke singsong-like.

Papa lowered *The Daily Oklahoman* with an affectionate smile.

"Marriage and teaching don't mix." The teacher candidate blotted her hands on her apron.

"His father asked about it today, that's all."

"I have my own plans." She set the shelling bowl on the table.

"You aren't the only McFarland girl who could step out with Frank." Viola all but growled and glanced at her father.

Papa ignored her. "No better plan than having a home, Ella."

"Teaching's an honorable vocation."

"What about a family?" He swatted the paper. "Frank's looking to settle down."

"He's university educated and ready to step into his father's shoes." Viola spoke above Joshua's babbles and slaps on the table.

"Normal school might not be the same as a university back East, but it trained me to teach. And teach I will."

Papa snapped the paper shut. "For all we know, Worthington won't hire you. Time to think of a home."

She leaned against the Hoosier cupboard. She'd hope for Worthington until hope died. But her calling to teach would survive. "I'll live as a spinster if I must."

Papa straightened in his reading chair. "Arguing with Ella McFarland's like spitting in the wind. A fellow ain't likely to come out ahead."

"Nor is a sister." Viola gave a mirthless chuckle.

Ella thrust a floured fist into the risen dough, scattering the rich bouquet of yeast. She dumped the lump onto the floured dough board and kneaded it with the heels of her hands. "Those stubborn Mexican petunias outside don't have a thing on us McFarlands." She flung a hand, flouring the floor.

Papa turned his eyes to the window. "It took a passel of folks as stubborn as mules to settle Indian Territory. And the good graces of the Chickasaw Nation."

"How many tales of McFarland stubbornness have passed around our supper table?" She rolled a section of dough into a ball.

"One or two." Papa chuckled.

"A daily affair, as surely as a pot of beans." She set the clump into an oiled baking dish and pinched off another portion.

"My big sister's saying she gets her stubborn streak from you, Papa." Viola scraped Joshua's bowl with a spoon. "But you're too stubborn to admit it."

As much as Ella loved her sister, Viola could conjure up her ire with a handful of words. Why did Mama and Papa put up with it? "If you're finished feeding Joshua, I need another pair of hands. There's supper and Lily's party tomorrow."

"But—"

"No buts." Papa tucked his shirt into his trousers, popped on his hat, and strode out.

"Why're we having a party for the likes of Lily Sloat?" Viola pulled Joshua from his chair and propped him on a hip.

"What do you mean by 'the likes of'?" A rush of indignation trundled over Ella.

"They're trash."

"We're having a surprise party for Lily, Vi." She slid the pan of rolls into the oven. "And you're going to help."

CHAPTER 10

"*M*ake a wish, Lily dear." Mama grinned as she lit the last candle.

Lily's face flushed as rosy a peach as the dress Mama had altered to fit her willowy form. "Ain't never blowed out no birthday candles. Sure 'nough not thirteen."

"First time for everything." Ella intended the celebration to be a never-forgotten event.

A bevy of lady friends from Christ Church had flocked to the community hall. They cheered and huddled close. Not the type to join social clubs, they embraced the birthday girl as kind-hearted and deserving of their affection, plain and simple.

"Wishin' won't get me no … anywhere. Gotta be doin'."

One matron brushed a hand on the child's shoulder. "It's your birthday, not your graduation. Time for fun."

Another harrumphed. "You'll be stuck in books soon enough."

Unlike other Needham women, these chatterers received the girl from the other side of Rock Creek as their own. Hopefully their acceptance would encourage her to attend church services. Thus far she'd shown no interest.

"I'm proud of you for setting lofty goals." Mama's eyes misted.

Lily dabbed a hankie to her eyes and settled her hands in her lap. She breathed in and blew over the candles, extinguishing all but one.

Viola pushed forward and puffed out the last flame. "Couldn't finish the job?" she murmured at Lily's ear.

Lily paled.

Ella spun, ready to do battle in defense of this innocent child, but

Viola had retreated beyond the circle of friends.

Unaware of the callous remark, the women cheered and shouted their jubilation.

Itching to set her callous sister straight, Ella shouldered past two women, but Lily's pleading gaze brought her up short. Making a scene at a birthday party was hardly the way to celebrate. If the target of Vi's animus could maintain her composure, so could Ella McFarland.

She regained her composure and returned to the cake table. Slipped the glass server under a chunk of decadent dessert. Slid it onto a china plate. And smiled. "First slice for the honoree."

When the last guest bid farewell and Cade drove Lily toward home, naught but crumbs remained of Mama's butter cake with strawberry icing.

Viola nabbed the server and licked it. "Hmmm."

"Be careful not to stain your dress. Got too much ironing as it is." Mama gave her thoughtless daughter's cheek a playful pinch.

Scowling, Ella stacked plates and cups into a wooden crate. "I was twelve when you marched me to an ironing board. Vi's eighteen and has yet to heat a flatiron."

"I heard that." Perched on a stool by the window, Viola spun and giggled and swirled her dark chestnut mane.

Mama extended a pointed forefinger. "Stop that. You'll make yourself sick."

The young mother gave the stool another twirl. She chose opposition when compliance would be the easier path.

Ella could restrain herself no longer. "You heard Mama. Stop it."

Her spinning sister laughed and gave the stool another twirl. "Make me."

Clenching her teeth, Ella stepped from behind the table.

Mama grabbed her upper arm. "Leave her be." She nodded at the remaining dishes. "We're almost done."

"But—" Movement outside the window drew her gaze. She squinted. And shivered. Good heavens. Frank was leaning against a sugar berry tree across the road. And conversing with an unsavory-looking stranger. Was Viola preening for him?

"What's Frank doing hanging around here?"

Mama looked up as the stranger shuffled off. Frank flicked a cigarette into the dirt and strolled toward the realty company. "Property dealings, looks like." She returned to the dishes. "Help us pack, Vi."

Viola replied with another whorl. No doubt Mama knew forcing her daughter to help would result in broken items she'd have to replace.

Would Viola watch their mother toil herself to death?

"I'll help. We'll get it done quicker anyway." Ella left off speaking the thoughts that rabbled in her mind. She wouldn't allow her mother to bend over a hot stove or hang clothing on the line or pack a single dish alone.

Mama scanned the room. "Where's Hannah?"

"Outside." Viola rolled her eyes. "What she gets from those stuffy books, I'll never understand." She turned to the window and twisted a silky strand around a finger.

Mama dried the last dish and set it into the crate. "It'll take both of us to get this into the pantry, Ella." They couldn't afford to replace a single saucer belonging to the Women's Club.

When the last dish was packed away, they locked up and climbed into their buggy.

"Come on, Hannah." Ella eyed her sister reading beneath a shade tree. "Hannah!"

Her head popped up, her eyes wide. "Wait for me!"

"Hurry. Papa's watching Joshua."

When Hannah's scrambling feet settled in the buggy, Ella directed Bunny onto the road. A banner announcing the church's upcoming quarterly singing stretched across Main Street.

Shoppers stopped and looked their way. Three women stared. A couple glanced at them and turned back to a window display. No one waved.

"See why I don't bring Joshua to town?" Viola wrinkled her nose. "I despise these people."

"Gotta live in spite of them." Ella figured her words were wasted breath, but at least Lily had enjoyed the birthday celebration of her life. There must be a way to help her in spite of the malice … and Worthington.

Ella woke Monday morning and stretched. Sunlight glimmered around the window shade. She swung her legs over the side of her bed and slipped into a cotton duster.

The laundry called. Thank goodness for a cooler morning.

"I'm awake." Hannah muttered from under her covers.

Stepping into the hallway, she opened Viola's door. "Rise and shine."

Viola growled and turned away.

Joshua stood in his crib, drooling around a rattle.

A substantial breakfast of boiled eggs and flapjacks fortified the women for the day's grueling labor. Heat from the stove and dishwater had consumed the morning cool, and perspiration beaded on Ella's upper lip.

"By the way, I can't help." Viola made the announcement as her elder sister and mother slipped on their aprons. "Frank's coming to talk about a teller's position at the bank."

"Who will see to Joshua while you're visiting?" Mama had fisted a hand at her waist.

"Hannah."

Such disregard enflamed Ella. "That'll mean less hands for chores."

"The worthy woman's productive." Mama leveled a pointed finger at her sassy daughter. "When Frank leaves, you'll join me in the wash shed. One sister is tending your child, and the other has the garden."

Viola flashed a sideways scowl but curbed her tongue.

The industrious mother-daughter pair headed for the wash shed.

Papa had built the separate outbuilding with a fireplace so Mama could run her laundry service without heating up the house. He installed a sturdy inside clothesline for rainy days and planted fruit trees outside so their fragrance would lift his wife's spirits.

The women sloshed garments in tubs. The fret of wet fabric over rub boards and the grating of each turn of the wringers settled into a gentle, mesmerizing rhythm.

"I'm sorry those Worthington men don't see what a prize they have in you, daughter."

"Until I know their decision, I'll keep dreaming." She sloshed a shirt in the clear rinse water, squeezing and wringing.

"Happy to hear it." Her mother ran a soapy skirt through a wringer and tossed it into the rinse tub. "I worry what will become of Viola and Joshua."

Ella eased the skirt hem between two rollers. "I pray she'll come clean about her boy's father. You'd think she'd want the man to know."

"If he could see his beautiful son, surely he'd claim him."

Would Frank declare himself as Joshua's father if he knew? Or would Viola's whining and the child's tugging on his coattail dispatch him back to Philadelphia?

A frown crawled across Ella's face. "What if the man's undeserving of Joshua?"

"Help!" A distant cry pierced the washday serenity like a dagger.

The women raised their heads, their hands suspended over the laundry, fingers dripping.

"Dear Lord, what now?" Mama laid a wet hand on her chest. Water spread across the fabric like flames in dry tinder.

"Coming from the trail." Ella wiped her hands on her apron and turned toward the door.

"Betsy!"

"It's Ruby!" The pair sprinted from the shed. Cleared the clothesline. Rounded the cow lot. And crossed the pasture toward the creek.

"Help!" Ruby's wail grew louder, more frantic. "It's Lily!" The distraught mother flailed her arms and pumped her legs, wild filly-like. Her mane fanned in strands, creek water flying.

"What is it?" Mama's arms enveloped her. Skirts billowed between them and settled.

"Blood's ever'where." Ruby grabbed great gulps of air.

"How?"

"Walter … home early. Took one look at Lily, the house. Lily got 'tween us." She collapsed against the stronger women.

Mama gave her a gentle shake. "Where's Lily?"

Seemingly out of her mind, she sobbed. "Blood … ever'where."

"Everything's gonna be all right." Mama soothed the frenzied woman and turned to Ella. "Get the honey salve. And the broom weed and sumac balms." She had assumed an authoritative tone. "Meet us at the barn."

Ruby tore away and charged toward the creek. "Gotta get to my girl."

A tremor passed through Ella, but she refused to give in to fear. Lily needed her. She covered the distance to the cellar in seconds. Her fingers shook as she lifted the wooden latch and entered the cool, dark space. No need for a lantern. She knew the cellar like her bedroom.

She stole into the back room with her arms extended, hands searching stocked shelves—jerky here, a smoked side of beef there, a ham. Her fingers lighted on crocks with corks waxed shut, honey and broom weed salves. Sumac balm. Cradling the stoneware, she dashed outside.

Mama issued orders. "Gavin, hitch up the wagon and meet us out front." She pointed to the crocks. "Set them in the back."

She turned to Cade. "Get your camping supplies."

"Bring me the rag basket, Hannah. And sheets and towels."

Viola, of course, was nowhere to be found.

Family members scattered. Ella charged into the kitchen alongside her mother. "I'd like to get my hands around Walter Sloat's neck!" Her fury had risen like a mama eagle's.

Chicken broth had cooled in an enameled pot on the cookstove. Ella dropped a funnel into a wide-mouthed Mason jar, poured the broth, and tightened the lid.

Mama pulled a basketweave satchel from the cupboard. She lifted two dark bottles of liquid to the light. "Plenty of laudanum. And ether."

Ella hiked the jar under an arm and jostled out the door. Her mother followed with the medicine case.

The family converged as Papa was leading Bunny and the wagon from the barn. "Ella, you drive. Cade'll ride behind you. I'll come over in a bit."

He secured the supplies in the wagon bed and lifted Mama to sit beside Ella. "The Good Lord'll be with you. Trust Him."

Bowing her head, Ella clenched her eyes. Her mother was trained in the healing arts and had tutored her herself. They'd do what they could. And trust God. But they must hurry.

"Heeya!" She cracked the whip, and Bunny strained forward.

CHAPTER 11

lla halted Bunny outside the Sloat house, fearful of what awaited them.

Donnie waited on the stoop, gnawing a fingernail.

Cade dismounted and slipped his rifle from its scabbard.

"Get the supplies while we wash up, son." Mama rolled a bar of carbolic soap in a towel.

Dropping the bucket into the well, Ella raised it, and water sloshed over the side. She sniffed. "Smells all right."

"Been a good well since John Glover dug it years ago."

They scrubbed to their elbows, rinsed, and dried on clean cotton.

Mama raised her face to the heavens. "Lord, you're the Physician. We're the handmaidens. Help us."

Cade waited at the stoop with supplies. "I'll check around."

"If the weasel shows his face, shoot him!" Ella spat her words.

"No. Wing him." Mama spoke in a commanding tone. "Sheriff'll do the rest."

Donnie faded into the interior shadows, and the women followed.

A dreadful wheezing led them to the far window, where the hem of its joyless flour sack curtain blew in the breeze. How stark the contrast between the Sloat and McFarland homes.

A column of light through a far window revealed Ruby kneeling beside a corn-husk mattress. "McFarlands're here, Lily girl." Her voice was rife with distress.

Peeking around her mother, Ella flinched. Ruby's hands cupped a visage of distorted features, blood-matted hair, and wounded flesh. It was savagery, plain and simple.

Lily's tongue had swollen beyond its boundaries, bulging out of her mouth. She battled for each breath. Her torso clamped, expelling air around the protrusion in great, noisy sputters. As her diaphragm contracted and released, her chest distended and collapsed, sucking air inward and forcing it out in ghastly wheezes.

How could a man do such to his child?

Mama knelt with her medicine satchel and rolled up her sleeves. "Need light. And hot water." Her voice matched her steady gaze.

Ruby tied the curtain panels into bulging knots and moved the lamp nearer, its wick yellow hot. She scooted to the fireplace and returned with a piping kettle.

With rag basket, sheets, and towels in hand, Ella knelt beside her mother. The knotted floorboards, hard and uncompromising, bit into her legs.

"We need Doc." Mama spoke in a measured tone. Sending for the doctor meant things were dire.

Ella raced to the door. "Get Doc, Cade!"

Her brother took a flying mount onto Braun. The thrumming of hooves faded as she returned to her mother's side.

Mama spread out a towel and prepared her surgical and medicinal supplies, bandages, and potions. Jars of dried herbs remained in the satchel, a sentry line harkening back to her Ozark roots. "Her skin's blue. Tongue's swollen, near bitten in two. Can't breathe."

"Don't let her die!" Ruby's fingernails dug into Mama's arm.

"Can't wait for Doc. Help me roll her to her side."

The three women rolled Lily over, and she groaned. Bloody spittle coursed over her cheek onto the homespun ticking, adding the finger-prints of brutality to the mercilessness of poverty. Ella wiped the brutalized face with damp cotton. They eased the girl onto her back with a rolled-up towel between her shoulders. Her lungs wheezed, battling for air.

Washing with carbolic soap, Mama issued instructions to her daughter assistant. "Give her laudanum. The big dropper. Force it inside along her cheek." Grandma Anglin, mountain woman and storied bonesetter, had received uncommon medical training and prepared her daughter for emergencies such as this.

Terrified and revolted by the violence, Ella washed the eyedropper in carbolic solution and extracted the reddish-brown liquid. Lubricating the tip with honey salve, she probed for access between tongue and cheek. *Please, Lord, make a way.*

The eyedropper eased inward. Like a mourning dove feeding her young, she dribbled the concoction, one precious drop at a time. Lily struggled. Her throat bobbled. She sputtered a cough. But she swallowed.

"My girl'll be all right. Tell me she will."

"Doing everything I can." Mama handed her a scalpel. "Run a flame along the blade."

Ruby retreated to the fireplace.

"I have to open up her windpipe, Ella. Here." She pointed to a spot at the base of Lily's throat just above her breastbone. "There's tubing in the satchel. Cut off a four-inch length."

Ella sliced off a section and dropped it into the carbolic solution.

"Need something stiffer, too."

Turning her head left and right, she searched for possibilities. "How about a pea shooter?"

"Fine idea, daughter."

"Get your pea shooter, Donnie!" She shouted over her shoulder.

The boy's heels hammered the wood planks like zealous carpenters. He and Ruby returned with the shooter and blackened scalpel.

Cleaning the implements in the solution, Ella joined the tubing to the shooter. A dab of honey salve lubricated the tip.

"Pull her chin up and back, daughter." Mama raised the knife. "Hold her head still, Ruby. Don't let her move."

"You're gonna cut my girl?"

"She'll smother if I don't."

"Want the ether, Mama?"

"'Fraid to use it with her struggling to breathe like this."

Ruby bent over at the waist. "Lordy. Lordy."

"No time for that!" Mama shouted at the terrified mother. "Do as I say!"

Ruby regained control and positioned herself at her daughter's head.

The wheezing picked up, wet and ragged.

Ella dabbed at blood seeping from the wound and leaned near her ear. "Gotta fight." She paused to settle herself. "When this is over, I'll get you out of here."

A moan gurgled.

"This'll help you breathe." Mama dabbed the site with alcohol and set her surgical knife at the proper spot. "Hold onto her." Swift and precise, she sliced and pushed aside tissue.

A sudden intake of air emanated from the opening, as if the child were gasping.

Ella leaned toward her. "You're a brave girl, Lily. Hold on."

Mama pushed the tubing inward until the shooter lodged at the opening. Air rushed through the apparatus. Lily's lungs pulled in long, steady breaths and released them in high-pitched whistles. Her body calmed, and her skin pinked as blessed oxygen flowed into her lungs.

"We'll leave things in place until Doc gets here." Mama snipped an opening in a length of cotton gauze and slipped it over the shooter, winding the remaining bandage around her neck. "Shouldn't be but a day or two before the swelling goes down."

"Before long you'll be whistling at the creek." Ella patted the poor child's head. "I won't let Walter harm you again, but we need to cut off your dress to examine you. Your ma'll cover you up."

The thin fabric slipped away in uneven strips, and Ruby spread a sheet over her daughter's reed-thin body.

"Tuck it around her good and tight." Mama instructed over her shoulder as she "And prepare warm water." She opened the peroxide. Uncorked the crocks. And gestured with her chin to the old sheets. "Tear one into strips. Soak 'em in alcohol. It'll evaporate quick."

Ella set about her bandage making with unspoken dread—rip, pause, rip, pause—the rending a fitting accompaniment to the drama playing out. How unspeakable, the injuries.

Ruby slid a pan of warm water beside Mama and knelt at her daughter's head.

Ella focused on her task. She must corral her emotions and her unrelenting questions for God. Lily's life depended on it.

Mama adjusted her spectacles and squinted. "Need more light."

Ruby hurried away and returned with a lantern. Close examination revealed surface cuts on face, neck, and shoulders. Some oozed bloody fluid; others were drying.

Mama saturated a cloth in the sterilizing solution and wrung it out, splattering fat droplets. She swabbed a bloody patch here, dabbed a lesion there, and applied ointment.

"See here, Ruby? Right collar bone and forearm are broken. Thank God it's a simple break, no piercing of the skin. It'll take Doc and me to set it though." She pointed to the bleeding gash traversing Lily's left shoulder and chest. "Gotta do something about this now."

"Oh, dear Lord." Ruby's chin quivered, and she folded forward to the floor.

"You're strong, Lily." Ella dropped a needle and fishing line into the carbolic solution.

Mama examined the laceration and threaded the needle. "Hold her tight." She set the needle tip against the child's skin and forced it into her flesh.

The girl's body twitched.

"You may be a butterfly, Lily." Ella whispered at the child's ear, her innards tumbling. "But you're a brave one."

Mama pulled the line taut and tied a knot. She completed the process, tying and snipping every quarter inch, and dropped the needle into the disinfectant.

Lily's wheezing cracked. And stopped.

"Do something!" Ruby pitched forward.

"Breathe!" Ella scraped a fingernail across the sole of her foot. The girl's lungs sucked in air, and her breathing resumed a steady rhythm.

Mama directed her focus to the battered girl's arm. "The break's below the elbow." She pointed to a bulging line of discoloration. "Still have that Sears-Roebuck catalog, Ruby?"

"Over yonder."

"Bring it here. We'll use it to splint Lily's arm."

As Ruby hurried away, Ella stacked the sheeting strips beside her mother. Mama would swathe Lily's forearm as she'd learned from her mother. Such skills were passed along from bonesetter mother to daughter in the remote areas populated by Mama's Ozark, Appalachian, and Blue Ridge Mountain ancestors.

Hooves thundered toward the house, and Ella peeked out. "It's Doc and Cade."

Doc halted his buggy near the well. Cade dismounted, led Braun to the trough and watered Doc's horse.

Ella met him at the door. "Thank God you're here."

"Where is she?" Doc growled.

"Over here." Mama called from the shadows. Eerie in the lamplight, the scene brought to mind the laying out for a funeral.

Ella shivered.

Doc knelt beside Lily. Ruby slid a pan of clean water and the catalog to him. He rolled up his shirt sleeves. "I'll need you, Betsy."

"My hands're strong. So's my back."

"Given her anything for pain?" he said as he scrubbed with carbolic soap.

"Stayed away from ether 'cause of her breathing. Gave laudanum an hour or so ago."

"Give her another dose."

Ella extracted a dropper full and eased it into Lily's mouth. The girl's throat bobbed as she swallowed.

"Take Ruby outside." Doc had assumed a commanding air.

The distraught mother pulled away. "Won't leave my girl."

What mother would answer differently?

He scowled. "Do what I say."

Placing a steady arm around Ruby, Ella nudged her out the door. "Let's take a walk."

Ruby wailed.

"Lily's in good hands." Tightening her hold, Ella set her mind on winning the tug-of-war to the creek. For Ruby's sake.

CHAPTER 12

The pair sat on the creek bank with their feet in the water. Time and again, Ruby turned toward the house with worry etched between her eyes, muttering, "Lordy. Lordy."

Ella murmured assurances and prayed aloud. "What do you say we go back?"

The distraught mother scrambled onto the trail with the younger woman on her heels.

A deathly silence greeted them as they neared the house.

Ruby shot toward the stoop. "Lily!"

Ella restrained her until the familiar whistle sounded from the darkened interior. A load lifted, and they stole into the house.

"Good you went for Betsy." Doc rolled down his sleeves.

With a self-conscious smile, Ruby kelt beside her girl.

"Arm's set in the catalog and plaster." The physician snapped his bag shut. "Keep the bandages clean. Use carbolic solution. Give her fluid, but boil the water. Broth, as tolerated. Send for me at first sign of infection."

"We've willow bark for pain and sumac for swelling." Ella gestured to their medicinals.

Doc leveled a forefinger at her. "You're a Betsy in the making."

Her cheeks warmed.

He turned to face Mama. "Get some rest. Your daughter can handle this." With a tap on his hat brim, he strode out. Reins snapped, and his buggy rolled toward Needham.

Ella fell into her mother's arms, absorbing her warmth.

"Doc spoke the blessing of a calling over you, lass."

"But I'm not called to tend the sick."

"Afflictions come in every shape."

"No. I'm afraid—"

"The woman who faced the Worthington lions is afraid?"

Mama was right. She had walked into a lions' den at Worthington. And she would again.

She straightened herself from her feet to her head. "Go on. I'll handle things."

Mama's gaze locked onto her daughter's. "I reckon you can." She tucked stray flyaways into her bun. "Get the team, Cade. I'm going home."

Early morning sunlight splashed Ella across the face, jerking her upward. "Lily?"

Ruby raised her head. "Still sleeping." She laid a hand along Lily's neck. "But fever."

Ella touched the girl's skin and frowned.

"What'll we do?" Ruby bent forward, keening.

"First, we won't lose our heads." She grabbed Ruby by her shoulders. "Watch and learn." She rummaged amid medicinals and handed Ruby a jar of a clear liquid and one of dried blood-red berries. "Sumac tea's good for swelling and vinegar for fever."

Ruby skittered away. The wash pan clinked, and water sloshed. In minutes she returned with a pan of the sumac-vinegar solution.

Ella submerged a towel and wrung it out.

Ruby removed the sheet, and Ella laid wet towels across Lily's chest, abdomen, and legs. "Got a pair of socks?"

"Walter's are over yonder." Ruby crawled to a pasteboard box and rummaged amid rags. She lifted the socks above her head.

"Soak them and put them on her feet."

Peeling towels from Lily's body, Ella rinsed and replaced them. Lily whimpered, but they kept to their task, repeating a half-dozen times until her skin cooled.

Ella's stomach grumbled.

Ruby motioned toward the door. "Donnie stirred up something to eat."

"Thank you." She stretched and stepped off the stoop, inhaling the aroma of beans and salt pork. "Morning." She sniffed. "Smells good."

Donnie spooned a serving onto a tin plate. She sat beside him and scooped with gusto.

"How's Lily?" Donnie said.

"Alive."

"Good 'nough."

"Never tasted beans so good. Is it the iron pot?"

"Naw. Possum."

The pounding of hooves coaxed Ella to her feet and spared her a response. She shaded her eyes and focused on the road. Cade barreled into the yard on Braun, and Papa followed on Cherokee.

Cade dismounted and tethered his steed. "Lily?"

"Breathing. Don't you have chores?"

"Got news." Papa joined his daughter and son. "Walter was sighted near Turner Falls."

"That's miles away." She dismissed the report with a flick of a hand.

A wrinkle formed between Papa's eyebrows. "Gotta get you out of here."

"Lily can't be moved."

Cade stepped forward, his expression fierce. "We'll figure a way."

"Do you need an ear trumpet?" She propped her fists on her waist.

Tension fired the air.

What right had she to lash out at her brother? "I'm sorry."

He hmphed. "You're at the end of yourself."

"Still, Lily can't be moved. Doc's orders."

"Stubbornest female." Cade kicked toward Donnie, stirring up dust.

Papa swiped his jaw and held Ella's elbow. "Let's talk this over."

She raised her chin. "Won't do any good." But what if Walter showed up? What then?

He motioned to the log as Cade watered the horses.

She gathered her skirt, yesterday's washday attire, and sat beside her father. Sweat circles lined her underarms. Lily's blood dotted her dress from her bodice's button placket to her skirt's hem. Scalding water reddened her hands yesterday and carbolic solution today.

"I'm not leaving you women alone with Walter on the prowl." Papa spoke firmly.

She leaned against him and inhaled the scent of shaving soap and pipe tobacco. "I'm staying with Lily and Ruby. You'll have to figure out something."

Ella pulled away and pushed to her feet. "Gotta check on Lily." Her head swam, and she swayed. "For heaven's sake." She held a hand at her temple. Her knees buckled, and she collapsed against her father.

"Plumb played out." Papa grumbled, struggling to remain on his feet.

"She had a bowl of beans just 'fore you rode in." Donnie slipped his comment between Papa's and Cade's.

"She needs rest."

Ella fought to pry open her eyes.

A plop and a swish sounded nearby.

"Lay her on this."

Papa adjusted his grip and lowered her onto a solid surface. Her cheek grazed a coarse fabric that smelled of leather and horse sweat. Cade's bedroll.

"I'll get some water." Donnie's bare heels thumped away.

Papa's hands felt warm on her arms.

"Here ya go, Mr. Mac." Donnie had returned. Soon water sloshed, and a cool cloth pressed her cheek.

"You need decent rest, daughter. I'm taking you home."

She opened her eyes. "I stood up too fast. That's all."

"That's *not* all. You'll be no good to Lily or your ma if you fall apart."

"I'll rest inside." She sat up and caught a whiff of her unwashed body.

"But I need a bath first."

Cade stepped to her side. "You can't be alone at the creek."

"If it'll make you feel better, you can wait along the trail. I'll yell if I need anything. Nothing wrong with my voice."

She extricated herself from the trio of menfolk and plodded toward the house. The rhythmic whistling through the pea shooter pulled her inside. Ruby lay beside her daughter, sleeping. Ella rummaged in the supplies and folded a towel around a bar of soap.

Papa and Cade talked with their heads together as if hatching a plan.

"One of you wait close to the house and listen for Ruby." She called to them over her shoulder.

"Be on the lookout. And holler if you need us." Papa's voice was strung tight as a fiddle string.

Cade's frown spoke for itself.

The morning sun infused warmth and color onto the path to the creek.

Bik! Kew! A pair of scissor-tailed flycatchers swooped from their roost in a sugarberry tree, grabbing insects for breakfast.

Suddenly exuberant, Ella called to the birds. "Lily's alive! She's alive!"

A mockingbird copied her declaration, tugging her lips into a grin.

Following the path to a bare spot on the creek bank, she surveyed her surroundings. Vines provided cover. Cicadas hummed, and a frog plopped into the water.

Sitting on a towel, she pulled off her shoes and stockings and wiggled her toes, grateful to be free of the bindings. The shirtwaist buttons slipped through holes worn with wear.

When her blouse fell from her shoulders, she laid her hands across her camisole-clad bosom. She'd never bathed outside the wash shed. She slipped off her skirt and cotton slip and glanced around. She wouldn't shuck her underclothes.

Never had she enjoyed a bath more. The water retained the night's coolness, but the sun warmed the air. She lathered her hair and watched soap suds float downstream with a turtle.

She contemplated her calloused hands and broken nails. Hardly suitable for Worthington.

A sudden stillness descended. Was that a shadow slipping between the shrubs? Had a finger of breeze rattled the vines? A warning rang inside her. She crept to the bank with her eyes trained on the vines. Drying her hair with the towel, she slipped on her blouse, petticoat, and skirt. And followed the footpath through the vegetation, under the sycamore boughs, and into the light of a pale, cloudless sky.

She studied the growth behind her. The flick of a squirrel's tail stirred the grass. But all else appeared motionless.

Still, unease nipped at her middle.

"Ella!" Cade's shout jarred her into a turn. "Doc's here!"

"I'm coming!" Holding her bathing supplies against her body, she raced toward the house.

CHAPTER 13

Ella bounded across the barren ground, and dirt stuck to her bare feet. She passed Cade and Papa and rushed inside. The pea shooter was whistling, so Lily was breathing fine. "How is she?"

"Stirring." Ruby nodded toward her daughter's rustling body.

Doc laid a hand across the girl's neck. "No fever. Her tongue's not so swollen."

"Is she in pain?" Ella knelt beside him.

"Could be. And hungry."

She blotted spittle from Lily's chin and neck. Disinfected the eye-dropper. And filled it with laudanum.

"Give it to her a drop at time." Doc turned to Ruby. "You can feed her next."

Ruby knelt at her daughter's side with a cup of broth in hand.

Doc raised Lily's head and shoulders, but the girl resisted. "Have to hold you up, or you'll choke. You're breathing through a tube. Swallowing won't come easy. Might hurt a bit, but you need medicine and a little broth. Ella and your ma'll take it slow."

Slipping the dropper between Lily's lips, Ella squeezed a drop of laudanum. Lily grimaced, and her jaw and throat stirred. Her breathing halted.

"She's choking!" Ruby reared backward and latched onto Doc's arm.

"Shhh." Doc leaned an ear toward Lily's mouth.

Lily's belly contracted, and a cough passed through the pea shooter.

Doc patted her head. "You'll be all right."

The patient settled, and Ella administered another drop. And another. Lily's throat churned, but she swallowed the last of the medication.

Ruby siphoned the broth and slipped the eyedropper tip between Lily's lips, repeating the process until the cup ran dry.

Lily's breathing steadied, and sleep overtook her.

Doc lowered her to the mattress and sat back. "Swelling's going down, so I'll take out the shooter soon. You're taking good care of her, ladies. Send for me if she takes a turn for the worse. Otherwise, I'll be back in the morning." He departed without a backward glance.

Ruby thumbed toward the door. "Your pa brought vittles. Go out yonder for a bite."

Ella's stomach grumbled. "But—"

"We need you strong. I'll eat directly."

Papa's and Cade's voices mingled with the clink of tin dishes. "All right. Call if Lily stirs." She ran her hands over her damp blouse and pushed to her feet.

Ruby slanted her head toward the kitchen area. "Apron's over yonder. To make you presentable."

Slipping the apron over her head, Ella tied the sash. The bib covered the dampness and protected her modesty. The apron front fell to the hem of her skirt. "Thank you."

She stepped outside.

Ella's guards sat at the campfire in a circle of shade.

She pushed open the screen door and stepped onto the stoop. Her legs trembled. Were her knees made of jelly?

She squared her shoulders. She wouldn't submit to fear. Or exhaustion.

Stepping toward the men, she sniffed. Beef stew. Her belly growled.

Cade emptied a ladleful onto a tin plate. "Hungry?"

She nodded. "I've barely eaten since breakfast yesterday." She sat on the log and tucked her skirt around her. "Any news?" She spoke between scoops of stew and biscuit.

Cade nodded. "Sheriff stopped by. Worried what Walter'll do next."

"Walter won't stand aside for any woman." Papa clenched a fist. "He's on his way, sure as I'm standing here."

What if Walter stole onto the property and into the house after dark? She pushed aside the fearful thought. "What're we going to do about it?"

"Since you won't leave this place, all we can do is stand guard." Cade spat and pitched a withered walnut shell at a black haw shrub.

"I can handle a gun."

"Can you be out here watching *and* behind the outhouse *and* inside with Lily at the same time?" Papa's forehead had drawn into telltale signs of vexation.

"'Course not." She set her empty plate on the ground.

Papa eyeballed his daughter. "Then you need us."

"I don't want you and Cade in danger."

"A bit late to be thinking that a-way. Sheriff's gathering sentries."

"I need a shotgun, Papa."

Cade strode to Braun and slid a 12-gauge Remington from a scabbard. He verified it was loaded and offered it to his sister. "Show us what you got."

She braced the stock at her shoulder and with a brief sighting, blew a sunflower to powder.

A corner of his mouth screwed upward, and an eyebrow peaked. "That'll do."

"I'm here to care for Lily, and no one will stop me. Leave me some ammunition." Heading into the house with shotgun in hand, she paused on the stoop. "Please."

Thunderclouds rolled in that afternoon, and a humid dusk settled.

Cade had set a box of ammunition on the stoop, but he and Papa were nowhere in sight. Ella brought the box inside. "We could use some milk if Milly'll give us some, Donnie. And eggs."

An hour later, she spooned potato gruel, fried eggs, and corn pone onto three tin plates and set aside portions for Papa and Cade.

"God be thanked for your kindness." Ruby murmured with bowed head.

"Thank God for his mercy over Lily."

Donnie grabbed a spoon and shoveled gruel into his mouth. Slurps and the clink of tin accompanied the steady rhythm of Lily's breathing.

"Walter never got around to making a proper table." Ruby indicated holes on one side of the table and leather hinges on the doorjamb. "In winter we hang it and eat on crates."

Would Ella display such resourcefulness in Ruby's shoes? Nay.

The wind picked up, rattling sheets of tin roofing and careening around the corners of the house. The screen door clattered, and Ella stepped onto the stoop, her skirt billowing. She cupped her hands around her mouth. "Cade! Papa!" Naught but the wind answered.

The men were out there in the darkness, but where?

What if Walter showed up? Could they hear her call over the storm?

A sheet of rain struck her face and stiffened her determination. She stepped inside and pocketed four cartridges. "We have to protect ourselves."

They cleared the table, upended it, and slid it into the door opening. Donnie reappeared with mallet and wood pegs. Ruby hammered the dowels into the hinges with unexpected strength, and the wooden latch anchored the door at the jamb.

A peal of thunder shook the house.

"Gotta cover the windows." Ruby ran toward the opening beside Lily. Two canvas strips held rolled oilcloth atop the window frame. She untied the strips, and the shade fell. Button holes at the bottom edge slipped around screws in the lower casement, securing the shade.

Ruby's ingenious creation was a product of desperation. She and Donnie lowered the other shades. A spatter of hail pelted the roof like stone peas. Water dripped into tin cans, the pings playing a tune. The mother renewed her vigil over her beloved daughter.

The wind and rain stopped as precipitously as they began.

Ella unlatched the door and pushed aside the screen. "I need some air. Won't go far." She glanced back at Donnie. "Keep watch at the window."

Donnie nodded, and she stepped outside with her Remington. The rain had cleansed the dark evening sky, and a few stars twinkled between cloud remnants.

She sent a prayer heavenward and leaned onto the doorpost. What could she do to ease the Sloats' impoverished state? Their unspeakable abuse had changed her. Come next week, would the Worthington board notice?

She imagined teaching Lily wearing the kid gloves Worthington required. The absurdity sparked a smile.

Returning to the darkened interior, she slid a candle lantern from a nail. Ruby had fashioned it from a Mason jar with clothesline for a handle. Ella formed the tallow candle herself, one of two dozen used as payment in trade for Ruby's help with the laundry.

Embers smoldered in the firebox. She lit a dry twig and touched it to the candle's wick, setting it aflame. She checked on Lily, readjusted the pea shooter, and spread beeswax along Lily's lips. The sheet nappy Ruby had fashioned for her daughter was clean.

"Donnie's turned in for the night. You need to sleep." Ruby hiked her chin toward a bedroll near a window. "Lily's bed's over yonder. No bugs. She keeps it clean."

"Can't sleep, Ruby. I'll keep watch at the window." Her candlelight revealed Lily's tattered pallet. The McFarland linen closet bulged with seldom-used quilts while the Sloats barely survived. Regret twisted her heart. She extinguished the candle and pulled aside the shade.

A dim sliver of the moon shone like an iridescent fingernail. She leaned her shotgun against the window casing and sat cross-legged on the floor, her forearms on the ledge. Lily's steady breathing provided a backdrop at once unnerving and reassuring.

Sentry duty gave her time to ponder. How was it some women could subdue a field of cotton, tend the sick, and defend their homes, yet cower before men like Walter? How could Ruby and Lily strengthen their loins like the woman of the proverb when their man wielded such control?

Trusting Papa and Cade were stationed outside, her thoughts drifted back home to Viola, Frank, and Worthington.

Mama and Papa tilled the soil and ran a country store. The Worthington parents lived in a world of private schools, social soirees, and the opera. Was she foolish to think a simple farm girl like herself could instruct such students?

The deepest night crawled in, and Ella's doubts wormed around a secret part of her soul, leaving her poorly tethered spirit restless.

CHAPTER 14

*M*ama nudged Ella awake. "I'll take over, daughter."

She sat up in the thick darkness, her thoughts cobwebs.

"Messenger boy delivered a telegram. Worthington Board wants to see you."

Ella snapped up. "When?"

"Tomorrow."

"What time is it?"

"Four o'clock Wednesday morning." Mama flapped her hands as if to scatter a brood of chicks. "Go on."

She finger-combed her hair. Worthington, so soon? "I don't want to leave Lily."

Mama drew nearer and pointed a finger. "Your papa and I have invested as much in this dream of yours as you have, so I'll speak my mind and you'll listen. If you don't show up at the appointed time, you can forget about Worthington and plan to pick cotton from now on."

"But my hands look a fright. And I'm exhausted." Was there time to repair herself? "I'll send a return wire asking for a delay ... until Monday perhaps."

Mama sighed, as if she'd known her daughter would protest. "You're keeping that appointment tomorrow. You can tend Lily until this afternoon, but I'm taking your place whether you like it or not. I'll tolerate no argument." She whipped a turn and stomped toward the door.

Moonlight outlined Ruby's bent form beside her daughter and a mound in a corner, no doubt Donnie. She followed her mother outside. "Where are Papa and Cade?"

"Your papa's in town talking to the sheriff. Cade's gone for another shotgun and ammunition. You'll stand guard alone until they're back."

She stepped outside with a lifted lantern, and the buggy rolled away. She'd face the board tomorrow and have her answer at last. Why wasn't she elated?

Soon Lily stirred, and Ella scooted to her bedside. The child's tongue, reduced in size, darted between her lips. An eyelid twitched.

Ruby set a hand on her daughter's head. "We're here, my Lily."

"You've been asleep two days. Your arm was broken, but Doc set it. Squeeze if you understand." She slipped her hand into Lily's.

The patient's fingers tightened.

"Thank God!" Ruby sobbed into the ticking.

Ella expelled her relief. "Mama put a breathing tube in your throat, Lily, but it'll come out soon. Doc checked on you yesterday, and he'll come by again today. Your ma'll give you a few drops of water, broth, and something for pain. We'll be here, so you can sleep."

Glimpsing a faint nod and a hint of a smile, she dipped the eyedropper into alcohol and hydrogen peroxide, and Ruby took over.

She slipped outside to the stoop and sat on an upended log with the shotgun on her lap. She released the action latch, and the barrel folded downward. Slipping cartridges into the empty chambers, she snapped the barrels closed and cocked the hammers.

Box elders, buckeyes, and bittersweet vines created a natural defense against wind and a cover from prying eyes. Until dawn Walter could slink through the shrubbery and get close to the house without being seen. She must remain alert.

Water splash inside the house. Ruby was rinsing a cloth in water, tending her girl.

Walter deserved to be thrown into a pit.

Movement near the chicken coop caught her eye. She stiffened. One of Papa's customers had reported a wild dog attacked his chickens. Whether a rabid dog or Walter, a monster lurked nearby. She raised her shotgun and aimed at the coop. The breeze tossed branches and vines. Shadows shifted, and a man's form appeared, his body upright and still.

Walter.

A string of shudders ran up her spine. Remembering Lily's battered body gave backbone to her fear. *Why, you miserable—*

The black haw branches rattled. "Get yerself off my place so I can tend my women." Walter slurred his words.

"You've done enough tending."

"I'll be the judge of that."

She'd thought the man more bluster than muscle, but Lily's injuries said otherwise. She lowered her right cheek to the stock and adjusted her eye position.

Walter emerged from the deep shadows.

She took a deep breath and let it out without sound.

He sidled forward, each drunken step bringing him closer.

Waiting for him to move into range, she trained her sight on his floundering form. "Move any closer, and I'll send you to your Maker."

"Where's Lily?"

"Where she's safe."

"Mind your own business and leave well enough alone."

"Well enough?"

"Well enough for a sharecropper's girl."

"Lily's smart. And beautiful."

Walter guffawed. "Ain't fit for nothing but cotton fields now."

She wouldn't let this monster near Lily, Ruby, or Donnie. She could send Walter to an early grave, and Sheriff Dawson would look the other way.

A cloud crept away from the moon, and a shaft of light illumined the wretched abuser. She curled her finger around the triggers.

"No! He ain't worth it." Ruby's voice from inside the shack startled her.

Walter gave her a drunken smirk. "Listen to my woman, girl."

"We can't let him get his hands on Lily."

"Your pa'll bring the sheriff." Ruby whisper-shouted through the screen.

A horse snorted in the distance, and Ella squinted toward the drive. Two riders emerged from the pre-dawn shadows, and Papa and the Sheriff Dawson rode up. Walter turned to run, but he stumbled and fell to the dirt.

"Thank God you're here, Papa." Ella lowered her shotgun. Behind her the screen door opened and whooshed shut. Ruby had joined her.

Papa jumped off his mount and yanked Walter to his feet.

Sheriff Dawson clicked handcuffs around the man's wrists. "Watch him, Gavin." He stepped onto the stoop. "Morning, Ruby."

She nodded. "Sheriff."

The pair strolled to the corner of the house, their voices fading to mumbles. In moments they reappeared on the stoop.

The lawman cleared his throat. "Ruby has a proposition, Walter."

"That woman can't proposition nobody."

Ruby stepped near to her husband. "I won't testify again' you and neither will Lily if you let her go with the McFarlands. But there'll be a peace bond."

"No." The thought horrified Ella. "You can't trust him."

"He deserves to face the law, but Ruby wants it this way." Sheriff Dawson grumbled.

"What good's a piece of paper to a man like Walter?"

"We've worked it out, Ella." He strode toward the cuffed no-account. "You'll stay away from this house, Walter. If you violate the bond, you'll be arrested. And those charges that were dropped over in Chickasha will be reactivated."

Walter spat on the ground. "I ain't gonna stay away from my own place."

"You'll stay clear until your daughter's well enough to be moved. I'll let you know when that is."

The abuser mumbled a protest but quieted, acknowledging the agreement.

Ella lowered her shotgun. "I'll be watching for you, Walter Sloat, bond or nay."

CHAPTER 15

Ella stepped inside Worthington School for Girls and smoothed her riding skirt. No corset constrained her, but her insides clenched.

"May I help you?" The receptionist's finely tailored suit reflected the school's refinement.

"I'm Ella McFarland. I have an appointment."

The woman ran a finger along an open diary. "Yes. Please take a seat."

She passed up the foyer bench—hard, straight-backed, and unfriendly. Instead, she strolled around the room, scrutinizing the portraits and plaques. And praying.

She glanced at a newspaper on a table. Its headline read *Suffragists Block Main Street!* She snatched up the weekly and read the dateline.

Women picketing for voting rights and perpetual prohibition blocked a main intersection in Westwood, clogging traffic and shutting down the trolley.

Audacious!

She muffled a gasp. The receptionist glanced up and returned to her filing.

Eight women had been arrested for disturbing the peace. She eased into a chair. How courageous. How bold.

Her spirit stirred as she pictured the women taking their stand.

"Miss McFarland?"

She set the paper aside. "Yes?"

Mr. Evans smiled a warm greeting. "Was the drive pleasant?"

"It was. Thank you." She walked beside him down the corridor to the library.

The same long table greeted her. The board members, their attire as formal as before, stood and extended greetings.

"Have a seat, please." Mr. Chairman pointed to the same empty chair.

Grateful that her soft leather gloves covered her broken nails and blisters, she laid her hands atop her clutch and held the man's gaze. The past few days had changed her in ways she never imagined. She wasn't the same Ella McFarland.

"We've rendered a decision." The man's voice was as gruff as before.

"It was difficult." Mr. Gray Vest glanced toward his more amiable colleague. "But we believe it correct."

Mr. Evans smiled. "Worthington School for Girls invites you to join the faculty as teacher of literature."

She repeated the words to herself, the fourteen she'd dreamed of hearing, and studied the three men. Mr. Evans's eyes exuded sincerity. Laugh lines bracketed his mouth. No doubt less genial attitudes had etched the channels between the other men's eyes.

Could she convey her gratitude? *Give me wisdom.*

"Thank you, gentlemen." She pulled in a steadying breath. "Worthington represents excellence. Being a part of this faculty ..." It would mean a dream fulfilled. Prestige and income, certainty and opportunity.

She imagined the girls arriving in their fancy carriages with abundant luggage and hatboxes, so like the girls she'd observed from a distance in Edmund. She'd be an integral part of the upbringing of future wives of bankers, lawyers, and railroad executives.

Not so, the students at Oklahoma Territory's Normal School who trained to be teachers like herself.

Could she muster the courage and boldness of the women in the newspaper article? She searched for honest words. "Worthington would bring my family honor."

The two dour board members adopted leisurely poses, one with a hand at his chin, the other tugging an ear lobe.

Mr. Evans leaned forward, his vivid, blue gaze intense, magnetic.

She shook off the effect. "But I've come to realize my family's reputation is as intact with those who know us as it ever was." She offered a lopsided grin. "Hardship comes and goes. It's what we do with it that matters."

Thy will, not mine, be done.

She caught her bottom lip between her teeth and studied the portrait of a society dame dominating other paintings around the room. How different from Mama, the woman appeared. How different from Ella herself.

"I'm grateful for the offer, gentlemen, but I must refuse it. I intend to do the McFarland name proud … but not at Worthington."

The chairman frowned. "That's a foolish decision. You'll not find a job anywhere around here."

Would she be forced to leave the Twin Territories to find a teaching position? Or give up teaching and accept grueling farm labor, perhaps marry someone she didn't love? She straightened in her chair. She must be strong and courageous.

"I suspect my decision has something to do with fancy carriages and hatboxes." She spoke just above a whisper.

Mr. Evans covered his mouth with a hand. Was he stifling another grin?

She stood, as did the three men. "Thank you for your consideration. I apologize for wasting your time."

Mr. Evans stepped forward. "I'll walk you out."

She nodded to the others and accepted his escort.

Outside, he turned to her. "I'm disappointed the Worthington girls won't have the privilege of your example."

She mounted Bunny. "Thank you. I fear it'll be a disappointment to my family as well."

As her mare trotted down the long drive, she glanced backward. Mr. Evans stood on the front steps, hands in his pockets, watching her.

She'd turned down the teaching position she'd always wanted, leaving her future in doubt and her family in uncertain circumstances.

Had she lost her mind?

Ella rode straight to the church. No time to change. Brother Percival Preston—a 250-pound mountain of a man standing six feet, four inches tall—had called the special prayer service and tagged it *for such a time as this*. What a time it was for Ella.

Bunny welcomed refreshment at the creek.

"Good girl." Ella tethered her faithful mare to Mama's buggy and patted her withers.

The windows and doors of the church stood open. Nary a breeze stirred.

Through the window she spied Mama fanning herself.

Cade rose from the front pew and faced the congregants. "Our first song is number 278."

He raised his hand to direct, and his sister walked through the open doors.

Mama smiled and let out a deep breath. She scooted over to clear a spot for her daughter. "I'll start your new suit tomorrow," she whispered.

Staring forward, unsmiling, she took her mother's hand. Mama would notice disappointment in her eyes.

Mama leaned back in the pew. "Lord, what now?"

Ella squirmed during the hymn and Papa's reading of First Corinthians 12, verse nine. "'And he hath said unto me, My grace is sufficient for thee: for my power is made perfect in weakness. Most gladly therefore will I rather glory in my weaknesses, that the power of Christ may rest upon me.'"

She lowered her head. *What do I do, Lord? I've not felt this weakness before now. Never been unsure of my decisions. Never second guessed myself. Until now. You must do something.*

Percival's sermon—entitled "If I'm God's child, why must I suffer?"— garnered nods from the congregation. Cade announced the final hymn, and they stood to sing "The Cross Is not Greater than His Grace," Mama's favorite.

Remaining seated, she folded forward, her hands covering her face.

The congregants sang the first verse from their songbooks of shaped-note music. Rather than instruments, they used their voices as sacred harps, a tradition that extended into the Appalachian Mountains and, some said, to the First Century:

> *The cross that He gave may be heavy*
> *But it ne'er outweighs His grace.*
> *The storm that I feared may surround me,*
> *But it ne'er excludes his face.*

Mama's arm encircled her. "Whatever's troubling you, take it to Jesus."

A sob escaped through Ella's fingers, and her mother traced circles along her back.

How could she admit what she'd done?

Had it only been two months since she returned home from college? So much had changed. Joshua. Frank. Worthington …

She struggled to control each breath. No job to support the family or to rescue their reputation. No husband prospects. And no way to make a living nearby, save in Papa's fields.

There was Viola's secret to keep, alongside her own. The thought of Frank in the family weighed her down. She felt a soul-deep need.

What am I to do, Lord?

A warm current wafted over her even as chills flitted along her skin.

Weak and dizzy, she thought of broken and battered Lily, a girl who longed to read but would never attend school, certainly not Worthington. Nor would countless others who lacked the resources she and her sisters enjoyed.

With a soft waft of breeze came a whisper in her heart.

Is that my answer?

Ella hadn't intended to stand, but stand she did, as if a power outside herself pulled her upward and set her feet in the aisle. Her eyes found Cade's. He set aside his song book, and the singing ceased. She fell into her brother's arms, and he lowered her onto the front pew.

Percival came to her. His hands, as big as buckets, swallowed hers. "What is it, dear?"

Women normally kept silent in their church. But couldn't she stand before these good people, friends she'd known always, and unburden her heart? "Please let me speak."

Percival frowned, studying her. His mouth stirred amid his gray whiskers. At length, he turned to the congregation. "This service is dismissed, but our Ella has something to say. Those who care to leave can do so. Those who have a lick of sense'll stay put."

He nodded to her, and the church members remained as still and silent as stones.

She daubed her eyes, filled her lungs, and exhaled on the wings of a whispered prayer. In that moment she knew what she must do.

She faced the gathering. "You're all beloved friends and family."

They nodded their assent, and she palmed a tear.

"When I was twelve, I gave my life to Jesus. Most of you witnessed my baptism in the creek. Eternity's settled for me. But the here-and-now's something else."

Frank slid into view behind Tad Thompson. He leaned toward the aisle, smirking.

"Everyone knows I've counted on teaching at Worthington." She gazed at her parents. "I got that offer today." Mama and Papa radiated joy, and murmurs of delight circled the gathering.

"But I turned it down."

Mama paled. A storm brewed on Papa's forehead.

Images of hatboxes and fancy carriages hopscotched through her mind. But they scattered like fairy sprinkles, leaving in their place tar paper, bowed legs, and quirt tracks.

She sucked in air, as if averting suffocation, and released it, clearing her mind. "I uncovered a viper's nest recently and learned not every woman's as blessed as I. Sure enough, not as blessed as the Worthington girls."

But doesn't every girl deserve an education?

She hesitated to voice the whispered calling in her heart. Was she really to do this? At what cost?

I heard You calling me, Lord. I know I did. Please give me strength.

"I'm opening a school of my own, not for daughters in fancy carriages with stacks of luggage, but needy girls with little to their names save the clothes on their backs and a desire to learn in their hearts."

Ella raised a hand like a witness in a courtroom. "So help me, God."

CHAPTER 16

$\mathcal{T}$he family gathered beneath glowing porch lamps.

"Are you crazy?" Even with the mild evening breeze, color had pooled into bright spots on Viola's cheeks.

Sensitive to Mama's aversion to tobacco, Papa puffed his pipe near the railing. "Worthington was the chance of a lifetime. All of us could've—"

"If the Lord wills it, such a blessing could happen yet." Mama's rocking eased the tension. "Tell us how it played out, daughter."

Somehow Ella must convey her strong conviction. And inspire her family.

She recounted her Worthington meeting. "I told them our family's reputation's as strong as ever among folks who know us."

Viola examined her nails.

"And that hardships come and go. What matters is what we do with them."

"God be praised," Mama said.

Papa puffed and nodded.

"I wasn't sure why I said no, only that Worthington didn't feel right. But standing in the church, I realized I can do something worthy of a McFarland right here in Glover County."

Viola raised a defiant chin. "Sounds ungrateful. Hannah and I've been tending the cottage garden while you nurse that Sloat girl."

"Sloats are as worthy of nursing as anyone. I thanked the board, and I thank you and Hannah. Any news about that teller's job, by the way?"

"No, but soon." The end of Viola's duster sash had taken custody of her eyes.

"Now you can court Frank." A cloud of smoke issued from a corner of Papa's mouth.

She withered. Would he ever give up on marrying her off? How she longed to explain in full. "Why can't you believe I'm serious about the school?"

"We've only just heard about it. Lots of details to figure out." The glow of the lamps highlighted Cade's dubiousness.

"Like where you'll put the school," Viola said.

"And how you'll fund it." Papa pointed with his pipe.

"Where will you find the students?" Hannah chimed in.

"I don't have those answers yet. But I will." Skepticism stared back at her. Truth be told, doubt rapped at her heart's door. "You think this is harebrained. But spending time with Lily has shown me the importance of women's education."

"Been telling you that all your life." Mama was reared in the mountains, but her mother had grown up in Boston where she received a fine education. Although Grandma Anglin moved to the Ozark Mountains when she married, she educated her children at home amid classical literature and home remedies. Mama transferred the same knowledge to her offspring.

"I guess I had to see it for myself. I haven't just read about the plight of women; now I've seen it. Why, suffragists—"

"That group of heathens is over the line, Ella Jane." Papa leaned forward and glared.

"I haven't joined them. Just read their positions on education and the vote."

Conversation halted. Mama's rocking, Papa's puffing, and Viola's sighing spoke for themselves. A summer azure moth fluttered around a lamp.

"Take that moth." She pointed to the lovely creature. "It does what it was created to do. I want to do what I was created to do."

Viola humphed. "Take care around a flame. Might be more than you can handle."

"And you could beat yourself up in the process," Papa said.

Mama laid a hand on hers. "Long as the Lord lights the flame, you're aiming right."

Ella sat tall. "Until I have a proper school, our guest room can serve as a classroom. Now that Doc has removed the breathing tube and reduced the laudanum, my patient will be up and about soon. When she recovers completely, she's coming over here. The school begins with Lily Sloat."

Viola stiffened. "White trash right under our noses?"

"What do you reckon Lily'll think of your idea?" Papa ignored Viola.

"Why, she's eager to learn."

"That was *before* Walter beat her to the edge of death. How do you know how she'll take to the idea now?"

"You blamed yourself at first," Mama said.

Their suggestion stunned. She leaned into the swing's back, her thoughts swirling. If Lily considered Ella responsible for her father's attack, it was as good as true. She must speak with her.

She wanted to rush to her at that moment, but ... "I'll be praying about this. I hope you will, too. See you at breakfast."

Next morning the family, save Viola and Joshua, assembled for a ride to the Sloat place. Ella dressed in a split skirt and tied up her hair with a rosy peach ribbon. She'd found one for Lily, a satin that shimmered in shades of blue and green. The girl was still recuperating, but her vision was unimpaired. The ribbon would spark a smile.

The Sloat bridge felt sturdier and the path less overgrown in the morning light.

Lily was seated outside with Ruby beside her. Small bandages dotted her face, and a larger one covered her throat. Her bound arm rested in her lap. She squirmed and turned her face away.

Ella slumped. "She doesn't want to see me, Mama."

"Go to her."

Ain't fit for nothing but cotton fields now.

Squaring her shoulders, she walked toward Lily.

Ruby stepped aside.

Lily's emerald eyes met Ella's. She extended her hand and mouthed one word: *friend.*

"Tragic, what Lily's been through." Julia Thompson leaned sideways in the pew, and her Sunday hat assumed a hazardous slant.

"That's very true."

"I'm sorry she isn't here today." The kindly woman fluttered a hand fan, stirring the gray tufts that peeked around her headpiece. Her cheekbones jutted through fine, delicate skin. The dearest of souls, Julia bore childlessness with sad dignity.

Ella returned a subtle smile. "Maybe in a few weeks." Ruby, as skittish as a baby calf, wouldn't permit Lily out of the house until she was completely well.

"My sister Josephine's son is coming from Colorado next week."

"You have a sister?" Julia had never spoken of family.

"Oh, we had a falling out years ago. That's behind us now."

Brother Percival stepped to the front, and Julia clasped her hand. "We'll talk later."

The sermon was well prepared and delivered, but it stirred no yearnings. Nor did the hymns, although Cade led them aptly. The problem lay not in her surroundings but in her mind. Her thoughts swirled like a rabble of butterflies as she recalled Lily's birthday party. The child deserved to be as happy and safe as she was then. When she was well enough, Ella would move her to the McFarland home.

But could she trust Viola under the same roof as Lily?

Cade announced the final hymn, and her thoughts returned to the service. The congregation rose, and she stood beside Julia.

"'There's a land beyond the river,'" the congregants sang.

She sat on the pew with a thumbnail tapping her lips, the words tickling a girlhood memory and her thoughts racing.

"'One by one we'll gain the portals.'"

Of course. She all but snapped her fingers at the sudden realization, but she'd hold her piece until the time was right.

The final amen scattered folks like a pistol pop on race day. Cheerful handshakes and hearty hellos carried the crowd down the front steps.

Frank and Viola stood beneath an elm. He hooked his thumbs into his trouser pockets, and she twirled her reticule, her color heightened.

Julia pulled Ella aside. "About Andrew—"

"Your sister's son?"

"He finished seminary and served at an Indian mission. A fine Denver church offered him a position, but he turned it down." Her enthusiasm sent poorly stitched primroses over her hat's brim. She pushed them aside. "He's coming to help Tad at the blacksmith shop. We're thrilled."

She corralled her thoughts. "Tad's bad heart?"

"I'll say. And I've been weak as a kitten myself. It's blessed news, having no children of our own, you see." Julia brought a hankie to her eyes.

She embraced the dear woman. Perhaps Julia's nephew would assuage her longing for a child.

"Come on!" Viola yelled from the buggy. "I'm hungry."

Ella offered Mama her arm, and they settled into the back seat. All but Viola raised their hands in farewell.

The team clopped along the road, and typical Sunday musings passed among the family. But Ella's mind scampered elsewhere … to her friend Adelaide Fitzgerald … and memories of their favorite play spot as girls, the old cottage where Addie's parents once lived. It nestled in a copse between McFarland and Fitzgerald properties.

Could she have stumbled onto a solution for her school?

CHAPTER 17

"I have an idea." Ella chucked her Sunday hat onto a chair. "Came to me while we were singing about portals up yonder."

Viola sat in the rocker with Joshua while Mama set out dinner. Fed up with baby tending, Hannah had vanished up the stairs.

Mama cocked an eyebrow. "What've you got up your sleeve now?"

"The Fitzgeralds' cottage."

Mama and Papa, the Fitzgeralds, and the Irvings, had been friends all their lives. They moved together from Arkansas to Indian Territory decades prior. Eli took up ranching and railroading and Zach, banking. Both men made fortunes while Papa struggled at farming, raising a few head of cattle, and keeping shop. The gap between their economic and social standings grew wider over time, but their friendship remained strong, as did their children's.

The Fitzgeralds had planned for the cottage to become Adelaide's one day, but upon their untimely deaths, Addie inherited Broadview, their grand estate, and everything that went with it. Her wet nurse, Margaret Gallagher, remained on as housekeeper and the only mother Addie knew. Addie was pursuing an opera career in Europe. Who knew when she'd return?

Mama closed her eyes. "Haven't thought of the cottage in ages."

"I could have a real school for Lily there." Excitement burned Ella's cheeks. "She's too bright not to be educated beyond learning to read. Besides, being off in the cottage would keep Lily out of Viola's reach."

Papa stepped into the kitchen. "The cottage, you say?" He hung up his hat and moved to the wash basin. "Been empty so long it might be beyond repair. And there's Walter to consider."

"It's worth a look, Papa. Besides, Walter knows he'll be arrested if he breaks the bond. As soon as Lily's strong enough, we can move her."

"I reckon we can ride over and take a look after dinner." He dried his hands on a towel.

The mudroom door opened and closed, and Cade tromped into the kitchen. "Smells good."

"Call Hannah, son. It's time to eat."

The family took their seats, and Papa gave thanks for the bounteous meal—pork chops fried with a crispy crust, mashed potatoes and cream gravy, snap beans with bacon, corn on the cob, and berry cobbler.

"Have you thought of how you'll contact Addie?" Mama held her fork aloft between bites. "Off in Italy, who knows how long it'll take to get word to her."

"I have no doubt she'll find a way." Ella was three years younger than Adelaide, but they'd been the dearest of friends all their lives. Kindred spirits, they shared a bond closer than many blood ties. Generous Addie gifted her friend with travel and social opportunities and supported her teaching dreams.

After dinner Cade returned to the horse paddock, and everyone but Ella and Papa stole upstairs for naps. When the last dish was dried, she picked up her mending basket. Her mind and hands stayed busy, it seemed, even on peaceful Sunday afternoons.

At length Joshua cried out. *Good. Mama and the girls would be waking.*

Mama entered the kitchen seeking a cup of coffee.

Ella set aside her mending. "Let's go to the cottage now."

"We can look, but it's bound to be a wreck."

Viola sashayed down the stairs and announced she was taking a walk. Hannah agreed to watch Joshua. Mama finished her coffee and urged Papa to hitch up the buggy.

The possibility lying over the way all but stole Ella's breath.

Just inside Broadview's gated entrance, Papa directed Bunny onto a bridle path that followed the fence line. They waved to Vernon Yancey, longtime estate overseer. The path skirted a gentle rise covered in wild-flowers. The buggy bounced over the uneven ground, and mother and daughter shared an anchoring embrace.

Papa reined in at a stone cottage nestled in a copse of oak and elm trees. His eyes snapped left and right and focused on the roof. "Roofline's straight. A few shingles have been blown away. Rocks and mortar look in good repair."

"It's as if Eli and Leona still live here." Mama covered her mouth with a hand.

"Someone's been keeping it up." Ella jumped down, her gaze roaming the structure's lines and angles. "Not a pane's broken. With the woods so thick, I'd forgotten it." She jogged to the side of the house with her parents following. They surveyed the house, outbuildings, and overgrown garden in the distance.

"It'll take some effort." Papa kneaded his chin with thumb and fore-finger, ruminating.

"Surely the inside needs repair, Gavin. And there's the cotton harvest facing us."

Ella's enthusiasm sputtered. How could they accomplish it all?

"Howdy, folks."

They startled and twisted around.

Vernon extended a broad smile. "Mr. Fitzgerald's last will provided for the upkeep."

Papa nodded with an approving smile. "You've done a worthy job,"

"Thank you, sir." The man ducked his head. "Anything for Miss Adelaide."

"May we look inside?" Ella's patience was wearing thin. Perhaps the interior was in better shape than they imagined.

"You're practically Miss Addie's family." The overseer pulled a ring from his back pocket, lumbered to the door, and inserted a brass key.

The lock clanked, and the door swung open.

"Oh, the memories." Stepping inside with a sharp inhalation, Mama motioned to the east wall of the great room. "Leona insisted on that wide bank of windows so she could see the sun rise." Oak casement outlined the windows.

Papa stared at a far corner. "Eli said an L-shaped counter would make things convenient for Leona."

Mama moved to sheet-draped mounds in the kitchen and slipped off the covers, sending dust flying. "Leona served many a meal at this table. Eli hauled the oak from back home. For the hutch and buffet too." The plain wood's patina was still lovely. The hutch's mullioned glass doors had survived the years.

Vernon pulled the sheet off a cupboard with an extension for sink and hand pump.

"Leona's work space." Mama said in a sigh. "I miss her still."

Ella surveyed a small separate room. "It's a pantry and larder." She ran her fingers over the pie keeper. "Flies don't stand a chance with this mesh on the door."

"I remember this well. Tiled walls and floor and counter. Didn't take much to keep it in apple-pie order."

More sheeted furnishings encircled a hearth: horsehair divan and easy chairs, matching settee with wooden swirls and knobs, and side tables with pie-crust edges.

The fine workmanship had been a labor of love.

"Sleeping quarters are down there." Vernon pointed down the hallway.

They entered the master bedroom, and the late afternoon sun struck a stained-glass window, sprinkling color as if from an artist's hand.

Mama's gaze glided up and down the large window, absorbing each detail. "The Blackthorn."

The tree's bark was dark, and its purple sloe, white blossoms, and vibrant greens created a stunning piece of art.

"The husband and wife tree." Mama pointed to a joint where the smaller trunk curved into the larger. "According to Irish legend, the husband and wife thus joined will never be parted." She turned a full circle, gazing around the chamber. A strange expression, fearful-like, flittered across her face, and she hurried out.

Ella found her at the sink. "You're pale. Are you all right?"

"Just missing Leona." Her eyes misted. "Go on. I'll wait outside."

Mama settled into the porch swing, wiping her face with her apron and gazing into the distance. Her friendship with Leona Fitzgerald represented a treasury of memories at once bitter and sweet. Leona died in childbirth, and Mama lost the friend of a lifetime.

But their daughters had played innumerable hours in the cottage, at Broadview, and on the McFarland farm. Their friendship knew nothing but sweetness. Would the coming years bring more of the same? Or would grief mar them?

Shaking off the dreary thoughts, she turned to the stairwell. A tour awaited her.

She followed Papa into the paneled upper passageway.

"I'd forgotten." She stole forward, examining the details. Two open doors on either side of the hall, a fifth at the end, each bedroom full of sheeted furnishings. "This is hardly a cottage. It's a mansion."

"Addie's mansion, not yours," Papa said in a commanding tone. "Way more than you need for lessons."

"This would make a perfect school." She scooted down the stairs, struggling to contain her joy.

"Don't know why you're celebrating." Papa grumbled behind her. "Addie's in Italy."

She scooted to Vern. "Will you send her a telegram?"

"And tell her what, Miss Ella?"

"Tell her I want to use the cottage."

"And what will I tell her you're wanting the cottage for?"

"Tell her …" She bounded through the door and down the steps, twirling onto the lawn. She stretched her arms wide as if to swoop the scene to her bosom. "Tell her I want to play house. This time for real."

CHAPTER 18

*E*lla straightened a framed telegram in the cottage foyer. *Proceed as you see fit*, it read.

"Addie's message gives us a license to do business, Mama. I've decided on a name. Broadview School for Girls."

"God be praised. You've made good progress in twelve days."

"Thanks to Addie's line of credit at Irving's Bank and Trust."

The tea kettle whistled, and mother and daughter walked arm in arm to the kitchen.

"My dream's about to be reality."

Mama seated herself. "The Lord provides."

The newly minted teacher snuffed the flame under the kettle. "This'll be a place where girls can find hope and purpose."

Hannah clattered down the stairs. "I want to go to school here."

Pouring hot water into the teapot, Ella replaced the lid. A string of mist threaded from the spout. "This is for needy girls, Hannah, girls who live where there's no county school. Not everyone can afford a boarding school like Worthington and others. So I need sponsors."

She took a seat, waiting for the tea to steep.

"I'm in need of something besides that grumpy tutor Addie hired." Hannah wrinkled her nose and plopped into a chair with a copy of *Sara Crewe*.

"Sheriff brought out a copy of the bond." A shadow clouded Mama's eyes.

Walter, unattended and free to do as he pleased? "We'll lock up and keep our guns handy. And have target practice." She rubbed the heels of her hands along her temples.

"I'll trust the Lord."

"Meanwhile, I don't intend to rely on Adelaide's generosity forever. I want this school to be a joint effort among like-minded women."

"Any leads on donors?"

"I've stirred some interest—and feathers—at women's clubs. Not everyone agrees with me about the vote. Or about educating girls. So far I've not had much success finding donors. Maybe that'll change when I identify students in whom donors can take a vested interest."

"Don't give up, daughter. You're helping to change women's thinking. You're turning clubs into classrooms."

"Aye. I'm not sure canned goods will produce the income I need in the long term." She poured the tea and inhaled its rich aroma.

Mama leaned into her chair's ladder back, sipping. "How's the garden?"

"Planted limas, cucumbers, and squash."

"A little late for string beans, but limas should do fine."

"The pantry and larder are stocked."

"You can share our milk and eggs. Just help with the milking and feeding."

"Five girls can live upstairs. They need sponsors, and I need a salary. But no one has shown an interest in investing in my idea. If I could only—" She set her cup in its saucer and angled an ear toward the front door. "That's a buggy."

She dashed to the porch with her mother and sister on her heels.

Cade rode up on Braun. Papa, Viola, and Joshua sat in the wagon with Lily.

Ella ran down the steps with her arms spread wide. "Welcome to your new home, Broadview School for Girls."

Cade helped Lily down and gestured to the cottage. Papa had trimmed the trees and vines and cleared the ground of deadfall. Mama swept the veranda, and Ella polished the panes until they glistened.

"Just waiting for you." Ella nudged her forward.

The girl's mouth eased open. "I'm really gonna live here?"

"This is your home now. Yours and mine and a few more students."

"It's a castle." She made her way up the steps. "You sure Pa won't find me?"

"He knows nothing about this place. But if he shows up, he'll be arrested. Besides, we'll teach you to defend yourself."

She halted, her eyes wide. "You'll teach me to shoot?"

"That and a great deal more. We'll start with Market Day tomorrow."

"You reckon I can go looking like this?" Small scars dotted her face and neck. Her blouse concealed the largest scar.

"You can have my wide-brimmed straw." Viola brushed past. "With a scarf over the crown and tied under your chin, those ugly scars'll barely show."

Ella rounded on her sister. "Viola McFarland, of all the—"

"What scars?" Grasping the carpetbag in one hand, Cade held aside the door with the other. "Glover County girls only dream of being as pretty as Lily."

The rosiness in the dear girl's cheeks deepened. "Don't reckon it matters, long as you ain't ashamed to be seen with me. But what about yonder field of cotton?"

Papa stepped onto the veranda. "Hoeing's done. Picking's a few weeks away."

"And today …" Ella waved her young friend inside. "You've come home."

Stepping over the threshold, Lily's mouth slackened further. Her eyes seemed to devour the interior stone walls dotted with paintings and framed embroidery work. "That there's a fine kitchen."

"We're blessed, aren't we?"

She turned to the hearth encircled by a davenport and easy chairs. "The firebox is for sittin' 'round, not cookin'?"

Mama and Papa nodded in a satisfied manner.

"My study and bedroom are down there." Ella pointed toward the hallway extending from the back wall. "Your bedroom's upstairs. Pick the one you want."

The child turned a full circle, the whites of her eyes bright and brimming. "There's even glass in the wall?" She pointed to the wide front panes that showcased the porch and the wildflower-strewn rise in the distance.

Viola had moved to the porch and sat with her nose pointed upward, bouncing Joshua on her knee.

"This is our grandson's first birthday, you know." Mama and Papa locked hands.

Bless him, Lord. Curb Viola's tongue. Mine too. And keep me strong. I've a job to do.

CHAPTER 19

Market Day, Ella's chance to socialize and introduce Lily to the townsfolk. How she enjoyed the energy. Two empty nail kegs for stools, a tool box, bolts of cloth, and a sewing basket bounced in the wagon bed. Ropes secured crates of canned goods and produce.

"Needham's vying for the county seat, so folks'll be heading our way. Bodes well for sales." She had chosen her usual split skirt, waist, and boots. A yellow rose festooned her curls.

"You reckon Pa'll be there?" Attired in a blouse with full, gathered sleeves, Lily radiated beauty. Her mane hung free, save the blue-green ribbon. Viola's erstwhile hat lay in her lap.

"Wouldn't think so. He's still shadowed by the deputy."

"Feelin' skittish, that's all."

"Sheriff makes his presence known."

As they rumbled into town, spiraled tendrils pulled loose and tumbled around Ella's face. She'd batten them with combs later.

The sun had risen just above the horizon. Few citizens were stirring, save the baker who'd been at work since before dawn. Ella's mouth salivated at the aroma, but passing the bank brought thoughts of Frank, and her stomach churned.

"Whoa," she called to Bunny at the square. "We're so early we get first choice."

"That one's best." Lily pointed toward a booth beneath a black walnut tree. "Closest to the street." She looked skyward. "And in the shade come afternoon."

They stepped down. Rejuvenated buttoned shoes showed beneath

Lily's skirt. Sunlight splashed her cheeks and tickled peach to the surface. She tugged on Viola's hat. "Help me with this?"

"Don't need a hat in the shade."

"Best I do." She tucked her chin.

Ella positioned the headpiece and tied the coral chiffon under the girl's chin. Viola was right. The scars were barely noticeable.

The pair unloaded the wagon. Lily helped as much as she could with the cast. Setting out her tools and tying a carpenter's apron around her waist, Ella wielded hammer and nails to shore up shelves. She unfolded a wooden carpenter's ruler and checked measurements. "The bunting should fit. But we'll add these." She waved two golden rosettes.

"Eye-catchin' with the red and blue."

When all was set aright, Ella nailed up a sign: McFarland Canned Goods.

"McFarland's a name to prize. Pa's made ours a bad word."

Ella's heart ached for her young friend.

Hooves thrummed. Wheels clacked, and she glanced to the street.

Viola's green plume fluttered past.

"Someone's going to be as green as her hat feather." Ella chuckled but experienced a wave of guilt. "Forgive me for voicing my uncharitable thoughts, Lily."

The child waved aside the apology. "You ain't got a uncharitable bone in your body."

"Well, well. Aren't you the early birds. Got a big fat worm?" Viola's lacquered voice intruded. Her amber eyes offered as little warmth as her tone. Her mane was mounded beneath a silk hat, green like her walking suit's lapels. "Everyone knows this is my booth."

Give me strength, Lord. And sisterly love. Vi makes it hard to show how much I love her.

Ella hailed a passerby. "Excuse me, but we have a question."

The man removed his hat. "Hello, fair ladies."

"You're a councilman. What's the rule for booth assignments?"

"Same as always. First come, first served."

Viola huffed and turned away. Ella was tempted to flash a self-satisfied grin, but regret tugged at her. She'd just prayed for strength and love, for heaven's sake. "We can move our things if you'll help, Vi."

"Why, I'll not—"

"Who's this lovely young lady?" The councilman tipped his hat to Lily.

"This is Lily Sloat."

"Are you Walt—Ruby's daughter?" The man failed to conceal his astonishment.

"Yes, sir."

"Like my new suit?" Viola preened for the man. "A Philadelphia purchase."

"Lovely." He spoke in a distracted manner and turned back to Lily.

"I must attend to errands." Viola backed away and bustled into Irving's Bank and Trust. She joined similarly two garbed women at the window, a pair who generated the lion's share of Needham's gossip. Had they gathered Viola into their fold?

"You're the subject of many a conversation." Ella bumped a shoulder against Lily's.

"I'll stay out of sight."

"You certainly will not. You'll sit out front. And point folks to our products."

A corner of Lily's mouth lifted, but she lowered her eyes and worried one hand across the other.

Shelving the last products, Ella stood back to admire the booth.

"Quite a display." An unmistakable rasp spun her around.

Frank swaggered up with Viola on his arm.

Ella's spirits tumbled.

He flourished his hat in a dramatic bow and slid his eyes toward Lily. "Who's this gorgeous creature?"

"Frank, you're an ornery rascal." Viola tugged his arm.

"An undeserved reputation, I assure you." He raised Lily's hand for a kiss.

She yanked it away.

Ella suppressed a grin. Good instincts, young friend.

"Care for a pretty for a special lady, Frank?" Viola pointed to the baskets of scented soaps and sachets in her buggy. Cotton bolls and vegetable gardens sent Viola into fits, so she cultivated herbs and flowering plants instead. She insisted on their palliative effects.

Frank leered at the lovely thirteen-year-old. "I was thinking of peach butter."

"Peach butter's twenty-one cents." She answered him with a smile.

He removed five coins from a pocket. "Will a quarter do?" He leered and winked.

Ella would like to scratch the man's eyes out, not give him change. She fished in her apron and handed Lily four pennies. "Four cents change for a quarter."

He extended an open palm. "You won't garner friends by undercutting their prices." He paused to appraise Lily. "Or by presenting such a tantalizing drawing card."

Lily blushed.

Viola twisted away.

Neither a skunk nor his worthless banter would distract Ella. She'd concentrate on making Market Day profitable. "We've much to do, Frank."

Unlike bank bookkeepers.

The fine-feathered pair of women emerged from the bank and joined Viola at her buggy.

Frank sauntered to the trio. "May I give you a hand, Vi?"

"That would be lovely." Viola twirled her drawstring bag with its potent blend of red roses, honeysuckle, and larkspur, her love potion.

Hogwash.

Frank signaled to his hired hand who carted Viola's supplies to her booth. The worker lowered his head against her onslaught of hard-edged instructions.

"Pennies're one cent, Lily." Ella whispered the instructions at her friend's ear. "Five pennies make a nickel. Five nickels make a quarter, which is twenty-five cents."

She raised a single shoulder, signaling her understanding. "Ain't hard."

"Not for someone as smart as you." Ella smiled and waved to approaching customers.

Lively voices marked the start of the day of commerce. Excitement crackled along Main Street and around the square.

A few ladies greeted Ella and Lily. Others nodded. Still others looked away. Some stopped to examine Viola's wares; others, the goods on Ella's shelves.

At noon Frank accompanied Viola to Marie's Cafe.

The two friends attending to McFarland products bowed their heads over slices of cheese and bread for Ella to pray. "Bring success to our efforts, Lord. And Vi's, too."

Lily laid a napkin in her lap, copying Ella. "You and your sister ain't cut from the same bolt of cloth."

Ella bit off a bit of cheese. "We're made from the same thread. Just woven together differently."

"Kind way of puttin' it." She guzzled from a pint Mason jar and raised the back of a hand to wipe her lips. She hesitated. Lowered her hand. And used her napkin instead.

A quick study. Ella must watch her step.

Viola and Frank returned. Try as she may, Ella couldn't divest herself of the revulsion she experienced in his presence. He lazed around their booths and doffed his hat to lady passersby. Shook hands with gentlemen. And chatted with the expertise of one trained in social graces.

The pair of gossips lingered nearby and spoke in hushed voices, their words muted and indistinct. But Lily's name sounded clear enough. Ella's eyes flitted to the dear girl.

Apparently she hadn't overheard the unkind words or noticed shoppers whispering behind their hands, their eyes flicking between her burnished locks and bound arm. News concerning the Sloats had been tickling their ears.

Menfolk paused to doff their hats and speak to the lovely girl at the McFarland stand. Some bought jars of marmalade or jelly. The women whisked their husbands away with their chins high. Still, Lily seemed unaware.

"Market Day produced a good profit." Ella made the announcement at day's end. "A worthy woman's merchandise is profitable." She placed the few remaining jars in a single crate.

Lily glanced toward Viola's well-stocked shelf. "I reckon it profits some more 'n others." She flashed a playful grin. The girl possessed a sense of humor too.

Taking her place on the buckboard beside Lily, Ella felt gratitude and hope brightening her spirit. She could support herself with regular profits like these.

When they rolled by Irving's, Frank was standing on the side street with a stranger. They had their heads together as if hatching a plan. What did the ne'er-do-well have up his sleeve?

At bedtime she snuffed her lamp's wick and released a satisfied sigh. Decided beauty such as Lily's was a sure drawing card on Market Day.

Her thoughts sobered. But beauty drew gossip. How fickle the winds of slander. A storm had swirled around Viola and Joshua just a month past. Now it nipped at Lily.

She went to her knees on her prayer pillow at her open window. "I've declared Lily and this school my life, Lord. I'm doing my best to work as if called by You. I vowed to trust You when I reach the end of myself. Trouble is, I have yet to discover where the end lies. And I fear the learning."

CHAPTER 20

A distant engine chugged, coaxing Ella from her Monday gardening. She shaded her eyes and strained at the new-fangled contraption's approach.

An automobile, black as onyx, bounced around the rise.

Honk!

Who would disturb the morning calm? She tugged off her gloves.

The auto braked, and the driver stepped out.

Frank.

Her chest and face heated, and she scampered out of sight. Perhaps he hadn't noticed her. She scanned the area. Bunny stood in the paddock. Smoke trailed above the chimney. She couldn't hide or expect Lily to greet the scoundrel.

How had he learned her whereabouts? Mama and the girls had promised to keep her secret. Her shoulders sagged in resignation, and she shivered at his knock.

Rounding the house, she found Frank on the porch in dandified garb—starched collar, tie, waistcoat, and bowler. "What're you doing here?"

He brandished his hat. "I hope you don't mind."

"I do."

He winced. "Been a long time."

"Not long enough." Was it just last night she prayed for an extra measure of grace?

He stepped off the porch. "Hardly the attitude of a friend."

"Don't speak of friendship. You ruined every amiable thought I once had of you."

Sweat slinked like a snake through his sideburn.

Bless them that curse you, pray for them that despitefully use you. Alright, Lord, bless Frank. But please get him out of my sight.

"Go." She headed to the shade behind the house. And to relief from the sight of the man. Taking a seat in a garden chair, she fanned herself with her apron. How dare Frank show up unannounced. She laid her head back and closed her eyes, pushing away the memory.

"You don't mean that."

She sprang to her feet. "I told you to leave."

"We could take a drive in my new Cadillac. Maybe take Lily."

Disgust lurched. "I'm going nowhere with you."

"Relax. May I sit?"

"You may not."

"Not even ... for Lily?"

She flinched. "What do you mean?"

"Your secrets are safe with me." He grinned and took a seat.

"What secrets?"

"Walter Sloat has no idea his daughter resides in this grove."

She twisted the edge of her apron into a roll. "That's no concern of yours."

"Sit. You make me nervous. Besides, you should be cordial to the new chief loan officer at Irving's Bank and Trust." He cocked an eyebrow and smirked. "I know you don't have a single contributor for your little ... school."

As she expected, Frank had enjoyed a rapid promotion. "I don't need a loan." She held her head at a prideful bent and spoke with a snippy tone. She couldn't manage to do otherwise.

Frank scrutinized the house. "There'll be upkeep, textbooks, and such. You need prominent citizens to speak on your behalf. Need I go on?"

Irving's support within the community could boost her efforts. But involving herself with Frank amounted to casting her lot with the devil. "What I do or do not need is my business, not yours."

He brushed lint off a sleeve. "Perhaps not. But I'd advise you to sit and listen."

She couldn't run a school without funding. Addie's line of credit aside, she had hoped she'd eventually build a cadre of supporters, a ministry. She'd find the money without Frank's assistance. "I'll have you know—"

"Too bad if word got out that Ella McFarland possessed … how should I put it? A certain ravenousness under her proper exterior."

Ice replaced the fire in her midsection. "You wouldn't."

"Try me."

The black in his eyes matched his heart. Could she lock away the memory of him in the moonlight … grabbing her?

"I cringe at the sight of you." Delicacy never had been one of her finer qualities.

"I like your fire." He stood and straightened his cuffs. "Don't know what you're missing. Ask Viola."

She backed away. "Leave. Don't ever return."

He donned his hat and whistled as he strolled to his auto.

She mustn't give in to Frank But how long could she endure?

Percival Preston's surprise visit the next afternoon sent Ella's worries onto the trash heap. She'd spent the morning reading and writing with Lily whose quick mind astounded her. Now a visit from lifelong friend, preacher, and eldest member at Christ Church, would highlight her day.

Percival relaxed in the ample easy chair. "You've made this a home."

"It's a home and a school." Ella's pride brimmed.

He turned to Lily. "You're blessed."

"Yes." She sat on the settee with her arm resting on a pillow.

"I need more students." Ella pointed upward. "Five bedrooms up there."

He nodded, his expression reflective. "I recently counseled a Westwood couple whose daughter's giving them trouble."

"I have in mind needy, not troubled or defiant girls." She paused, considering her words.

His mouth churned, as if gnawing on a response. "Troubled girls could be the most deserving."

Taken aback, she floundered for a proper response. "I have yet to secure funding to run the school this coming term. And this being my first endeavor ..."

"The quarterly singing's next Sunday." Percival set his stoneware mug aside. "All six county preachers should be in attendance."

"Perhaps they'd have recommendations."

"There'll be dinner on the ground. Singing. Scripture. And prayer instead of the sermon."

"So Lily won't get to hear you preach the first time she attends?"

Lily cleared her throat. "Just so you know ..." She lowered her chin, and the fiery line along her neck puckered. "I ain't goin' to yonder church come Sunday. I 'preciate all you're doin' for me, but I ain't ... I *won't* go nowhere ... I won't go *anywhere* with you fine folks." She touched the scarlet welt. "Not after all the stares on Market Day."

Would Ella's heart rip in two? She'd hoped the child hadn't noticed. Kneeling, she hugged her. "You mustn't think ..." The plaster cast was hard and cold. "You're a beauty, a butterfly. Remember?"

The first of the child's tears eased onto Ella's shoulder. They bled through her thin cotton house dress and beckoned others to follow.

Percival cleared his throat. "I better get home."

Ella wiped her eyes with her apron hem. "Thank you for coming. You're our first guest."

"'Cept Frank."

Percival's easy manner stiffened. "Frank Irving, a guest?"

Ella waved a dismissive hand. "Not a guest. We chatted outside is all."

His brows knit, and his jaw set firm.

"I'll walk you out." She directed him to the veranda.

"Frank isn't to be trusted."

"He wasn't invited. I sent him off in no uncertain terms."

He grabbed her by her shoulders. "I regret not telling your parents back then. If anything should happen to you …"

She hugged the bear of a man. "I made myself clear."

"Let me know if you need me." Settling his hat, he prepared to mount his steed but stopped as if in thought. "At the feet of that poor child, I could see you've found a calling."

First Doc, now Percival.

"Such a calling will do others a heap of good." He spoke in a tone tender. "But what'll it do to you?"

She blinked and left Percival's question unanswered. His words ricocheted in her mind as she returned to Lily's lessons. They accompanied her to the well before supper. And to bed.

She'd never wondered what a calling might do to herself.

Her thoughts scampered to Cade at sheep shearing the previous May. Lightning had struck, endangering both a lone lamb and Cade. Now Viola and Frank had stirred up a mighty wind. Walter's cruelty turned it into a gale. Ella vowed to shelter Lily and other girls as helpless as Cade's newly shorn lamb. But what would the wind do to her own self?

The moon flung its light through the blackthorn stained glass and transformed the bedroom with eerie colors. Drifting clouds cast deep shadows and bade her to her kneeling pillow. Best not search for answers alone. Tree frogs joined night creatures in song, and she folded her hands, lowered her head, and prayed.

"I'm fed up." Leaning against the Hoosier in the McFarland's kitchen, Viola buried her face in a towel.

Ella looked up from her notes. She'd left Lily alone at the cottage so she and Mama could write curriculum. But a stack of dishes waited to be dried, bread dough kneaded, and laundry ironed.

An urge to help her sister threatened, but she ignored it. Viola must learn to help out.

"A home requires effort." Mama positioned a needle and thread above

Papa's shirt.

"I have Joshua."

Viola's grumbling knew no match.

"That you do."

She slapped the towel on the counter. "I'm tired. Can't that Lily creature help?"

Ella pulled in a hard breath. Her eyes blazed. "Why—"

"You'll either do your chores now, Vi," Mama said, "or when your father gets home."

"It isn't fair." Viola's eyes slung amber-colored spears.

"What's that?" Mama pondered a loose stitch.

"Making me do chores while my sister tends to riffraff."

Ella set down her pen. "You talk as if I'm not present."

Mama raised a calming hand. "Your sister tends the cottage and teaches."

"A school of your own's a harebrained idea. And for a Sloat, no less."

"Lily's worth every ounce of effort, sister. So are others. Only yesterday Percival asked me to speak with a troubled girl—"

"Is there no end to the vermin you'll drag home?"

"I won't have you disparaging your sister or Lily," Mama said. "If you can't speak kindness, do not speak."

"All right, Mama, how's this?" Viola huffed. "I fear others will take advantage of my good-hearted sister." Her words reeked of sarcasm, and her grin extended no further than her mouth. She whisked a plate with a dramatic flair and swirled to the cupboard.

Ella put away her writing utensils and gathered papers. "Our plan has disintegrated, Mama. We'll meet at the cottage next time."

A dish crashed, and her head jolted up. Shattered stoneware lay scattered on the floor.

"I can't take this anymore." Viola ran outside.

"I'll finish the dishes, Mama."

"No. Your father won't allow it. They can stack to the ceiling."

"I can iron then." Doing so would rob her of an hour of sleep and relieve Viola of the lesson she needed—that she wasn't the center of creation. But far better Ella ironed than her weary mother. Curriculum planning could wait.

Mama appeared to chew on the thought. New creases showed around her eyes and in her forehead. She angled her head, as if listening. "We have a caller."

Ella hadn't noticed. She peeked out the front window. A single horse neared, its gait too quick for a social call.

They stepped outside.

CHAPTER 21

Sheriff Dawson dismounted.

"Earl." Mama greeted him with a crinkled brow.

He nodded. "Good day, Betsy. Miss Ella."

"Join us." Mama gestured to the porch chairs.

He took a seat after the ladies. "Sorry to bother you, but Walter Sloat's home. Took him myself."

Mama sat up straight. "All right."

"How was he acting?" Ella's belly had tightened.

"Hasn't had a drink in two weeks. He's in a foul mood."

"What about Ruby and Donnie?" She wished she hadn't left Lily alone. Would Frank betray her and tell Walter about the cottage?

"He'll be arrested if he lays a hand on them or steps onto your land."

"Might be too late by then."

"Can't watch him every hour, ma'am, not without locking him up. You know what Mrs. Sloat wants."

Mama nodded. "We must trust the Lord."

"Yes, ma'am." He replaced his hat. "I'll be going then."

Mama stood. "Thanks for letting us know, Earl."

Leaning on a porch post, Ella watched the sheriff ride away. "Where's peace, Mama? Knowing Walter's home is like living on the edge of a war zone."

"The fruit of righteousness is peace."

Might have known her mother would answer with Scripture. She pushed away with a heavy sigh. "Better get along. Lily's alone."

"What do you think Walter's presence across the way will do to your prospects for enrollment?" Mama followed her daughter inside. "What he did to Lily's bound to have reached every eager ear in the territory. Now he's just beyond the creek."

Parents and donors would expect a secure environment. Could Ella provide it?

She must.

Sunday morning dawned bright and clear, boosting Ella's spirits. Folks from all around would show up at the singing. Surely she'd return home with names of prospective students.

All the McFarlands, save Hannah and Joshua, were attending. They'd be along soon. "Won't you go too, Lily?" She stuffed a hunk of bread in her mouth to ease her stomach rumbles. Checking her reflection in the entry mirror, she brushed crumbs from her chin and tidied her curls.

"I 'preciate it, but no."

"Rest while I'm gone?"

Lily raised her bound arm, her smile rueful. "Not much choice."

Ella had donned a frock Adelaide sent from Paris—a cream-colored crepe de chine with ruffled sleeves and shaded embroidery along the hem. Her amethyst-studded choker, another of Adelaide's generous gifts, matched the trim. According to her generous friend off in Italy, amethyst brought out the hint of purple in Ella's eyes.

Harness traces jingled, and hooves thudded. Papa drew the buggy to the porch.

Ella joined her mother and Viola in the patched leather back seat. "Lily's not coming."

"Thank heavens." Viola's words emerged as a barely audible hiss.

"Lily deserves better." Her sister's heartlessness irked Ella.

Staring through powdery dust out the side opening, Viola hiked a hankie to her mouth and coughed. "We're wedged together like Grandma Mac's false teeth." The closeness of the ride presented unde-sirable conditions for the puffy sleeves and delicate smocking of Viola's gown. Ollie had purchased it in Philadelphia, insisting the bold pink petals in the floral fabric highlighted the rosiness in Vi's cheeks.

Morning light tumbled around Christ Church, which sat on a rise at the edge of town. Wild petunias and Indian blankets surrounded it. The clapboard building was a yellow rose among the carefree wildflowers.

A sturdy bell tower reached heavenward, its bell clanging. Automobiles chugged, wagons rattled, and buggy wheels whirred as they delivered families. The Irvings' green Packard and the Yorks' red Buick sat side by side, their polished surfaces gleaming. Frank's steel-gray gelding Flint, a handsome Thoroughbred, was tethered to the hitching post. A new black saddle matched the horse's mane and tail. Keeping books at the bank apparently paid well.

"Welcome!" Brother Percival greeted folks from the open doorway. "Just look at the food!"

"Viola, take a couple baskets." Mama pointed to the containers in the back seat.

Viola grimaced but complied.

Securing the pickles and bread basket, Ella helped Mama maneuver the uneven ground.

Frank stood just off the porch. "Hello, young lady." His smile barely creased his face.

Viola flushed pink "Don't you look handsome."

Must this man's leer or her sister's foolishness mar every joyful moment?

"Let me take that." He reached for Ella's pickles and bread.

She shook her head—and with it, memory's cloak, hot and heavy. "No. Escort Mama to the back."

A frown bunched, but he guided the older woman inside.

The ladies had transformed the church into a party room. Pews lined the walls. Deep etchings recorded innumerable moves across the wooden floorboards. Serving tables covered in blue gingham supplanted the pulpit.

The aromas of seared roast beef, fried chicken, and sweet and tangy fruit pies made her mouth water.

"Smells like Heaven." Papa patted his belly.

"Mighty near." Zach nodded and smiled at his friend.

The two men shook hands with the earnestness of lifelong friendship, their banter friendly. Zach, a straight-forward businessman, made low-interest loans to struggling folks. Many a night he and Papa prayed and studied the Word at the kitchen table.

How did such a man produce a son who strutted from one girl to another?

Ella took her place at the serving table and signaled Viola to join her. But her sister turned away.

The table overflowed with the ladies' best offerings, an immersion in bounty. Mama showed her pleasure as she arranged her chicken and dumplings and butter beans alongside fluffy hot biscuits and preach preserves.

The chatter quieted as if an invisible conductor had stepped to a podium.

Ella looked up.

Thaddeus and Julia Thompson had arrived with a dark-haired gentleman.

"Is that their nephew?" someone whispered behind them.

The man turned.

Standing stone still, Ella's eyes widened. Her cheeks twitched around a hesitant smile.

"That's Andrew, Julia's nephew." Mama leaned toward her eldest daughter. "Isn't he handsome?"

Ella steadied herself against her mother.

"What is it, daughter?"

Rendered speechless, she struggled to comprehend what her eyes beheld. "The Worthington ..."

"What?"

She jerked her head toward the man. "Mr. Evans. The Worthington Board of Directors."

Mama squinted. "How in the world ..."

She steeled herself to tend the table.

"Betsy, this is Andrew Evans, our nephew." Julia and her guest had neared. "Andrew, my friend, Betsy McFarland."

Mama extended a hand. "Haven't seen you since you were a tyke. How are you?"

"Doing well. Thank you." He was as warm and friendly as she remembered.

One matron pushed her daughter forward. Other mothers positioned their girls so the handsome gentleman could meet them.

Frank leaned against the door frame, eyeing Ella and grinning. Refusing to be intimidated, she faced the Thompsons and their guest. "Hello, Julia."

"Good Sunday to you. Ella McFarland, meet Andrew Evans, my sister Josephine's son."

"Welcome to Needham, Mr. Evans." His sapphire eyes sparkled, as she remembered.

"Thank you, but call me Andrew." His voice was as deep and mellow as before.

She extended a hand and looked up at him, a full head taller. "I'm Ella ... as you know." His palm felt as rough as she remembered; his grasp strong but gentle.

"The women of Christ Church certainly know how to serve dinner on the ground."

She smiled. "We moved it indoors long ago" She handed him a plate and plopped a chicken leg onto it.

"Here." Mama added scoops of side dishes.

"Looks delicious. But that's plenty. Thank you." Muscular arms emerged from the rolled sleeves of his tab-collar shirt. His boots were scuffed but clean. This was a man acquainted with physical labor, not educational endeavors alone.

"Join me?" He indicated a pew.

Hungry members lined the wall, waiting to be served. "No, I—"

"I'll take over." Mama proffered a filled plate.

Ella's hands showed a decided tremor. Where had her strength gone? The plate slipped from her fingers and upended in a splat. Mashed potatoes clung to her skirt.

Andrew knelt, and the moist lump disappeared into his napkin. He righted the plate and wiped the floor. Mama grabbed the mess and retreated behind servers.

"Take mine." He settled her blushing self on a pew. "I'll get another."

He smiled as if nothing awkward had occurred, but the wet floorboards testified to her clumsiness. Embarrassment heated her skin.

Mama handed him a freshly filled plate.

He turned to his aunt. "Join us?"

"We'll sit with the Prestons. You young folks enjoy yourselves."

He sat beside Ella with the proper distance between them.

She gave her head a shake and cleared her throat. "I had no idea the kind Worthington board member was Julia's nephew."

He offered her a lopsided grin. "Nor did I know the remarkable young woman we interviewed was my aunt's friend." His expression sobered. "I'm sorry you—"

"I made the right decision." Composed at last, she spilled her ideas about a school like buttons from a button tin, everywhere at once.

His eyes twinkled. "You have a grand plan, but I'm sorry the Worthington girls won't have the privilege of your example."

Warmth rushed up her neck. "Tell me about yourself." She managed four words but nothing else.

Andrew expressed pride in his and Tad's work, casting bells for rail stations, churches, and schools. His little sister was enrolled in private school, and his parents resided in Denver.

She touched a napkin to her lips. "You were a seminary student?"

"Had my finger in a few pies." He took the conversation to a Colorado

Indian mission. To railroad lines near Oklahoma City and Sapulpa and cattle drives in Texas.

"You've had a world of experiences."

Mama approached. "Julia needs you, Andrew. She isn't feeling well."

He stood and gave her a half-bow. "It's been a pleasure. I'd like to visit you if your folks approve."

Her heart fluttered. She must contain her enthusiasm. She had a school to plan and a student to teach. No time for dalliances. "The McFarland door's open anytime." She left out the part about living at the cottage.

He paused, as if evaluating her tone. "Until then."

Andrew and the Thompsons made their way to the door. He looked back and smiled, and she returned his gesture.

Meanwhile, Frank leaned on a window casement. His grin had turned into a hard-edged glare.

She flipped a curl over her shoulder and pivoted. Neither the painful memories Frank stirred, nor the agreeable ones Andrew engendered would claim Ella McFarland.

CHAPTER 22

*A*ndrew Evans was nothing short of a distraction. He'd proven his tenacity over the past week. According to Hannah, his handsome horse Kieran stood at the McFarland's hitching post each evening. Ella couldn't imagine what he and Papa had to talk about.

But what did it matter? Her commitment to Lily and the school came first.

Standing at the cottage's clothesline, she fanned her face with her apron. She'd written six letters of inquiry for the school, tended the garden, and mucked the small barn's stalls. The cottage was starting to feel like home.

She lifted the empty laundry basket and scanned overhead. Not a single rain cloud. Perhaps the sky would open soon and water Papa's cotton field.

Today was the first day of Hannah's new school term. Chuckling, Ella wondered how it was going. More rightly, how was the tutor holding up? Hannah groused that Ella was too much a schoolmarm and too little a sister. But Ella had no interest in listening to more of her sister's complaints. The new teacher at Broadview was good for her.

A finger of smoke inched from the kitchen's chimney pipe. Lily would have dinner on the table soon.

Passing the rose arbor she'd trimmed earlier, Ella's steps slowed at the sound of hooves. Who could be visiting at this time of the day? She hurried inside.

Lily stood at the stove, a task she insisted she enjoyed after having nothing but the Sloat's open firebox or campfire. How did she manage with her arm in a cast? Thankfully, Doc would remove the plaster in a week.

"Someone's coming." Hanging her hat on the hall tree, she tucked stray locks behind her ears and stepped onto the porch. The sight of Andrew Evans astride his ink-black horse halted her midstep. He'd pulled the brim of his hat down low in the sunlight. What fine form he presented.

He drew up and doffed his hat. "Good morning."

She moved to the top step. The man was more handsome than she remembered. "Same to you. What brings you our way?"

"A visit with you. If you don't mind."

Garbed in a sweat-stained work dress and boots, Ella felt ill prepared for a visit. Her insides cartwheeled. "Come in."

He dismounted and took the steps two at a time. She caught a whiff of horse sweat. And aftershave.

"Lily's putting dinner on the table. You're welcome to join us."

"Thanks, but I can't stay." He gestured to the porch chairs crouching like guard dogs. "Can we sit here?"

"Of course." She snatched up a hand fan from a chair seat and settled into the wicker piece.

"You have a fine place." He ran his hands over his thighs. A hint of stubborn blacksmith grime hid beneath one nail.

"This cottage belongs to my friend, Adelaide Fitzgerald. I'm just … we're just … using it for a time." *Calm yourself, Ella Jane.*

"It's more than a cottage." He took in the gables and stonework.

"Aye."

"I hear an Irish lilt. Your mother, too."

"Great-grandma Anglin brought the brogue with her from Ireland."

"Aye." His mischievous grin revealed straight, bright teeth.

She set her fan in motion. "May I get you something to drink?"

"No, but thank you. I won't be staying long. I have something to ask."

Her fan fluttered. "How intriguing."

"I've been a frequent visitor at your parents' home."

"Oh?" It wouldn't do for him to know she'd peeked through the sumacs for the sight of his gelding at Papa's hitching post.

"They've been gracious to me, a newcomer."

"Mama and Papa are nothing if not hospitable."

"I asked your father for permission to court you."

Her fan stopped mid-flutter.

"Your father gave his permission. I'm here to ask for yours."

The idea robbed her of breath. Would the man divest her of every shred of composure? "I beg your pardon?"

"I'd like to come calling … as a suitor, I mean. If you approve."

Her mouth slackened. Courting hadn't occurred to her. Andrew was handsome beyond reason, but she had plans, commitments. She came to herself with a jerk. "I'm flattered and honored, sir."

"Please call me Andrew."

"I'll do my best. It's just that …" She mustn't dissolve into a puddle. "The first time I laid eyes on you was across an interview table." She reached for the right words. "It's one thing to share conversation on a church pew and something altogether different to court."

"Very different."

"Courting leads to …"

"To deeper friendship. And love." His mouth drew into a smile.

"You don't know me. Not really."

"I began to know you when I read your application. That knowledge grew at the first interview. As I listened to your responses and observed your composure and grace, knowledge became admiration."

"I appreciate it; truly I do." She must set this fine man straight … if she could manage to speak more than two words.

"When you showed courage and integrity in your decline of Worthington's offer, I must confess admiration turned to intrigue. I knew you came from Needham, where my aunt and uncle lived. They were bound to know you, so I paid them a visit."

"After—"

"After you turned down the offer. I came away with renewed family ties and a certainty I'd ask what I am asking today. May I call on you,

Ella?"

The blue of his eyes was striking, even distracting. Marshaling her thoughts, she looked to the hillside where the wildflowers had begun to fade, past the windmill, and back to Andrew. "I'm committed to Lily and building a school. It's my calling. But I want to help women find their voices too. My life has no room for … other interests." A shadow passed over his face. "Not at the present time. Though if it did …"

"I admire your commitment. I'd expect nothing less. But I'll keep asking. Until you say yes."

"I give thanks for your friendship."

"Your mother's been feeding me. Invited me to supper tonight. Will you be there?"

So Andrew was the reason Mama had insisted she and Lily come to supper. Her own mother was matchmaking. "We will." Her response surprised even herself.

He donned his hat and settled it firmly. "Until then?"

"Until then." Her gaze held him as he strode with certainty to his horse and reined him toward the bridle path. And as the sound of hoofbeats faded and the pair receded from sight.

The door opened and closed behind her. "Who was that?"

"Andrew Evans."

"The Thompsons' nephew?"

"Yes."

"I'd've liked to meet him."

"You will. Tonight. In Mama's kitchen."

During Lily's reading lesson, Ella's thoughts wandered to Tad's blacksmith shop. How disconcerting, Andrew's visit. Surely he wouldn't persist. No time for courtship. Still …

"I've completed the first McGuffey. Now to the second?"

Ella brushed away her musing and scanned the bookshelf. "It's the green binding."

Lily opened the text with an expression of awe. "I never knew whole worlds live inside book covers."

"Aye. Many more await you."

Lily brightened. "Let's get started. There's numbers waiting at the canning pot."

"Where you'll measure. And add and subtract."

The remainder of the afternoon passed in pleasant conversation with a pot of tea and scratch pads at hand. Ella checked the wall clock more often than she liked. The hands crept along. Would they ever reach six o'clock?

By four she'd had enough. "Let's change and go on over. No need to saddle up. The walk'll do us good."

Freshening up amounted to more than she'd intended. A bit of rosewater in the wash basin. Dabs behind her ears. A yellow cotton dress, belted with a sash embroidered in golden rose buds. And a late summer rose in the coils atop her head.

"Help me?" Chemise-clad Lily held up a green muslin dress Mama had made full-sleeved to accommodate her cast. The garment covered her in one solid piece and buttoned in the back.

Brushing the girl's shimmering locks, she tied a deep green ribbon in the back.

"I'll practice my table manners."

"You'll do credit to Mrs. Vanderbilt I'm sure."

CHAPTER 23

*T*he walk energized Ella for what lay ahead—Andrew Evans. She refused to notice the dark wave that threatened to fall on his forehead. Nor the black lashes that rimmed his eyes—those cobalt pools—or his broad shoulders. She'd busy herself at the stove and dishpan and let Papa converse with their guest.

But Andrew entered Mama's kitchen, and her plan crumbled. Her intended glance transformed into a stare. The man proffered two nosegays.

"Thank you for feeding me again." He handed Mama the rose verbena and extended the remaining bundle to Ella. "I hope you like purple asters. They've just begun to bloom."

She accepted the posy, breathing in its pungent bouquet. "Julia's asters put others to shame." Her eyes slid upward. "Thank you."

"Hear about the ambush in Millersville?" Papa called to Andrew from his reading chair.

Ella assumed kitchen duties, and the men's voices droned. Joshua babbled. Viola and Hannah chatted, and Lily laughed. Cade stepped inside and extended a warm greeting.

Andrew's voice transcended the din. How was she to resist the rich timbre?

Spread with roast beef and country trimmings, the supper table worsened her plight. Mama sat their ever-so-distracting guest across from Ella, making it impossible to avoid his eyes, absurdly blue even in the lamplight. Papa said grace, and turnips, potatoes, and beets circled the table.

"Aunt Julia's attending the Glover County Temperance Union meeting tomorrow night. Are you ladies?" Andrew spoke between bites, his eyebrows raised. "A suffragist will speak."

Seconds stretched into a long, uncomfortable pause.

His eyes searched the family circle. "Have I spoken out of turn?"

Papa's frown spoke volumes.

"Certainly not." Ella gave a pert nod. "We're open-minded."

Mama's eyes squinted closed.

Viola turned to Joshua with a spoonful of potatoes. "We're so open-minded my sister's taken to living with riffraff." She mumbled barely above a whisper.

Please close up Lily's ears, Lord.

Papa swallowed and grimaced. Likely, he'd deal with his insensitive daughter later. "Depends on what you mean by open-minded." He pointed a fork at Andrew. "The Temperance Union women are godly, but I have yet to know a woman of faith in this movement for women's voting rights. From all accounts, heathens make up their ranks."

Andrew set down his fork and mopped his mouth with a napkin. "I share your concern, Gavin. But everything I've learned about the local effort reassures me the Twin Territories' suffragists are the finest ladies. Like Aunt Julia."

The lines around Papa's eyes softened.

Mama leaned toward their guest. "Julia's joined the suffragists?"

"I don't know that she'd put it that way." He ran fingers over a shadow of shaven beard. "From what I hear, a speaker will explain statehood and the need for the state constitution to provide equal suffrage. Why don't you attend, Betsy?"

She gave her head a staccato round of shakes. "No. My girls maybe, but not me."

Papa harrumphed.

Ella held her fork poised over her plate, and gravy dripped onto a mound of mashed potatoes. Six pairs of eyes sought hers.

Until women won the vote, they possessed no voice in lawmaking. Could she add the movement to her overflowing agenda?

Her involvement would keep Papa stirred up. Still, how could she teach Lily and her future students to stand up for themselves otherwise?

"I'd love to."

Lily perked up. "May I go?"

"Of course." Andrew answered without hesitation. "I'll drive you. And take you home tonight. You ladies mustn't walk alone after dark."

"Thank you." What had happened to Ella's iron will? She must find it. Quickly.

The Temperance Union meeting the next evening couldn't come soon enough. Ella planned to socialize and make at least one contact.

She examined her appearance in the entry mirror and smoothed the bodice of her embroidered afternoon dress. Mama had fashioned it from lightweight honey-toned muslin with equally airy petticoats. Not that the temperature was all that warm. But a case of the jitters had overtaken her. She fanned her rounded neckline. "Whew."

"Will this do?" Lily gazed over Ella's shoulder. She'd begun to accept her image in the looking glass.

Ella faced her young friend.

Lily's frock was similar to her own, a floral Viola had chucked aside, insisting the color washed out her alabaster complexion.

"Peach is beautiful on you. The appliqués are stunning. Turn around."

The sweet girl did a half-twirl. Long lace sleeves covered her cast. "Never seen anything to compare with it." She settled a hand at her high neckline. "Covers the scar. Can't do much for the freckles, though."

Ella straightened the silk peach blossom in her ward's hair. "Someday you won't see the freckles. I don't." She touched a fingertip to the spots on Lily's nose and cheekbones. "Angels kissed you there."

Lily lowered her head with her hands clutched. "Hope I don't embarrass you, what with learning a new way of talking and all." She raised her right arm. "And being trussed up still."

"If only you could see yourself through my eyes. I'm sure you'll charm those ladies." A carriage jangled up, and she peeked between the curtains. "There's Andrew and Julia." She threw aside the door and took Lily's hand to descend the steps.

Joy somersaulted through her at the sight of Andrew. Attired in his black suit, he held open the carriage door. His smile invited the women to step inside. Thankfully, he'd lowered the top so they could enjoy the balmy evening sky.

Julia patted the facing seat. "Sit here so I can look at you."

Lily lifted her skirt like a debutante, a quick study, and Andrew helped her up.

He offered Ella his hand. "May I?"

She touched her fingers to his, and her heart fluttered. What had come over her? Andrew Evans was just a man. Why should his touch affect her so intensely?

She should've pulled on her gloves, irksome social requirement. "Thank you." She raised her skirt and set a well-maintained leather shoe onto the step.

His fingers caressed hers. "Be at ease. You are most beautiful, Miss McFarland."

She calmed. "Thank you, Mr. Evans." She settled into the tufted seat. Refusing to force herself into an instrument of torture on a hot summer night, she'd stuffed her corset into a drawer. Her wide belt that dipped to a point in front and fastened with hooks in the back was as far as she'd go for a gaggle of women.

As they drove through town Ella glanced toward Irving's Bank. Frank stood outside, drawing on a cigarette. He tapped the ashes toward the buggy, and she turned away.

Andrew delivered them to the Glover County Women's Club. Lamplight spilled out the windows onto a small rose garden, replete with arbors and trellises dripping blossoms.

She alighted with his helping hand holding hers, and when the carriage clattered away, a wash of disappointment rolled over her.

She must keep her head. She'd printed a handful of calling cards in her finest script and slipped them into her reticule. She'd concentrate on distributing them to at least six potential contributors.

"I hear Mrs. President won't be here tonight. She's come down with a cold." Julia inclined her head toward Ella.

Perhaps they'd be spared the woman's daughter as well, the silly girl who rejected Cade.

"Glad you've come, ladies." A greeter met them at the door.

The women chose seats near Maude Preston and two church ladies who greeted them with warm smiles. One woman moved to another section, and a cadre of her friends followed. Did she consider sitting near a Sloat beneath her? Or a McFarland? How could Ella make important contacts with women who avoided her? Disgruntled, she crossed her arms and mused.

She mustn't let unkindness mar the evening for Lily or herself.

Mistress of Ceremonies Winifred Norris wasted no time. As she presented the required but painfully dull reports, Ella glanced around. Who were the women of means who might invest in the education of needy girls? Some would contribute if they saw the social benefit. But she needed more.

"The speaker's Catherine Barnard, angel of Oklahoma City's down-trodden." Julia spoke behind her hand fan. "I'll introduce you. She'll have a name or two for you."

Mrs. Norris quoted Susan B. Anthony's plea for woman suffrage in the Territory: "'For if it comes into the Union without this in its constitution it will take a long time and a great deal of work to convert over one-half of the men to vote for it.'"

Ella mulled on the idea. Women could use the ballot box to benefit children and women.

Miss Barnard spoke about her efforts with the indigent and the inhumanity of child labor. Her emotional plea for compulsory education, regardless of gender or race, stiffened Ella's spine. Surely this woman would understand her passion.

What if Miss Barnard had heard about Viola's disgrace? Or what

Walter had done to Ella's first student? Might Lily's presence—even the McFarland name—be a stumbling block for the school? Surely a woman who rescued homeless women wouldn't look askance at Lily.

The young leader from Oklahoma City had caught her dark hair into a casual knot atop her head. Her large brown eyes flashed under dark, untamed eyebrows.

Ella knew such zeal. She was certain the Lord had brought her here to meet Miss Barnard. And meet her she would.

CHAPTER 24

hile Lily sipped punch and munched lady fingers, Ella filled a china plate and planted herself beside Miss Barnard. Steadfast in her goal to find support for her school, she handed the public official—the first such woman in the Territory—a calling card.

"So you're Ella McFarland? You're opening a school for needy girls."

Ella's mouth nudged open. "How did you know?"

The young leader leaned sideways conspiratorially. "When women like you and me stir the waters at places like Worthington, people sit up and listen."

"Then you understand I must find donors."

"Winifred Norris is a good contact." She glanced around. "But I see she's returned home." She slipped a card from her skirt pocket. "Here. Send me your mission statement and needs. And call me Kate."

"Thank you. I'm Ella."

Kate eyed her card. "Broadview School for Girls. Is that Adelaide Fitzgerald's estate?"

"Yes. Adelaide and I are lifelong friends. She donated the property for the school."

Kate tapped the edge of the card against her chin, her expression thoughtful. "I'm determined compulsory education will be included in the new state constitution."

"So you share my aspirations."

She waved to a pair of chairs with a table between them. "Let's sit over there. My feet are killing me."

While the grandfather clock chiseled away the minutes, they conversed like friends. Helping the indigent. Educating all children. Kate kept her views on women voting to herself. Ella had heard her father disapproved and she remained neutral out of respect for him.

Julia breezed to Ella's side. "Andrew's here."

How the time had flown. "I'll be right there." Ella turned to Kate. "I hope I haven't monopolized you this evening."

"I've a feeling more was achieved in our conversation than in all the others put together. Give me the rest of your cards. I'll distribute them in Oklahoma City."

"Thank you."

Kate's expression turned pensive. "If you have an interest in reaching out to unwed mothers, I can keep you busy."

"I promise to think about it." She took Kate's hand. "Thank you for your time and recommendations."

"I'll be eager to hear from you." Kate tossed her a mischievous grin.

Across the way Lily was exiting near a trio of matrons who'd decidedly *not* abandoned their corsets. They stopped to eye the dear girl, one through a lorgnette, the other two under peaked eyebrows.

"Is that the girl?"

"I believe it is. Of low birth."

The third snapped open her fan. "I had no idea Needham allowed dregs into such gatherings. You can be sure Hackensack possesses higher standards." Her upper lip curled backward.

Ella's insides boiled. She brushed past the corseted trio. "Pardon me, ladies. I must join my *friend*." She nodded toward Lily. "Ready?"

Lily turned and smiled.

"Come here, dear. These ladies would like to meet you."

The women recoiled.

Lily proffered her hand. "Hello. I'm Lily Sloat."

Limp-wristed, they mumbled their names.

"And I'm Ella McFarland. Will you excuse us?" She glanced back at Kate who smiled and winked.

Andrew stood on the porch. "I've been here an hour. Couldn't wait to see you."

A flush stole her poise. She'd spoken confidently with Kate Barnard and faced the Hackensack snobs. Why was she reduced to a bundle of nerves at the sight of this man?

Lily's and Julia's chatter consumed the ride home. With Andrew close enough to touch if she were so inclined, her inner tempest refused to still.

Later, when she turned down her bed covers, she considered the flood of unexpected blessings the evening had presented. Lily had socialized with ladies of privilege who looked down on her. Yet she appeared comfortable expressing herself in spite of the bulky cast beneath one sleeve.

Julia had beamed with good health and joy while Ella and Kate Barnard shared their common dreams for girls like Lily.

She remembered a word spoken here and another there about a principal for the school, a superintendent, and a board of directors. Her spontaneous declaration that she was starting a school for underprivileged girls weeks past had come with such ease. But with statehood impacting women and children, her endeavor was growing into more than she imagined. As were her questions.

Then there was Kate's concern for unwed mothers and children laboring in sweat shops. Might Ella consider talking with the girl Percival spoke of, the one whose parents were pleading for help? She worried that taking on too much could distract her from her calling.

Surely answers lay right around the corner. She wouldn't rest until she found them.

Her thoughts flew to Andrew, who stirred her fervor in an altogether distinctive way. Handsome, kind, educated, and godly, he was supportive of her interest in teaching and women's rights. Could she deal with matters of the heart when Lily's education and the demands of the school sapped her of time and energy?

Andrew Evans deserved a woman's full attention. She must find a way to tell him.

For a month Ella had tended the garden and cottage with the devotion of a swallow building her nest, everywhere at once with apron strings aflutter. Some mornings she found Lily dressed and waiting in the kitchen at sunup.

"Rain's expected the next three days." She and Lily had just cleaned up the breakfast dishes. "Even with the irrigation system Addie's father built from the creek, there's nothing like rain for growing plants."

Lily slipped a hand into a glove. "There's some weeds in the new plantings."

"Aye, but you can put away your gloves. I'll not have you in the garden with the cast still on and your studies waiting." She nodded to her desk. "I've drafted a letter to Kate Barnard with our mission statement and what we need for the school. You can copy it for your writing lesson."

Lily studied the message. "You reckon ... *think* I can read this?"

"If I didn't know better, I'd think you'd been reading for years. Circle what you can't read. That'll be your reading lesson." She scooted down the steps.

"Miss Barnard seemed a lively sort," Lily called from the open doorway.

"You could say that." She tied her hat strings. "I want to mail the letter tomorrow."

The garden plot lay in a bold patch of sun near the creek. How she enjoyed tending her own garden. Her gratitude for Papa's generosity knew no bounds. He contributed to the school effort by hiring field hands to replace Lily and Ella.

Thank you, Lord.

She hummed as she toiled. Kate's enthusiasm for the downtrodden inspired her. Perhaps she'd speak with the couple Percival mentioned.

Certain purchases were required. A sewing machine and supplies. Every level of McGuffey and lots of classic literature for girls. A microscope for botany. And boxes of school supplies to make a real classroom.

She had yet to enroll a single student, so her plans must remain general. For now.

Taking notes, Lord?

Andrew had met her the previous day in Mama's kitchen to discuss curriculum. He possessed a storehouse of knowledge, and his enthusiasm for the school had grown to match her own. Perhaps he'd serve on a board.

She imagined him dressed in his black suit, his hair combed back, his shaven beard shadowing his jaw. That hint of a dimple. And his eyes, pools reflecting the deep blue sky. She pressed a hand against her middle, suppressing those troublesome feelings again.

She wiped her forehead. The temperature was rising, which could account for the sudden flash of warmth beneath her blouse. She lifted her apron and dried the moisture dotting her chin.

Truth be told, she could listen to Andrew's voice, mellow like a stream of honey, all day. Like it or not, the man sent her heart into palpitations.

"Ella!" Lily called from beyond the garden.

She cupped a hand around an ear, straining Lily's way.

"Andrew's here."

Ella's heartbeat kicked up a notch, and she pushed herself to her feet. "Be right there."

Strengthen my will. A war's raging inside me.

Rounding the corner of the cottage, she found Andrew on the porch, hat in hand.

"I brought the books." He'd offered to share from his own collection.

Five huge wooden crates had been stacked in the wagon. "So many? I'll need more bookcases, and you'll need help getting them inside."

"I'll see if Vern can help me unload and bring over bookcases later."

"How can I thank you?"

He motioned to the porch. "By sitting with me awhile. Don't have long."

The door opened, and Lily stepped out. "Juice? Made it from plum paste."

"What a treat. Thank you." Boot-clad Ella clomped up the steps with Andrew following. She pulled off her hat and ran her fingers through her hair to settle stray curls.

Lily delivered a tray of refreshments. "Daisy and me're ... Daisy and *I're* itching for a ride." Vernon had given her a young filly, and girl and horse had bonded.

Ella settled into her chair, as did Andrew. The heat produced little effect on his rich complexion, but there was a hint of rose in his cheeks.

He captured her in his gaze, a deep pool of blue. "Gardening suits you. You're beautiful." Dimples came and went when he spoke.

Her hands flew to the flattened heap crowning her head, the swirly tendrils that resembled a stubborn trumpet vine. "Goodness."

She simply must find a way to tell him courting was impractical for someone wedded to her work. "Andrew ..." The rattle of a conveyance halted her.

"It's a wagon." He set his glass on the railing.

And the two of them stood.

CHAPTER 25

A mule-drawn wagon rounded the rise.

Ella shaded her eyes with a hand. "Not anyone I recognize."

Andrew's brows knit. "Who knows about this place except family?"

"Only close friends." She glanced up. "Like you." She moved down the steps with him beside her.

A man drove the team. A woman sat beside him, a bright-haired girl in back.

They came to a halt, and the overalls-clad driver in work boots jumped down. The woman, as thin as paper, followed like an addled baby chick.

"Howdy." The stranger removed his hat. "I'm Clyde Harper. This here's my wife, Lucille. You Ella McFarland?"

"What can I do for you?"

"Percival Preston said you're looking for girls for a school."

Ella's determination to send them on their way disintegrated. This was the couple Percival mentioned. Why hadn't he asked her if they could visit? She glanced at the towhead in the back. "Won't you join us, have some plum juice?"

Clyde's eyebrows formed one hard line. "We'll sit on the porch, but not for juice, if it's all the same to you. Not much on socializing today."

"All right."

Andrew introduced himself and turned to Ella. "I'll see if Vern can help me unload." An expression of wariness marred his high spirits. "Unless you want me to stay."

The Harpers wanted to speak privately, that was plain to see. Ella shook her head. "You can go. But thank you."

"You folks have a good day." Andrew spoke the parting words, donned his hat, and drove away.

Clyde turned to his daughter. "Go over yonder under the sycamores, Nell. We'll be along directly."

With a raised chin and a flip of hair the color of pale butter, the nearly grown girl slid off the tailgate.

Ella sat in a chair, and Clyde and Lucille took the porch swing.

The Harpers wore sodden expressions. Lucille's nose was red, and she'd twisted her handkerchief into thick twine.

"We're here about our Nell." He hooked a thumb toward his girl.

The girl stood in the shade of a sycamore with her arms locked over her chest. She dug lines in the dirt with the toe of one shoe.

"Percival told you about our trouble?" Clearly, this man had downed a lump of pride.

"He didn't give details."

"She's giving us a heap of worries. Been sneaking around with Billy Redmond. Has a harebrained idea she'll marry him. He keeps pestering us, but I'll be six feet under 'fore I'll let a redskin darken my door as a member of the family."

Lucille blew her fire-red nose.

He heaved a sigh and continued. "Lucille can't bar Billy from the house when I'm gone. Nell won't listen to either of us." A storm brewed on his face. "Somebody needs to talk some sense into that girl, a young somebody with a good head on her shoulders, minus the wrinkles her ma and me sport. Someone like you."

"But I'm not trained to counsel a troubled girl."

"I'm asking you to do more 'n talk. I want you to keep Nell here out of Billy's reach, your family being righteous and all."

She scrambled for a response. On the one hand, her heart went out to the Harpers. On the other, Lily and the school consumed her time and energy.

"I'm only twenty-one and planning for a school. My hands are full, and . . ."

"If you'll take Nell ..." He twisted his rolled-up hat brim. "And give her some learnin', I'll pay for her keep."

The wind rustled and stirred. The front and back doors stood wide open, creating a draft and flinging sand like it was peeved. Walnut saplings bent, and the air smelled of rain.

Kate Barnard had mentioned homeless girls, desperate for someone to take them in. Just three days later such a one was standing on Ella's porch.

She turned to Clyde. "Nell can stay. I'll keep Billy away."

The father, no longer a stranger, sighed. "We thank you kindly. We sure do."

He rushed down the steps and pulled a knapsack from the wagon. Weeping, Lucille stumbled to her daughter and held her.

Clyde shooed his wife into the wagon and gave the reins a shake. "Keep that redskin away," he called over his shoulder.

An old saying of Grandma Mac's came to mind: *Sometimes regret comes a-calling.*

Ella shivered. And opened her arms to welcome Nell.

CHAPTER 26

*E*lla examined Bunny's left forearm, knee, and fetlock by lantern light. The mare grunted but stood still, switching her tail in annoyance. She'd found her in the pasture with blood dripping down her leg. Thankfully the wound wasn't deep. The fence had slashed her, not a crazed animal. Cade lost a lamb last year to a mad dog.

"That's a girl." She soothed the animal as she worked.

"Ella?"

Startled, she jumped up, and her brother strode into the barn.

Cade kicked aside a stray clump of hay. His face twisted into a scowl. "What've you done, taking in Clyde Harper's daughter?"

What had come over her good-natured twin?

"Why, the Lord's opened the spigot." She ignored the lines that marred his features. "Percival told me about the Harpersand their daughter. So when they showed up with Nell, and Clyde said he wanted me to keep her away from Billy Redmond and school her myself, our family being righteous and all, I said yes. Nell's in the house." She paused to take a breath.

"Without talking to your family first? Billy Redmond's trouble."

"I thought—"

"That's the problem! You *didn't* think. Did you even pray about it?"

Truthfully, she hadn't.

She took a step back. "Why, Cade McFarland, you ought to—"

"It's *you* that ought. Ought to think before you speak. Talk to your family before you take such action. What effect might this have on Lily? Don't you know Billy Redmond's dangerous? You women are out here by yourselves."

She stood with her arms at her sides, as deflated as a circus tent on moving day. Her heart ached for Clyde and Lucille, for Nell and Lily, even for Bunny.

She leaned against the tack room door. "I admit I made a spontaneous decision."

Cade raised his eyebrows.

"But the promise is made. We've plenty of room. Lily will be delighted to have a classmate." She kicked her chin up a notch.

Cade crumpled onto a hay bale and ran his fingers over his forehead. "What about Billy Redmond? He got out of jail only a few months ago. Know what he was in for?"

Her stomach knotted.

"Beating up a woman." He let his head fall against the stall rail.

"I won't pretend I made the wisest decision. If I'd taken more time, I might've told Clyde I'd think it over. But I saw Viola in Nell and Mama's and Papa's pain in her folks' eyes." She shrugged in resignation. "I won't send her home."

Ella would've said the Lord hadn't given her a spirit of fear, but she hadn't stopped to pray about it.

Her brother slapped his hat against his thigh. "Percival and our mother can counsel Nell. Maybe Andrew can advise you, sister."

"Aye. The Lord provides the power of a sound mind through godly counsel."

He surged away and halted mid-step. "How did the Harpers know where you live, anyway?"

"Percival told them."

"He didn't. I asked him. He would've talked to you first, let you meet them at the church, not send them out here unannounced."

"I assumed ... How *did* they know about the cottage?" Odd.

"What's done's done, sister. I'll keep watch." He strode toward the barn's wide open doors. "Let me know if Nell acts like she's about to bolt. I'll come over in the morning for Lily's target practice."

Ella trudged across the yard to the cottage. Perhaps a good night's sleep would bring tranquility, and a bright new morning would lift her spirits.

Lily met her on the porch. "I saved you some beans and cornbread."

She smiled at her young friend. "Did Nell eat?"

"A bit. She's upstairs in the bedroom next to mine."

"You're a dear." She gave Lily a side-hug. "Cade'll come over tomorrow as visiting professor. For target practice."

The ever-so-innocent child's eyes went wide. "A real professor?"

"No, silly." Ella chuckled and nudged her inside. "That's a McFarland's way of teasing."

Lily joined her at the table. "Nell moped around and huffed like a riled-up mama cow while you was … you *were* outside with Bunny."

"We'll make tomorrow different."

Four and a half inches of rain kept them indoors the following three days. They got to know Nell while time drizzled past them. The Haper girl's mood mirrored the drooping clouds, but Ella and Lily included her in their conversations, and gradually she relaxed. Until Sunday afternoon when Viola showed up.

"What're you thinking, for pity's sake? First you take in a Sloat and now a Harper?"

"I refuse to discuss Lily or Nell, Vi. So unless there's something else …"

"Don't you know no one will contribute to a school with such undesirable students?" Her eyes blazed. "It puts a blight on the McFarland name, just when we were being received again."

She waited until the tirade ended. "The school's my affair." She spoke evenly, refusing to allow her sister to ignite her temper.

The golden-eyed beauty leaned toward her with a forefinger pointed. "Having to do your chores *is* my affair. So is leaving our little sister to tend my baby and living on pennies because Papa's replacing both you and Lily in the field." Her words reverberated off the porch's ceiling.

Ella sagged. A flurry of harsh responses corkscrewed in her mind, but she chucked them away. "I'm sorry you're unhappy, Vi. I love you, but you may not bring your misery to this place. I've enough on my mind without adding rancor." She couldn't remember a time when Viola represented anything else. "Bring encouragement and assistance or stay away."

Viola leered. A dreadful darkness had overtaken her. "Make no mistake, you haven't heard the last from me." She tromped down the steps.

"You mustn't be out with another storm coming. Come in."

Ella's perpetually irate sister stomped across the yard, stopping once to scrape mud and leaves from her shoes.

Nell stepped onto the porch. "I'm causing you trouble, ain't I?"

"Not at all." Ella opened the door and waved her back inside.

The girl twisted a pocket around a finger, drawing up her skirt. "I heard what your sister said. I don't belong here. And I ain't givin' up Billy."

"He doesn't know where you are, and that's that."

The defiant sixteen-year-old flipped a blonde tress over her shoulder. "We're gettin' married."

"Your father will have something to say about that. You're not grown yet. Besides, don't you want an education?"

"Don't need no educatin' to keep house."

What would it take to reach this girl?

Grandma Anglin came to mind. She'd pored over newspapers and great literature alike. She was informed in uncommon ways.

"What would've become of Jane Eyre if she'd not been sent to Lowood?" Grandma had said when Ella fussed about school assignments. "Education, my dear, made the difference between Gateshead and Thornton Manor."

An idea, featherlike, tickled her teacher mind. "Ever hear of *Jane Eyre?*"

"Jane who?"

"It's a made-up story. You know, a novel. Writers show through such stories that we all share some of the same problems. I'll introduce you to Jane. But you must promise to try."

Nell lifted a shoulder in a nonchalant manner.

"I'll make you a deal. If after one school term you're still convinced education doesn't matter, I'll talk with your father about how you feel about Billy. Will you agree to that?"

Nell tilted her head with a snippet of a smile. "I reckon."

Ella sat back in satisfaction.

Would one term be sufficient? If not, she must face Clyde Harper.

Perish the thought.

CHAPTER 27

*I*ntent on completing her chores, Ella unhooked the well bucket from the rope. Nell and Lily had milked and fed at dawn and finished their lessons. Doc arrived at noon to remove Lily's cast. All three of them would organize the cellar later that afternoon. But first, there was canning.

Yesterday's rain had left the ripening cotton bolls soaked, reducing the market value of the raw fiber and adding strain to the McFarland household. But improved sales at the store eased Papa's worries. The representative of a wealthy new resident of Glover County had purchased most of the store's inventory and asked for more. Odd.

Two horses with riders loped around the rise and into view—one a man and the other a woman. She sported a hat secured by a length of fabric that trailed behind.

Frank and Viola.

Ella raised her eyes to the heavens and sighed. *What now?*

She entered the cottage and set the bucket of water beside Lily. "Pump pressure's down, so here's some for the first round of canning. But we have guests, Vi and Frank. I'll get rid of them. We have work to do." She stepped onto the porch, and they reined in.

Dressed in a teal riding suit fit for a queen, Viola dismounted and approached with a skewed smile. "Don't you look the worse for wear." She removed her scarf and hat and shook out her mane. It fell in dark chestnut waves to her waist.

Ella ignored the remark. "Why're you here on a workday?"

Frank twisted one end of his newly grown mustache. "An ordinary day for the working class, but for the rest of us it's a fine occasion for a ride in the country."

"Everyone's idle at home, sister?"

"Rain kept us inside yesterday. Still too wet for the garden or fields. Papa's store stock has sold out again, so there's nothing to do at the store." She strode toward the cottage. "Charming, don't you think, Frank?"

Her cavalier escort slid his hand around her waist. His thumb grazed her arm in intimate circles. "In a quaint sort of way."

Give me grace. I haven't a speck of my own. "I can't tarry, Vi."

"Surely you have time for a chat." Viola sashayed onto the porch.

No time to waste in idle conversation. "I must get busy."

"Where's that girl you have living here? Nell, is it?" She looked around.

"Why?"

"Thought I'd say hello. Be friendly."

What was her perpetually plotting sibling brewing? "Busy with her schoolwork. So enjoy your ride." She abandoned the couple on the porch, visiting in conspiratorial tones. At length they claimed their mounts and headed not back to the road but toward the woods.

Lily peeked between the curtains. "There's some bad blood."

Ella's skin pebbled, scattering thoughts of chores like sand in the wind.

The ever-observant girl let the curtains flutter closed. "Want to talk?"

"Is Nell in her room?"

She nodded. "With that novel you've been reading her."

"Good." Ella chose the high-back chair that afforded a clear view out the window. "By bad blood, do you mean Frank or Viola?"

Lily sat beside her. "Both of them, from the looks of things."

"You are indeed perceptive. Vi's my sister, so I won't say there's bad blood between us. It's more like …"

"*Animosity* is a vocabulary word this week."

"I don't feel animosity toward Vi. I love her."

"Viola's the one with battles. Something's not right inside her."

Ella tapped a tooth with a thumbnail. "Surely it's a phase."

"Was she different when she was a young'un … a *child*?"

"Viola was caught in the middle. Cade and I are twins, but I'm the eldest by minutes. He was the only boy, and Hannah the baby. That left Viola … nowhere special."

"Her beauty's special." Lily leaned forward with her elbows on her knees. "A copperhead's beautiful, but it's full of poison. Sorry if that gets your hackles up, her being your sister, but I fear what she'll do."

Hadn't Ella thought the same herself? Even when Vi was a child? "We four are as different as a patch of wildflowers. Don't know why Mama and Papa don't take a firmer stand with Vi. I suspect they're waiting for life to teach her."

"Having a baby without a pa is a step in that direction."

"The Lord'll get hold of her sooner or later. But what's in store for the rest of us in the meantime?"

"Bad blood destroys, Ma says."

Ella restrained a shudder.

Nell completed her daily chores without sniveling, but she often meandered around the property. On one occasion Ella had discovered her and Viola in Broadview's gazebo with their heads close together, as if they were close friends. What was her scheming sister cooking up?

Another time she found Nell at the creek near the Sloat place. "You can't be going off like this. Isn't safe."

She'd shrugged and tossed her pale mane over a shoulder.

The girl cooperated with mathematics assignments. But she listened with her face aglow when Ella read *Jane Eyre* aloud, hour after enchanting hour.

"If me and Billy have us a girl, I'm gonna name her Jane." The Harper's daughter insisted she'd marry the boy in the face of her father's opposition. Clyde Harper was no man to get crosswise of, but she was in love and might go to any length.

"I'll marry Billy, pa or no pa." The unyielding girl insisted, her eyes ablaze. "And I won't read or write another word in no lesson if you don't leave me alone 'bout Billy."

Determination was stamped on her face and in her voice. She likely would come to heartache. But she was in God's hands, wasn't she? "Jane's a fine name, Nell."

You'll have to figure this out, Lord. I'm stumped.

On a morning in mid-September, Nell pushed aside her breakfast plate and smiled at Lily. "I'll go with you out yonder to the garden." The rains of the previous week had given rise to abundant growth.

The girls hitched baskets over their arms, and Ella called from the back porch, "Don't stay long. We have a history lesson to complete."

They sauntered toward the garden, their hair bright gold and copper in the sunlight. The breeze carried their voices like daisy petals.

A knock on the front door drew Ella into the house. She hooked a finger around the edge of a curtain and peeked outside.

A stranger stood on the porch with his hands in his pockets. No sign of a horse or wagon. Dark haired and dark skinned, he looked to be in his mid-twenties, dusty and tired. Who was he? And where had he come from?

She pulled her pistol from the drawer in the entry table. "Who is it?"

"Billy Redmond."

A rush of panic zipped through her. She caught her lip between her teeth, mulling over her options.

For God gave us not a spirit of fearfulness; but of power and love.

She slipped the pistol into her pocket and opened the door. "Can I do something for you?"

He removed his flat cap. "I could use some water." Clearly exhausted, the young man possessed a rugged form. Surely he was dry as powder in the ninety-degree heat.

She couldn't refuse a man a drink of water. But she couldn't let Nell see him either. The well was on the other side of the house from the garden. And Lily and Nell would be working for at least an hour. "It's around there." She gestured with a thumb. "I'll bring a dipper."

"Thank you, ma'am." He trudged off the porch and around the house.

She hurried through the house to the back porch and snatched a tin dipper from its hook by the door.

She found Billy at the well, hauling up a sloshing bucket. "How'd you get to our place?"

"Walked."

"From where?"

"Westwood."

"That's twenty miles."

"Yes, ma'am."

She squinted. "You still haven't told me what you're doing here."

He drained the dipper and filled it again. "Nell."

She hiked her chin. "Nell who?"

"Nell Harper, ma'am. I know she's here."

"Where'd you get that idea?"

He pulled a kerchief from a pocket and mopped his forehead. Heaving a sigh, he trained his eyes on hers. "Best I not tell where I got my information." He raked a hand through his hair. "Let's just say I know and leave it at that."

What was she to do with this young man? He didn't present himself as dangerous, but the sweetness of a cobbler couldn't be judged by ogling the crust. If Nell caught sight of him, all the progress they'd made in the past ten days could be destroyed.

"You're welcome to a drink but not to Nell. I promised Clyde."

He ran his eyes up and down her petite frame. "You think someone as puny as you stands a chance with a man like me?"

Pushing away from the rock-and-mortar well, she turned with her pistol pointed. "Until I hear different from Clyde, I'm sticking to my promise."

Fire blazed in Billy's eyes. "I'm gonna talk to the man."

"Knowing you've done time for beating up a woman tells me I don't want you around Nell. Neither does Clyde." Her voice was strung tight as fence wire.

"I didn't touch that Chickasha woman. She was lying." His lips and chin quivered.

Could the sheriff have been mistaken about Billy? "Until Clyde Harper says otherwise, you need to leave. I'll give you a jug of water and a bite to eat."

He slapped his hat on his pant leg and gazed at his feet. "You ain't gonna keep us apart."

"Then change Clyde's mind." The young man's shoulders drooped and tugged at her heart. "I'll meet you out front with a bit of sustenance."

Minutes later, she handed him a sack of food. "Stop at the caretaker's house. Maybe he can give you a ride."

The bedraggled young man dragged himself beyond a stand of elms and over the rise. Defeat hung on him like a shroud.

Nell came into the house grumbling. "Billy was here."

Ella turned from washing squash. "How do you know that?"

"I went to the well for a drink." She opened a fist. A heart-shaped rock lay in her palm. "I gave him this. He must've left it for me."

Exhaling, Ella pulled out a chair. "Yes. He was here."

Nell ran to the front and hurled the door aside. A stiff breeze pasted her shift against her body. She sprinted down the steps and up the drive crying, "Billy!"

Ella ran after her. "He's gone. Besides, you can't just run off. Give him a chance to talk to your father. And remember your promise to me."

The girl grabbed her middle and bawled. Her shoulders shook. Tears raced down her cheeks. She turned around, and Ella drew back.

The light in her eyes had gone out.

CHAPTER 28

Ella woke with a headache the next morning, the Lord's Day. She'd tried to comfort a weeping Nell, and by nightfall she felt cranky and out of sorts. Lily saw to their simple meals, but appetites had abandoned them.

Andrew and Cade had paid them a visit after supper, but Ella was poor company. Nell dragged herself upstairs and closed her door, and Ella read until the regulator struck midnight. She slept fitfully, hurting for the love-sick girl and questioning her own judgment.

She splashed water over her face and checked her reflection above the wash basin. Morning light revealed dark circles ringing her eyes. A crease had taken up residence above the bridge of her nose. She dampened a cloth and ran it around her neck.

Shuffling to the kitchen, she put on a pot of coffee and dissolved a packet of headache powder in water. She must get on with the day.

She downed the medication and sat with her elbows on the table and her head in her hands. The pot blub-blubbed.

Footfalls above told her one of the girls was up. Soon the stairs squeaked, and Lily appeared beside her. "You don't look like you feel good."

"Headache." Ella massaged her neck.

Dark liquid shot into the glass knob in the pot's lid.

"I'll fix breakfast." Lily busied herself with the slicing of a slab of bacon.

"Nothing but a bit of oats for me."

"I'll give you some buttered bread too."

The redolence of the coffee filled the room. Ella savored the richness.

"Did I decide right, not allowing Billy to see Nell?"

"What else could you do? She's the Harpers' daughter."

"It hurt seeing their pain. Both of them. But I'm not sure Clyde's making the right decision. I may ride over to Westwood."

Lily moved the gurgling coffee pot off the stove and poured her out-of-sorts mentor a cup. "Nell carries a burden, that's for sure."

Still dressed in her nightgown, Ella padded across the hardwood floor to the stairs. "I need to wake her." Trudging up the stairs, she knocked on the closed door. "Nell?"

No answer.

"Breakfast is almost ready." Lily called up the staircase.

Ella opened the door and found the room tidy, but no sign of its occupant. She threw open the wardrobe. Empty.

The bed was made up as she'd taught her. And on the pillow lay a sheet of ruled paper with crude script. "Pa'll never change. Me and Billy have money. Don't look for us."

Clyde Harper barreled up the porch steps and glared at Ella. "You said you'd take care of my girl."

"I had no idea—"

"Percival Preston said I could trust you."

Her strength had abandoned her. She held onto the porch rail, trying to explain, but the Harpers were beyond hearing her.

The irate father jabbed a finger in her direction. "Folks are gonna hear of this."

"Come on." Lucille hooked her arm through her husband's, and the two tramped away.

Heartsick and discouraged, Ella watched their wagon rumble around the rise. Later that evening Andrew tried to encourage her, but she could get no further than the simple truth.

This was her fault.

"How can I go on with this burden of guilt, Andrew?"

His arm around her shoulders and his strong body to lean into kept her on her feet. "Who'd send their daughter to this place now? Broadview School will be known as the place where the girl ran off with her lover. Gossip will spread, and all of Indian Territory will know. I'll be a disgrace to the McFarland name."

That night she buckled over with the weight of disappointment. Nell's words returned, words Ella hadn't responded to at the time. *That girl Jane, she had her some backbone. Would Jane've done what her pa said if she'd had one? Billy'n me'll live in a manor one day, just wait 'n' see.*

Billy's words lingered too. *I didn't touch that Chickasha woman. You ain't gonna keep us apart.*

Their voices rang in her ears, and in her confusion and doubt, she raised her fist at God. "I trusted You! Is there no end to troubles? What can I do to please You?"

Whitecaps of regret peaked and waned and peaked again over the coming days. If only she'd sought counsel and prayed with Nell. Why didn't she kneel with the Harpers and ask for the Lord's leading? She listened to Clyde and her prideful self instead.

"Ma says hindsight's sure enough crystal clear." Lily crooned, her empathy on display. "It's the foresight that stumps us."

Loved ones shared their wisdom and prayers, but regret had captured Ella's spirit. Even a visit from Percival and Maude made little difference. The future of Broadview School for Girls had turned bleak indeed.

CHAPTER 29

$\mathcal{G}$radually Ella drew upon her McFarland stubbornness to meet each new day, her eyes on her original goal—educating Lily. Starting a school was impossible amid the Harpers' accusations, so back into the field she and Lily trudged for the cotton harvest. At least Papa no longer had to hire their replacements.

She straightened from between two cotton plants and focused on Lily. "You feeling alright?"

"Two months of good vittles and living in safety have made me stronger." She nodded toward two slight forms on the far side of the field. "Can't say as much for Ma or Donnie."

Since Lily moved into the cottage and began her schooling, Donnie was doing his best to replace her in the field. But his crippled legs limited his mobility. Often, he could do little more than work his way down a single row before collapsing under a bur oak. Papa had agreed to pay Lily double wages, so she could share with her mother.

Pulling her sack of cotton nearer, Ella felt its wide strap slacken at her shoulder. "They appear stronger since you're getting good food to them." The child made nighttime visits to the creek with supper buckets for her mother and brother.

"I'm hankering to do more than send them leftovers across the creek." She swabbed her neck with her apron.

"Finish your studies, and you can attend normal school if you want. I'll move with you and look for a teaching job where no one knows how foolish I've been. We could both help them then."

"What'll happen in the meantime?"

"Statehood's coming. So is compulsory education. As a ten-year-old,

Donnie will attend school whether your pa likes it or not." If only the law had been in place for Nell, she would've been in school, not sitting at her father's produce stand, the day Billy stopped for a peach.

But Ella mustn't let regret bring her down. Her eyes traced the fence line surrounding Papa's acreage. Thick growth outlined the creek.

Across the field Ruby yelped as she struggled with her load and fell backward.

"Ma!" Slipping the strap over her head, Lily let her sack plunk into a heap and ran toward her mother.

Eager to help, Ella stepped toward them. *Sloat women are proud.* Best leave them be.

Lily knelt at her mother's side. Helped her stand. And tugged on Ruby's sack.

A vertical field scale hung on a tripod, rocking in the breeze. Its rusty rasp sliced through the tract's weary wordlessness like a dull blade through hardened leather.

Ella, the teacher, must speed up her student's education. They both needed to get away. Someplace where Walter couldn't find them, where they could be known as something other than a sharecropper's daughter and a teacher too foolish to be trusted.

Unable to watch her young friend tug a hundred pounds of cotton alone, she took off, hurtling the plants and calling, "I'll help!"

Together, they pulled Ruby's sack along the turn row toward the trailer. Cade met them at the tripod and lifted the exhausted woman's load with a grunt. He wrestled the strap onto the scale and eased the burden off his shoulders.

The tripod's legs spread outward, struggling to contain the weight.

Ruby stood with her head down and her hands worrying her apron pockets.

Ella returned to the field and took note of her own calloused hands and scuffed boots, far from the form she'd presented at Worthington. The board members would raise their eyebrows and sniff in disapproval

What did they know of life on a farm? A cotton field could fray the sturdiest fabric, a shredding Viola and Hannah had yet to endure. She hoped they never would, although a little more exertion would do them both good.

Her failure with Nell had given rise to more of Viola's unkind remarks about the girl's lowly background and Billy's undesirable reputation. As if they were unworthy of Ella's efforts.

She was forced to endure Frank's insincere condolences and his hand lingering at her back with untoward intimacy. Would she never be rid of him?

Then there was Andrew, beautiful in all his ways. She closed her eyes and let her imagination carry her where it hadn't dared to venture. There in the field amid row upon row of beckoning bolls of white fiber, Ella smiled.

She swayed, and her eyes popped open. She ran the back of a hand over her forehead and slipped her fingers beneath her collar, coaxing a whiff of air against her chest.

Why would Andrew want to court an imprudent woman such as herself? Slipping the canvas strap over her head, she settled it on her shoulder, tapped the crown of her hat, and dragged her sack to the next plant.

She must stop daydreaming. Work called.

Ella slept in her marriage bed, her body cupped alongside her husband's like spoons in a drawer. His arm draped over her waist, warm and tender. His hand cupped her cheek. His thumb moved in lazy circles across her chin. She stirred, brushing aside a curtain of curls and nestling into the cradle of his body. 'Twas a day to wallow in her loved one's arms.

"Go to sleep, Ella love."

She shot upright. Her eyes searched the shadows beyond the lamp's glow. She ran a hand over the surface beneath her. Slats. She was in the swing. Her head jerked left. "Andrew."

The man in her dream sat next to her.

She pulled away. "I thought ..." She couldn't tell him . . . "I just ..."

"You're exhausted."

Were the inches between them sufficient to keep her consternation at bay?

He stood. "I'll sit in a chair, and you can lie down."

Regaining her composure, she leaned over, and he slipped a throw pillow beneath her head. He moved his chair closer and stroked her hair.

She sniffled. "It's been a month now. Cotton harvest is complete. Everyone's gone back to living. And you've comforted me more than you know. But when will regret ease for good?"

"You did nothing but love Nell. And try to help her."

"If I'd kept a closer watch ... If I'd refused to let her come here in the first place ... Where could she and Billy have gone?"

He traced a line on her forehead, and she closed her eyes.

"When Nell realized her father would never let her marry Billy, she made her choice, Ella."

She covered his hand with hers, savoring his warmth on her cheek, the bulging knuckles and sinews. Andrew Evans possessed more common sense and kindness in one finger than resided in most folks' bodies. Seemingly born to the task of binding up broken spirits, he took to heart the Apostle John's admonition to love one another.

He leaned forward and kissed her hair. The scent of manly hair tonic tickled her senses. Every semblance of restraint stole from her body.

Suddenly he was in the swing, slipping her onto his lap and easing them into a rocking motion. She nuzzled into the curve of his neck. And wept.

He cupped her head, stroked her back, and hummed. Her tears coursed and pooled against his skin, saturating both their necklines.

Her sobs subsided, and he spoke. "Your labor for Nell was pure love."

The rhythm of his heartbeat matched her own.

He lifted a ringlet, and it curled around a finger. "God knows you tried." He brushed away her tear and kissed her hands, his touch like a lightning dance across the prairie. "I won't coat my counsel with sugar. You've drunk from a bitter cup. But if you'll drink the Balm of Gilead, He'll seep into the lifeblood of your soul and sweeten the gall in ways a sugared cup can't."

She nuzzled deeper into a place where his heartbeat grew louder. The swing rocked, and she lifted her eyes to the ever-darkening sky.

The beneficent moon scattered a frothy glow amid the low-hanging clouds that had let loose an inch of rain. The light reached down to the sycamore and pecan trees, grazing their tops and resting its palms along the plains beyond. It was the kind of moon that could settle a pen of hogs while it woke an owl, yet surrender its place in the heavens to an impatient sun come daybreak. And leave the fingerprint of God all around.

Together in the porch swing, Ella and Andrew spoke of ordinary things: the sweetness of spring water in a dry gullet on a hot summer day. The lowing of contented cows with full bellies and babies at their sides. And the spreading of the moon's October frock amid the sycamores and plowed fields beyond.

She breathed in his heady scent and recounted each moment she'd known him, each word he'd spoken, each spark of his eyes, and each of her secret longings. The day's rain and warm humidity gave way to a cool evening breeze, and Ella's broken, weary spirit absorbed the sweet balm Andrew offered.

"Yes," she whispered at his ear.

"Yes, what?"

"Yes. You may come calling. Please."

CHAPTER 30

A full month after Nell ran away, lingering regret still pestered Ella. But since she told Andrew he could come calling, her joy had soared. Perhaps witnessing Nell's and Billy's forbidden love had awakened her own sleeping need. How could she have thought she could live without love? She wanted nothing more than to love Andrew and receive his love in return.

Would her longing for a school ever fade? On the night of her bold vow before family and friends, she hadn't questioned her calling. Nor had she doubted she was wedded to teaching. Had she misunderstood? Or was there a way in spite of scandal's shadows?

Idleness opened the door to dark thoughts. An image of Walter emerged like a pesky gnat. She batted it away. She must stay busy and trust the Lord.

Cotton harvest had passed, but a garden needed tending and required fall canning.

And there were Lily's lessons.

She stepped outside to the well. Would Andrew cut down the sickly black haw that obscured their view of the rise after work as he'd promised?

Viola and Frank appeared in his Cadillac without invitation and lazed on the porch again. Didn't they have better to do with their time?

Andrew arrived and waved. Ella paid her uninvited, bedeviling visitors no mind and joined him in the circular drive.

"Good day, Ella." Dressed in work shirt and trousers with suspenders, he untied the leather binding around his tools and set them near the black haw. He removed his hat and took her hand.

"Want a bit of sustenance before you begin? Lemonade maybe?"

"Well water'll do." A model of decorum, he strode alongside her to the porch.

Viola plucked a hand fan from its chain at her waist and unfolded it. "Blacksmithing slow today?" She fanned her cheeks. They'd reddened in the eighty-degree weather.

"Matter of fact, we've been busy." He thumbed toward the haw. "I've come at your sister's request."

"Finally." She rolled her eyes. "That old thing's unsightly, so near the house." She clicked her tongue against her teeth.

Ella supplied a pitcher of water and glasses, and Andrew drank his fill. Pauses in the conversation grew dense, but she refused to relieve the strained silence with pointless chatter.

"I must be about my task. Good day." Resettling his hat, Andrew strode to the haw.

Viola glanced at him over her shoulder. "Why'd he ride out here for a chore our brother could dispense?"

Should Ella keep their courtship to herself? Viola would know soon enough. Having a man to answer to would be good for Frank. Still … "Cade has plenty to do."

"As does a working man like Mr. Evans." Suspicion glinted in Frank's eyes.

"Speaking of plenty to do, Lily and I are canning. Excuse me." She swept into the house, leaving the couple to stare after her.

She secured the curtains with tie backs. Frank and Viola returned to his automobile and puttered away.

Andrew stopped to wave, but they ignored him. He returned to his task, chopping at the roots of the old haw. He hefted a sledge hammer above his head and struck a tamping rod, splitting the root ball in two. Such a task required uncommon strength.

He wedged a shovel under the mass and forced both halves to the surface.

"He's almost finished, Lily. Let's take some berry juice to the porch."

They met him at the front with a tray of refreshment. He came up the steps swiping a rag across his face. She smiled at him in a brand-new way. "Sit for a while. You've earned a break."

He took a chair, turned up the glass, and guzzled. "That hits the spot." Was it his heightened color that deepened the blue of his eyes? He shoved his fingers through his hair, settling the damp strands and smiling.

"Black currants." Lily answered with pride, as she had picked the berries in August and stored a paste.

Ella closed her eyes, imagining the porch devoid of Andrew. Doing so lowered a curtain of gray. Another head of black hair came to mind, this one paired with eyes as black as soot. She laid a hand across her middle. Her spirit rebelled at the thought of Frank.

Unlike the haw's roots, such rottenness was best left buried.

She opened her eyes and experienced a rush of joy at the sight of Andrew. What would the mysterious social tradition called courtship entail? Observing others from a distance was a far cry from doing so herself.

"I'll leave you two to visit." Lily cleared the dishes and left a sense of calm in her wake.

Andrew wasted no time. "I need to talk to you about last night."

Her face flamed at the memory of her dream and the swing.

He dipped his head. "I shouldn't have taken you onto my lap that way. It's just that I long to comfort you. I won't do it again. Get that close, I mean."

"You're right. I needed comfort. But I trust you."

"Even so, I can't forget God's set boundaries for every living soul. And the line between unmarried men and women like us is wide and tall. For our protection." He leaned forward and grinned with a twinkle in his eyes. "Shall I call on the God of Boundaries to be a witness between us?"

She chuckled. "Like I said, I trust you."

"From the first time I saw you at Worthington, you've invaded my life."

He'd overtaken her every waking thought. And her dreams.

He expelled a long sigh and leaned back in his chair. "I intend to speak without touching you. So I can keep a clear head. I requested your father's permission to call on you because I wanted there to be no misunderstanding about my intentions."

"What are you intentions?" She hoped her boldness wouldn't put him off.

"To be at your side. To know how you think and feel ... if you'll let me. And to tell you the same in return. Do you approve?"

She forced down the rush that livened her pulse. "Aye, I do."

He cleared his throat. The prominent knot jiggled. "What about the school?"

"I closed the drawer on that dream and locked it."

"You still want to open a school, don't you?"

"If you call a single student a school, I have one now."

"Do you want more? And what about your passion for women's causes?"

This man deserved nothing less than honesty. "Aye, I want both. But what happened here with Nell is bound to have ruined my chances."

"Don't sell yourself short. Or the good people of Glover County." His features softened, the effect mesmerizing. "Yours is a good name. I'm a newcomer, so I can see things to which others have become accustomed. You've earned the admiration of many. I'd place no restrictions on what you might achieve."

She brought fingers to her lips, heedful of the trembling. What did he mean by no restrictions? Though all creation was swimming, she must keep her head.

"I see your beauty, of course, Ella. Your golden hair and remarkable eyes. They're blue but green and tinged with brown and gold. And all of it's rimmed in blue, like multicolored jewels. Did you know that?"

"I never heard them described in that way."

"I see a woman I admire, one who has claimed my ..." He took her hand with earnestness. "I know how to finish that sentence, but you deserve to be courted first."

CHAPTER 31

The bracing October temperatures approached freezing, which triggered Papa's scowl and complaints about a poor crop of fall vegetables.

Mama had sewed Ella a stunning suit of light worsted wool in an eye-catching peacock blue trimmed in dark green piping. With its long appliquéd peplum jacket, it rivaled the fashion plates in *The Delineator*.

Not that she cared a whit about the latest fashion. She'd don her new suit and hat with every intention of holding the eye of Andrew alone. She must remember what truly mattered was what resided in a woman's heart.

If the citizens of Needham were unaware of the courtship of Ella McFarland and Andrew Evans, they could make no such assertion on the fourth Sunday of October. When the couple strolled into Christ Church with Ella's hand tucked into the crook of his arm, every head turned. She smiled, grateful for her simple hat made extraordinary with peonies of blue muslin and green organdy.

How could she concentrate on a sermon in Andrew's presence? His strong baritone and Cade's tenor blended in a pleasing manner. Best of all, Lily had consented to attend. With Andrew on one side and her wide-eyed, flush-faced ward on the other, she felt she had entered the vestibules of Heaven right there in the McFarland family's pew.

Frank eyed her sideways from across the aisle. The sight unearthed what hid in her heart: bitterness. Would his presence forever mar her world?

Devoid of a smile, he stood and leaned over to speak at Viola's ear. And the two took seats in front of the McFarlands.

Throughout the service Ella was forced to gaze at Frank's and Viola's heads. His neatly trimmed hair and side whiskers were glazed with pomade. Viola's hat feather plunged downward along her left ear. She leaned against his shoulder, and he smiled.

Dear Lord, bring my willful mind under Your control. Divest me of every unholy thought.

Andrew slipped his hand toward hers. The touch of his fingers ignited a flash that traversed her body. Her eyes flipped open, and her head turned toward him.

He smiled, and she composed herself.

After services she urged him out the door ahead of Frank and Viola. Percival and Maude greeted them.

Andrew shook the preacher's hand. "Enjoyed the sermon."

The man smiled. "Ella's a keeper."

"I'm tickled to see you on Andrew's arm." Maude beamed as she spoke to Ella.

Ella's skin warmed. "So am I."

"You ready to preach soon?" The preacher laid a hand on Andrew's shoulder.

"Be happy to."

"How 'bout next Sunday? We'll be visiting our daughter in Fair Valley."

"Thank you for the invitation. May I stop by early this week?"

"Come any time before Friday."

Andrew guided her to Aunt Julia. "How happy I am to see you together." The older woman spoke amid a nest of smile crinkles.

Ella glanced up at him. "It's official, I guess. For now, anyway."

A crease dashed across his brow. "I'll take now. And later too."

Others paid their respects. Were they analyzing the couple for signs of the mysterious state of mind called being in love?

Mama and Papa thanked him for removing the black haw. Hannah sidled up, obviously enthralled with her sister's handsome suitor. And why shouldn't she be?

Needham's pair of gossips drew a circle of twittering girls no doubt vying for the next opening in the Cotillion Club.

She searched the crowd for Lily and found her and Cade beneath the hackberry tree. The jittery lass stood with one hand grasping the other and rocking on the heels of her buttoned shoes. Cade would put her at ease.

Whispers coaxed Ella's focus over her shoulder. She ducked her head and peeked sideways. A mother and daughter held their heads close and spoke behind their hands. Their eyes homed in on Cade and Lily.

The mother frowned at the couple, and Ella glowered at her.

Frank rode off with Viola in his parents' Packard, leaving Ollie and Zach to seek transportation for themselves. Andrew extended an invitation, and the Irvings accepted.

The women settled into their seats, and Ella stiffened at the thought of sitting next to the woman who birthed Frank. But she'd known Ollie always. They were the dearest of friends. Yet here she sat, thinking not of their friendship but of Ollie's son. On the one hand, she longed to scream the truth about Frank. On the other, she wanted nothing more than to spare her friend.

"What a lovely ensemble." Ollie ran a hand over the fabric of Ella's skirt. "Your mother's creation?"

"An anonymous buyer purchased every item in the store. More than once. Mama kept back some fabric."

"Anonymous?"

"Aye, a gentleman entered the store on more than one occasion saying he's the representative of a new citizen of Glover County in need of a great deal of products."

"How curious."

"Papa thought so. But he thanked the man for his business."

Dressed in a coral bolero dress, Ollie leaned as near as her plumed hat would allow. "Andrew's a fine man. I've always dreamed you and Frank …" She cleared her throat and dabbed at her chin. "But if it cannot be, there's no one more deserving than Andrew."

Had Ella been avoiding this lifelong friend without realizing it? The dear woman would be appalled to learn of Frank's unwholesome ways.

"And the school? Surely you've given up on it. Marriage and a career don't mix."

No, she hadn't given up on teaching. How could she? But marriage? She'd barely gotten used to the idea of courtship. "There's time enough to think about that. Andrew and I are—"

"You're falling in love. I see it in your beautiful eyes." She tapped Ella on the knee and grinned like a cat with a secret.

Ella put a finger to her lips, as if to whisper. Surely the men couldn't hear their conversation amid the rumble of hooves and wheels.

"If falling in love means the sight of a man all but suffocates a girl with joy and her breath catches at his touch, then perhaps ..." She gave Ollie a mischievous grin.

The older woman squeezed her hand. "I'm happy for you, dear."

What was Ella thinking? She must bring her emotions—and this conversation—back to Earth. "I haven't given up on teaching. We're only getting acquainted, you see."

Ollie chuckled. "Oh, yes. I see."

CHAPTER 32

The McFarlands feasted on Sunday dinner, and when eyelids grew heavy, Andrew invited Ella to stroll to the creek. Cade and Lily accompanied them for propriety's sake.

Lily's gaze flitted along the line of foliage. "You sure Pa can't see us here?"

"I'm sure." Sitting beside her young friend, Ella was grateful for the shade and her lightweight cotton batiste blouse. "Besides, these two strong men can protect us."

Lazing against a sycamore, Cade rolled a toothpick between his teeth. "Walter wouldn't dare."

"He values his freedom." Andrew skipped a pebble across the water.

"Ollie's going to the town hall meeting Tuesday evening, and I plan to attend." Ella couched her announcement in nonchalance. "County schools are on the agenda. They're actually allowing a woman to speak." She left off Mrs. Norris's reputation as a territorial firebrand for women's rights.

"A woman's place is at home." Cade grumbled, as he was wont to do of late. She had thought his uncharacteristic blazes of irritability were based in his brotherly concern. Now she wasn't so sure. What could be afoot?

"We do such an admirable job tending our homes, brother, just think what all of us could do with the great house of this United States."

Lily fell silent. She twisted an emerald green waist ribbon around a finger.

Something was troubling her ever-talkative young friend. "Want to go too? It'll make a real-life civics lesson."

Lily smoothed the front of her pale green dotted Swiss dress. "Seems to me, when men gave women the vote in school elections, they made schools women's business." She stared straight ahead, acknowledging Cade would siphon off her courage.

He blinked hard. He opened his mouth and closed it without speaking another word.

Andrew glanced at him. "I'm taking Uncle Tad and Aunt Julia to Fair Valley tomorrow. Won't return until Wednesday. Can you escort these ladies?"

"No need." The last person Ella needed to escort them to such a meeting was her brother with his insufferable views on woman's suffrage. "Lily and I can ride Bunny and Da—"

"No. You won't." Cade's tone said he'd brook no argument. "I'll accompany you."

Lily slid a corner-of-the-eye gaze at Ella and stifled a grin. "I'll take along my journal. For notes."

Monday crept along, and Tuesday evening seemed destined never to materialize. Ella finished her chores early and gave her student an assignment on the suffrage and temperance movements based on a collection of newspapers and the writings of their leaders.

She coached her pupil as she read, helping her with the more difficult words, but the ever-so-bright girl drew her own conclusions. "Tonight's meeting's a step in the right direction, Ella."

"Indeed, but it'll take many more to win the hearts and minds of over fifty percent of the men."

"That's called a majority?"

"A simple majority. Suffragists and prohibitionists expect Indian and Oklahoma Territories to merge into one state and are pushing for inclusion of both in our state constitution."

"This constitution would make it so women could vote?"

"Indeed. Meetings like tonight's lay bricks on the road to full suffrage and permanent prohibition." What would life be like in such a state?

Ella mulled through Tuesday afternoon and chose a simple skirt and shirtwaist with a cameo at her throat. Lily appeared pensive, but she was dressed by six o'clock. "Is this all right?"

"A skirt and waist are perfect. You look lovely."

They entered the Methodist church early and sat near the front, two of a handful of women in attendance. One of the town gossips targeted the seat beside them, but at the sight of Lily, she turned away.

A frown skipped across the child's brow.

"A few have turned out to support their sisters." Ella whispered at her ear. "Doesn't matter where they sit."

Lily's frown danced away.

"Get your hands off—" A loud, raspy voice cut through the pre-meeting chatter.

Cade glanced over his shoulder. "Sit tight. Walter's here." He hurried toward the back.

Lily blanched. Ella took her hand. "He'll take care of things."

The commotion increased. "I've a right to be here. Ain't no place for womenfolk."

"Your right's superseded by an order of the court." Sheriff Dawson spoke in a commanding tone. "Miss Sloat arrived ahead of you. I won't send her home. So go on."

"I'll see you in—"

"Grab him!"

A scuffle. Howls and protests.

"Get him outside, men." The sheriff's voice rose above the din, and the commotion faded away.

Lily's body stiffened.

"Don't hang onto it." Ella squeezed her hand. "Not worth it. Open your eyes and ears and take in your first public meeting as a concerned female citizen."

Winifred Norris represented the Women's Temperance Club in Westwood. Dressed in a flamboyant gown of black and white striped taffeta, the white-haired matron spoke with passion. "Liquor's the bane of families across our great nation, save a few bastions of Christian virtue in Indian Territory.

"Only a vote by the U.S. Congress and President Roosevelt's signature separate us from full statehood. But we'll battle our sister territory over constitutional prohibition."

She traced a bold line across the assemblage. "The Canadian River alone separates our good citizens from a nest of unholy vipers in Oklahoma Territory, men who'd sell the souls of their loved ones for a drunken dollar."

Mrs. Norris excused herself for her journey back home and joined her husband who had stood at the back while she spoke.

"A woman can speak like this in a mixed gathering?" Lily's eyes had gone wide.

"A brave few." Ella shivered at the memory of Walter's trash heap of empty liquor bottles and his drunken state at the Sloat cabin.

The Needham Women's Club representative emphasized the importance of equal voting rights and a compulsory education law, although with less fervor. "Now I believe Ella McFarland has a word to say."

Gathering her thoughts, she took to the podium. "Gentlemen, it occurred to me while reading the history of the women's rights movement that women like your good wives have been crying out since the first conference in Seneca Falls in 1848. Six decades is a long time for husbands to turn deaf ears to their wives' pleas for what's guaranteed to men by virtue of their gender—the right to vote.

"You trust your wives with your children and homes. Why not trust them to partner with you as ably in managing the greater house of America?"

She scanned the gathering, pausing at each familiar face in turn. "As a teacher I want nothing more than to see girls being educated as widely and as thoroughly as boys. I, for one, intend to flood the mailboxes and offices of every territorial official with this argument. I invite everyone— male and female—to join me. I pray our pleas won't fall on deaf ears for another six decades. Nay, not for another day."

Silence swallowed the assemblage as her last words faded away. The women turned to one another as if seeking a sign of mutual agreement. Lily bounded to her feet, and the other women followed. Their applause reverberated off the walls of the clapboard church like clangs from the Liberty Bell.

As she returned to her seat and the meeting proceeded, Ella felt a sense of awe. She could inspire others for good. But she mustn't let her feelings for Andrew dim her zeal for Lily's education. And for meetings like this one where she could emphasize the importance of the woman's vote in improving education for all girls. She'd almost given up her dream of a school for girls like Lily, but she mustn't. Tonight's meeting had shown her that much.

Cade escorted the women to the buggy at the close of the meeting. When he gave the reins a shake, the team bolted, leaving the buggy suspended momentarily. Lurching forward, it collapsed onto its shafts, and he plummeted head-first to the ground. The women tumbled forward, landing in a flurry of arms, legs, and petticoats.

He scrambled to his feet. "Are you hurt?" He lifted them from the broken conveyance.

"We're all right. What happened? No one cares for their livery like you and Papa."

Men ran from the church with lanterns aloft and yelling, "What's going on?"

Cade removed the dash lantern and examined the buggy and leather gear. "Someone cut the traces." He squatted. "And shaft loops."

Sheriff Dawson examined the harnessing gear. "Someone cut through the loops enough that they'd break when you climbed in."

"Walter," Cade said.

Trembling, Lily reached for Ella.

Could she ever keep the child safe?

She mustn't let down her guard.

CHAPTER 33

*E*lla opened her wardrobe. She'd be on the arm of the preacher today. She must dress with care and deport herself appropriately. A flutter like damselfly wings drew her hand to her chest. She mustn't in any way distract Andrew.

Tad and Julia would join them for dinner at the cottage after church. She hoped the stubborn pie crust had turned out all right and that the Chickasaw plum filling would make up for any lack.

She'd make an announcement after dinner. She believed the news would be well received. If not, she was prepared.

She laid a tobacco-brown broadcloth suit with an appliquéd skirt across her bed. Ollie had tagged the ensemble a cast off, but not a single frayed thread could be found. The fabric's golden undertones complemented her hair. She suspected Ollie bought it in Philadelphia with Ella in mind.

She opened a simple wooden dresser box, Cade's first attempt at wood crafting as a boy. She chose a brooch hand-painted with a bouquet of blue orchids, green ivy, and twirls of brown ribbon. The lovely piece had arrived at the store just before she departed for normal school. Papa presented it to her at her going-away party. No occasion had seemed special enough to wear it until today.

She slipped on her heaviest stockings and camisole. Her knickers came below her knees, important on a cold morning. She wouldn't force herself into her old corset, a contraption that imprisoned her lungs. Her new lightweight piece would do nicely.

"I'm going with your family," Lily called from the kitchen. "See you there."

Thankfully, Ella needn't worry about her ward's safety. The sheriff had ridden to the Sloat property to speak with Walter about the sabotage and found the place deserted. Later he reported seeing the bedraggled family heading south in a wagon loaded with household goods.

Lily agonized over the loss. She'd been managing secret meetings with her mother and brother at the creek. Having lost her family, she wept bitterly, but by Sunday she was dressed for church on Cade's brotherly arm.

At least they enjoyed relief from Walter's lurking presence.

Andrew was pulling up when Ella stepped into the entry. Stopping at the hall mirror, she checked her pompadour and pinched her cheeks. She positioned her brown felt hat with the saucy tilt and simple ribbons and anchored it with a hatpin.

He knocked as she was pulling on her gloves. She opened the door and felt a flush.

"How lovely you look." He spread open her long woolen cape.

She turned and leaned backward onto his chest, longing for his arms to linger around her shoulders, their warmth cushioning her from the cold that crept around the doorjamb.

But he behaved like a gentleman. He released her wrap as she put her arms through. She hooked the clasp. Did he notice how she leaned into him? Had she been too forward?

As they strolled to the buggy, she peeked at him, but his face was a mask. He tucked woolen coverlets around her feet. She smiled, a gesture he didn't return. Was the sermon consuming his thoughts, or something else?

When Andrew stood at the pulpit, he took command of his audience. "I have a new appreciation for you farmers. You've given me fresh insight into Jesus' Parable of the Sower."

Needle-sharp and precise, his closing packed a powerful punch. "If I

were a betting man, I'd wager you could forgive your children anything."
He looked one matron in the eye. "Isn't that true?"

She nodded.

"Can anyone out-forgive God?" Heads moved side to side around
the room. He stepped into the center aisle. "Of course not. He forgives
every foolish soul who comes to Him with a humble heart. But too often
pride stands in our way."

He paused to observe the assemblage. "Every last one of us must
answer one question: What will you do with Jesus? We can answer now
or wait until it's too late."

Moving up the aisle, he paused at the pew Viola and Frank shared.
"No farmer can grow a decent stand of cotton when the soil's soaked
with brine." His gaze spanned the room and rested on Viola. "It's time I
let the plowshares of the Spirit break up the clods in my heart. Will you
join me?"

She responded by stomping out the door.

Ella choked back an urge to go after her, but Frank leaned forward,
glowering, as if ready to strike a blow.

She closed her eyes in a tight squint. *Dear Lord, what's happening?
Andrew's message pricked my heart, but he seemed to target my sister, hardly
a way to repair our bond. And Frank's ready to do him harm.*

What could she do? Should she speak to Andrew? The last thing she
wanted was to discourage him. Or elicit a sour response to the bold idea
she planned to present after dinner, one that had sprouted in her heart
weeks before.

*Yet every word Andrew spoke is true, Lord. I've brine in my own heart,
haven't I?*

She opened her eyes and raised her head.

Andrew knelt at the front while Cade led a hymn. The words—*Purer
in heart, oh God, help me to be*—accompanied one member after another
as they made their way forward.

Ella did the same, bowing alongside Andrew at the foot of the cross.

The results of the message were plain to see. Each face shone.

All but Frank's.

CHAPTER 34

"*Y*ou made a good harvest, Andrew," Julia said at the dinner table.

"Percival prepared the soil and planted the seed. God harvested."

"May He give the increase." Tad spooned a second serving of boiled potatoes onto his plate, his mouth half full of the previous helping.

Ella mustn't wait to make her announcement. "I have something to say."

The foursome looked to her with smiles of expectation.

"I intend to join the suffrage movement."

Julia beamed. "We'll be glad to have you. Do you plan to travel?"

"May I go too?" Lily exuded enthusiasm.

"Where will your support for travel come from?" Tad held his fork midway to his mouth.

Andrew stilled, uncharacteristically quiet.

"I don't plan to travel, and I won't need support to participate locally. I'm acquainted with Kate Biggers, the territorial organization's president. I'll let her know my plans to speak to women's groups and community meetings and to write to officials. But my emphasis will be on girls' education, and I won't let it take away from Lily or plans for the school."

Andrew smiled broadly. "Glad to hear it."

Conversation resumed, and soon her guests sat back, sated. Julia invited Lily to join her near the fire where Tad had moved, his eyelids drooping.

"Is it too nippy to step onto the porch?" Andrew had shoved his half-eaten third pork chop around his plate until it hardened.

Eager to leave the stuffy indoors, Ella checked the outside thermometer. "It's fifty degrees, not too cool with our wraps."

She settled in the swing, and Andrew in a nearby chair. Leaning back with her hands in her cape pockets, she enjoyed the gentle sway. "Thank you for all you've done for us, Andrew. You've helped with chores, carted water, chopped wood. Even cleaned the flue." And he'd opened windows in her heart she was unaware were shuttered.

"Been a pleasure." He took her hand. "That's the way it is when you care for someone."

A corner of her mouth twitched.

He ran a thumb over the back of her hand. "You know the admiration I spoke of earlier?"

She nodded.

"It's changed."

Her insides pitched. Was he preparing her for disappointment?

"To love."

Her smile congealed as if painted onto a doll.

"I want to look on your face. Touch your hand." He stared at her mouth. "And kiss your lips. Every single day from now on. Will you marry me, Ella? Will you be my wife?"

Her lips parted. She breathed in the crisp air and attempted a reply but found naught but the rising warmth of affection.

What of her declaration, her calling?

She sprang to her feet, unable to contain her thoughts. "When I failed with Nell it stole my voice, you might say, for a time. But I've found it again. I can use it for teaching and as an advocate for voiceless women like Lily and Ruby, like Nell. I'm wedded to this calling, you might say. I can't relinquish it."

"Who said you can't do it all as a married woman?"

"There's barely enough time to tend to the cottage, see to Lily's schoolwork and hopefully add more students. How could I be a wife too?"

"As I said before, I'd place no restrictions on what you might achieve."

"You'd marry a teacher who speaks at suffrage meetings and writes to officials all over the territory?"

"Indeed, I would."

"Wouldn't my loyalties be divided?"

"The man who spoke those words didn't know Ella McFarland."

She laid her hands on his chest, savoring the rise and fall beneath his coat. "Nothing would make me happier than to be a teacher and your wife all at the same time. But I can't promise without Papa's blessing."

"Your father and I took care of that."

"And your parents? They don't know me."

"I've written them. So has Aunt Julia. Father gave their blessing."

She lowered her hands to her sides. Her fingers brushed her cape's rough woolen fabric. She gazed at Andrew face to face, eye to eye.

"I'll never love anyone but you." His words rang true. His eyes were blue windows to his soul. If she could, she'd tumble into them, unafraid, for he was good.

The image of a dreaded set of black eyes blurred her vision and struck her heart. Could she pretend they didn't exist, didn't creep into her thoughts like a cancer, stealing her joy? Could she, for love of Andrew? "I'm sorry. I can't."

An expression of shock passed over his face.

"Not until I tell you something."

He nudged her onto the swing and drew her near, but she held herself apart.

"It's about another man."

He paled.

"The summer of '02, just before I left for normal school ..." *Give me the strength, Lord..* "At my going-away party at the Prestons', I went outside in the dark. I knew Mama and Papa would've said not to go out alone. But I did it anyway. Told myself it was to see the moonlight, but I knew the truth. I wanted to be alone with this man."

Andrew's eyes searched hers.

"He was waiting in the peach orchard. I thought we would stroll and talk, but he cornered me. And smothered me in kisses. My heart raced, I'll admit, but it frightened me too. I told him to let me go, but he wouldn't listen."

Andrew's eyes glinted like polished steel.

"He forced me to the ground. I fought him. Tried to scream. But he covered my mouth. I couldn't move, Andrew. I tried, but I couldn't."

He grasped her hand.

"He fumbled with my skirt, my petticoats, my—"

"You don't have to go on, Ella dear."

The memory welled inside her. She drew her lips into a firm line. "He would've taken my innocence if not for Percival."

Andrew's shock registered in his eyes.

"Percival had seen me step outside and was checking on me. My attacker skittered off like a possum."

"Did he catch the good-for-nothing?"

"No, but he identified him."

Andrew caught her by the shoulders. "You reported it, didn't you?"

"I couldn't."

"Surely Percival did so himself."

"I said I wouldn't darken the door of the church again if he told Mama and Papa. Later on, he found the weasel. Slammed him against the side of the house. Told him if he caught him with his hands on me again, he'd kill him."

"I know how he felt."

"You mustn't harbor ill will. Not on my account. I'm handling him. But tell no one."

"I understand the sensitivity of your position, but—"

"It's because of Mama's and Papa's lifelong friendship with his family."

"Which family? Tell me."

"The Irvings. The man who attacked me, the one who almost stole my innocence, was Frank."

Andrew's hands fisted. "He'll not come near you again!"

"There's something else."

He sat forward, his eyes blazing. "Has he done something else?"

"Not really. He makes his presence known and sidles near, but he doesn't scare me."

How she longed to throw her arms around Andrew, to cast aside every foul thought of Frank, and to replace it with loving reassurance for this man who loved her. But she couldn't. She must tell him the whole truth. "Frank cast his spell on Viola. Joshua's his son."

CHAPTER 35

*A*ndrew dropped his head to his hands. "This can't be kept another day. The man should take responsibility for his child."

Ella gave her head a vigorous shake. "There's too much at stake."

"You deserve to be relieved of this burden. And Frank needs to be dealt with."

She must make him understand. "Mama and Papa and the Irvings go way back. I won't disturb their friendship." She paused, eyeing her thumbnail. "I must confess I was a bit startled when you singled out Viola in your sermon. Now you know why."

"I hadn't planned to stand at their pew and focus on her, but--"

She placed a finger on his lips. "Shhh."

He discharged a full-chested sigh and leaned backward, gazing at the ceiling. "I'm listening."

"Viola will tell Mama and Papa soon enough. The news will upset our families and strain our friendship, but Zach and Ollie will see that Joshua has every advantage, and the boy will be better for it. There's no need to add to their distress with what Frank did to me."

He clasped his hands behind his head. "Your sister hasn't your integrity. She needs to hear God's truth, just as I presented it. And she needs to know what kind of man Frank is."

"She refused to listen when I tried to tell her. Besides, it's too late."

"I'll have to think on this. Don't know that I can live with such a secret, at least not until Frank makes an honorable woman out of Viola."

"As far as I know, she hasn't told him he's Joshua's father."

He planted his feet on the floor planks and brought the swing to a halt. "Why not?"

"I figure she wants him to propose willingly."

"If they marry and Frank's in the family …"

"He'll never go away. He'll sit at our dinner table and around our Christmas tree. He'll pose in family portraits and jostle Joshua on his knee."

Andrew rubbed his eyes with a thumb and finger. "You've endured this alone long enough. I'll talk to the man whether you want me to or not."

"What do you mean?"

"I'll confront him." He blasted out of the swing with both hands fisted. "He'll never come near you again. He'll know I'm watching him, that his selfish acts have been exposed. I'd be half a man if I didn't stand up for my wife."

Ella understood. She couldn't respect a man who would do less. But she wouldn't let her happiness tear her family apart. "Percival's already talked to him, so whatever you do, do it privately." She grabbed his hands. "I won't marry you otherwise."

He turned away. Running fingers through his hair, he leaned against the railing and stared beyond the porch, as if answers could be found in the depths of the woods.

She waited, stone still. A lowly creature scampered beneath the porch's floorboards, perhaps a squirrel preparing for winter.

She laid a hand at her throat. Her pulse produced a steady thrum, but would her heart beat another day? How could it without Andrew?

At length he turned, drawing her to him. "This is a hurdle for both of us. But it's one we can mount. Together."

Relief flooded her. She leaned into him, absorbing his warmth.

"My feelings for you are God-given, Ella. I'll not traipse on such a blessing. I'll talk to Frank privately. No one will know but us. But I must ask you …"

"Yes?"

"May I have a kiss?"

"Now and forever."

He grazed a thumb on her cheek. "I love you with my whole being. I always will." He inched his mouth closer, paused, and pulled back.

Had he thought better of his proposal? *Dear God, no.*

"You haven't told me you love me. Or that you'll marry me."

She blinked. Disarmed, she dug her fingers into his back. "Andrew Evans, you're everything God intended a man to be. You're my first waking thought and my last before I sleep. You visit me in my dreams. You're far too beautiful for a man. I'll never tire of gazing at ..." Heat rose to her face. "All of you."

He gulped a breath.

"Of course, I love you. And yes, I'll marry you. With joy and thanksgiving. As long as you understand you're marrying a teacher and suffragist."

He lowered his mouth, touching her lips lightly, then with an earnestness that drew her hands to his face, hungry for his very breath.

He pulled away sooner than she would've liked. Her surroundings swirled as she stood with her eyes closed and her mouth seeking his.

"Will you accept this?"

She opened her eyes. A diamond ring lay in his palm.

"For my love." He slipped it onto her finger. "Forever."

Joy catapulted her into his arms and headlong into the house. "Andrew asked me to marry him!"

Julia, Tad, and Lily rose in tandem, their faces shining.

She scurried to them with her left hand extended. "We're engaged!" She and Lily waltzed as hugs and congratulations circled the room.

"I can't keep the news another hour. We must tell the family."

The group traipsed through the woodland toward the McFarland home. Autumn's crispness saturated the air. The ground carpet laid down hues like Ella's spice rack—nutmeg, saffron, and sumac.

Leaves crunched beneath her feet as she danced in circles toward the clearing, taking her ahead of the others.

She stopped abruptly, and her smile faded.

Viola and Frank stood beneath an elm tree, their limbs entangled in an altogether passionate, intimate way.

"Never seen a real kiss, sister?" Viola shot her a daring grin.

Frank chuckled and drew her closer.

Voices neared, and Ella thumbed over her shoulder. "Julia and Tad. Andrew and Lily."

Viola pushed away from Frank. He shoved his hands into his pockets and slouched in a devilish manner.

The group emerged from the woods unaware of the couple's tryst.

Julia rushed to them. "It's wonderful, isn't it?"

Viola flashed a disinterested shrug. "What?"

Andrew gave Ella a nudge. "Tell them."

Viola and Frank maintained expressions of indifference.

Slipping an arm around his intended, Andrew took a protective stance. "We're engaged. What a blessed man I am." He pulled her closer.

Viola crossed her arms. Glowering, Frank crushed a toothpick between his teeth.

Ella drew back at Frank's expression of hostility.

"We couldn't be happier." Julia squeezed Ella's arm. "Show them your ring."

Dare she bring on more animosity?

Viola cocked an eyebrow. "A ring?"

Andrew took charge, extending Ella's hand. The diamond blazed in the golden sunlight. "It's a Tiffany cut in a filigree setting." He gazed down at her. "This woman deserves nothing less."

Tension hung like icicles.

Viola turned in a casual manner. "Rather lovely, if you're inclined toward ... simplicity."

Frank followed her toward the house, kicking leaves into whorls.

"Shall we?" Andrew motioned the group forward.

Hatred simmered in Frank's eyes. If Andrew confronted him, would it overflow?

Inside, Ella's family whooped and cheered and encircled the couple, extending glad hands and pats on backs. She'd treasure this occasion, the unbreakable bond of family and friendship in a complete circle that not even Frank would break.

He and her sister were nowhere in sight.

She slanted her eyes toward Andrew. Love lighted his.

Surely they'd find answers. They must.

CHAPTER 36

*E*lla longed for a sweet bond of family devotion between herself and Viola. She must take steps to bridge the gulf. If her sister will let her.

Conversation among the friends continued as they walked through the copse back to the cottage. The dusk's lengthening shadows created fingers of mystery in the undergrowth. An owl hooted and fluttered between trees. A few resolute tree frogs chattered and crickets chirruped.

She paused at the tree where she'd come upon Frank and Viola.

Andrew turned to her. "What is it?"

She leaned against him, sensing a weighted cloak drifting onto her shoulders. "I wish my sister and I …" She straightened to regain her composure.

"You'll find a way." He held her hand until they reached the cottage. "Will you ride with me to take Aunt Julia and Uncle Tad home?"

"We'd better—"

"Go on." Lily shooed them like a hen. "I'll leave the lantern burning."

What a delightful thought, being with Andrew unattended. "I will. Thank you."

Julia and Tad sat in the back with the newly engaged couple up front. Ella tucked her hand around his arm, enjoying his warmth.

Andrew called to the team, and they clopped around the rise. A light burned on Broadview's ground floor. No doubt Maggie had the house in order and was preparing for bed.

He pressed a shoulder against hers. "Happy?"

"Very."

"Still want to open a school?"

She gazed at the heavens. Stars winked in the clear autumn sky. Some emitted golden light; others cut through the darkness with silver luminance. "The finest man God ever created put a ring on my finger that outshines those stars, and he's agreed to marry a teacher suffragist. What more could I want?"

"You can have it all." The dash lantern illuminated his mischievous grin.

"Do you really believe I can run a school and be your wife and keep house and be a suffragist and have babies … and do justice to any of it?"

"You're an amazing woman. You'll figure it out."

"What about Lily while we're on our wedding trip?"

"I've wondered the same."

"She misses her mother and brother. Now I'm marrying and going off on a wedding trip. I've been full of joy and my mind on so many plans I haven't stopped to think how this will affect her."

"We'll take it to the Lord."

"Aye." Only God could come up with a solution for Lily's future.

Later that night, Ella knelt on her prayer pillow. Astonishing possibilities swirled. Knowing what to worry about first felt akin to a burden.

Cast thy burden upon Jehovah, and He will sustain thee.

How difficult, baring her soul even to the One who knew her completely.

"Lord, I made teaching Lily and starting the school my life, but You showed me my work can fail. I reached the end of myself on my knees after Nell disappeared. Now Andrew has opened the door to love. Every dream and those I never dared imagine are within my reach.

"Aside from You, my love for Andrew ranks above all else. You created me a teacher. You gave me a calling for girls like Lily. But I must get my house in order—starting with Viola."

A telegram from Adelaide arrived at the cottage on the first day of November. She'd arrive on the twentieth.

Andrew suggested Sunday, the twenty-sixth, for their wedding. "I'll announce it tonight at prayer meeting."

Lily picked at a nail. "I need to be somewhere else when you come home from your honeymoon."

"You've barely settled into the cottage." Ella sat straight, leaning toward the child with earnestness. "This is your home now."

"Not with newlyweds. I'll go back to the cabin."

"You'll do nothing of the sort."

"Pa's gone. The house is empty. No reason not to."

Andrew's brow creased. "We've no idea when he'll crop up. Besides, you're thirteen years old."

"Pa's moved on to where he's not under a bond."

"None of this is fair to you." Ella released a deep sigh.

"Life isn't fair. Gotta live it, though." Grown before her time, Lily traced the scar at her neckline.

Ella closed her eyes and lowered her head. Her young charge's remark echoed her own oft-repeated words. The child was as pliable as the moss on the creek bank while Viola was as resistant as river rock. Yet Ella longed for each to find resolution.

Andrew stood abruptly. "I best be going. I have an appointment in town." He kissed her on the cheek. "At the bank. With the newest loan officer."

CHAPTER 37

$\mathscr{A}$ndrew returned to escort Ella and Lily to prayer meeting. "Frank wasn't in his office. But I'll find him."

Ella struggled with conflicting emotions—gratitude for his protection but niggling unease at Frank's likely response. Her relationship with Viola sat precariously in the middle.

Andrew checked his pocket watch.

She caught her bottom lip between her teeth and glanced toward the stairs. "Lily's taking more time than usual to dress."

"Have you thought more on her dilemma?"

"There's no dilemma as far as I'm concerned. She can't go back to the Sloat place."

Zach's Packard and a brand-new Buick were parked near the front of Christ Church. More buggies and horses than usual were scattered about the grounds. Andrew parked at the bottom of the hill and hobbled the horse.

"Big crowd." He set his hand on Ella's back as they approached the building.

Light streamed from the windows, as did laughter and chatter. The service hadn't begun. He pulled the double doors wide, signaling the women to enter.

Lily waved Ella ahead and followed her inside.

"Surprise!"

"Congratulations!"

Ella stared. The church was bedecked with ribbon streamers and silk flowers.

Andrew put his arm around her. "Word got out before I could make the announcement."

Lily stepped to her side. "I stalled as long as I could. I was afraid you suspected something."

"I had no idea." The honoree gazed around the room, her eyes resting on each family and memories flooding back.

Percival and Maude stepped forward. "Congratulations. You better take care of this girl." He flashed Andrew a jovial grin.

"On behalf of everyone, may you enjoy a long and happy marriage." Maude spread her arms wide. "Let's have some cake. And you two, dig into those presents."

The ladies at the serving table stepped back, revealing stacks of wrapped packages.

Joy surged through Ella. "Am I dreaming?"

Papa stepped to their side. "I'm mighty happy you'll be a part of our family, Andrew."

"You're getting the top of the cream, daughter." Mama stood alongside Hannah and Cade. "You're both blessed." She patted Andrew on a cheek.

Her future groom turned to the gathering. "Thank you, everyone. You've been most kind, accepting a stranger into your midst. Kinder still to share this ..." He gazed down at Ella. "Thank you for sharing this remarkable woman."

"Come on and cut the cake." Percival rubbed his paunch. "Been eyeing it long enough."

The couple received blessings on their way to the refreshment table. Ella set the point of the cake knife on the delicate frosting.

"I have an announcement too."

The male voice brought on a shudder, and Ella's body seemed chained in place.

The crowd stepped aside.

Frank and Viola stood arm in arm with Joshua.

"We were married in Fair Valley today at noon." Frank shifted his son to the other arm. "Meet my boy. He looks like me, don't you think?"

Mama's knees buckled, and Papa caught her.

Ollie paled, and Zach stiffened.

Why must Vi and Frank ruin the party? He was her sister's husband now. *Give me grace.*

Ella set down the cake knife. "May God bless you."

Viola pushed a strand of hair off her boy's forehead. "Told you he comes from handsome stock."

Papa's face reddened, and Mama held a hankie to her mouth.

Ella faced the crowd with a smile. "Looks like this party's for two McFarland girls." She extended a hand, inviting Viola to join her.

The sisters cut the cake and handed out refreshments together, Ella with a twitching smile and Viola with a pout.

The crowd's stiffness eased, and they commented on Joshua's beauty as if nothing untoward had occurred. But the surreality of the evening's turn of events was difficult to absorb.

Ella and Andrew were being honored with a surprise engagement party that had become Viola and Frank's marriage celebration and a birth announcement of sorts. Was it only last night she prayed to find a way to reconcile with her sister?

"Better get started on those presents." Maude pointed to the gift table.

Ella's gaze flew to Viola. Like sheets of sleet on a wintry day, unbidden childhood memories returned: Vi running away when Ella tried to babysit, kicking and spitting, daring her to react. But they were girls no longer. Ella could continue to chase after her, but then what? Would she run like the child of long ago?

Maude reached for Viola. "We'll shower you with presents, too."

Viola's nose creased. "We'll furnish our home as we please." She stiffened her neck and headed for the door.

Gasps and murmurs sounded here and there.

The McFarland beauty, as haughty as a bantam hen, swung the door open, and it banged against the wall like a rifle blast. Frank followed her with Joshua in his arms.

Scanning the crowd, Ella reminded herself she was surrounded by friends who'd prepared a party and given of their limited resources. She'd receive their gifts with gratitude.

"Come, everyone." She took a seat beside the mound of offerings, some wrapped in fancy paper, others in nothing but twine. She tore into one package and held up a doily of crocheted pansies. "Isn't this lovely?"

There was a crate of canned tomatoes. A box of recipes. Two embroidered pillowcases.

But Andrew was nowhere in sight.

When he finally entered, his expression was stormy. He sat beside Ella with his elbows on his knees. She pulled a ribbon from another gift, and Andrew jiggled a leg, inhaling noisy drafts. Two spots blazed on his cheeks.

What had happened outside?

When the last guest extended a final blessing and departed, Ella and Andrew and Lily and Cade loaded the gifts into their buggies and returned to help clean up the church.

Zach and Ollie stood stone-faced beside Mama and Papa.

How Ella longed to assuage their pain by explaining away their children's callousness. But she couldn't. She must wait on the Lord.

"It'll take a while to understand what's happened. And why." Papa nodded to a pair of pews in a corner. The friends sat facing one another.

Ella and Andrew, Cade and Lily, and Hannah started for the door.

"Come back." Papa called to them in a commanding tone.

Lily shook her head. "I don't belong, Mr. Mac."

Andrew gestured outside. "We'll give you folks some privacy."

"This is family business. All of you belong." Papa pointed to an empty pew.

The five lined up on the bench, hands in their laps.

"We've been through some hard times." Zach stared at the floor.

Mama nodded. "And plenty of good ones."

Ollie gazed at her hands wrestling in her lap. "Why didn't I see it? Joshua's the image of Frank."

Ella could've spared them this public embarrassment if she'd told her parents what she suspected. And what she, herself, had endured. She sagged with regret.

Was this the time to tell them about Frank's attack on her?

"It isn't right for parents who've only loved their children to suffer at their hands." Zach lowered his head, and Ollie reached over to comfort him.

No. Ella wouldn't add to their pain.

Papa's expression grew pensive. "Frank came home from Philadelphia just that one time."

"Thanksgiving of '03." Zach spoke as if in a daze.

"I didn't notice a thing untoward." Ollie turned to Mama. "Did you, Betsy?"

"Not a thing."

Papa gazed at his friends. "Our children did a mighty disrespectful thing tonight."

Zach hmphed. "To say nothing of how they begat that little boy."

"Joshua's here because God willed it." Mama's hands had drawn into fists.

"That's true." Zach vented between clenched teeth. "But just wait until I get my hands on *my* boy."

"We should've gotten our hands on him long ago." Ollie shook her head and stared at the floor.

"The same could be said of Betsy and me." Papa gestured to Mama. "We all did what we thought was right. Our children bear a responsibility for their choices."

"Aye, but it's what's in their hearts that troubles me." Mama spoke with resignation. "Now we can only pray for them."

Ollie brightened. "We always wanted to share grandbabies."

Mama smiled. "Got what we wanted., didn't we?"

The tension broke. The thread of friendship that bound them had refused to snap. The couples stood, embraced, and shook hands as if they hadn't just witnessed an astonishing display of defiance and disrespect. How amazing, God's healing touch.

"Mind if I pray?"

The group turned to Andrew.

"It would be an honor." Zach gazed at the future groom, the man who stood beside the girl he'd hoped his son would marry.

Andrew said the amen, and Zach shook his hand. "You're the man who deserves Ella."

Her mouth screwed up, stifling a tremor. Her eyes misted.

Zach stopped midway to the door. "Almost forgot. A wire arrived for you at the bank, Lily." He handed her a sealed message.

She slipped a finger between the folds. "It's from Miss Adelaide."

CHAPTER 38

"*M*iss Adelaide's inviting me to move to Broadview." Lily's chestnut lashes spread as if her eyes were sunflowers greeting the sun. She covered her lips with her fingers.

A sense of resolution spread through Ella. Why hadn't she thought of this herself? Lily could continue her education and have a wonderful home near the cottage, a perfect solution.

The group of friends congratulated her on her newfound favor, and she blushed. Mama and Papa offered to drop her at the cottage, and she appeared content.

The engaged couple drove to the cottage with their buggy full of gifts.

"Where did you go when you slipped out tonight, Andrew?"

"I got to Frank and Viola as he was climbing into his car. Told him we needed to talk."

She gripped his sleeve. "And?"

"He laughed and motored away. Left me standing there."

"I'm sorry."

He leaned toward her with kindness in his eyes. "Let's not let Frank ruin our evening."

They arrived at the cottage having spoken little. She could think of nothing but Frank's and Viola's outrageous display. Her parents and the Irvings had dispensed with their shock, but her own ire bubbled.

Take this indignation, Lord. I can do nothing about it.

She set Maude's labor of love—a bundle of kitchen towels with crocheted edging—on the sideboard.

Devoid of chatter, Lily helped them bring in the rest of the gifts. "I'll finish my writing assignment upstairs in my room."

"You can finish in the morning, dear." Lily offered no response, only crept up the stairs as if in thought, withdrawn. Ella would speak with her tonight.

Andrew invited Ella to join him on the living room settee. "When I asked if you were still interested in starting a school, I had something particular in mind."

What more could this man lay before her?

"We're both educators. We can found a school that'll put Worthington to shame."

She leaped to her feet and paced, her mind aflutter with possibilities. "I can think of nothing more wonderful than running a school with you. Where would we build it? Could it be for underprivileged children, boys and girls? How did I come to be so blessed?"

When Andrew departed, her first thought was of Lily. She knocked on her door but found her fast asleep. She'd speak with her in the morning. Meanwhile, she'd put aside the evening's shock and dream of her future with Andrew. She'd relish the love of dear friends. And dream of Broadview School for Girls.

Frank and Viola departed on a three-week honeymoon to New York City, leaving Joshua with Mama and Hannah. They'd return in time for the wedding. Honestly, Ella preferred they stay away.

Meanwhile, a whirlwind descended on the cottage as they prepared it as their own. Some of Andrew's furnishings arrived on the cold, wet morning of the sixteenth of November, ten days before the ceremony. He refused to enter Ella's bed chamber, so Cade set up the fancy armoire, chest, and bed.

As the day warmed, she invited Lily to join her on the settee. "Tell me how you feel about moving to Broadview. How you *really* feel, I mean."

"Broadview's a palace."

"But do you want to live in a palace?"

She shrugged. "Never lived in one, so I can't say." She pinched her bottom lip between her teeth. "What really matters is who'll live in the palace with me. I don't know Miss Addie."

Ella took her hand. "Oh, Adelaide Fitzgerald's a fine woman. As fine as you'll ever meet. Her heart's as big as all outdoors, and she'll love you like you're her own blood."

Her eyes spread wide. "Me, a Sloat?"

She took Lily's face in her hands. "Addie can't help but love you. But you can stay right here in the cottage with Andrew and me too. You know that, don't you?"

The dear child smiled, pensive-like.

"Now. Help me explore my wedding chest."

The friends sat crosslegged beside the trunk, and Ella lifted the lid. "Look at these bed linens. It's all Mama's handiwork."

"Embroidered roses."

"Daffodils and lilacs. Pillow shams trimmed in tatting. Why, there's a needlepoint stool cushion and a table runner."

"That there's a a lap quilt."

"When did Mama have the time?"

"Bound to have been working on it for years."

Ella recalled her mother in her sewing chair with her mending or needlework, her hands rarely still, her eyes straining over the stitches. Many evenings her shoulders bent over the sewing machine with its treadle racing. Her fingers kneaded the small of her back, but she never complained. Such scenes had become commonplace in the McFarland home.

She'd taken for granted such signs of her mother's love. "I wish I could repay her for everything she's done for me."

"Ma says love can't be earned. It's a gift."

Ella turned her gaze on Lily. "Sometimes love takes the shape of a doily. Other times, a palace."

The unseasonably warm temperature beckoned the couple to the porch swing in the evenings. Ella cuddled under Andrew's arm. "The Lord gave us eighty-degree weather in November, so I could sit out here, close to your heart."

His hand grazed her shoulder. "Forever."

A thrill passed through her.

"I can build you a home of your own."

How like Andrew to think of giving her a home before he could afford it, surely not on a blacksmith helper's pay. She must never take such a love for granted.

She smiled. "The idea of a place where no one but you and I have lived sounds lovely. Maybe someday we can afford it. But I'm content here for now."

"Want to know where we're going on our honeymoon?"

"No. Surprise me."

"I'll take you away for months if you'll let me."

As if he could afford it. *Bless him, Lord.* "With Christmas coming and Addie here soon, a day or two will do."

"Has Lily adjusted to the idea of moving to Broadview?"

"Appears so. She's a bright girl. It's as if there's not enough knowledge in the world to fill her up."

He drew her head onto his chest. "Hear my heart?"

"It's picking up."

"That's what you do to me, love."

She nuzzled closer. "Will you say such lovely things when we're old and gray?"

"Always."

"Will we speak of ordinary things too?"

"The commonplace becomes extraordinary with you beside me. A full moon on the rise and the geese that fly across it. They're nothing short of a pot of gold and a flock of angels because of you."

"That's beautiful."

"The changing sketches in the stars are a canopy of diamonds." He pointed skyward. "See? And burning wood becomes the heat of my longing for you. It's a fire that'll never die." He lowered his mouth to hers. "I'm under your spell, my love. Always."

"Only nine days until you're married." Mama removed the fruit of her labor—Ella's wedding gown—from a dress bag.

"Mama …" She ran her fingers over the lace. "It's like sugar flowers and lattice work. Never seen a shade like it."

"The color of tea, heavy with cream. Grandma Anglin made bolts of it."

"But you haven't measured me." She slipped off her house dress.

"I've sewn for you since you were a baby. I know how the Lord made you." She unfastened the covered buttons, revealing built-in staves. No corset required.

Ella stepped into the gown, and Mama secured the back.

Yards of ecru taffeta and lace tumbled to the floor like a gushing spring. The high neckline showed a hint of skin through the swirls in the lace. Sleeves, gathered at the shoulders and elbows, hugged her arms to her wrists. Belting, adorned with dark ecru velvet ribbons that swirled like rose vines, shot tendrils down the front.

Tears welled. When had her mother found the time and strength to sew such a creation? A familiar sense of unworthiness crept in and settled around Ella's heart, forcing her head lower. A tear fell from her chin onto the lace, leaving an expanding blotch.

"Oh, no. I've spoiled it."

Mama brushed a finger over the spot. "Nay, daughter mine. Tears dry."

Love cannot be earned. It's a gift.

Could Ella remember this truth beyond today? Nay, beyond this instant?

Mama spread the lace veil over her daughter's head.

"How did I not know you possessed such lace?"

"Been in my wedding chest. Waiting for you. The Good Lord's answering a lifetime of prayers." She smiled and drew her beloved one to her.

Ella inhaled the scent of rosewater in her mother's hair.

"No one must see it until you walk down the aisle." Mama unbuttoned the gown. "Into the wardrobe it goes."

Smiling, the bride-to-be donned her everyday dress. Papa had been working less as store sales picked up inexplicably. He'd even hired a clerk. Thank God for the prosperity.

Mama leaned against her. "Sometimes the weight of God's love takes me to my knees."

She knelt beside the bed and pulled her daughter alongside her. "Lord, You've given Your grace in ever-increasing measure. You've bound up Lily's wounds that reach deeper than her scars. Eased Ella's disappointment about Worthington and healed her grief over Nell. And now You're blessing her with the man of Your choosing." Her voice broke.

Ella took over. "Oh, Lord. With each passing day, Your grace grows greater still. I'll never forget."

CHAPTER 39

*A*ndrew's parents arrived on the Fair Valley train nine days, four hours, and thirty-seven minutes before Ella and Andrew were to be declared husband and wife.

Ella's first sight of Josephine Evans would be seared forever in her memory. Rather like the tintypes Mama kept in her chest to protect them from the light, she'd hide her impression, telling no one. For Andrew's sake.

Tall, striking, and in perfect pigeon-breasted form, Mrs. Evans stepped from the train in a dark brown traveling suit that matched her bounteous hair, the same rich shade as her son's.

Andrew waved. "Mother, over here." He nudged his intended forward.

His mother turned, her posture perfect, her head tilted as was proper. Her brown woolen hat with its stylish swept-up brim moved not an inch. Ella's headpiece sported ribbons while fur trimmed the dignified older woman's.

"Meet my soon-to-be wife, Mother." Andrew's features glowed as he bent to kiss her cheek.

Mrs. Evans lifted a lorgnette and appraised her son's future wife beneath carefully penciled eyebrows. She proffered a limp, leather-clad hand. "A pleasure, Miss McFarland."

Their fingers touched. "Happy to meet you, Mrs. Evans. I'm Ella."

"When you are my son's wife, you may call me Josephine."

A distinguished gentleman approached, and Andrew reached for him. "Hello, Father."

"Come here." Mr. Evans pulled his son to him. "This must be your Miss McFarland."

"How do you do, Mr. Evans." With blue eyes in a nest of laugh lines like Andrew's, Owen Evans was as handsome as his son.

"You're perfectly beautiful, my dear." He took her hand. "But let's dispense with formalities. Call me Owen."

"Thank you, sir. I'm Ella."

"And I'm perfectly parched." Mrs. Evans marched forward and scanned the parking lot. "Where's your automobile?" Glowering, she halted at the sole conveyance. "A second-hand buggy? Is that all?"

"It's all we need, Mother. Here, take my hand."

Lifting her skirt, she stepped into the back seat on kid-covered feet. Her shoe buttons shone. She arranged the yards of fabric and straightened her jacket.

Andrew assisted Ella to the other side. "You outshine your diamond."

How would she converse with this elegant woman? She repositioned her tortoise shell comb and sneaked a peek at the Denver socialite's jacket. Its puffy sleeves tapered to the elbows and hugged her arms to the wrists. Her high-collared blouse, no doubt made of the finest silk, was encrusted with lace and delicate edging.

Ella felt positively underdressed in her cotton gloves, simple skirt, and embroidered waist. She offered Andrew's mother a tumbler from a picnic basket and poured water from a decanter. Conscious of her work-reddened hands, she kept on her gloves.

"Thank heaven." Mrs. Evans flipped open a hand fan. "My, but it's warm."

"Not yet eighty degrees, Mother."

Owen smiled. "Perfect."

As Andrew directed the team into the thoroughfare, Ella recalled her lessons on social conversation. "Tell me about your family, Mrs. Evans. And Denver."

The dissertation continued as the road skirted Needham, taking them into the countryside. She eyed the farmland to the right and ranch property to the left. The road curved, revealing the wide, elegant entrance to Broadview, and she inhaled loudly. "My, you have a lovely—"

"That's Broadview, my friend Adelaide Fitzgerald's home." Ella caught the inside of a cheek between her teeth.

"And yours is nearby?"

"My friend Lily and I live in a cottage on Adelaide's property."

She pointed to the left. "Over there, perhaps?" Her countenance had taken on a sign of hopefulness.

"That ranch land belongs to Zach Irving."

The woman pressed a handkerchief to her lips. "Mr. Irving's prosperity shows."

Indeed. Ella pointed across the vista to the right. "Our cottage is over there, in the woods. But we're heading to my parents' home first."

Mrs. Evans coughed into a handkerchief.

Beyond the copse between Fitzgerald and McFarland properties, Andrew slowed the team and eased them up the broad but simple drive to the country home of Gavin and Betsy McFarland.

Her hopes no doubt dashed, the society dame crumpled into the seat back, no longer speaking.

Ella's insides shriveled into a tightly drawn ball. Her soon-to-be mother-in-law had pulled the end of a length of yarn, stretching and tightening it around her heart. She'd never attain this woman's level of refinement. But could she hold her head high before her disapproval?

Aye. She'd remember her mother's love, her father's, and those who came before.

Andrew helped Josephine alight, and Owen assisted Ella. The foursome stepped onto the porch with its simple handmade furnishings. Should Ella point out Grandpa Mac's bent elm chairs? Grandma Anglin's swallow gourds? Mama's ticking cushions?

Andrew held open the door.

Would Ella deny her roots? No. She couldn't. "Family crafted these furnishings. They represent a great deal of love." She forced a thread of brightness into her voice. "Welcome."

"Who do I hear?" Mama came through the kitchen doorway wiping her hands on her apron. She stopped mid-step, gazing at Josephine. She rallied and extended a hand. "I'm Betsy McFarland. Come in."

"Josephine Evans." She touched Mama's bare fingers with her own encased in fine kid.

Ella removed her gloves and hat. Glancing into the entry mirror, she straightened her crimped hair.

"Betsy, this is my father, Owen." Andrew extended hands between the two.

His father doffed his hat and gave Mama a half-bow, kissing the back of her hand as if she were a duchess. "I see where Ella gets her beauty."

His wife sniffed.

"You're just in time for warm apple pie." Mama pointed a thumb over her shoulder. "Gavin's seeing to an ailing calf. He'll be along directly."

What did this affluent woman think of Mama's simple parlor furnishings, some built by Papa and others, gifts from prosperous friends?

Ella removed a pie from the keep and set it on the dough board for slicing.

Their ever-so-proper guest pulled off her gloves with a decidedly dramatic flair.

Mama poured coffee, served pie, and made conversation.

When Owen finished his dessert, he mumbled his pleasure.

"May I get you another slice?" Ella scooped up his plate.

"You're as gracious as your mother." He patted his midsection. "But that's all I need."

Mrs. Evans pushed aside her plate. "I assume you learned your mother's fine pastry tricks. Our cook's a marvel."

"I try, but I can't touch Mama's skill."

"I'll show you around, Father. And introduce you to Gavin." Andrew s escorted Owen outside.

Ella felt at ease with Owen surveying the property. Not so, his wife.

Mama turned her attention to the proud matron. "Tell us about Denver. I hear the railroad's brought prosperity."

"Indeed. Owen has more real estate business than he and our other son can handle. There are our daughter's school friends and Owen's associates and The Ladies' Auxiliary and Brentwood Men's Club. I simply had to purchase new dining and parlor furniture. Our position demands it."

Her words were sharp points beneath a covering as smooth as molasses. They flowed as if they were planned in advance.

Mama's were drawn in a lovely, old-fashioned script, simple and laced with sincerity.

Mrs. Evans's nails, neat and trimmed, spoke of a life of ease. Mama's shouted homemaker and the labor she wouldn't relinquish. Her hands were carved by love.

"In what activities are you involved?"

The woman's question jarred Ella from her reverie. "Teaching, keeping house, and tending the garden fill my days. I sometimes speak about women's right to vote. And I serve in church ministries."

"You're like Julia, foolish about the vote, missionaries, and wayward souls. My sister will work herself to death. You'll do the same if you're not careful. Come to Denver. I'll introduce you to my circle of friends. How does that sound?"

It sounded perfectly miserable, but Ella managed not to say so. "Thank you."

They met the men in the front drive, and Andrew prepared to deliver his parents to Tad and Julia's. He kissed Ella on the cheek. "I'll see you tomorrow." He hugged Mama, gave Papa a firm handshake, and whisked his parents away.

Andrew's mother wouldn't relinquish her son to just any woman. Her sister Julia's assessment aside, Josephine Evans would render her own verdict.

Before Ella saw Andrew on the morrow, she must find honest but kind words to describe her initial encounter with his mother.

Daunting.

CHAPTER 40

$\mathscr{D}$elighted to see Julia arriving in her buggy later that day, Ella waved from the cottage's front porch. "What a lovely sight." She helped Andrew's aunt down, noting the contrast between her frail hands and strong bearing.

"I've something to say." Determination flared in Julia's eyes. "Can't keep it any longer."

Leading her to the kitchen, Ella set out coffee and reminded herself to listen and guard her tongue.

"I'm ashamed of my sister. I love her, but it's hard to tolerate her ways."

Ella sat with her elbows on the table and a fist at her jaw. "You mustn't—"

"Josephine's always been prideful—which is why we parted—but I've never known her to be mean-spirited. Not until now."

What had Andrew's mother said about the McFarlands that riled this meek woman? "She's your sister, Julia."

"I told her where I was headed and what I'd say. So, I'm not gossiping."

Intent on hearing her out, Ella sat straighter.

"She's planned for her eldest to marry a society girl in Denver. You're in the way."

Ella blinked. Had Andrew's mother apprised him of her plans?

"I told her there's not a better girl anywhere. Nothing has made me happier than knowing you and Andrew are marrying."

Touched by Julia's devotion yet scrambling to make sense of the news, Ella tented her fingers. "This girl ... Andrew knows her?"

She flipped a casual hand. "Oh, he knows the girl, but he has eyes for no one but you." She patted Ella's hand. "Don't let my news distress you. You have Andrew's heart. Just wanted you to know my sister's attitude reflects none of mine and Tad's. We love you. There isn't a time more special for a girl than her wedding, so enjoy it."

Ella embraced her slight frame. "Thank you for loving me, Aunt Julia."

Andrew arrived at the cottage at sunset. Dishes were done. Lily had excused herself for the evening.

"It's best we discuss my mother." Grim-faced, he stood before Ella. "I'll be nothing but truthful. Please sit down and listen." He paced. "My mother's society ways don't appeal to me. You don't need fancy clothes, hairdos, or parties. You're perfect as you are."

He pulled her to her feet. "I'm leaving my mother and father and cleaving to my wife, a near-perfect woman."

"But do we have her blessing? It isn't my intention to take you from your family but to join your circle. If she'll let me."

"Already taken care of that."

Did he believe he could dispense with his mother's objections so easily? "If you say so. But I can't help but think—"

"I can't stay." He gathered his coat and hat and gave her a kiss on the cheek. Mounting Kieran, he smiled. "When the sun rises tomorrow, I've only eight days to wait."

The wind picked up, and bits of debris struck Ella. She covered her face, fearing the blast bespoke a deeper dread—that Josephine Evans would have her way.

As she pulled down her bedcovers and slipped beneath her quilt at bedtime, she couldn't erase the image of her future mother-in-law stepping from the train. And crumpling into the seat back at the sight of the McFarland home.

How was a common farmer's daughter to withstand such a force?

Could a Denver socialite accept a simple, rural girl like Ella?

Unease scratched at her, but she closed her eyes and begged sleep to come.

"I'm going to the Prestons, Lily. Maude asked for a drawing of the cake I have in mind. Want to come?" The morning was new and the air fresh and crisp.

"Thank you, Ella, but I have a reading assignment."

When she pulled up at the Preston place, Percival waved from outside the barn. He wore a sweat-stained hat, field-scuffed boots, and a smile. "You're a sight for an old man's eyes. What brings you out?"

To the right behind the house stretched the peach orchard where Frank had …

Pushing the memory aside, she held up the drawing. "Wedding cakes and … a hankering to talk with you … privately, if that's all right."

He beckoned her onto the porch. "Have a seat. I'll let Maude know you're here and get us something to drink."

The couple's voices in the kitchen and the gentle stirring of a breeze calmed her. She prayed to find the proper words.

Percival returned with lemonade. "Friends brought us a peck of lemons from San Antonio. A shipment had just come in from down Mexico way. Maude got the sugar just right. She'll be out in a bit. What's on your mind, Ella?"

They sipped and rocked while she gathered her thoughts. How could she recall the images and speak the words? "Percival, about that night with Frank …"

He nodded.

"I thank God Frank didn't actually … hurt me. But I've never thanked you."

"No need. The Lord nudged me to check on you."

The memory gripped her, and tears sprang to her eyes. "Thank you for being His shield over me. I've loved three godly men besides Andrew: Papa, Cade, and you. But I've never told you. I do love you, you know."

"It's an honor to be a part of that list."

"It's an honor to have been watched over by a man like you." She smiled. "But there's something else troubling me. It's about Andrew's mother. She's from a different world, from society, if you know what I mean. I'm worried about her accepting me."

Percival worked his lips as he was wont to do and gave a deep-chested growl. "Oh, I know Josie, all right. Known her for years. Since way back before she and Julia had the falling out. You don't have to worry about Josie. Her bark's a whole lot worse 'n her bite. What's Andrew say?"

"Oh, he assures me there's nothing to worry about."

"Then I'd take him at his word and let it be."

Maude joined them, and they visited about stubborn mules, wedding cakes, and how to pitch a song just right. Maude announced she'd fix a bite to eat, and Ella knew it was time to depart.

"You're a fine young woman." Percival stood beside her at her buggy. "Stand on your faith. It'll keep you peaceful, even in storms. If you need anything, call on me."

"I'll do that." She smiled within the gentle embrace of his powerful arms.

He helped her into the conveyance. "Have you told Andrew? About Frank, I mean?"

"Couldn't marry him if I didn't."

"You did the right thing."

"Andrew won't rest until he sets Frank straight."

"Best take care. Frank could do most anything." He shook his head as if to rid himself of a pest.

"You don't think Frank would hurt Andrew, do you?" No. The Lord wouldn't allow it.

"Don't mind me." He shooed her with a flutter of fingers. "See you in the morning."

"I love you, Percival." She waved and directed Bunny onto the road. The mare undertook a spritely pace with her ears pointed forward.

The steady whir of the buggy wheels and the familiar click of hooves did little to blunt Percival's warning. Should she share it with Andrew right away? *Dear God, keep him safe.*

Remembering Julia's encouragement, she pitched aside her misgivings. At the edge of town, the ring of metal on metal and the smoky scent of burning coals drew her eyes to Tad's blacksmith shop. She drove past the cotton gin, another of Zach Irving's astute investments. Frank had claimed an office spot, but he rarely used it. His Cadillac was parked outside.

So Frank and Viola had returned earlier than expected.

She turned Bunny toward the gin. She'd speak with Frank before the day ended. Ordering her thoughts like shirts on a line, she headed for the office.

Frank opened the door before she could turn the knob. "To what do I owe this pleasure?" His gaze blistered. Behind him stood the same shifty stranger she'd seen with him before. The man ducked his head and stepped out a side door.

"May I speak with you outside?"

"My pleasure, ma'am." He donned his hat.

Stepping outside, she turned to face her adversary.

He stepped back. "What's on your mind, soon-to-be Mrs. Evans?"

"You."

"So, your thoughts're on me now?" A mirthless grin crinkled his cheeks.

"Not willingly. But since you got my sister with child and eloped with her and you've marched in and out of church and family gatherings as if you have no conscience, I intend to utter a handful of words and try never again to speak to you." Her mouth tasted of bile.

He raised an eyebrow and brought his face so near she could smell his breath. "No one—least of all a McFarland—tells me what to do. Watch your step."

Taken aback, she moved away. Never before had she witnessed the expression on his face. Would he harm her? Surely he was bluffing.

Determined to stand her ground, she stretched to her full height. "Treat my sister kindly. Be a decent father. And never come within six inches of me."

Not waiting for his reply, she stepped into the buggy and gave the reins a flick. She had Lily's lesson to think about. And wedding details to review with Mama.

As the buggy rolled out of town, Andrew approached on horseback from the opposite direction, his expression thunderous. What was troubling him? His mother, no doubt.

Ella waved and blew him a kiss. No need to take him from his parents. She'd tell him about her talk with Frank tomorrow, the Lord's Day.

CHAPTER 41

*L*ily completed her history and mathematics lessons and retired to the gazebo to read. Ella packed lingerie into a travel trunk. Imagining wearing the pretty nighties as Andrew's wife stirred thoughts she hadn't dared consider.

At the sputter of a motor car engine, she abandoned her task and strode to the front window. What brought out Quentin York, Needham's chief attorney and a McFarland friend, mid-afternoon?

She stepped onto the porch. "How're you doing, Quen?"

He slid out of the driver's seat and left the engine purring. His shoulders drooped, and he twisted his hat into a roll, his gaze on the bed of marigolds around the front porch. "There's been an accident."

Heat surged, and her hands fisted. "Who?"

"Andrew."

Her knees threatened to buckle. She leaned onto the railing. "What's happened?"

"Cotton gin." He gestured northward. "Don't know details."

She'd heard descriptions of gin-mangled bodies. "How bad is it?"

He tugged on his hat. "All I know—"

"Is he alive?" She took the steps two at a time and stopped, eye level with his breast pocket. "I'll know the truth, so—"

He raised both hands, as if to ward off her ferocity. "They've taken him to the Fair Valley Sanitarium."

She dashed inside and pulled a straw hat and scarf off the hall tree. What might she need? Scanning the living room, she snagged her embroidery basket and Bible and turned off the flame under the field peas. Pinning on her hat, she stepped outside.

Lily rounded the corner with a book in her hands.

"Andrew's been in an accident." Ella's legs wobbled as she descended the steps. "Quentin's taking me to Fair Valley." She stopped to embrace the startled child.

Quentin opened the passenger door and gave her a steadying hand. She tied her scarf around her hat. "What was Andrew doing at the cotton gin? I'll bring him here tonight and take care of him myself."

"He won't be coming home tonight. It's … well, it's bad." He steered the car onto the road.

She caught his sleeve. "Tell me what you know."

He shook his head and drew his lips into a firm line. On a good day Quentin was as closed-mouthed as a rusty lock. She didn't expect him to open up on a day like this one.

Dear God, take anything but Andrew.

The hour-long drive gave her time to imagine the worst. When the tires bumped the curb outside the medical facility, she was strung tighter than a clothesline. Forging into the building, she aimed for the receptionist. "I'm Ella McFarland."

"We're expecting you." The woman led her to the end of a hall. "Wait here." She opened a door and peeked inside.

Ella removed her hat. Her fingers dug into the weave.

"The doctor will be right out." As the woman returned to her desk, her heels produced a dreadful tapping on the hardwood floor. Like a dirge.

A doctor wearing a white coat and a kind expression approached. He took her hands. "I'm Dr. Williams. Mr. Evans has been calling for you. I'm glad you're here."

Grateful for his steadying grip, she trained her eyes on his. "Is he alive?" Her right eye twitched. "Tell me what's happened."

"He's alive." He gestured to an alcove. "Let's sit." He guided her to a grouping of easy chairs. "Mr. Evans has suffered a profound injury."

"What, in heaven's name?"

"From what I'm told by others, he entered the cotton gin looking for a man named Frank. Do you know the gentleman?"

"Yes. Frank's father owns the gin. What does Frank Irving have to do with Andrew's injury?"

"Witnesses say Mr. Evans was giving the man a piece of his mind. There was a scuffle, and Mr. Evans tripped. Apparently, the gin's mechanism had been left uncovered."

She covered her lips with her fingers. "But you're caring for him. He'll be going home."

"He's lost a great deal of blood. I'm sorry, Miss McFarland, but we couldn't save his left arm. I'm not sure he'll live."

A tidal wave as thick as overcooked oats threatened to suffocate her. Images rendered her speechless—her loved one's strong arms holding her close, encircling her. She clenched her eyes to dispel what she'd imagined with the greatest joy—his hand extended for his wedding ring.

"No!" She fell to her knees and rocked, her arms locked around her like steel traps. "Tell me it isn't so!"

Color evaporated from the alcove. A smoky haze moved in. She collapsed, and the doctor caught her before she hit the floor.

She woke on a divan in the physician's office. Quentin stood nearby, wringing his hat.

"Are you all right?" The physician had knelt beside her.

"I think I am."

"The news you received was traumatic. Sit up and let me take a look." He checked her pulse and blood pressure, eyes and respiration. "I won't mince words or paint a pretty picture. Mr. Evans isn't out of danger. If he survives the loss of blood, gangrene can set in."

Why have You permitted this, Lord?

"Mr. York tells me you and Mr. Evans were to be married in a week."

She pitched forward with a whimper.

"We've applied a carbolic solution to his bandages and will continue to do so until the danger of gangrene has passed. He'll remain here more than a week, however."

The doctor placed a hand on her shoulder. "I hear you're a strong person. It'll take a great deal of strength to face what's ahead. Once the danger passes …" He shook his head, as if visualizing the possibilities. "Let's just say Mr. Evans must adjust to a new way of living. He'll need your support."

"Of course." She raised her eyes to his. "I'll do whatever it takes, but …" She shook her head to dispel the nightmare. "I'm sorry. It's just …"

"You've sustained a shock. I'll take you to him."

"He will live, won't he?" She ignored the stunning warning of gangrene.

"I can't promise. I'm sorry."

Following the physician down the hall, she struggled to absorb his dire words. She stopped to speak to Quentin. "Has anyone contacted Andrew's parents? They're in Needham in advance of our wedding."

"Percival was on his way to the Thompsons when I left." As distraught as a family member, the man had aged years in a day. "Go home, Quen."

"I brought in your things." He pointed to a table where he'd set her sewing basket and Bible. "Anything else you need?"

"Mama and Papa'll come. But thank you."

He eyed the door and shifted his weight from one foot to the other. "I'll see about your folks, too."

"You're a good friend. Thank you." She turned to the doctor. "May I see Andrew now?"

"Your name's all he's spoken."

Ella entered a room as stark as the day's news.

Andrew lay beneath a sheet on a bed near a window. The sun offered its waning rays, but the wall sconces and bedside lamp provided the bulk of illumination.

His right arm lay at his side. His left was bandaged between his shoulder and elbow, where it ended abruptly.

She moved nearer, checking for signs of life. His chest rose and fell.

Her body swayed. The doctor slid a chair behind her.

"Thank you." She steadied herself against the chair and inched into its cushioned seat.

"I'll leave you alone." The door opened and closed. All sounds faded, save the feather-soft passage of air in and out of her loved one's lungs.

Andrew was alive. Ella would live alongside him as long as he drew breath.

But why, in the name of all that was good, had this happened?

CHAPTER 42

Owen and Josephine arrived just before visiting hours ended.

"Where's my son, Andrew Evans?" Like a crow's caw across a cornfield, her words traveled from the receptionist's desk all the way to her injured boy's room. "I demand you take me to him."

Sitting at Andrew's side, Ella imagined the skittish receptionist abandoning her task to escort the daunting visitor down the hall. Ella must remember to thank the girl.

Recalling the sight of Mrs. Evans stepping off the train--the tilt of her head, her voice--and her reaction to the McFarland home ignited a shudder.

Ella braced herself and stood. She'd put aside her heartbreak for the sake of Andrew's parents. And she'd extend kindness.

She laid a hand on his shoulder. "It's your mother, my love."

His eyelids twitched open. "Mother?" He sighed. "Poor Mother."

Ella straightened her blouse.

Crinolines announced her arrival before her properly attired form graced the simple room. She entered like a bantam hen claiming her territory. Dispensing with formalities, she targeted her son.

"Andrew." Her eyes roamed the length of his body and settled on his left side.

"Where's Father?"

"He's coming."

Ella nudged the chair toward Mrs. Evans and eased her into it.

The mother laid her head on the mattress beside her son. "How will we endure this tragedy? No one in our family has ever been maimed."

"I'm sorry, Mother."

Her eyes blazed. "If you hadn't left in a huff when I was merely explaining what opportunities lie in Denver, this wouldn't have happened. But off you rode to that horrid place. Why a cotton gin, of all places? How could the owner have let this happen? What redress can you expect?"

"No one's fault but my own."

"If you'd taken your father's offer at the agency, you'd have both arms and a bright future. Now you're lame." She crumbled at Andrew's side.

So, his mother had been behind his stormy expression. He'd ridden into town rather than endure her tirade about Denver. Ella couldn't blame him.

How could such insensitivity reside in a mother's heart?

She backed away. An urge to spew her thoughts, to describe the woman in miserable terms, blasted through her chest. She fisted her hands, her exasperation ready to spill.

"Oh, Mother."

Ella staunched the rage she was tempted to vent. Hadn't she vowed to extend kindness to Andrew's mother? "I need air." She shoved open the door and ran down the corridor.

Bursting out the entrance, she stopped short. Owen was speaking to the hansom driver. "Thank you. Can you wait while we visit our son? I'll pay you for your time."

"Be happy to, Mr. Evans."

Andrew's dear father turned to Ella. Creases ran between his eyes and around his mouth, etchings of suffering. He drew her into his arms. "Ella dear, how's my son?"

"Dr. Williams says each day will be an answered prayer."

"My heart's broken for both of you. Tell me what I can do."

Stunned by the contrast between Andrew's parents, she lowered her head to his chest and wept.

"Andrew's asking for you." Ella spoke through a stuffy nose and his manly handkerchief.

They walked the corridor with her hand in the bend of his arm.

At Andrew's room, the grieving father closed his eyes and took a deep breath. Turning the knob, he entered.

Andrew's weak smile brightened the dreariness. "Father."

Owen pulled a chair alongside his son. They spoke in low tones, each comforting and assuring the other while Mrs. Evans squirmed and sighed.

Ella wouldn't intrude on the parents and son. She turned from the intimate scene and ducked into the hallway.

Ella trudged to the tiny sanitarium chapel, little more than a prayer closet. A portrait of Jesus on the cross hung above a makeshift altar and kneeling bench.

She collapsed on the first of three pews, her shoulders slumped, head bowed. Her hair had come undone and hung in scraggly strands. She sighed and raised her eyes to the portrait. Nails pierced His flesh. Blood seeped from His hands and feet, His side.

A man of sorrows, and acquainted with grief.

She closed her eyes, coaxing the drops of moisture from between her lashes. They oozed down her cheeks, but she hadn't a care to wipe them away. She'd leave the spigot open until it ran dry.

And He shall wipe away every tear from their eyes; and death shall be no more; neither shall there be mourning, nor crying, nor pain.

If she'd taken Percival's warning straight to Andrew …

If she'd turned around when she passed him at the edge of town …

Could she have stopped him before he found Frank?

Must her happiness forever be marred with pain?

Ella struggled to pray, but words refused to come. Only tears. She sat like a crumpled cotton sack, stained with sorrow. Voiceless.

She'd reached the end of herself.

The doorknob clunked, but she paid it no mind.

Fabric rustled. Someone sat beside her and put an arm around her.

The redolence of pipe tobacco. Papa.

He nestled her against himself, sitting in silence until she could speak. "Where's God, Papa?"

"God's goodness runs through every hard place like veins of gold, Ellie."

"If He can't be trusted to protect a man like Andrew, He can't be trusted at all. I thought He'd called me to start a school. Instead, Andrew and I are shorn to the skin in the midst of a storm." Agony studded her voice. "And the storm's hardly tempered."

"How do you know He's not calling you still? Have you thanked Him for His mercy today?"

"I'm to thank Him for this heartache?"

"Andrew's alive. Hard as it is to hear, He brings His loved ones closer through suffering."

Her Bible lay in Andrew's room. The thought of opening it sickened her. "I'm no closer to God because of this."

"Give it time, sugar. And keep praying."

Ella would give Andrew all the time left to her. But pray? What good would it do?

Ella slept in a chair in Andrew's room, his parents in the hotel across the street. Two days later they left for Denver, and she checked into the hotel at Owen's insistence. It provided a measure of rest, hot baths, and meals. And quick access to Andrew.

The sheriff interviewed witnesses, including Frank, but Andrew insisted he'd tripped on a ladder and fell into the machinery. A gin like Needham's consisted of many ever-moving parts that transported raw cotton from bulging trailers, through separate mechanisms in which blades removed the seeds from the fiber, and to the baling platform.

Accidents such as Andrew's could occur when the protective cover was removed from a row of ribs and blades without stopping the engine.

Carelessness, inexperience, and inadequate training resulted in serious accidents each gin season.

What was Andrew doing in the gin in the first place?

She wired Adelaide, who cancelled her travel arrangements.

A rainy Thanksgiving devoid of feasting came and went. Mama and Papa delivered leftovers, but neither Andrew nor Ella partook.

Three days later their chosen marriage date brought not a hint of joy.

Andrew sat in a straight-backed chair in the alcove. His empty sleeve dangled uselessly.

Ella sat beside him. "We don't need a wedding. Percival can marry us here."

He shook his head, his expression grim. "You deserve a wedding."

"And you deserve two arms." She leaned backward, ashamed and discouraged. "I'm sorry. I don't know that I'll ever bridle my tongue."

"You speak the truth."

"Dr. Williams will discharge you soon. We need to be married so I can take you to the cottage. No sense getting stuck on foolish details."

"A wedding isn't a foolish detail."

She rested her forehead on her tented fingers. "What do you suggest?"

"It'll take time for me to heal and for you to adjust to a new way of seeing me."

She fell to her knees at his feet. Sunlight brightened his eyes. "My darling Andrew, nothing can change what I see when I look at you. You're everything beautiful, kind, and good."

He touched a finger to his lips and pressed it to hers. "We've endured a traumatic event. It'll take time to recover. For both of us."

"Time seems to be on everyone's minds, as if it matters. It doesn't, I tell you. My every moment is yours. You mustn't deny me the privilege of looking after you as your wife."

"You'll not tend my wounds. Nor teach me to dress, wash, or any other thing."

She laid her head on his knee. The wool of his trousers scratched her skin. She welcomed the chafing, insignificant compared to her heartache.

He set his hand on her head.

Only days ago she'd donned her wedding gown and worried about cakes. Had Maude hidden away the drawing or kept it nearby in hopeful anticipation?

She could continue to conjure up painful images. Who would reprove her? She longed to swipe them away like chalk from a slate board. But where was she to find such strength?

Not in prayer.

He straightened in his chair. "I don't belong at Aunt Julia's and Uncle Tad's now. I can rent a place and hire help."

"How about Broadview's west wing? Addie said to use it for whatever I need."

He gazed at the ceiling. "Vern's been kind to visit. I respect him. Perhaps he'd be willing to help until I can care for myself."

"Only the hill will separate us. And not for long." A shred of hope emerged.

He cupped her head with his hand. "Know what I'll miss most?"

"No, dear, what?"

"Holding you with both arms. And wearing a wedding ring."

Could she bear any more? Drawing in a trembling breath, she reminded herself to remain strong. "I'll hold you tight enough for both of us. And your ring fits as well on your right hand as your left."

He turned toward the window. The barren branches of an elm tree danced on a breeze beyond the polished pane.

The day's forecast was seventy-five degrees.

Perfect day for a wedding.

CHAPTER 43

*E*lla rubbed away the haze from the hotel window glass and peeked down. Horses and buggies dotted the street. Vernon had parked the motor car, Adelaide's enclosed limousine, and visited with Andrew. Now he was exiting the sanitarium.

A baggage boy carried her single piece of luggage downstairs, and she donned her muffler, woolen hat, coat, and gloves. She wouldn't miss the four walls that had enclosed her grief and pent-up anger for twelve lonely nights, but she departed the hotel with gratitude for Owen's generosity.

Had she opened her Bible or prayed a single time in twelve days? No.

"It'll take time," Papa had said.

Striding down the staircase, she promised herself she wouldn't look back.

"Morning, Miss Ella." Vernon awaited her in the lobby. "It's nippy out. The clerk said I can heat the warming bricks on yonder grate."

She smiled at the hotel employee. "How kind of you."

He nodded and smiled.

Kindness in more than one form had arisen from unexpected sources. Home-cooked meals. Fall flowers. She must thank the church ladies and hotel staff for their encouragement.

"I brought some of Miss Addie's things." Vernon indicated a bundle of furs on the counter. "A moleskin motor cape. Lap robes and a fur-lined storm apron that's big enough for the both of you. I'll leave them here where it's warm while we get Mr. Evans."

"That's lovely."

"I brought the Acme, it being enclosed and all."

"You're very thoughtful. Thank you."

"Would you care to don the cape now?"

"Of course."

He spread the fur-lined garment wide and laid it across her shoulders. She slipped her hands through the side slits.

"Shall we?" He waved her out the door.

A brisk draft stung her cheeks and nose. She lowered her hat's fleece-lined brim and stepped into the street. The packed dirt was dry. A train whistled in the distance, long and low, as they crossed the thoroughfare.

When they stepped inside, Dr. Williams greeted them. Beside him stood Andrew, dressed in a smart navy-blue wool suit with an ample sack coat and matching cuffed trousers. The coat's left sleeve had been tucked into a pocket.

Her beloved's black hair was parted and combed down with pomade. A hint of dark beard outlined his jawline.

She smiled. "Who's this handsome gentleman, Dr. Williams?"

"A man who's been waiting for his bride since dawn."

Stretching to give him a kiss on the cheek, she turned to the physician. "So he's ready to walk out?"

"Ask your groom."

Andrew hadn't spoken. He'd exchanged his warm manner and ease of conversation for a grim expression and stiff posture. She put out a hand. "Let's go home."

"Not without bundling up." Vernon held out an overcoat, hat, and neckerchief. Settling the neck wrap, he slipped the coat onto Andrew's right arm and over his shoulders. Secured the buttons. And tucked the left sleeve into a pocket.

Andrew gestured Ella forward and over the threshold.

The threesome crossed the thoroughfare. Unlike his former purposeful gait, Andrew ambled, leading with his right side. Vernon opened a car door and signaled Ella to enter. She held onto the side post and stepped into the auto.

The men rounded the Acme to the other side. Andrew lifted a specta-tor-clad foot onto the running board and leaned forward, struggling to lift his weight. Twelve days in bed had weakened him.

The overseer laid a hand on either side of the younger man's waist. "I'll help you, sir."

"I can do it." Andrew latched onto the side post, flexed his body into the narrow space, and stretched upward. His hand slipped, and he pitched forward.

Vernon caught him before he tumbled headlong into the floorboard.

How dreadful, the sight of self-sufficient Andrew falling with a grunt, his eyes wide with alarm. Appalled, Ella reached out but grabbed naught but air.

Vernon held the flush-faced amputee around the waist. "There's more space up front, sir."

Andrew pushed backward, his eyes downcast. His skin had reddened.

Vernon gave him a strong-armed lift into the front seat. "I'll get the furs and brick warmers. Won't be but a minute."

Strained silence reigned in the overseer's absence.

Ella cleared her throat. "Isn't it wonderful to be going home?" She reached forward to touch his shoulder and stopped with her hand mid-air. Could she touch him … there?

"How many times will you reach for my arm or hand and find them gone?" He stared straight ahead.

"I'm sorry." At a loss for words, she exhaled a cloud of vapor.

Vernon wielded a fireplace shovel to arrange the warmer bricks in the front and back heater drawers. He laid a fur on Ella's lap and another on Andrew's.

Andrew frowned. "If you can do without a fur, Vern, so can I. Let Ella have it."

She ached in a way she'd never imagined.

The kind, patient servant settled the furs around her legs and feet. He stepped to Andrew's side window and pulled an article from his pocket. "Here's your glove, sir."

Andrew stared as the man pulled the fur-lined leather onto his hand.

What adjustments he must endure.

Vernon cranked the automobile, and they clattered onto the road toward Needham.

Travel conversation was as chilly as the weather. When they pulled in at the cottage, the family—Mama and Papa, Julia and Tad, Cade and Lily, and Hannah—ran outside.

"Welcome home!" The girls waved and hopped in place.

Andrew opened his door and lowered his feet to the running board.

Vernon put out a helping hand.

"I'll try it on my own but thank you." Andrew gripped the side post and slipped his feet over the running board onto the ground. When he stood, the family cheered.

He nodded with a hint of a smile. Leaning to his right as if seeking a new sense of balance, he stepped forward. He was the same man who walked through the cottage door only two weeks prior, yet he'd changed. Something besides a limb was missing.

Hanging her coat on a hook, Ella took his and gazed into his eyes. They had misted, and the sparkle had dimmed.

Mama's and Julia's baked sweets and hot drinks filled the sideboard with a cheery spread and the cottage with welcoming aromas. But the guest of honor tired quickly. Ever watchful, Vernon offered to take him to Broadview, and Andrew agreed.

Standing on the porch as the Acme bounced around the ridge, Ella crossed her arms to ward off the biting wind and the pain in her heart. What a dreadful sight, her beloved sitting stiff and unsmiling as the conveyance clambered away. Her natural urge was to run after them, screaming her need for him to marry her that very day.

But she mustn't. For Andrew's sake.

CHAPTER 44

lla opened her travel trunk and ran her fingers over delicate fabrics. Aunt Julia had gifted her with lace-trimmed sateen and soft batiste lingerie—chemises and camisoles, stocking and petticoats, and a simple ribbon corset. But she had no need of them now. She placed the frilly items in her wardrobe alongside the morning and afternoon frocks, evening dresses, and nightgowns intended for her honeymoon.

She closed the wardrobe door, and air whooshed against her skin. How she longed to throw wide the door. Fling her clothing back into trunks. And set out to claim her groom.

She collapsed onto her bed, racked with sobs.

Lily tapped on the door. "Mr. Yancey's here."

Sitting up, Ella dried her tears. "Thank you. Be right there."

How had Andrew slept? Had he eaten a good breakfast? She trudged down the hallway and managed a smile. "Morning, Vern."

The man wore a troubled expression, his appearance harried. "Mr. Evans won't be visiting today. Not feeling well. Said it'd be best if you stayed away. Could be coming down with something catching, don't you know." His fingers clutched at his hat.

Could he have developed an infection this far into his recovery? Her eyebrows scrunched together. "Does he have a fever?"

"Not that I can tell, ma'am. There's phantom-like pain. But he got himself out of bed. Ate breakfast. I helped him with his shaving. And dressing."

"I'm sure he appreciates it." If only she could soap Andrew's shaving brush and sharpen his razor, prepare his breakfast and help him dress. She collapsed into an upholstered chair, struggling to hold back tears.

He eased toward her. "Mr. Evans'll need time, don't you know, to feel at ease in his own skin. To accept what he sees in the mirror. To dress and comb and shave with half of what he had before. He must learn to saddle Kieran. And that fine steed must learn his master's new ways. It'll take time."

She reached for his hand. Calluses covered his palm and fingers, but his voice and touch were tender. "Hearing the truth is difficult. Forgive me."

"Nothing to forgive. You're grieving. But you'll get past it. Trust the Lord."

Hadn't she trusted God always?

She'd turned down the teaching position of her dreams to follow a higher calling. And vowed to trust Him with the school. Yet that dream lay in shambles.

She'd opened her heart to love, and trusted Him to supply the joy of a family. Yet her wedding day had come and gone with no vows spoken.

Worst of all, she'd trusted God to keep Andrew safe. Yet the dear man sat a world away, maimed in body and spirit.

Ella gazed into Vernon's kind eyes. "Thank you for caring for Andrew."

"It's my privilege and honor, ma'am." He ducked his head, his expression solemn. "May I speak plainly?"

"Please do." She pointed to the easy chair. "Have a seat. May I get you coffee?"

"No coffee but thank you." He eased into the chair, a twin to Ella's. "Mr. Evans is a fine man. You've chosen well. But he must find the path to his new manhood in his own way. So he can come to you doing what a man does for his lady, not hanging his head, you see."

Could she put aside her yearning and give Andrew time to grow strong on his own? Her soul cried out to mend the broken wing of her loved one.

Vernon's mouth quavered, as did his hands. "Forgive my boldness, but Mr. Evans needs your trust as much as he needs your love."

Ella was broken herself. "I don't know how much more I can endure." A heavy pall weighed her spirit down. Weariness reached to her bones and heartsickness to her soul. "Thank you for everything, Vern." Turning, she shuffled toward her room.

"Give it time." His response followed her down the hallway. "I'll be praying for you."

She closed her door and gazed at the stained glass. *The husband and wife who sleep beneath the blackthorn will never be parted.*

Ella's *never* hadn't even begun.

Give it time. Time was all that remained.

Glancing at her kneeling pillow, she turned away and folded herself into a wingback chair. She wouldn't waste her breath on prayer.

Ella left her diamond ring in its box Sunday morning. Her gloves helped hide her secret brokenness, but her friends' well-meaning queries into Andrew's health were knife stabs to her heart.

Monday promised to be the warmest in weeks. By mid-afternoon, the back porch thermometer read fifty-six degrees.

Leaving Lily to write a report on Nellie Bly, she donned her work gloves and headed for the garden. She turned dirt with a spade. Pulled up the last of the Brussels sprouts and parsnips. And shucked the last of the fall vegetables into a basket.

She sat on her haunches and kneaded her lower back. She grimaced. Vernon said Andrew complained of phantom pain. Would it do any good to pray for him?

The tromping of boots drew her gaze to the trail from Mama's and Papa's place.

Viola.

Attired in a simple dress she hadn't worn in months, she'd tied her hair into a tail and wore old boots, a picture of the sister Ella remembered. Dark circles ringed her eyes.

"Morning, Vi."

Head lowered, Viola treaded toward the cottage without speaking, rather like a toy in need of winding. Was she ill? Or something else?

Ella pulled off her gloves and shook dirt from her skirt. She stomped, hurling chunks of dried mud from her boots.

Viola stopped at the well. She turned up the bucket and guzzled, sluicing water over her head and scattering droplets.

Ice traipsed up her spine, and she froze. Something was amiss.

Movement drew Ella's gaze to a corner of the house. A mangy dog rounded the cottage, yapping and swaying. Foam encircled his mouth. The fiend bared his teeth and gave a deep-throated growl.

Her skin prickled.

Hydrophobia.

She scanned her surroundings. A tree limb lay a few feet away. With her eyes on the brute, she scurried forward. Seized the branch. And moved toward her sister.

The dog drooled foam and stumbled forward.

"Get in the house, Vi! Run!"

Viola appeared welded in place.

Ella raised the bludgeon and raced forward. "Heeya! Get!"

Viola jerked to awareness, dropped the bucket, and bolted up the steps, flinging water from her hair and hands.

With crazed eyes and bared teeth, the creature careened toward the fleeing form. His mouth spewed a brew from perdition.

"Dear God, help me!" Ella met him at the bottom step. She swung as he lunged, and her club struck his skull, sending him reeling.

She moved up the steps backward, and Viola sped inside.

The dog barreled forward.

She jabbed and kicked and clubbed her way to the porch.

The animal attacked, as if to sink his teeth into the wood.

The club thudded against his head, but he yelped and shook off the blow.

Ella dashed inside and slammed the door. The cur's body smacked into the jamb, snapping and snarling and ramming the door.

Trembling like a sapling in a whirlwind, she slid to the floor with the blood-streaked wood in her hands.

Lily peeked between window sheers and knelt at Ella's side. "Dog's out yonder by the well, chewing up the bucket."

"Poor creature. Get the rifle."

Lily retrieved the firearm and stepped onto the porch. Two rounds sounded, and the foul snarling ceased.

"I'll get Mama." Viola rushed out the front door.

Lily entered and squatted beside Ella, offering her arm. "Let me help you up."

Mama found her daughter in a daze at the kitchen table. "Let's get you to the bedroom."

"I'm fine."

"Gotta look for teeth marks and scratches."

Ella stood and wobbled.

"Fear's left you weak, daughter."

She leaned on her mother down the hallway to her room.

Mama nodded toward the bed. "Sit." She pulled Ella's dress over her head, unhooked her boots, and set them aside with her stockings. She wiped her daughter's face and hands with a warm cloth, soothing her with her gentle touch. Her murmurings were more drones from her heart than words.

At length Mama released a deep sigh. "Nary a scratch." She slipped a robe around her daughter and drew her into her arms, singing her favorite hymn barely above a whisper. "'I am satisfied to know that with Jesus here below I can conquer every foe.'"

Papa rode up at sunset. "Where's everybody?"

"In here." Mama called to him from the kitchen.

Mother and daughter had rested and woke refreshed. They prepared the evening meal, and Lily completed a history assignment as if naught untoward had occurred.

His focus moved between his wife and daughter. "Vi said there was a mad dog over here. What's going on?" Worry lined his features.

"Just shook up." Ella shrugged and set out supper dishes.

"What happened?"

"I fought off a mad dog."

He hustled to her side. "Let me look at you."

"She's all right, Gavin. I checked her myself."

He leaned against the cupboard with a relieved sigh. "Tell me about it."

"I was in the garden. Saw Vi headed to the house. Something told me I needed to follow."

Mama flicked a nod. "It's second sight, I tell you, a gift from the Lord. Same as your Grandma Anglin."

"Vi stopped at the well and splashed water over her head. The dog came for her. I picked up a limb and used it on him." She pointed to the back wall. "That's it."

He hoisted the club. "Where'd it come from? Looks like Texas ebony."

Ella shrugged.

"Heavy. Who'd've thought you could handle a piece like this?" He examined it in the light and grinned. "There's blood on it. Looks like you got in a good wallop."

Mama grunted. "'Twasn't Ella who raised that wood above her head. 'Twas the strong arm of God."

He nodded and grinned. "Thank the Lord."

Ella turned away. *She* had wielded the wood and conquered her foe. For the first time, she doubted her family's inexplicable faith in God's power to protect and save.

Mama was wrong. Ella had protected herself this day.

CHAPTER 45

"*E*lizabeth Jane Cochran showed a heap of courage, setting off alone like Phileas Fogg in *Around the World in Eighty Days*." Lily had woken with a bee in her bonnet and sat at the kitchen table with a biscuit, coffee, and newspaper.

Ella had forced herself from bed. Dressed in a heavy robe and slippers, she poured herself a cup of coffee. "Miss Cochran was indeed courageous." She stirred cream into the brew and hoped she could muster enough enthusiasm to encourage Lily.

"Reporter Nellie Bly, she was. Says here her articles about women's working conditions set folks on their heels."

"Aye." Ella split open a scone. "She went undercover as a journalist in a woman's asylum, too."

"She allowed herself to be treated like an animal."

Ella slathered butter on the scone but set it down, devoid of appetite. "Asylums are still tragedies in some parts."

"She made the world listen." The copper-haired thirteen-year-old lifted an eyebrow. "Amazing what one woman can do."

"Aye." Ella thought she could change the world not long ago. A foolish dream spun on a loom of fantasy.

The corners of her pupil's mouth tugged upward. "We can too."

Ella kneaded her temples, coaxing away a headache. Mustn't let her melancholy taint Lily. "Of course. In time."

"What's that verse about doing for the Lord?"

She gave a shoulder a careless lift. "'Whatsoever ye do, work heartily, as unto the Lord.'"

"We ought to be acting like we believe that."

Could Ella believe again? Did she want to? Bitterness danced on her tongue, but she corralled it. For Lily's sake. "You've a glint of steel in your eyes."

"Thanks to Ma. And you." She gestured to the books Andrew had donated. "That's a library. You're a teacher. And I'm a student. So this cottage is a school waiting to be filled."

Dare Ella consider her former plans?

Could she find her voice?

"We've both known sorrow, but we shouldn't let it stop us."

Only months ago, Ella would've let nothing stop her. Zeal reared its head, as if peeking over a window sill. "I need more students. And income."

"Let's start there then." Lily's features had brightened.

Ella tapped a finger on her chin, ruminating. She could wither away here or reach for something meaningful. "There's several years of study on those shelves. but I need a sewing machine and supplies. That takes money, hard to come by nowadays."

"How much you reckon it'll cost?"

"The sewing machine in Papa's store is priced at less than fourteen dollars. The Sears catalog has one for under twelve. Start-up supplies will require about that much."

"Do other towns have Market Days like Needham's?"

Ella nodded. "Some are weekdays, others Saturdays. Christmas Markets will open soon."

"Would the church ladies donate? For the sake of the school?"

Ella's attitude brightened. "The school could be a ministry. Like Miss Barnard's work." She slid away from the table and paced. "I wrote Kate, by the way. Should hear from her soon. Meanwhile, we can strike out and sell at local markets. Best we not go far until warmer weather. If we make Westwood's Christmas fair, I can speak with Winifred Norris about students."

"That's where the Harpers live, isn't it?"

The corners of Ella's mouth turned up in a rueful grin. "Another reason to travel to Westwood. Something about the Harpers hasn't set right with me. Percival counseled them, but he didn't tell them where we live. How'd they know about the cottage?"

The friends tossed ideas from one to the other, and Ella laughed in spite of her despondency. Munching on scones, they added to their list of ideas until the fire died to embers.

Lily laid another log on the grate. "What about Andrew?"

Flinching, Ella slouched into the chair back. She'd managed to confine thoughts of the man she loved to the recesses of her mind. "As much as I want to be his wife, I want to be a teacher, too." She sat straighter. "He needs time to adjust, but I can't wait to make this place a school." She narrowed her eyes into slits. "I fought off a mad dog alone." She waved their list. "And I can overcome these obstacles."

Lily gazed into her mentor's eyes. "You sure you fought off that dog alone?"

What had Ella cried out when she faced the creature?

Dear God, help me.

From where had her plea come?

He that dwelleth in the secret place of the Most High shall abide under the shadow of the Almighty.

Scenes from the past two days flashed. She raised fingers to her lips. And bent over in her chair. Her pulse raced.

What was real and what was false, her former faith or present denial?

Never would've thought you could handle a piece like this, Papa had said.

Had Ella wielded the wood alone? Or had Someone helped her?

The air stirred around her feet and corkscrewed upward, pebbling her skin. She leaned back in the chair, and the whorl touched her cheek, as gentle as a breath.

She'd wallowed in self-pity and faithlessness. Railed against God. And denied Him. But now ...

She doubled over and moaned. "No. I didn't fight that mad dog alone. Jesus fought beside me. I've been a fool."

Lily laid a gentle hand on her rescuer's head. "Ma says He'll never leave you or forsake you."

What sweet assurance, Lord. Thank You.

The girl from the other side of Rock Creek seemed to have grown up overnight. "I must trust Him give me the voice to speak out for others." Ella raised her eyes heavenward, recalling the Chorus of the hymn Mama loved:

> *The cross is not greater than His grace.*
> *The storm cannot hide His blessed face;*
> *I am satisfied to know*
> *That with Jesus here below,*
> *I can conquer every foe.*

CHAPTER 46

*E*lla strode to the hall tree and coiled a woolen scarf around her neck. "I'm off to ask Vern to watch over things while we're away. And to check on Andrew." Batting away heartache, she pulled on a sock cap and fluffed the curls that hung to her waist.

"I'll bring some things up from the cellar while you're gone."

"Thank you. See you in a bit." Ella wouldn't hide at the cottage. Nor would she turn her face away when she passed the estate. Not another day.

Risking a return of despair if she found Andrew mired in hopelessness, an enemy she battled herself, Ella crammed her hands into her pockets and marched across the rise.

The dry prairie grass stubbles crunched under her boots, and her cheeks tingled in the brisk air.

She followed the pebbled pathway to Broadview's rear entrance. Evergreen topiaries dotted the landscape. She passed beneath Addie's rose arbor overrun by dormant vines. How she missed her friend. And needed her.

Vernon held open the door. "Look who's here. Come in."

Stepping inside, she looked around. "Where's Andrew?"

"In the study I'd reckon. Spends most of his time there."

"Has he ventured outside? Tried his hand at grooming Kieran?"

"He hasn't gone past the garden since he visited you."

"I was hoping he'd made progress." She tried not to show her disappointment.

"He accompanied me to burn the mad dog's carcass. Seems the warmer weather a while back brought woodland critters above ground.

And hydrophobia with them."

"I see." She glanced around. "May we speak in private?"

"Good idea, Miss Ella. I've something to ask of you." He waved her into the spacious and well-appointed pantry. Counter tops gleamed, as did the bright white built-ins.

He closed the door. "You see, I've a sick nephew in Ardmore. Need to tend him. But Mr. Evans needs meals. Could you help?"

Her shoulders sagged, and she stifled a sigh. It would be a joy to tend her beloved ... under different circumstances. Could she prepare his meals without her heart breaking?

And what about the marketing trip?

Vernon had been so kind. She couldn't turn him down.

"I'll be happy to, Vern."

He reminded her of the flour, sugar, and oatmeal bins and the arrangement of other staples. The new icebox with four separate sections—for fresh produce, meat, milk and eggs, and baked goods. "Ice delivery was yesterday, so we're stocked up. Barnyard boy leaves milk and eggs on the doorstep mornings at five. Housemaids were here two days ago. They'll return in another five. Can you think of anything else?"

"I'll be right at home. I've spent many a day in this kitchen."

"Yes. I leave on the morning train from Westwood. Your brother'll take me."

"Lily and I can take you." And look up Winifred Norris.

"I won't have you out by yourselves, not with it wintry and all. Who knows what rascals could be abroad."

"But—"

"Even if I'd consider such a thing, your brother and father would tan my hide." He escorted her into the hallway. "What was it you were wanting to talk with me about?"

"It can wait, Vern." She breezed past him as if delaying her plans was altogether insignificant.

He helped her bundle up, and she promised to return at five o'clock the next morning.

The plan she and Lily devised had stalled, but they'd make use of the time by preparing their stock and working ahead on assignments. Christmas around the world made a dandy history theme. They'd created a timeline of dates, places, and events. But history was more about the people who lived in the spaces between the dates.

At present, one person in particular, a beautiful man God had placed between the dates in Ella's life, had claimed her heart

If Vernon stayed away a week, they could peddle their wares in Westwood and a handful of surrounding towns and still make it back for Needham's Christmas in the Park on the twenty-third.

But most importantly, she'd see to Andrew.

"What're you doing here?"

Ella whorled from the stove where ham was frying. "For heaven's sakes, Andrew, you startled me." She tapped her chest. She'd arrived at dawn and spent the last hour familiarizing herself with the kitchen.

"Where's Vern?" He stood in the doorway with a fierce frown. A loose garment hung to the knees of his trousers.

"Gone." She returned to breakfast preparation.

"Gone where?"

"To the train station."

"Why?"

Sliding the skillet off its burner plate, she set ham, boiled eggs, and flapjacks on the round oak table. She pulled out a chair, forcing gentlemanly Andrew to do the same. "I take it he didn't tell you."

"Tell me what?"

"His nephew in Ardmore is ill. Asked me to see to your meals."

Andrew's scowl eased. "Vern's family's in Ireland. Seems he's gotten the best of us."

"Broadview's estate manager wouldn't take off without ..." She scooted to the entry table.

An envelope addressed *Mr. Evans and Miss Ella* had been propped against a crystal candleholder.

She handed it to Andrew.

"You expect me to open this with one hand?"

How thoughtless of her. "I'm sorry." She tore the seal loose and read aloud, "Forgive me for deceiving you, but what else could I do with the two of you so stubborn? You've a week to get your heads turned straight. Vernon. P.S. If you have need of me, you may contact Quentin York, Solicitor."

Andrew snatched the paper and crumpled it into a ball. "Of all the harebrained ideas, thinking to throw the two of us together against our wills."

"Don't speak for me."

"You're bound to have better things to do than babysit a mutilated man."

Her ire spiked like a riled bull's. "I'll decide how I spend my time. Furthermore, I've no interest in babysitting a thirty-year-old man. So if you have any such ideas, you'd better think again. Besides, you're lame the day you decide to be."

"Oh?" Flames of indignation seemed to lap at his face. "What do you call a man who can't even dress himself? Answer me, Miss McFarland." He edged closer.

"I call it a man who's so caught up in self-pity he can't see beyond his nose. To prove it, I won't help you put on your socks and shoes or your hat or a single other thing. It's time you got out of that filthy night shirt you're wearing as if it's day clothes."

He drew back. "I've lost my appetite. And I can take care of my own meals."

As he stomped from the kitchen, the tail of his night shirt hung askew under his suspender clasps. His hair stood on end like blackened corn stalks. But he walked at a hefty pace and with a purposeful gait.

Ella could follow. Insist he clean up. Face life. She could beg him to talk to her. Unload his burden. Accept her love.

Or she could leave Andrew in God's hands.

She leaned against the door with her mouth turned up in a grin.

Andrew's sour attitude aside, Ella must keep her promise to Vernon.

The following morning, she prepared breakfast and left it on the table in a covered dish. By noon the contents had congealed. She emptied them into the slop bucket and set out dinner, chicken and dumplings.

As she reached for the back-door handle, a grunt halted her. The sound had come from down the hall toward the study.

Andrew? Or someone—perhaps something—else?

Creeping into the passageway, she hugged the wall to avoid boards that creaked.

A guest room door stood ajar.

She inched nearer. A floor mirror reflected the room's occupant.

Andrew stood in his undershirt and trousers with his back to the mirror. One cuff had caught in the dip at the upper edge of a boot, and the other trouser leg was a bundle of wrinkles.

He slipped his hand into a shirt sleeve and wriggled it onto his shoulder. It hung in folds at his back, his left arm useless to pull it around. He grappled, twisted and snorted, and threw the garment onto the bed.

Ella experienced a pang of guilt. She hadn't meant to spy. Still, she longed to understand Andrew's needs.

Seizing the shirt, he squeezed as if to wring blood from the fabric. He swatted it across the mattress. Clenched his teeth. And lashed the shirt like a whip. Again and again. His eyes blazed and he grunted with each thrust.

Should she go to him?

No. His pride wouldn't permit it. Besides, he must learn.

A bundle sailed through the doorway and plopped onto the hall floor. She retrieved it, and Andrew dropped onto the bed.

She returned to the kitchen feeling as if she and Andrew were scraggly cuffs and button holes, tattered and coming apart. But she forced away self-pity and wondered …

Could *she* dress with one hand?

Immobilizing her left arm beneath her apron, she struggled to don and button the shirt. She wiggled her topknot loose and broke a sweat. Vented a blast that stirred tendrils on her forehead. And gave up, musing over a cup of tea.

Andrew entered the kitchen as forlorn as an orphan calf.

Her heart ached, but she wouldn't pity him.

He snatched the shirt and returned to his room without speaking.

That evening he came to supper dressed and buttoned. The shirttail hung free on one side, and the left sleeve flapped, but he'd made progress.

CHAPTER 47

Andrew's dressing skills visibly improved over the following week. When a telegram arrived, he opened it without assistance. "Vern arrives in Fair Valley at ten o'clock tomorrow. He asks that Cade pick him up."

That meant Ella and Lily could leave for Westwood at dawn. Eager to prepare, she cleared the table. "Best be going. Lily's world history vocabulary is challenging this week."

"The girl's bright. No telling how far she'll go." He gazed out the window. "You still want to start a school?"

"Lily's a student. I'm her teacher, so the cottage is already a school." She lathered soap in the near scalding dishwater. "I'll put your clean laundry on your bed before I leave."

"You shouldn't be doing my laundry."

"Couldn't wait any longer." She rinsed a teacup and set it on a kitchen towel.

"When Vern returns, I intend to learn to saddle Kieran."

"Wonderful." She scrubbed a pot with an extra measure of fervor.

"Mind if I visit when I've learned to ride properly?"

She pivoted, hands dripping, and knelt at his side. "That would be perfectly lovely."

He ran his fingers over her hair. "Only to visit. As friends."

"And why's that?"

"You deserve a whole man who can embrace you properly. Someone who can harness and drive a team." He flashed her a rueful smile. "And dig up worrisome shrubs."

She pressed his hand to her cheek. "I need the man I love—you,

Andrew."

"You can love again."

Disheartened and a tad frustrated, she slipped off her apron and slapped it over a peg. "I'll see you for supper." Slinging the back door aside, she let it pound against a sidelight and stomped across the rise, kicking up dry stubble as prickly as herself.

Lily mastered her vocabulary. Ella delivered a platter of fried chicken for Andrew's supper but didn't wait for him. She must inform her parents of their plans for the morrow.

She and Lily found the McFarlands bundled on the porch, Papa puffing his pipe.

Cade stomped in protest. "No need to travel to Westwood. You'll sell out in Needham on the twenty-third."

"We've collected far more stock than we'll sell at home, brother. You mustn't worry. We won't travel at night, and we'll stay at the parsonage or hotel. Time we stopped depending on men. Besides, I want to look up someone."

"Who's that?" Mama had assumed a curious expression.

Ella picked at a hangnail. "A prohibition activist who spoke at the community meeting, Winifred Norris."

Papa grumbled. A trail of smoke snaked above his head. "One of those suffragists?"

"She's a prominent citizen with contacts, perhaps leads to potential students."

"When will you return? Shouldn't be out after dark." Mama's curiosity seemed to have turned into motherly worry. "Travelers've been waylaid on country roads, the women attacked."

Newspapers had reported the incident. A girl was kidnapped, some feared forced into white slavery. Even so, a successful sales trip would prove Ella could live independent of her family. And without benefit of a man.

Cade shook his head, grumbling. "If you get into trouble, remember I warned you."

"It's a deal." Lily folded her arms with a sharp nod.

"Meanwhile, brother, will you share your strong arm? Come to the cottage to help us load?"

He jerked to his feet. "I wouldn't want two perfectly capable women to strain themselves, now would I?"

When Cade packed the last item onto the wagon, a thick darkness had settled. Wrapped in a shawl, Ella walked him to the edge of the woods. She held the lantern aloft until the shadows swallowed him. She returned to the cottage with the light bobbling around her.

Lily opened the door and waved her inside. "Something troubling you?"

Ella's insides tightened into knots. "I've an unhappy task to attend to." She donned her coat and stocking cap. "Go on to bed. I won't be long."

"I'll leave a lamp burning."

She forged toward Broadview, her boots kicking her split skirt outward and grinding deadfall into pieces.

A light gleamed in the Vernon's cottage, delivering a spate of relief.

She plodded to Broadview's rear entrance. How many happy hours had she spent in this home as a child? Too many to count.

But there was no joy in what she now must do.

"Ella?" Andrew held open the door. "Something wrong?"

Pain, sharp as glass, slashed her heart. "I've something to tell you."

"Come in. Let me take your coat."

"No, I won't be long." She stood with her hands in her pockets near a bench and small mirror. A riot of curls fanned over her shoulders. Her nose glowed red.

"Care to sit in the parlor?"

How she'd love to rest at his side, her hand in his. She blinked. "No. But thank you. We're leaving for Westwood tomorrow."

One dark eyebrow collapsed downward. "Who's taking you?"

"We're taking ourselves. You see—"

"You can't go alone." The lines around his eyes compressed.

"Indeed, we can. Cade loaded the wagon. We'll peddle from here to there and back."

He let loose a blustery huff. "No need when there's a fair in Needham."

"We'll sell everywhere, and I'll use my voice to speak for uneducated girls."

"You could be accosted. You need protection."

"Don't need a man."

"But—"

"I've made up my mind." She knew the dangers, and she struggled to control the waver in her voice.

He thrust his fingers into his hair, shoving it back. "This is unnecessary. I can give you—"

"I'm not your wife. You've said we're only friends. I'm a woman set on providing for herself. And finding support for a school."

He eased onto the bench and stared at the floor.

"I came to ask Vern to check on the cottage." She reached into a pocket. "And to return this." The ring lay on her palm.

He pulled back. "It's yours."

The wick of a slender wax candle on a side table was as lifeless as her engagement. She slipped the ring over the taper. "This came with a proposal that, from all I can tell, has come and gone like our wedding day. I won't sew with threads of illusion another hour."

She dashed out, along the pebbled pathway, and over the lawn as dead as her insides. Topping the rise, her breath came in ragged gasps. Faithful lamplight shone on the cottage porch. *Bless Lily.*

She stumbled forward, and tears blurred her vision. Her shoe caught on a long-forgotten stump, and she fell headlong onto her face. Pain exploded from her nose. Her hands came away wet and sticky. The dry, cropped bluestem grass had chaffed her chin and cheeks.

Again, the old hymn came to mind:

The thorns in my path are not sharper
Than composed His crown for me;
The cup that I drink not more bitter
Than He drank in Gethsemane

Composing herself, she stood. She mustn't delay. She must move forward.

She found Lily reading with her finger sliding along the page and her lips moving in whispers.

The copper-haired young one looked up. "What happened?" Casting aside the book, she rushed to her friend.

Ella hung her coat and cap on hooks. "I tripped. Nothing to fuss over." She leaned toward the mirror. Blood oozed from a nostril. Her hair stood on ends. Already the grass burns had splotched red. Discoloration and swelling mustered around her eyes.

How could she sell to strangers looking such a mess? She set a thumb and forefinger on either side of her nose. "Don't think it's broken. Unlike my heart."

Like a hapless creature in a hailstorm, Ella fell against her friend and wept.

CHAPTER 48

*E*lla slept in fits. Dreaming of mad damselflies that swarmed and devoured her breath, she fought the bedcovers. And rose before dawn.

The pair of friends consumed a simple breakfast and bundled themselves in Addie's furs.

Ella leaned toward the entry mirror. "I look a fright." Bruises marred the flesh around her eyes. She pulled on her stocking cap and fluffed her mane over her shoulders. "Can't be helped."

They stepped onto the porch, and Ella gazed overhead at the cloudless sky. "Morning stars are winking at us. Scripture says they sang with joy at God's creation." Would she rejoice again? Perhaps not, but she must move forward. Others depended on her.

Vernon had harnessed Bunny and Daisy to the wagon and set heater boxes into the buckboard. "It's twenty degrees, but it'll warm up. I've rigged up a locking box for your valuables."

They set their lunch pails under their seat and burrowed into the double wrap, grateful for the warmth.

Lily buried her hands in her muff. "We'll keep the furs safe."

He waved. "A new day's upon us. God be with you."

Ella peeked through her muffler's eye opening at the beams of molten gold streaking the sky. She jiggled the reins, and the horses moved forward.

Broadview wore a bleak and forlorn raiment. A lone figure stood beneath the grand oak, his one hand in his pocket, as lonely a sight as her heart. She stifled a sob. For Andrew. For herself. For all they'd lost. But she couldn't walk his path for him. He must find his way. And so must she.

The team maintained a brisk pace along the cold-hardened roads. They stopped for a rest in Edwards Springs and pulled up at the Westwood depot at half-past ten o'clock.

Ella located the depot master. "Do you know Winifred Norris, sir?"

He chuckled. "Who wouldn't know Winnie? Her husband's a prosperous merchant, and she's ... Winnie's just as fine but rather like an unbroken filly."

She followed his directions to Superior Mercantile on Main Street. Door chimes welcomed them inside.

The handsome middle-aged matron Ella remembered from the Needham meeting held court near the pot-bellied stove. Dressed in a flamboyant, bright purple suit, she sported a matching wide-brimmed hat. Billows of white hair provided a more than an adequate base for her headpiece.

The pair sidled down a row of goods, watching and listening.

The woman spoke to a semicircle of six wide-eyed, plainly dressed young women. "If the state constitution includes no provision for woman's suffrage and the perpetual prohibition of liquor, we've no one to blame but ourselves."

One devotee raised a hand. "What can *we* do about it? We've no vote."

Mrs. Norris's eyes blazed. "You can speak, write, and walk, can you not?"

"Of course."

"Then sign this petition." She waved a sheet of paper. "The placards are prepared."

"But who knows when the constitution will be written?"

The boisterous leader vaulted to her feet. "These Twin Territories will become a state—maybe two. Either way, time's fleeting. Word must go out or our mule-headed men won't get the message through their thick skulls in time for the convention—whenever that may be."

She marched past astounded Ella and Lily. "Join us, ladies. We're on a mission."

Was this the group Ella had read about in the paper? The ones who stopped traffic and ended up in jail? Should she align herself with such controversy?

The semicircle folded and formed a single line behind the firebrand. Each woman signed the petition and nabbed a placard.

Ella and Lily did the same and traipsed onto the street as if they belonged.

Was she leading this innocent child into a den of lions? Risking imprisonment?

If women's lives would improve, so be it. Ella possessed a voice, and she'd use it.

She raised her poster and straightened her spine.

Lord, please keep us out of the jail.

Dodging buggies, automobiles, and a streetcar, Mrs. Norris led them down the middle of unpaved Main Street. Horses snorted. Horns blasted. And their little bank of women skittered and grabbed their hats.

"Oh, my." Ella reminded herself to hold her placard aloft.

Mrs. Norris marched them to the newly constructed Santa Fe Railroad depot. "Hook arms, ladies. We'll stop foot traffic into and out of the building. But speak not a word."

Ella's mouth eased open. "Surely this is prohibited by city ordinance."

The woman peered at her. "I had no part in making such a regulation. Did you?"

"Why—"

"You did not. Here, take my arm."

Ella glanced at Lily. "What have I led you into, child?"

Lily snapped a nod. "Don't worry yourself. This is a just cause."

Tugging her bottom lip between her teeth, Ella pushed aside her uncertainty. Determined to set an example of independence and courage she locked arms with Mrs. Norris. The other ladies followed suit, forming a solid line of opposition to would-be travelers.

A gentleman approached and doffed his hat. "Pardon me, ladies."

Mrs. Norris hiked her chin.

The gentleman's bare-headed companion raised his cane. "Get out of the way!" He waved a hand as if scattering a brood of hens.

The women tightened their grasps.

The hatted gentleman cleared his throat. "We all know your position on woman's suffrage, Winifred. Please move aside."

Mrs. Norris only tightened her hold.

Ella never dreamed she'd participate in civil disobedience. Surely Mrs. Norris would relent. If not, Ella would herself.

A police officer strolled up with billy club in hand. "What's the trouble here?"

Now the law was involved? The newspaper article came to mind, and her pulse sped.

The hen-shooing gentleman signaled the law officer. "These women are interfering with the free flow of traffic and commerce."

The policeman stepped toward Mrs. Norris. "What did I tell you the last time you pulled such a prank, Winnie?"

She stared straight ahead, as silent as a wintering owl.

"I told you I'd haul you down to the jail, that's what."

Ella's gaze traveled along the line of fellow protestors. What would become of her influence if she were a known lawbreaker? But what did her influence amount to if she refused to stand for women at the cost of her own comfort? Ultimately, she was standing for girls like Lily and Nell and those she'd enroll at Broadview School for Girls.

And stand for them she would.

An enclosed wagon drawn by a team of burly horses pulled to a stop outside the frame depot. A pair of policemen hopped out and held the back doors wide.

"Join us, ladies." The officer waved them inside as if doing so was commonplace.

The ride to the sheriff's office required the women to cram themselves onto benches. Their headpieces rubbed together, a problem they remedied by leaning forward alternately with their hands on their hat brims.

The driver called the team to a halt, and the second officer jerked open the back doors. "Out."

Mrs. Norris hopped down and led her band of followers into the building. "Heads high, ladies. You represent all disenfranchised females."

Would this tactic alienate the men further? Ella bit back her query.

The sheriff looked up from his desk and shook his head. "Again, Winnie?"

She straightened her suit jacket. "Indeed."

He scratched his pate. "Don't have room for you tonight. So you'll pay a fine."

Ella's enthusiasm melted. A fine might erase their earnings. How could she have been so foolish?

One follower moaned. "Philip will—" She muffled her words with a hand.

Another nodded. "He won't let you out of the house for a month. Steven won't allow me a word sideways."

Both women paled.

Ella hadn't the wherewithal to worry about repercussions now. She must see to herself and Lily. The fine would reduce their profits, but what choice had she?

She stepped forward. "How much is the fine for two, sir?"

Mrs. Norris waved her aside. "Mr. Norris will cover all our fines when he returns. Now ... Where do I sign?"

CHAPTER 49

The sheriff assured Ella no record of the event would appear in official paperwork, and she sighed in relief.

Outside, Mrs. Norris extended a hand. "I'm Winifred Norris. You look familiar."

How could this woman throw off the day's event with casual ease?

They had traveled to Westwood to sell their wares and make contacts for the school. She must remember her goal. "I'm Ella McFarland and …" She paused for Lily to introduce herself.

The child stepped forward with a smile. "I'm Lily Sloat." Her dark brown suit and high-necked blouse covered all evidence of Walter's assaults.

The bold leader's brow puckered. "McFarland and Sloat? Sounds familiar." She flicked a wrist. "But never mind. You joined us. That's all that matters. We're a small group, but …" Her smile broadened. "We're enthusiastic."

Indeed. Did all suffragists cause such a stir? "Actually, we're here to sell our wares." Ella pointed to their wagon down the street.

"What kind of wares?" She examined Ella through her lorgnette. "What, pray tell, happened to your face?"

"A clumsy fall." Ella tapped the tender flesh around her eye. "We're selling canned goods. And Christmas items. We're from Needham."

"Needham? Any connection between you and Gavin McFarland? He owns a fine general store."

"He's my father. And you might've heard of my friend, Adelaide Fitzgerald."

"I've spoken to Adelaide on several occasions, at temperance meetings and women's clubs. She's an aspiring opera singer, if I remember right."

Did Mrs. Norris know every soul in the Territory? "Addie's in Italy, but she's due home for Christmas."

"Our Christmas on the Square is tonight. You can set out your wares." She flashed a conspiratorial grin. "No problem getting approval. I'm in charge."

"That would be lovely." This meeting appeared positively providential.

Mrs. Norris turned to the other women. "Thank you, ladies. See you on the square tonight. Don't forget your *Votes for All, Liquor for None* buttons."

As they strolled toward the store, Ella gathered her thoughts. "Kate Barnard suggested I contact you."

She chortled. "I don't hesitate to speak my mind. Or get arrested."

Ella double-stepped to keep up and pulled a calling card from her coat pocket. "I'm set on starting a school for unfortunate girls." She chanced a furtive glance around. "If I can stay out of jail."

The matron halted and stared at the card. "Did you enroll a student by the name of Harper?"

No doubt the citizens of Westwood had heard a batch of distortions, but Ella could straighten the record. "I wouldn't call her a student really, but Nell Harper lived with me for a time."

Mrs. Norris stared at them in turn "Do you ladies have a hotel reservation?"

"Not yet."

"Good. You're staying with me."

"No, we couldn't impose, being strangers and all."

"I enjoy entertaining friends." She winked. "Especially when my husband's out of town."

Without waiting for a response, she traipsed into the store, and the twosome followed. She called out instructions to her clerk and shooed Ella and Lily back outside. "Follow me. And call me Winifred. Or Winnie." She clambered into a white carriage and slapped the reins, sending her gray steed into a trot and her hat scarf into a gale of flutters.

They hurried into their wagon.

"What're we doing?" Lily fixed her gaze on Winifred's conveyance.

"Getting answers." Ella gave the reins a shake. "I hope we don't regret it." She guided the wagon toward the carriage disappearing in a dirt cloud.

Winifred pulled in at a spacious two-story home with a broad veranda. Topiaries, fountains, and bird baths sprinkled the lawn as if from the hand of a benevolent giant. Studded with finials and spindles, dormers and gables, the ornate structure drew Ella's gaze in every direction at once.

"Come in, ladies. Take off your coats. We'll visit over tea." Their hostess charged into the house, leaving the door ajar for the Needham pair to amble through.

She hung her coat on a hook, removed a hat pin, and deposited her headpiece onto a hall tree. "Leave your things here." She sat on a bench, unbuttoned her shoes, and kicked them aside. "And your shoes."

Her guests followed suit.

Winnie cupped her hands around her mouth. "Tea for three, Myrtle. Tell Isaiah to tend the horses. Our guests are staying the night." Her robust voice careened down the hallway, and she collapsed onto a parlor davenport.

Their stockinged feet sank into the deep pile of an Oriental rug. And their eyes roamed the well-appointed salon.

Winifred wasted no time. "Have a seat and tell me about yourselves."

Ella hesitated, questioning how far to delve into her story. Miss Barnard had advised her to consult with Winnie. And she trusted Kate …

An unexpected sense of relief eased her apprehension, and she laid out her dream for a school, her love for Andrew, his accident, her broken heart—all to a woman she barely knew.

The housekeeper wheeled in a tea cart, and the three newly found friends shared personal tales between sips of tea doused with sugar and laughter.

Winifred bombarded them with questions. "Tell me about Nell."

Ella leaned back in her chair, gratified her hostess had targeted the heart of her visit. But how was she to sate Winnie's curiosity and get to the answers she sought, yet steer clear of gossip? "You see ..." She hesitated.

Winifred seemingly understood her quandary. "Why don't I tell you what I know. If you feel comfortable recounting the rest, I'll keep the information confidential."

"Perhaps that would be better."

With her manicured hands wrapped around her teacup, Winifred gazed at the chandelier. "I've known the Harpers for years. Some weeks ago, soon after the temperance meeting in Needham, a smartly dressed young woman showed up in the store asking about Clyde." She sipped her tea and mulled.

"Something about her didn't sit right with me. So I watched her through the store's front window. She stopped to speak with a black-haired gentleman, a local bank clerk as I recall. Before I could exit and cross the street, she was rumbling out of town in a Cadillac.

"I might not have remembered the incident, it being common for folks to ask directions and all, but ..." Again, she took a long sip of tea, eyeing Ella over the brim of her cup. "When news got out about Nell, I thought of that woman. I haven't the foggiest idea why."

Lily raised a hand. "I'd reckon you've the gift of second sight." She spoke just above a whisper.

Ella's hackles stood on end. "Can you describe the woman?"

"Ah, she was memorable, to be sure. Thick chestnut hair. And enough beauty for ten women. Never seen eyes like hers before or since. They were golden, amber-like."

Ella's eyelids snapped shut, and she lowered her face into her hands.

"What is it, dear?" Winifred placed a warm hand on her knee.

Viola in Westwood? What was Ella to make of this bit of news?

Fabric rustled and tousled the scent of lemon verbena. Lily had moved to the floor at her feet. "Ella's had a shock, Mrs. Norris. Even so, she needs to get to the truth."

Ella claimed a long, deep breath and lowered her hands to her lap. "Our preacher recommended me to Clyde and Lucille. He thought I might have an influence on Nell." She tugged a kerchief from a pocket and twisted it. "As it turned out …"

"I'm a recipient of Ella's kindness," Lily said. "According to my ma, she wears the mantle of a calling across her shoulders. To help unfortunates like me."

"I don't doubt it a minute. Please continue."

"The beauty you described no doubt is my sister, Viola. She was astounded I'd taken in Nell. Wanted her removed from all things McFarland. And yet Vi pretended to befriend Nell. She and a family friend—Frank Irving—hung around while Nell lived with me.

"Any connection to Irving Bank and Trust?"

"Yes. His father Zach is the finest of men, but I can't say the same about his son. I've no idea why Viola came to Westwood." Her eyes tightened. "But I'd guess the Harpers can enlighten us. Where do they live?"

Winnie's hand flew to her chest. "Oh, my dear, you can't go to their place."

"I need the truth. Nell's disappearance marred my chance of starting a school."

Her mouth puckered. She rang a hand bell, and the housekeeper appeared as if from the woodwork. "More tea, Myrtle dear. And a plate of cookies." She spun to Lily. "Your name's Sloat?"

Lily jerked a nod and leaned backward, as if wary.

The woman squinted in perusal. "Any native blood in your family?"

"Not that I know of. Why?" Clearly, Lily was taken aback.

What other subject would Winifred broach?

The regal dame tapped a fingertip on her chin. "A Sloat man married a half-blood Chickasaw decades ago. Got his hands on her father's Indian allotment. Got in trouble at a poker table and traded the property for an inferior parcel over Needham way. On Rock Creek, if I remember right. When he died—under suspicious circumstances, I might add—his son inherited the land."

Lily audibly inhaled. "My father inherited a piece of land on Rock Creek. He's dark haired and black eyed, and so is my brother, but I never heard about Chickasaw blood."

"You don't look native, but then …"

Ella's frustration kicked up a notch. "What does this have to do with Viola and the Harpers?"

Winifred closed her eyes and kneaded the bridge of her nose. At length, she sat up, as if resolved. "I wouldn't send two women to the Harpers alone—not if you paid me."

"But—"

The daunting woman raised a forefinger. "But I trust my stable master with my life. He can ride out and see if the Harpers are around. My husband and I present Christmas baskets to less fortunate families like the Harpers, so an unannounced visit won't appear suspicious."

"When?" Surely Ella's eagerness was showing.

"He's helping with festival preparations and will remain until it closes. He won't return until the last customer has tasted my spiced cider. So, you might as well settle in and prepare for a wait."

"I won't sleep a wink." Ella's posture slackened.

Their hostess bounded off the sofa. "You need rest. Follow me." She showed them to their upstairs room, a chamber as ornate as the parlor.

Lily fell asleep, but Ella's thoughts created such a racket she could find no relief. She never dreamed they'd find lodging with a stranger who'd become a friend in a day's time. A friend acquainted with the entire Territory, it seemed.

She stared through the dark shadows toward a sliver of moonlight creeping around the window shade.

What in the world did Viola have in common with Clyde Harper?

CHAPTER 50

Church bells clanged, and a band blared. The forty-degree weather beckoned Westwood citizens outside. Christmas on the Square rivaled Needham's tradition with one exception: Mama's pastries. Her cherry and apple pies would've outsold everything.

Ella glanced around the square. "Might the Harpers attend, Winnie?"

She flashed a face. "Oh, no, dear. They avoid public gatherings."

Nell's parents were country folk devoid of social graces, but Ella had hoped the holiday festivities would draw them to town. Their faces materialized in her memory, grief-stricken and weary.

She batted away the images. "Let's stroll around the square, Lily."

Pine boughs burned in barrels. Festooned awnings graced rows of booths. And warm lamplight dazzled, displaying tempting wares: spiced cider, cotton candy, popcorn, peppermint, and handmade toys.

Aromas mingled in a heady combination of pungent, sweet, and savory cheer.

Andrew would've enjoyed the event in better days. A rare spate of weakness wrapped itself around her, and she grabbed her middle. Stumbling, she fell forward.

Lily caught her. "Are you sick?"

"No, but how clumsy me." She smoothed her clothing and her composure. "Let's head back."

Winifred escorted two ladies to their booth, a display hastily created from the wagon's lowered tailgate. "Ella. Lily. Come. You must meet someone."

Ella set aside her candied apple, as did Lily her cotton candy, tagged fairy floss by some. Local ladies had discovered the recipes at the World's

Fair in St. Louis. They swiped the backs of their hands across their mouths. Hopefully no vestige of the sticky candy remained.

Winifred's friends, officers of the Westwood Women's Temperance Club, twittered over Ella's jam. They invited her to speak at their Sunday Club meeting the following afternoon.

Exhausted and weaker, she welcomed the closing bell. The festivities had sapped her strength. They rolled into Winifred's drive at midnight, and they prepared for bed in dim lamplight. Ella settled under the covers, grateful to rest at last.

Andrew's struggles and their shared heartbreak plagued her sleep. Her throat was sore and her body weak. Rest would be hard to come by in coming days. The thought nudged the old hymn to life:

> *The light of His love shineth brighter*
> *As it falls on paths of woe.*
> *The toil of my work groweth lighter*
> *As I stoop to raise the low.*

She forced her eyes closed and prayed for brighter light and a lighter load. She possessed the strength of a newborn kitten.

While they took coffee and bread pudding in the parlor, hooves clacked up the drive. "He's back." Winnie jumped to her feet and swirled to the door, her floral skirt flipping around her black pumps. "Come in. Have you any news?"

Ella hoisted to her feet in anticipation.

The man removed his flat cap. "Of sorts, ma'am."

"Have some coffee and bread pudding. There's cream." She gestured to the dining sideboard.

"Thank you, ma'am." He served himself with the ease of a friend. "It's a far piece out there. No one around the Harper place."

"Might neighbors know their whereabouts?" Ella hoped against hope they would.

"No, ma'am." Seemingly ill at ease, he scooped up a spoonful of pudding.

She wrung her hands. "Did you ask?"

Winifred sighed. "It's best we tell you the truth about Clyde." She waved them back to the table. Glancing at the horseman, she cleared her throat. "As you know, prohibition's the law in Indian Territory, but that doesn't mean liquor isn't distilled and distributed, bought and sold in many a locale. Glover County tries to maintain strict adherence but ..."

"Clyde Harper's the chief distributor," the stable master spouted.

Ella's mouth eased open. "So Nell was reared in—"

"A law-breaking home." Winifred nodded. "And a drunken one. In fact, Billy was a regular customer."

"Nell didn't meet Billy at her father's peach stand?"

"Hardly."

Winnie's friendly employee scraped the last bit of pudding from his bowl and leaned backward in satisfaction. "Myrtle's bread pudding's the best." His napkin muffled his words.

"What we're saying ..." Winifred reached across the table to Ella. "Showing up at the Harper home unannounced without protection is unthinkable."

"Poor Nell." Ella's shoulders slumped. "No wonder she set her hopes on getting away."

"Billy's wrong for any girl." Winifred muttered, as if to herself. "I hope she doesn't live to rue the day she met him."

Ella kneaded the ropes in her forehead. "What does my sister have to do with it all?"

The stable master sat up. "Lucille's the one to ask. She wanted better for Nell. I suspect she has a heap to tell."

"Let's find her then." Ella's enthusiasm had kicked up a notch.

Winifred extended a hand, as if in warning. "Clyde's a suspicious one."

"Then how am I to find Lucille?"

"They come to town on Fridays." She tapped a fingertip on her chin. "He goes his way, and Lucille goes hers. They steer clear of folks, but she isn't unfriendly. I've spoken to her more than once. I can again."

"We must wait until Friday?" Tears threatened Ella's composure. "Loved ones are waiting on us in Needham. Christmas in the Park is Saturday, and the next day's Christmas Eve."

Winifred raised her shoulders and lifted open palms toward the ceiling. "Wire them."

"I guess you're right ..."

"You're bound to sell some products at the meeting this afternoon. That is, if one old biddy isn't there. She's a stickler about doing commerce on the Sabbath." She rolled her eyes.

Ella preferred not doing business on Sundays herself. "What about other days this week?"

"That's it!" Winifred jabbed a forefinger skyward. "Easton's club meets Mondays. Burlwood's Tuesday. Hackensack's Wednesday. And Forrester's Thursday. We'll travel to a different town every day. There's a hotel in each community. We'll return Thursday evening."

The thought of four days on the road exhausted Ella. But she must find the strength.

Lily headed for the sideboard. "In that case, we can have us ... we can *enjoy* another serving of pudding."

"And a cup of coffee." Winifred reached for the silver pot.

In preparation for Westwood's Sunday Club meeting, Winifred dabbed dollops of makeup on the dark circles around Ella's eye. Little good it did. Truth be told, she wasn't feeling herself. Still, she spoke with spirit as she laid out her plans for the school and distributed calling cards. The ladies prayed over her efforts, and a few agreed to the club's support of the school.

As she munched on a light supper in the Norris kitchen, her throat burned. The night stretched long, and her sleep, brief. Her imagination swirled, and she ached for Andrew.

She crawled from bed Monday morning with a headache and chills but ignored it.

Duty called.

CHAPTER 51

*E*lla learned she could inspire a group of ladies. From Easton to Forrester, she ignored her ever-increasing weariness to ply her wares and to speak against injustices to women and children. She found her voice in spite of her weakening physical state. But her eagerness to locate Lucille made the week seem interminable.

The threesome returned on Thursday evening. Winifred instructed Myrtle to prepare a light supper and deliver it to their rooms. Lights blinked out well before ten o'clock.

Squirming, Ella sought comfort but was unable to close her eyes, let alone sleep. Feeling ill and ready to explode with a desire to find Lucille, she threw off her bedcovers. She refused to return to Needham without talking with Lucille.

"Thinking about the Harpers?" Lily said in the dark.

Ella sat up with a hand at her throat, and Lily followed suit. "I want to race across the countryside to the Harper place. And learn what Viola has to do with all this."

"What if Lucille isn't in town tomorrow?"

"We'll take a run down every road hereabouts if we have to." Ella slapped the mattress.

"What about Clyde? And his liquor business?"

"We have weapons. And know how to use them." She crooked her lips into a pucker. "Besides, I faced a mad dog and Walter Sloat both. Why fear Clyde Harper?"

Lily flopped backward onto her mattress. "What trouble are we getting ourselves into?"

Ella coughed, spreading thorn pricks through her chest. She wouldn't complain. No time for illness. "We'll know that soon enough."

The pair dressed by lamplight the next morning and arrived in the kitchen ahead of Myrtle.

The housekeeper flurried in, tying her apron sash. "Land sakes, you two're up early."

"What can we do to help?" Ella pulled an apron off a hook.

"Not a thing. You're our guests."

"Not too fancy to help a little," Lily said.

"Well, if you insist ..." Scanning the kitchen, she pulled cream and butter from the icebox. "I'll stir up some oatmeal. And, Ella, you can bring in the milk and eggs. They're on the back step."

"I'll set the table," Lily offered in a bright tone. "I've learned to do it right."

Myrtle turned to her with a grin. "Have you now, miss? There's tableware and napkins in the sideboard. Put them out while I fry the ham."

Devoid of appetite but in need of fuel, Ella forced down a small bowl of oatmeal. "Delicious, Myrtle. But we must be on our way." She wiped her mouth with a napkin and led Lily upstairs to freshen at their wash basins.

Winnie joined them at the stables, and the threesome stepped into Superior Mercantile at eight o'clock.

Ella stationed herself at the front display window. "What'll the Harpers be driving today? They brought Nell to us in a rickety wagon."

"They'll be in the same." Winifred busied herself, straightening bolts of cloth.

Two clerks took their places for a day of commerce, and Lily joined Ella at the front.

"Try not to be too obvious," Ella whispered to Lily, "lest the employees grow suspicious."

Winifred moved nearer. "No need to worry. My employees are loyal."

Ella sincerely hoped so. Crossing her arms at her middle, she tapped a foot, and her eyes roamed Main Street. An automobile puttered past. Several buggies and a fancy carriage. A gentleman checked his pocket watch.

She spied a haggard horse pulling a weathered wagon. The driver turned toward the store, and she stepped into the shadows. "It's Clyde and Lucille."

He reined in across the street and dropped to the ground. Leaving his wife in the wagon, he entered the hardware store.

Ella's foot tapping picked up. "How do I make contact without alerting Clyde?"

"Neither of them knows me. I can talk to Lucille." Lily nipped at a thumb nail. "But slap me first."

"What?" Ella drew away in astonishment.

"Just do it." She bent forward, offering her cheek.

"No. I can't make myself slap you, Lily."

Winnie stepped between them. "I know how. I've slapped many a cigarette from a man's mouth." She held an open palm aloft and swatted Lily's cheek with such force it hurled the girl backward.

Winnie's eyes went wide. "Oh, Lily. Did I hurt you?"

Lily patted the fiery handprint. "I've had a whole lot worse." She flung aside the door and trotted across the street to the waiting wagon.

"Help me!" She reached for Lucille, displaying the red welt. "Pa's gonna kill me."

"Has Lily lost her mind?" Ella muttered from the safety of Quality Mercantile.

Winnie harrumphed. "I'd say she's found it."

Lucille slid across the buckboard. "Go away."

"Please, can I hide in your wagon?"

The older woman dropped her chin to her chest. "No."

Lily plunged over the wagon's tailgate and wriggled beneath a tarpaulin.

Lucille turned sideways. "Get outta there. My man'll kill you and me both."

Trepidation snaked through Ella. "She won't cooperate, Winnie."

Winifred joined her as a watcher at the window. "Give her time."

The hardware store's welcome bell ting-a-linged, and Clyde clomped out. Mounting the buckboard, he snapped the reins, and the wagon rolled away.

Winifred pressed her cheek against the window glass. "Oh dear, there goes Lily."

Ella sneaked a peek. "He's pulling up at the barber shop. Let's take a stroll like we're window shopping." She twirled around and swept her gaze over the store's interior. "Got something to cover my face?"

The store owner gestured to a clerk. "Bring me that bonnet, the one with the extra-wide brim."

Ella tugged it onto her head and tied the ribbons. "Will it draw undue attention?

Winnie chuckled. "Not in Westwood, dear. Too many farm folks."

Ella tucked her hand around her arm. "You do the talking. I'll do the watching."

The pair undertook their promenade outside Quality Mercantile.

"Clyde can afford a barber, Winnie?" Ella spoke just above a whisper, aiming her words around her bonnet brim.

"Every Friday." Winifred maintained a friendly pace and chatted with browsers.

One shopper stopped to converse. "Who do you have with you, Winnie?"

Winifred leaned toward her as if sharing a secret. "A distant cousin. She sustained a shock weeks back. Today's her first time out of the house."

The shopper tsk-tsked conspiratorially and twittered off.

They halted at a bench outside the barber shop. "Go inside, Winnie, and draw the men away from the window. I'll sit here and talk with Lucille."

"Are you sure?"

"Dead sure."

Winifred settled her supposed cousin and entered the barber shop. "Hello, gentlemen," she called out. "I'm looking for a new shaving set for John …" Her voice faded away as the door closed.

Lowering her head and leaning forward, Ella set her gaze on the sidewalk planks at her feet. "You all right, Lily?"

Lucille sat motionless, as if Ella hadn't spoken.

The tarp stirred. "I'm fine."

"Get out of there. Now."

"Lucille won't talk to me."

"Too dangerous." Lucille rasped against her left shoulder.

Lily's freckled face appeared in the space between buckboard and tarpaulin. "We wanna talk about Nell. And get you away from that man."

"Get down!" Ella peeked backward around her bonnet brim. The barber was accompanying Winifred to the back and leaving a draped Clyde reclining in a chair.

His beard was soaped, but he was squirming.

Ella leaned forward with her elbows on her knees. "Lily's right. Tell us when and where to meet you."

Lucille gasped.

The sound trundled from the wagon as if from a bullhorn. Had someone heard?

Ella sat stone-still. "I can keep you safe, Lucille."

"Like you did my Nell?"

The tarp rustled. "Ella didn't tell Billy about Nell."

"I can find out who did, but I need your help."

Laughter swelled in the barber shop, and Ella forged onward. "Clyde's getting antsy. Tell us where to meet you. Do it for Nell."

Lucille's shoulders rose and collapsed. She looked toward the wagon bed with her chin set in a firm line. "East toward Hackensack. Left at the third road. Take the first right and wait at thicket. Two a.m."

Thank you, Lord.

Winifred opened the barber shop door and stepped outside. "Set that shaving set aside for me." She let the door click shut behind her.

"Ready to go home, dear?" Winifred nudged Ella to stand and glanced sideways at the shop. "Clyde's face is covered with a hot towel. Now!" she whisper-shouted.

Lily slid over the tailgate and scrambled to their side.

Winifred set off at a jaunty pace.

Her two companions scurried to keep up.

Barely.

CHAPTER 52

"*We* need to tell Winifred." Lily whispered to Ella as they washed up.

"No. She won't hear of it. Gotta do this on our own."

"What if a drunk …"

"You can stay here." Ella grabbed her by the shoulders. "I understand."

"You think I can sit here while you get yourself killed?"

"No. Neither could I. So let's strengthen our loins with a good supper and be done with the chit chat." She dared not reveal her poor state of health. Each swallow shot pains through her throat. And her chest ached.

Winifred retired at ten o'clock. Myrtle snuffed lamps and closed her door off the kitchen. Ella and Lily waited in their room with furs in hand. When the clock struck one o'clock, they bundled up and stole out the back door.

Bunny clip-clopped out the drive, and Ella steered her onto the road to Hackensack. They counted off two roads on the left and eased onto the third.

Bathed in silence, fallow pastureland lay on either side.

"Moon's so bright I feel plumb exposed." Lily shuddered.

"We are. Just pray."

Lily pointed ahead. "There's a section of timber up yonder."

Grateful for the generous moon, Ella nodded and stifled a cough. The wagon rounded the next corner, and she halted Bunny midway along a swath of brush and trees, Lucille's thicket.

"Now we wait." She scanned the area. "I figure Clyde has one way into his place so he can keep an eye on who's coming and going. This must be the back side." She clicked open her brooch watch. "It's one forty-five. Let's wait at the fence line."

Sharing the double motor wrap, they huddled beneath a tree. An eerie stillness blanketed the landscape. Night critters had gone to bed for winter. A distant train's whistle—a lonely, desolate wail—cut through the hush.

"I ain't goin' with you, so don't ask." Lucille had emerged from the thicket, as silent as thistle down. "What'd'ya know about my Nell? Not that I trust the woman who let Billy get to her."

"It wasn't—"

Ella nudged Lily to silence and reined in her own tongue. "We intend to find your girl. But we need information."

"What sort o' information?"

"We heard a fancy stranger came to visit awhile back. Who was she, and what did she want?"

"Don't know. She talked about a man named Frank that's in cahoots with Clyde."

Ella stiffened. Frank was behind this in some way. "Doing what?"

"Liquor."

"What in the world . . . They're distilling it?"

"No. Frank's got connections back East. He moves superior liquor along the Canadian River as far as Keystone. Brings it our way 'stead of going into Oklahoma Territory. Clyde stores it, and folks like Billy Redmond pick it up to sell. Or get drunk on."

She forced down her outrage. "Is that how Nell met Billy, through Clyde's liquor business?"

"Yes. When Nell and Billy went sweet on each other, Frank told us about Percival Preston. And you. Said he'd get her into your school and she'd be close to someone him and Clyde do business with over Needham way."

"Who?"

"Name's Walter."

Lily gasped, and Ella caught her arm. "Walter Sloat?"

"Don't know his last name. Clyde stored liquor at his place now and again and wanted Nell to be a go-between. But just when Clyde suspected Walter and Frank made some sort of deal, our girl disappeared."

"But how did Billy find her?"

"Been thinking on that. Who wanted her off your place?"

"Only one I know is …" Lily's voice trailed off.

Ella jerked a nod. "Lucille, did that fancy woman come before or after Nell ran away?"

"'Fore. No more 'n three days, I'd say."

"Did she ask about Billy?"

"Clyde's loose-lipped when he's drinkin'. So, yeah, he would've carried on about his girl."

Ella searched her memory. Viola showed up at the cottage unexpectedly more than once. She pretended to be Nell's friend. And walked the property with the poor girl. She could've transmitted a message.

Puzzle pieces plinked into place.

A horse nickered, and Lucille whipped around. "Better go. Privy's out this way."

"It isn't too late to come with us." Ella whisper-shouted into the darkness.

Lucille pushed aside the brush and stepped through it.

Guilt plucked at Ella. "I'm sorry about Nell, Lucille. Sorrier than I have words to express."

Winter-dead foliage rattled a bitter reply.

Ella woke with a fever. She hoped the two bright spots on her cheeks wouldn't give her away. No one must fuss over her.

Bundled against the numbing cold, she and Lily thanked Winifred and headed out as the sun was gilding the eastern horizon. The empty wagon rattled, but Ella carried a full load of questions.

Her chest ached with each breath, and she shivered, but they faced a journey home in temperatures below freezing all the same. She longed to crawl into bed and rest for days, but Needham's Christmas fair was tonight, their last chance for sales before the worst of winter.

Would she make it home before collapsing?

She directed the team through Westwood to the train depot. "I need to send a wire, please," she said at the ticket window. Lily was warming her hands at the pot-bellied stove.

The clerk prepared to jot on a pad.

"It's to Gavin McFarland at the Needham office."

"Yes, ma'am?"

"Just say *Headed home, Ella*." She handed over the proper coins and joined Lily at the stove.

"Look." Lily pointed out a window. "Is that Clyde?"

Ella squinted through the frosted pane. A man was conversing with a baggage handler. Sprigs of gray hung beneath a battered hat and grazed his turned-up coat collar. "It is."

She ducked and turned to the clerk. "You have a place where I might lie down? I'm feeling faint."

The man's gaze darted around the station.

"Please?" She plopped down another coin.

He pocketed the currency and pointed down a short passageway. "Last door."

She laid a bill atop the blotter. "There's more for staying quiet." They entered a tiny room packed with clutter and a sagging divan. A blackened pot sat atop a coal stove. The space reeked of scorched coffee.

Lily held the door ajar. "Clyde doesn't know me. I can sit in the waiting room and keep an eye on him." She stepped out before Ella could respond.

Ella perched on the edge of the divan. The depot's outer door clanked open and slammed shut.

"See the woman driving that rig out yonder?" a male someone asked.

"Hmmm," the clerk replied. "Now that you mention it, there was a lady, maybe two. Walked over yonder toward Third Street."

Ella sat motionless, listening. A smatter of indecipherable chatter trickled around the door jamb. Boots hammered floor planks. A door clanked. And a slammed.

Hot coals sputtered and spit in the stove's belly, and she grabbed her middle. What had Lucille endured before she confessed to Clyde?

Lily reemerged in the storeroom. "He's gone. Hurry."

They scurried to the front. No sign of Clyde, but how could they avoid him in town?

The clerk shuffled papers and averted his eyes.

Ella approached him with a bill held aloft. "How do we get to Needham without … being seen?"

The man thumbed over his shoulder. "Over the tracks. Past the residences. The road on the other side leads to Meyersville. And from there, to Needham."

She reached for his hand and deposited another bill. "Thank you."

He slipped the currency under the ink blotter.

The women pulled on their hoods and returned to the wagon.

"You reckon that clerk was telling the truth? What if he and Clyde're in cahoots?" Lily appeared jittery as a June bug.

"We'll do our best to stay out of sight. And we won't stop for anyone."

They rolled past homes and turned onto a side road that paralleled the main thoroughfare. Ella stopped at a crossroad a couple of miles outside town.

"I'm scared." Lily admitted in a weak voice.

"So am I." Ella loosened her cloak and fluffed it around her neck.

Lily leveled an appraising gaze. "You're feeling worse, ain't … *aren't* you?"

Each breath burned Ella's throat. "A bit. I'll be fine."

"Maybe that clerk was God's way of helping us out."

Ella scanned the surroundings. Farm fields here and yon. A road to the left and one to the right. "We'll see."

The perky, courageous girl slid over the seat and into the wagon bed. "I'll keep my eyes peeled."

"And your rifle ready. We're going home."

CHAPTER 53

The pair wandered along country roads and pulled over at the Myersville town square at noon. Seated on a bench outside a pavilion, they shared Myrtle's corned beef on pumpernickel and apple dumplings.

Ella tugged at the neck of her wrap. "Help me out of this." She waved a handkerchief near her face. "It must be fifty degrees."

Lily laid a hand on her forehead. "Fever."

"Mainly I'm boiling about Vi's part in all this." A shudder passed through her body. "I could wring her neck!"

"You think your sister meant to harm Nell?"

"Six months ago, I wouldn't've dreamed a speck of what I know to be true today."

"Your sister's carrying a load. Seems she's hurting inside."

"I'm sure she is. But she's done a lot of damage to others." Ella blew her nose on her kerchief and hoisted her weary body to her feet. "Come on."

Lily trailed along behind her. "I've been thinking on how the human heart can darken."

"We've seen plenty of it recently."

"It's easy enough to see the light in Ma. And the blackness in Pa. But aren't most of us somewhere in between?"

"Is there more than one shade of black?"

"Don't figure there is. But the black of sin stains ever'one of us, don't it … *doesn't* it?"

If Ella felt her usual self, if her voice were stronger, she'd teach her student God's view of sin. "I shudder to think how black Walter's heart is. Or the rest of them."

"But ain't it … *isn't* it wrong for those with a bit of black to throw stones at those with a heap?"

No farmer can grow a decent stand of cotton when the soil's soaked with brine, Andrew had said in his first sermon at Christ Church.

She flung a dismissive wave at Lily. "Viola's traveling a road that leads to destruction."

It's time I let the plowshares of the Spirit break up the clods in my heart, more Andrew.

Burdened with a sudden load, she leaned against the wagon. Was her own heart a mound of clods?

This child had witnessed and received the worst inflictions sin offered. But she hadn't uttered a word of condemnation in Ella's hearing. Now she cared about Viola, who'd shown her nothing but cruelty.

Ella set her foot on the wagon's side step, and the world swam around her.

Lily caught her elbow. "You feeling worse?"

She ran the heel of a hand over her forehead. Would she make it home without collapsing? "Better or worse, we've gotta keep going."

"Get in the back. I'll drive." Lily let down the tailgate.

Ella crawled into a corner of the bed near the front. She grabbed a rifle and straightened against the hard wooden slats. If only she could rest. But she must watch for Clyde.

She chambered a round. "The quicker we get home, the sooner the sheriff can throw *official* stones at those who deserve it."

Lily popped the whip, and Bunny and Daisy stepped into a smart trot. Seemed they longed to be home as surely as Ella.

She retreated into her thoughts. *Lord, my heart's soaked with brine. It needs a good plowing too. Give me a heaping measure of Your grace, or I'm liable to fly into Viola and do some damage.*

As the team slowed for the final turn toward Broadview, Ella spied a rider in the distance. "Someone's coming." Had Clyde really followed them all this way?

The team maneuvered the turn, and Lily urged them into a trot toward home.

As the wagon bounced over the wash board lane, Ella positioned the rifle stock against her shoulder and supported her arm on a bent knee. "Stop inside Broadview's gate. I'll lock it behind us." She scooted to the tailgate.

As the team slowed at the gate, the rider turned off the main road in their direction. "He's coming, Lily. Hurry." She unlatched the tailgate and let it fall flat.

"Is it Clyde?" Lily called over her shoulder as she steered the team through the entryway.

The wagon teetered sideways, barely missing the entrance pillars. Ella's weakened fingers lost their grip, and she tumbled to the ground with rifle in hand. She rolled into a kneeling position, prepared to defend their lives.

She wouldn't fail now.

Lily slowed the team in the bridle path. "You all right?"

"Get out of sight!" She swung the gate closed and secured the locking mechanism.

Lily urged the horses toward the cottage, and Ella ducked behind an ancient tree in Broadview's oak grove.

The pounding of hooves grew louder. A horse neighed. "Whoa." Hooves clopped one direction. And another. The rider appeared to be considering his options.

Broadview's front door opened, and Vernon stepped out. Ignoring Ella, he strode toward the front gate with his gaze steady on the rider. "What can I do for you?"

The man spoke in throaty grumbles, his words indecipherable.

"Sorry, I can't help you. Have you checked with the sheriff?"

The man mumbled, and horse and rider galloped away.

Crunching leaves and bits of dead fall announced Vernon's approach. "You can come out now. He's gone."

Ella stepped from her hiding place.

"Who was that?" Crinkles had crept across his forehead.

"I didn't get a good look." She was unprepared to reveal their dealings with Clyde Harper. Not until she knew how deeply Viola's involvement ran.

He frowned. "You're looking poorly."

The air had turned colder, the sky grayer, and Ella could barely get a good breath. How she'd enjoy a warm bath and her soft bed. But her task wasn't complete. "I'm fine, Vern. But thank you." Heading toward the cottage, she wondered if she possessed the strength to round the rise.

Ella and Lily unharnessed the mares and gave them rubdowns. They'd have longer to rest after the fair.

Cade showed up while they were loading the wagon with the last crates of jams. "When did you get home?"

"Couple hours ago." Ella groused inwardly. She'd no time—nor voice—for questions.

"I restocked the woodpile." He kicked a clod. "Been watching for you all day."

She shucked away her brother's concern. "We're here now. But we're headed to town."

"You don't look or sound good. You oughta go to bed."

"Just hoarse. We've more wares to sell."

He flashed an expression of resignation and took over the re-harnessing. "Go on inside and put up your feet. I'll finish here."

"Thanks." She buttoned her coat and tightened her muffler. How she longed to sit by the fire with a hot cup of tea. "But if we don't leave now, our customers will have come and gone."

Lily joined them, and Cade waved and turned toward home.

Ella checked the tailgate. The freezing air nipped her warm cheeks. Had it gotten colder or was she running a higher fever? She pulled her muffler over her nose. "I'll drive."

They mounted the buckboard with Ella's rifle under the seat and Lily's over her lap.

Products rattled in crates as the wagon rolled around the rise. Vernon met them at the entrance and unlocked the gate. Andrew stood at a window with his hand in a pocket. Ella recalled their last shared words, and heartache slashed through her. She glanced down at her ring-less finger.

"God be with you," Vernon called.

"And with you," Lily answered.

They rolled onto the road, and Ella waved overhead. Hopefully their menfolk wouldn't worry. Lily scanned in all directions, but Ella's thoughts plagued her. Her stubborn—even prideful—streak was showing, but if she didn't stand on her own now, when would she?

Was she endangering Lily unnecessarily? Could Clyde be lying in wait up the road? She pulled Bunny to a halt.

Lily stiffened. "What is it?"

Rays of the late afternoon sun filtered through the sky's dome of gray and produced a mysterious green glint in Lily's eyes. "Are you sure?"

"'Bout what?"

"Being here. With me. With Clyde looking for us and all. I can take you back."

Her eyebrows tugged together. "Where would I stand if not beside my friend?"

"It's dangerous. He could be anywhere."

Lily raised her rifle. "What was target practice for, if not times like this?"

Ella managed a smile. She faced forward and shook the reins.

As they neared the outskirts of Needham, dusk was settling.

Lily pointed over her shoulder. "Someone's coming."

"Get him in your sight."

"He's gaining on us."

Ella gave a sharp tap of the reins, and the mares picked up their pace toward the light above the housetops, Christmas in the Park. At the edge of town, she directed the team not toward the glow outlining the park but toward the dark behind the livery.

They would wait out the rider.

CHAPTER 54

The muskiness of freshly mucked stalls alerted Ella to the nearby livery. She steered the team into the darkened alley, and the pair scampered down.

Ella patted Bunny and Daisy. "Good girls."

Positioned on either side of the alley and with their rifles read, they had a clear view of the road.

Seconds ticked by.

No sign of their pursuer.

Ella peeked around the corner. Buggies, wagons, and a few automobiles lined the street ahead. A few lanterns bobbed in the distance, buggies making their way toward town.

"No sign of him." She scrambled onto the wagon, and Lily followed. She signaled the team to move forward, and they eased onto the main thoroughfare.

A horse with rider barreled from a side street, blocking their way. The horses startled, and she tightened her grip on the reins. "Whoa, girls."

Lily sucked in a sharp breath. "It's Pa." She grabbed Ella's arm. "What've you done with Ma and Donnie?"

Walter dismounted and approached. The lantern revealed a trimmed beard. Fresh haircut. Buckskin duster. And a holstered pistol. Had Lily not called his name, Ella wouldn't have recognized him. Lucille guessed right. Walter was in a new line of business, a prosperous one.

What unholy endeavor had the scoundrel entered into?

He grabbed Bunny's harness collar, and the mare laid back her ears. Shook her head. And bared her teeth.

He slid his hands along the shaft and moved nearer.

Ella raised the riding whip. "Get!"

"You don't want no harm to come to your sister, do you?"

She pulled the reins taut. Walter had Viola?

He stole closer. "Ready to deal? Your sister for what's mine—Lily."

Her pulse pounded. "You don't have Vi. You couldn't get past Frank."

"You ain't sounding so good, missy." He chuckled. "Coming down with something, are you?"

Lily's fingers trembled on Ella's arm. Her rifle lay across her lap, but she wouldn't point it at her father.

Ella must take charge. "I won't let you have your way." She'd stand her ground as she'd preached to others.

Lily tightened her grip. "Gotta go with him." She spoke as if resigned to her fate. "For Vi's sake. He'll hurt her if I don't."

How could Walter have gotten his hands on Vi? Was he bluffing? What had he planned for Lily?

Heat flashed through her core, and her vision blurred. Her fever must've risen.

Dear Lord, help me.

Tranquility settled over her like a gentle cape. She'd call the scamp's bluff. And refuse to waver. "You mistreat women and children, but you're a coward."

He ducked into the shadows, and his laugh, as brittle as old glass, echoed down the alleyway. "You don't have no idea what's waiting' for you."

His pistol hammer clicked.

"I'm going with Pa."

"You'll do nothing of the sort, Lily." Setting the footbrake, Ella grabbed her rifle from under the seat. "We won't dance with the devil."

She steadied the rifle stock against her shoulder. "Threaten all you want, Walter, but you'll not get your hands on this innocent child." She cocked the firearm. "And I'll find Viola."

"Take the reins, Lily."

She moved closer to Ella, and the buckboard shifted. The footbrake clunked in release.

"I hope you're right." Lily flicked the leather guides. "Get along, girls."

Ella slipped into the wagon bed, and the conveyance eked forward. She maintained her aim as the team trotted toward the glow around the park. They halted at an empty space in the buggy lot, and she scanned their surroundings.

The park overflowed with celebrants, their voices rising and falling. Snowflakes landed with the quietness of down, as if no danger threatened.

Lily set the brake and grabbed a bucket from the bed. Dipping it into a nearby water trough, she held it to Bunny's muzzle.

Walter wouldn't dare threaten them among the fair-goers, but she needed to speak with the sheriff. She lowered her rifle and coughed, grimacing at the pain. Her chest and throat blazed, and heat flamed through her core.

"You shouldn't be out in this." A note of worry tinged Lily's tone.

Ella glanced around and chin-nodded toward the booths. "Looks like the stalls are all occupied. Let's haul our goods near the fire pots."

Lily transferred the bucket of water to Daisy. "You need to see Doc first."

"He's closed."

"He never wanders far."

Ella set her rifle aside and mustered the energy to lower a foot to the step. But had she the strength to stand?

A woman screamed, and Ella tightened her grip on the sideboards.

"No!" the female cried.

"Who's that?" Lily scanned left and right.

Ella searched the mass of conveyances. "Sounds like—"

"Get away!" Scuffling and grunts sounded from across the parking lot.

"It's Vi!" Ella vaulted down the wagon step.

"I'll kiss my wife when and where I please." A man's gruff voice. And a slap.

Frank.

She raced toward the commotion.

"Help!" A thwack resounded, hard and biting.

Dear God, no!

"Vi!" Ella raced forward, and Lily's boots pounded behind her. They skirted a buggy here, an automobile there, and darted between conveyances.

"Look, Lily. It's Frank's Cadillac.

Viola screamed, and Ella rounded the automobile's backside.

Frank had pinned her against the automobile with her hair twisted around his fists.

"Let her go!" Ella had left her rifle in the wagon, but that wouldn't stop her. She lunged between the pair.

Frank flailed backward but scrambled to his feet with his hand raised to strike.

"Hold it." Lily eased forward with her rifle aimed at Frank's chest.

Ella shuddered in rage. "What sort of evil has gotten into you, Frank? Where's the boy I knew?"

Dear God, give me eyes to see Frank and Viola as You see them.

Viola cowered against the Cadillac. Blood trickled from her nostrils, her hair a riot of dark, unruly strings. Snowflakes clung to her cape like colorless spiders.

"She's my wife. I'll do with her as I please."

A man like Frank could do most anything with his wife. Married women possessed few rights. Viola had made her bed, but her bed was a sorry place to lie.

Viola raised her arms to ward off her husband's blow.

Ella threw herself against him. He stumbled. Righted himself. And grabbed for her. "Why, you little vixen."

"Oh no, you don't!"

Ella whipped around.

Andrew emerged from between two buggies with Vernon beside him. What a glorious sight! Neither man carried a firearm, but they appeared ready to fight.

"Am I to fear an old man and a cripple?" Frank leaned his head back and guffawed.

"I'll show you what I can do with one fist and strong legs." His expression thunderous, Andrew eased toward Frank with Vernon close at hand.

"Should've known you'd show up." Frank sneered. "Like at the gin. You followed me right to the ribs and saws." He chuckled and chin-nodded at Andrew's missing arm. "Too bad you didn't lose both of them."

Ella banished every merciful thought and lunged for the fiend. "How dare you!"

Andrew subdued her with his strong right arm. "No." She struggled, but he stood like an oak. "God ordained a way to deal with the likes of Frank Irving—the law. Besides, he's God's child."

How could he forgive in the face of such evil? If he expected Ella to do so, he'd be sorely disappointed.

Andrew stood his ground. "You admitted to purposely endangering my life, Frank. No doubt there's a laundry list of lawless deeds to be laid at your feet."

Ella jerked her coat straight. "We learned about that laundry list in Westwood. Starting with bootlegging with Clyde Harper and Billy Redmond."

Frank assumed a cocky stance, his hands on his lapels. "Crazy ramblings."

She refused to be deterred. "You used the Harpers' misfortune for your twisted purposes. How the girl's father could be in league with you

I'll never know."

She stared at Viola. "You put Billy onto Nell's trail."

Frank scoffed. "She was to talk Billy into leaving the Territory, not tell him where to find Nell." He raised an open palm.

"Hold it." Lily assumed a confident stance and cocked her rifle. "Lift a hand to a woman again, and I'll pull the trigger."

Before Ella could stop her, Viola pulled away from Frank and skittered off into the night, a sob on her lips.

CHAPTER 55

A dark figure emerged from the shadows with a pistol in one hand and an arm restraining Viola. "Thought you'd seen the last of me?" Walter growled.

Ella all but wilted at the sight. But she must remain strong.

Lily sucked in air. "Where's Ma and Donnie?"

"Stop your yapping 'bout those two." He angled his eyes toward Ella. "Think any more on my proposition?"

"You're still bound by a bond, Walter," Andrew said. "If I were you, I'd head back where I came from."

The foul abuser tightened his grip on Viola. "Not without Lily."

Frank glared at him. "You double-crossing—"

Ella's gaze dashed between the two lawbreakers, Walter and Frank. "You two're in cahoots, aren't you?"

Smirking, Frank leaned against his car with a foot hiked on the running board. "Mighty slow to figure things out, Miss McFarland."

Puzzle pieces fell into place.

"Maybe not." Ella jabbed a forefinger at him. "With statehood coming, the Chickasaw Nation will no longer have control of the land. By exerting financial pressure on Papa and marrying one of his girls you figured you could get your hands on the land he farms."

Frank shrugged. "A man's gotta do what a man's gotta do."

She inched closer. "You made a deal with Walter to kidnap Viola for ransom. But he double-crossed you. He came for Lily instead."

"Maybe you're right. Maybe you're wrong."

Walter pressed the pistol barrel against Viola's temple, and she yelped.

Ella resisted a flinch. "You convinced Clyde I'm responsible for Nell's disappearance. You encouraged him to take vengeance on me, leaving one less McFarland to stand between you and a prime piece of land. You married my sister for her part in the inheritance."

"Frank made me do it!" Viola's haughtiness seemed to have melted like candle wax. Had remorse taken its place? "I was to find out where Billy was so Frank could get rid of him. If I didn't cooperate, he'd harm my loved ones."

Eyes blazing, Ella moved toward Frank. "You made my sister do your dirty work?"

He clenched his teeth, glaring. "Your sister there struts and makes declarations, but she's a weakling. I should've gotten rid of both of you."

Her shoulders collapsed. "Where's the boy I once knew?"

He chuckled, a deep rumble from his chest. "Didn't know me as well as you thought. I came back home to pick up where I left off with you." He head-nodded to Andrew. "But a certain stranger came to town. So, I went after your sister." He snickered at Viola and ran his focus from her feet to her head. "I liked her willing ways. Besides, I wanted a son to raise up in my likeness."

Viola growled and wrenched away from Walter, shoving him to the ground. His pistol discharged above their heads and plopped to the ground. She came at Frank with her nails bared, and he grabbed her by her wrists.

"Sheriff," Andrew called out, and the players halted. "Heard enough?"

Sheriff Dawson moved into sight with Cade beside him, pistols drawn. "Put up your hands."

Frank halted with his arms raised, and Andrew scooped up his pistol.

"I've heard enough, and so have these folks," Sheriff Dawson said.

Mama and Papa and the Irvings stepped around a buggy.

Ollie looked away, but Zach focused on Frank. "We love you, son, but you squandered every advantage. Power isn't about controlling others." He lowered his head. "God, have mercy on us."

He gathered his wife under an arm, and they merged with the deepest shadows.

Mama and Papa eased toward Frank. "We treated you like our own." Papa's voice broke.

"And you defiled our daughters." Mama gawked as if Frank were a stranger.

"You'll not defile our grandson." Papa put an arm around Viola. "We won't permit it."

"Turn around." The sheriff prepared the handcuffs. "You're under arrest." Cade helped him snap the restraints onto Frank's wrists. "You're gonna spend a lot of time as far from these folks as I can manage." He jerked the bank bookkeeper-turned-criminal away.

Viola fell against Ella. "How foolish I've been. Jealous. Mean-spirited. I'm sorry." Sobs racked her shoulders. "Forgive me." She raised her eyes to Andrew. "My heart's soaked with brine. I want to root it out. Truly."

"Humility grows good fruit." He smiled and nodded.

Ella's fingers inched to shake her sister. Vi had thought of no one but herself, taken advantage of every act of kindness. She deserved …

Isn't it wrong for those with a bit of black to throw stones at those with a heap?

Her skin blazed. Energy dribbled from her body. She sucked in a rattling breath and shivered.

God's ordained way to deal with the likes of Frank Irving is the law.

She mustn't feed the monster of hate. She must let God work. Wasn't His grace greater than her pain?

She offered Viola a sisterly embrace. "I've been hard to live with, always bossing and fussing. I'm sorry."

Viola drew her parents near. "I've been ungrateful and disrespectful."

Mama and Papa spoke gentle and low and eased Viola away.

Andrew looked around. "Where's Walter?"

"And Lily!" Ella rasped, and her strength faded.

Andrew grasped her around the shoulders. "What's wrong?"

Blackness closed in.

Water splashed. A hand pressed a cool cloth onto Ella's forehead. She coughed. Moaned. Thrashed beneath quilts.

"There, there." Mama patted her hand. "You're in your own bed, child. Sleep."

"Hot," she croaked.

Her mother pulled off a layer of quilts. "Rest, daughter mine."

Ella succumbed to the encroaching darkness and woke with a single quilt covering her. Firebrands popped in the fireplace, scattering embers like fireflies. The heat inside her had dissipated.

How many hours had passed?

Lily was kneeling at her bedside.

"You're safe." Ella forced the words between chapped lips.

Lily's head popped up, her eyes wide and bright. "You're awake."

"Walter?"

"Got away."

"You … Are you all right?"

"Cade brought me back."

Thank God.

"Water."

Lily poured from a pitcher on the bedside table.

The cool liquid soothed Ella's throat. "Thank you." She pushed upward and leaned against the headboard, coughing without pain. "How long?"

"Three days. Doc feared pneumonia, but the Lord had other plans."

"Andrew?"

"He'll be along directly. Your ma went home after your fever broke. She'll be checking on you later. Hungry?"

Her stomach grumbled. "Aye."

Lily returned from the kitchen with a piping bowl of chicken broth. She ladled the liquid, a spoonful at a time, until the spoon clinked in the empty porcelain mug.

Ella smiled. "The strength of ten women is coursing through my veins."

"Naw. You don't have the strength of one woman. Not yet."

"An unfamiliar state of affairs."

"It is for you. But what are friends for, if not to be strong for one another?" She extended an envelope. "I found this tucked inside the front door."

"Who's it from?"

She shrugged.

Ella tore it open, her curiosity piqued. "It's from Zach Irving. Someone has opened an account for the school. And made a deposit."

Lily's mouth dropped open in surprise. "Who?"

She reread the message. "Women we talked to. But the bulk is from an anonymous source." She stirred, her excitement all but getting the better of her. "I've been abed long enough."

"Not without my help." Lily folded back the quilt and offered her arm.

Ella set her feet onto the chilly floor. A wave of dizziness came and went. Lily helped her with slippers and robe, and they shuffled into the living area.

Sitting in the rocker beside the fire, Ella rested her feet on a footstool. "Thank God."

"Aye, my friend. More than you know." Lily tucked a lap quilt around her friend and pulled an armchair to her side. "I feared for awhile I wouldn't have a chance to tell you …"

"Tell me what?"

"What I've been thinking on."

"And what's that?"

"Jesus is our friend. I wouldn't have known what that meant if you hadn't made me yours."

"What a lovely thing to say."

"It's the truth." Her eyes glistened bright green. "You found me when I was covered in dirt and couldn't look you in the eye. You cleaned me up and dressed me in your own clothes."

Ella's eyes brimmed.

"You said the Lord's preparin' me a mansion and a feast." Her voice faltered. "You set out a spread yourself, the likes of which I'd never seen. Even fed me the nectar of Heaven." She paused to blow her nose on a kerchief. "You gave me a home, and you took up the cause of women like me."

She glanced out the window where dusk approached. "Like when Cade rescued that shorn lamb, you stood between me and my pa's evil plans. And I'm not even a McFarland."

Lily's gratitude struck Ella with such force she gasped and covered her face with her hands.

How hadn't she realized it earlier? That night at the church when she made her bold declaration, she hadn't fully comprehended God's calling on her life. When she blamed Him for Andrew's misfortune ... when she fought off the mad dog ... even when she acknowledged Jesus had saved her from the mongrel, she hadn't understood. Not completely.

Ella bent forward. *I've shown the constancy of a dust mite, Lord. Please forgive me.*

CHAPTER 56

A rap sounded after dark.

Lily entered Ella's room, breathless and wide-eyed. "He's here. He rode Kieran and tethered him himself." She whipped around. "I'm going upstairs."

Wearing her robe and slippers, Ella pulled on a cardigan. Her prayer time had strengthened her, but she felt as breathless as Lily.

She greeted Andrew in the front room and hung his hat and coat on hooks. He stood tall and proud, his left sleeve tucked into his pocket. The outdoor cold radiated off him.

He settled her into the love seat and sat beside her.

The two stared at the fire. An ember popped. Heat reached out like fingers, caressing the couple and coaxing memories of better days.

Andrew cleared his throat. "Glad you're doing better."

"You brought me home that night?"

"You were burning up with fever."

"Don't remember much, only that you were with me and then—"

"I never left." He turned to her.

Her heartbeat quickened. "Never?"

"I stayed by your bedside. Outside your door. And here before the fire. Praying."

She laid a hand on his and he drew her close. She curled into the comfortable spot under his arm.

He eased her head onto his broad chest. "I love you, Ella."

Her breath caught. "And I love you."

"There's not as much of me now—"

"None of that." She touched a fingertip to his lips.

"I can't do everything I once did. But I can do more than I dreamed. I regret—"

"Only a foolish man drinks from the stream of regret once he's tasted its brackishness."

He reached into a vest pocket and held out an open hand, her ring in his palm. "Will you marry me the way I am? I'll make the best life I can for us."

She cupped his face. "How I've longed to hear those words. Yes, I'll marry you. I love you more than all the world."

He slipped on the ring. "There's something else."

She sighed, gazing at the diamond. "We're getting married. What else is there?"

"I'm a wealthy man."

She blinked and sat upright. "You're what?"

"I sold my interest in a silver mine in Colorado."

"So …"

"I've more money than the two of us can spend in a lifetime. I've furnishings stored that would fill up several cottages."

Her thoughts raced. "You're the one who bought Papa's stock." She ran her fingers across her forehead. "You filled the store's coffers and eased Papa's worries. You put the bounce back into Mama's step and the childish lilt in Hannah's voice."

"Guilty as charged. A family friend from Oklahoma City represented me in those purchases."

Only weeks past she'd refused Andrew's assistance with the school. Now she gazed into the sapphire depths of his eyes and saw what she hadn't seen before: God's grace in this man's generosity. Her pride had blinded her.

"How is it a foolish McFarland like myself could be so blessed?" Her eyes widened. "What am I saying? Blessedness has nothing to do with any good I've done. It has everything to do with *God's* goodness."

He applied a gentle pressure to her cheek, easing her head to his chest. "Aye, my love. When we think He's given His all—"

"His grace grows greater still."

A rumble in his broad chest transformed into a great melody. "'The cross is not greater than his grace. The storm cannot hide his blessed face.'"

Five days after Andrew returned the ring to Ella's finger, the Lord's Day dawned with a light covering of ice. The Lord had healed her and blessed her with uncommon strength. She gazed out her bedroom window and caught her bottom lip between her teeth, anxious their plans wouldn't stall.

The sun came out, and Sunday services were conducted as usual at Christ Church, with Ella on her beloved's arm, worshipping beside her family. The McFarlands consumed a light meal, and she excused herself to her room.

Mama peeked in, her face flushed from the wedding commotion. "Time to dress, lass."

Ella opened the wardrobe and removed petticoats, stockings, and slippers. She paused to imbibe the room's sweetness a final time: rose sachet; maple bedstead with a glaze like honey; a bedspread the color of old pearls; and the old dressing screen, conjuring memories of playtime dress-up.

Mama steadied her daughter as she stepped into her gown of old lace. She pulled the skirt to Ella's waist, eased the sleeves onto her arms, and secured the bodice in back.

Ella turned to the mirror that stood watch over the long awaited, never repeated scene and its intimate cast of characters. Grandma Anglin's diligence and artistry created the lace. Mama's steadfast devotion sewed a gown fit for a fashion plate. And Ella's hourglass shape emerged beneath the gown's staves. Twenty covered buttons traipsed up her back.

Mama set the veil atop her mound of curls. "Lord, cover Ella in your joy."

The Irvings' fancy carriage awaited the bride. Bundled in Adelaide's furs, Ella and her parents rode to the church in silence, as if speaking would break a mood as delicate as fine crystal. Delicate flurries of snowflakes danced outside and stuck to the windows like spun sugar.

The bell tolled the bride's arrival, its peal strong in the thirty-degree air. Festoons of white ribbons outlined the church porch. Snowflakes adorned the pathway for her final walk into the church as Miss McFarland.

Standing alongside Papa in the church vestibule, she trembled, but not from the cold, this final day of 1905. Her wedding day. She closed her eyes and imagined gazing at Andrew and never looking away.

Papa patted her hand. "You all right, Ellie?"

Her thoughts turned to the previous night. She had slept in her old bedroom with her loved ones scattered about. The day ended with a visit from her father.

"I'm happy, Papa, but sad, too, thinking how different things'll be."

He set a hand on her cheek. "It's been hard, not having you in the house these months. Now you'll be gone permanently." He swallowed hard. "Best we think on the joy."

"How can I be elated and despondent at the same time?"

"A man and his daughter share their own kind of love. But the love of a man and a woman in marriage is ... Well, it's a God-given blessing."

She had laid her head on his shoulder.

"Keep your conscience clear, and follow your calling. Love won't smooth the road, but it'll put springs in your wagon."

The treasured memory sparked tears there in the church vestibule. She slipped her hand from her father's arm and pulled a hankie from her sleeve, dabbing at an eye. "Just happy."

The church doors swung open, and the gathering stood.

Ella caught a glimpse of a shock of auburn tresses, thick and luxurious, on the last pew. A flash of russet in a hat, a nose veil. The woman turned, and Ella gasped.

Adelaide had made it in time! She stood and embraced the bride, her kiss soft against Ella's cheek. The fragrance of violets lingered around her.

Mama smiled from the first pew.

Ella gazed at her sisters and Lily at the front, dressed in shades of golden velvet. There was Hannah, her cheeks pink and dimpled; Viola, no longer sporting a proud tilt to her head; and Lily, her posture perfect and her nails clean, flexing her wings. Their nosegays, like Ella's bouquet, were fashioned of silk, Ollie's gift in lieu of garden posies this frosty day. All three rivaled confections in Stewart's Bakery.

Twin fiddles played "Amazing Grace," drawing Ella along the aisle where her growing feet had skipped and stumbled and her knees had bent in prayer. Each step took her closer, quickened her breath, deepened the flush spreading across her skin.

Where was Andrew?

He stepped forward, wiping his eyes with a handkerchief.

Would Ella ever rein in her smile?

Papa spoke a blessing and took his seat beside Mama.

She handed Lily her bouquet and faced her life's love in the presence of family and friends, imagining a troupe of angels, unseen but real, surrounding them.

All faded away, and only Andrew remained.

Her simple band on her left hand and Andrew's on his right symbolized their vows. Percival pronounced them husband and wife and proclaimed, "You can kiss your bride now."

"I love you, Ella Evans." Andrew spoke in a strong voice that rang true. "I'll never love anyone else." His kiss, deeper and more earnest than ever, lasted longer than Ella expected. And promised more to come.

"And I, you," she whispered.

CHAPTER 57

*T*he Irvings hosted the wedding reception.

Putting aside thoughts of Frank's confinement in the Fair Valley Jail and Viola's emptiness, Ella celebrated with abandon alongside Andrew.

The frothy punch tingled and left lazy trails of foam on the crystal cups. White and ecru frosting adorned the delicate cake. Ollie had it shipped from Charleston's Lady Baltimore Tea Room, and Maude added the golden sugar roses.

Percival gave her a grizzly-bear hug. Owen did the same, his sole adornment a pocket watch on a gold chain. Her tears soaked into both men's lapels, Percival's black and Owen's steel gray.

Josephine's perfume permeated the room. Elegantly attired and coiffed, she carried herself like one accustomed to fancy parties. And reigned over her rose-throated morning glory phonograph which provided the music. Some guests abandoned the cake ritual to pore over the new-fangled contraption.

"I hope you'll be happy." She spoke the words and turned away.

A wash of unworthiness threatened, but Ella batted it away. She faced Josephine Evans with confidence as Andrew's wife. She longed for her mother-in-law's love and tenderness, but with or without her approval, Ella belonged to the King of Heaven, didn't she? Would she allow unkindness to spoil her future?

No. She'd love Josephine anyway.

Cade spoke the family's blessing. "Ella, you've made it hard to look out for you, but I'm proud to call you my sister. Like the prairie rose, you're tougher than you look."

He paused as chuckles subsided. "Andrew, you're the only man Papa and I would let step into our boots. Welcome to the family."

Cheers and amens made their way around the assemblage. Friends and family toasted the couple with the bubbly punch.

Slipping her hand into the crook of his arm, Andrew nodded toward the waiting carriage. She shared another round of hugs with loved ones and smiled through tears.

The resonant contralto of a lone fiddle played the decades-old Scottish hymn "O Love That Will Not Let Me Go," weaving a benediction around the guests and urging the bride and groom out the door.

Dusk was deepening when Andrew settled himself beside Ella with new familiarity. He took the reins in hand, and she gazed over his shoulder. "Look!"

The house glowed. Light streamed out the windows. Oil lamps dotted the footpath. Loved ones stood as silhouettes against a background of radiance.

Andrew snapped the reins, and she glanced back once more. The family waved with their hands above their heads. She leaned against her husband's shoulder and smiled.

What lay ahead this first night as Andrew's wife? Her former uneasiness in Josephine's presence returned, causing her to squirm. But she flung it away.

Andrew's gentle whoa brought the buggy to a stop at the cottage. He stepped down and extended his hand. "I have a surprise on the porch."

She rushed to a new oak swing. "It's beautiful!"

"I hung it while you were at your folks' yesterday." He pulled furs from a wicker chest and spread them out.

She ran her hands over the pelts. "How soft. What are they?"

"Beaver. I cured dozens. Care to sit?"

They bundled up and snuggled close. The frigid air encased them like crisp sheeting.

She laid her head on his chest. "The sweetest music is the sound of your heart."

"It beats for no one but you."

"We spoke once-in-a-lifetime words today." She gave the swing a nudge with a foot on a floorboard. "But I love speaking of ordinary things, too."

"Like the frost that'll blanket our world come morning?"

"Aye. And the smell of coffee at daybreak. The twinkle of morning stars. Will we mark such common things when we're old and gray?"

"Yes, even then, dear."

"And when the crackle of the fire invites us into one another's arms …"

He moved his lips to her ear. "There's a fire inside me."

Ella wanted nothing more than to be Andrew's wife … in every sense. Nervousness beset her, but she'd let nothing stain this night. She eased her lips to his. "You've never seen the bedroom." Her lips tingled against his.

"A gentleman doesn't visit a lady's chamber."

She bounced to her feet and opened the door. "Unless he's her husband."

He put out his hand, palm toward her. "Wait. I dare not try to carry you over the threshold, but I can do this." He backed inside and pulled her across.

"Look. Vern stoked the fire." She ran her arms around her husband and received his lingering kiss. "Hallway light's on. Shall we see where it takes us?" She led him to their bedroom, and he stepped inside.

His eyes flicked to the stained glass the moon spun in silver.

"The husband and wife who sleep beneath the blackthorn are never parted," she said.

"The universe can spin apart for all I care, as long as I have you."

He snuffed the lamp and turned to his wife, his shirt and coat tossed to the side with his shoes. The moon bathed the bedchamber in beauty.

"I'll need help with the buttons, husband mine." She turned her back to him.

The fire crackled.

His fingers moved down the line of covered buttons and slipped the last one from its hole.

Ella trembled.

Later, when her husband's steady breathing told her he slept, Mama's words returned.

"You stewing about sharing a bed?" she had said days before.

"A little."

"You reckon the Lord would design a wedding gift to put angst in His daughters' hearts?" She chuckled. "'Course not. Now, about this fancy furniture ... looks to me like it'll keep you dusting ... when you aren't holed up under the covers." She had tossed Ella a wink.

Mama's words of assurance faded, and Ella's dream in the swing took its place. Sure enough, she and Andrew fit together like two spoons in a drawer. They'd mark the coming days and years folded around one another in their marriage bed. The Good Lord would carry them in ever increasing measure through whatever life served up. Even when they were old and gray, the moon's slender fingers would reach through their window and soothe them into blissful, restful sleep.

Ella cuddled against her husband and smiled.

EPILOGUE

*E*lla feasted on the sight of her loved ones. She would treasure it always.

The men had voted that day for delegates to Oklahoma's Constitutional Convention. Ella led women picketers outside the polling site. Some men ignored them. Others shouted objections, but the women stood as one. With Papa smiling at her side, Mama led a prayer that the constitution would include woman's suffrage and education for all.

Afterwards the family gathered for what would be a tradition: the Baby Blessing. The aroma of the noon meal's yeast rolls filled the house like an offering of incense, combining with others the likes of which many a home never enjoyed. Peach and berry cobblers waited on the stove. Mama's homespun curtains adorned the windows. And the family spoke of their love for one another. All combined in a new level of contentment.

Papa took his place at a chair in the center of the room. Mama stood beside him. "I was negligent, not doing this for Joshua, so I'll do it now. Come here, son."

Joshua crawled onto the chair and stood straight as his tin soldier with his mother beside him. Sheriff Dawson had investigated Viola's part in Frank's dealings and cleared her of wrong doing, save that of the heart. She carried a load of sadness, but she was learning to trust the Lord. A sweet bond of family devotion was growing between Ella and Viola.

Papa turned to Andrew and Ella. "Bring me that girl."

They joined him with their month-old baby swaddled in a blanket

Aunt Julia crocheted before she died. "I suspect I won't be around when the baby comes," she had said. "It'll be a girl. So I chose pink."

Percival and Maude sat beside Uncle Tad. As frail as a dry reed, he wilted a little more each day. Soon he'd join his Julia.

There sat Adelaide, home for a long while, she said. Ella suspected there was a story behind her friend's decision, but that could wait.

Cade settled next to Lily, a picture of transformation. Living and studying at Broadview School for Girls, she was no longer ashamed of her freckles. She still hid scars, but Ella prayed she'd one day see them as evidence of God's healing power.

Hannah perched in the midst of five girls who'd filled the cottage with laughter the past ten months. Shortly after Ella and Andrew had returned from their wedding trip, Kate Barnard appeared on their doorstep with the orphans, daughters of the Worthington board member who suffered the tragic death. The cottage's five upstairs bedrooms were now filled and Ella's destiny realized, albeit in an altogether different form than she imagined.

Were they equipped for the task? Not of themselves. But God was faithful, and Papa had wrapped the family tight in a blanket of love and faith.

Mama smiled at her and put an arm around Viola. How Ella treasured her mother.

Zach and Ollie took their places beside Viola and Joshua. At one time Ella wanted nothing more than to spare her friends and parents the pain of knowing what Frank had done. As it turned out, the Irvings held up well. They saw off their son to prison, trusting the Lord to bring him home a changed man. Shared pain deepened the McFarland-Irving friendship.

Would memories fade? Perhaps. But one truth was certain: Ella Evans would focus on the Lord.

She gazed at Andrew standing tall, his eyes moving from hers to their daughter. His first sermon at Christ's Church had made an impression. Percival asked him to gradually take over, as he was declining. The prospect delighted Andrew who encouraged Ella to move beyond the local Woman's Suffrage Club.

As the Lord gave her strength, light to see the way, and a voice to speak, Ella would help tens and hundreds find their voices at the Constitutional Convention in Guthrie. And she'd do so with joy, as the hymn's final verse proclaimed:

> *His will have I joy in fulfilling,*
> *As I'm walking in His sight;*
> *My all to the blood I am bringing,*
> *It alone can keep me right*

Papa placed a hand on each child's head, gazed upward, and recited what would become the family's pledge: "We offer up to You, Lord, Joshua Owen Irving and Julia Jane Evans, the fruit of generations of faith. May they tell of Your goodness to the generations who follow from this day forward and always. Amen, amen, and amen."

ACKNOWLEDGMENTS

The writing of this story began as a seed planted in my imagination at my grandmother's and mother's knees in the '40s, '50s, and '60s. Germination occurred when I fell in love with stories like *The Secret Garden, Little Women, Anne of Green Gables, Gone with the Wind,* and *Jane Eyre.* And in college in the '60s when an English professor asked me if I had ever considered a career in writing. This story was watered by life's showers and torrents in the '70s, '80s, and '90s, and it was fed by the Lord's faithful nourishment and Son-light in the '90s and 2000s.

Its first buds appeared in 2005 when I became a first-time grandmother three times over at the birth of our daughter's triplets—Ella, Davis, and Ethan. Another bud appeared in 2006 when their brother Daniel was born. A grafting occurred when granddaughter McKenna's mother married our son, and the last bud opened in 2007 with Braden's birth.

My ancestors' legacy of faith and its weight for my grandchildren brought me to the keyboard in 2007 with a longing to keep alive the stories of the past for the generations to come. My great-grandparents, Gove and Louisa Alexander Pyle, settled in Indian Territory prior to the turn of the twentieth century, years before Oklahoma became a state. Their eldest child Ella, my grandmother, married my grandfather, William Tribble Banks, in 1904 Indian Territory. He had lost an arm in a cotton gin accident. My mother, Goldie Banks Brooks, was born in Oklahoma in 1919, and because she loved her mother's and grandmother's stories, she passed them on to me.

In this novel I continue my mother's and grandmother's storytelling tradition through the circumstances of characters' lives, historical realities, and the living out of faith through failure, tragedy, and loss. Needham, Westwood, Fair Valley, Glover County, Jackson Academy, Rock Creek, Broadview, and the rural environs are imaginary, as are Christ Church and the characters themselves. I alone am responsible for any historical errors. They result not by design but by frailty.

The three historical persons named in the story are Kate Barnard, Angel of the Downtrodden in Oklahoma City; Kate Biggers, first president of the Woman Suffrage Association of Oklahoma and Indian Territory; and President Theodore Roosevelt. Although parts of the novel are based on the lives of family members, it is not my grandmother's or mother's story. It is the story of Ella Jane McFarland, a fictional character who came to life when I set my hands on the keyboard and asked the Lord to help me tell of His goodness to the generations that follow.

I owe a debt of gratitude to many without whom *The Calling of Ella McFarland* would not exist.

Thank you, Jerry B. Jenkins, for creating the Operation First Novel contest to recognize aspiring authors like me. You are an instrument in God's hands in the development of many writers, the extent of which you will understand only in Heaven. I thank God for your ministry and influence.

Thank you, my mentors: Susan Titus Osborn, the first person I trusted to critique my work; Allison Pittman, whose unselfish advice and encouragement have cleared fogs and buoyed me in more ways than I can count; and DiAnn Mills, who carried me through a year of mountain tops and valleys and showed me what it means to put your heart and soul into a project.

Thank you, Dr. Bennie Cleveland, for your medical expertise; Bill Bush, for reliving your firsthand experience as an amputee; my brother and sister-in-law, Jerry and Teresa Brooks, for offering up the prayers that have sustained me; and my readers Dale Brooks, Teresa Brooks, Penny Brooks, Jean Billingsley, Charlotte Largen, Ailie Harriger, Mark and Cindy Sharp, Sarah Kennington, Cheryl Green, and Denalyn Lucado for peeking into Ella's world and sharing your impressions.

C. J. Darlington and Mountainview Books, thank you for your careful editing and for ushering me into unfamiliar territory with grace and sensitivity. Ella McFarland thanks you, as well.

And thank you, Al Davis, my husband and life's love. Your unwavering devotion and belief in me have carried me through discouragement and exhaustion. I could not have completed this project without your faithfulness and selflessness.

Above all, thank you Jesus, for calling me and standing at my side. You are my next breath.

Mama's Nectar of Heaven

Whisk in a pan (preferably thin-bottomed) 1 egg and 1 c. sugar until smooth and fluffy

Add ¼ c. butter and ⅛ c. water

Heat over medium-high heat, whisking continuously, until the mixture comes to a fast boil.

Continue to boil while whisking and scraping until the mixture is sprinkled with browned specks/flakes and is the consistency of syrup.

(Mama's secret tip: The flakes add the distinctive flavor. Using a thin-bottomed pan facilitates the browning. Whisk and scrape--adding another ⅛ c. water if needed--until the syrup is thoroughly speckled with flakes.)

Remove from heat and cool slightly.

Add a dash of salt and ¼ t. vanilla and whisk until smooth.

To serve: Pour over buttered biscuits and enjoy!

Serves about 4 (unless you're a McFarland, in which case you may want to double it)

ABOUT THE AUTHOR

*L*inda Brooks Davis was reared on a farm in the Rio Grande Valley of Texas and holds bachelor and master degrees from Abilene Christian and Houston Baptist Universities. A retired 40-year veteran of speech pathology and public-school special education and administration, she adores her husband Al and her daughter and son, Lynn Lee and Lane, veterinarians who practice together in San Antonio, Texas.

Since the 2005-2007 births of six grandchildren, she has been pursuing God's calling to write, the seed of which was planted in her girlhood. Her mother and grandmother told tales of the wilds of Indian Territory and Texas at the close of the nineteenth century and the turn of the twentieth.

As a grateful sinner saved by God's grace, Linda writes to portray the blackness of sin, the amazing grace that covers it, and the hope and healing He provides through Jesus Christ. She prays her readers, like her characters, will experience a beyond-the-ordinary love for Jesus Christ. *The Calling of Ella McFarland* is her first novel. It won first place in the 2014 Jerry Jenkins Writers Guild Operation First Novel contest and the ACFW Carol Award for Debut Novel of 2016.

Discussion Questions

1. Ella McFarland heads to Worthington in a squeaky buggy, but she oozes strength of character. Which character traits do you see in the first sentence? The first chapter? Thereafter? What does the Bible say about God's developing an individual's character? [See: Jeremiah 1:4-5, 18:1-6; Job 10:8-12, 33:4; Ephesians 2:10, 4:24; Isaiah 64:8] How has God molded your character?

2. Other character traits emerge throughout the first chapter. Which equip Ella for the day's demands? Which serve to challenge her and others? What does the Bible say about an individual's responsibility in the development of his or her character? [See: Matthew 4:18-20; John 1:12; 1 Corinthians 9:27; Colossians 3:1-17; James 1:27; 1 John 1:9] How have you taken responsibility for the development of your character?

3. Which of Ella's character traits do you admire most and why? Read Proverbs 31: 10-31. Which traits noted in Questions 1 and 2 are seen in this proverb of the Worthy Woman? Which of the Worthy Woman's traits do you claim? Which remain elusive?

4. Ella faces the Worthington Board with certain preconceptions. What are they? Which are grounded in reality and which stem from naiveté? What does the Bible say about naiveté? [See Matthew 10:16; Ephesians 5:15] Can you point to a time when

your naiveté got you into trouble? Or would have gotten you into trouble had God not intervened?

5.   Ella demonstrates an array of practical skills from the first page to the last. Which of these skills are common or needful in today's world and which are relegated to the past and why? How does your life differ from Ella's on a practical level? Do you long for such "good ol' days?" Why or why not? Compare Ella's skills to those of the Worthy Woman of Proverbs 31. Do you see the development of such skills as God-honoring? Why or why not?

6.   Ella conforms to certain societal norms. Do you see this as a strength or weakness and why? In what ways have those norms changed over the past one hundred years? What did the Apostle Paul have to say about conformation to societal norms? [See 1 Corinthians 8-10] Share times when such norms have affected your walk with Christ negatively.

7.   Ella challenges other societal norms. In what ways does she do so openly? In what ways does she exercise discretion? Do you see challenges to the norm as positive or negative and why? In what ways or under what circumstances did Jesus challenge societal norms? [See: John 4:1-42; John 8:1-11; Luke 7:36-47; Matthew 15:1-9, 21:12-13; Luke 19:1-10] Share times when your walk with Christ has challenged societal norms.

8.   Do Ella's challenges to the norm change or become more entrenched over time? How does either approach benefit or hinder her? What did Jesus have to say about entrenched societal norms? [See: Matthew 9: 10-13, 14-17; Mark 7:1-23; Matthew 15:1-28] Have you found societal norms in the church to be an encouragement in your walk with Christ? Why or why not?

9.   Ella's view of herself in relation to her family changes over time. How does it change from the first page to the end of Chapter

15? How does it change by the end of the story? What does the Bible say about God's perspective on family? [See: Numbers 1:2; Leviticus 19:3; Psalm 100:5; 1 John 3:1-2] About about Jesus' perspective on family? [See: Mark 3:32-35, 10:29-31; John 19:25-27; 1 Timothy 3:4-5] Share your view of family, how it has molded you for good or otherwise, and how it has changed over time.

10. Ella's view of the world in general changes over time. In what ways and why? Do you see these changes as positive or negative? What does the Bible say about the world and the believer's place in it? [See: John 15:18-22; 1 John 2:15-17, 4:2-6; James 4:4; Colossians 2:20-3:17] How has your view of the world changed over time, and has the change been for the worse or the better?

11. How does Ella's view of God change? Do you now or have you ever shared such views of God? What extremes in his view of God did King David experience? [See: Psalms 1, 3-8, and others] How have your views of God changed over time and why?

12. Ella's calling is the central theme of this novel. In what ways does her calling change? What does the Bible say about God's calling on an ordinary person's life? [See: Hosea; Jonah; the apostles; Ephesians 2:10; 1 Corinthians 3:16; John 15:16] Have you felt God's calling on your life? If so, how did you respond? If not, will you seek a calling from the Lord? Why or why not?

OTHER WORKS BY
LINDA BROOKS DAVIS

1910. Readers first met Lily Sloat in the award-winning *The Calling of Ella McFarland*, a novel set in 1905 Indian Territory prior to Oklahoma statehood. In *A Christmas Measure of Love*, Lily stands on the cusp of womanhood and her mother at the nadir of her life. Lily's as straight as her starched collar, but Ma's as bent as a shepherd's crook.

Joined by blood and separated by circumstance, mother and daughter reunite. But what will they find in the old shack where their sweat and tears once mingled? It's Christmas, and Lily's in for a Yuletide surprise she hasn't reckoned for.

Purchase novella *A Christmas Measure of Love* at
https://amzn.to/2z36Mwy

1914. American women are demanding the vote. The first flames of the Great War are igniting Europe. But a battle of a different sort rages in Oklahoma. The thermometer registers one hundred six degrees, an out-of-the-ordinary occurrence, even for the twenty-eighth day of July.

But this is no ordinary day. A murder trial has concluded, and the jury has reached a verdict.

Lily fidgets in the old church pew. She's lost enough, given more than her share. Hasn't she? The answer rests in the hands of twelve men. Not a single woman sits among the jurors.

Lily eyes the judge. And the courtroom holds its breath.

Purchase *The Mending of Lillian Cathleen* at
https://amzn.to/2q36mCl

DEAR READER,

I thank you sincerely for purchasing *The Calling of Ella McFarland*. By doing so you have validated the story of one young woman's quest to rise above the clamor of human voices to catch the whisper-soft voice of God. I thank you in a tangible way by offering at no cost to you in digital format the companion novella, *A Christmas to Remember*.

To access this Christmas novella, follow this link:

http://www.lindabrooksdavis.com/BonusEbook

and enter the promo code:

EllaChristmas

JOIN THE
CHRISTIAN INDIE
AUTHORS & READERS
GROUP

If you enjoyed this book by Linda Brooks Davis, please join **Christian Indie Authors & Readers Group** on **Facebook**. You will find Christian books in multiple genres and opportunities to find other Christian authors and learn about new releases, sales, and free books.

facebook.com/groups/291215317668431